OFF THE GRID

ALSO BY C. J. BOX

THE JOE PICKETT NOVELS

Endangered
Stone Cold
Breaking Point
Force of Nature
Cold Wind
Nowhere to Run
Below Zero
Blood Trail
Free Fire
In Plain Sight
Out of Range
Trophy Hunt
Winterkill
Savage Run
Open Season

THE STAND-ALONE NOVELS

Badlands
The Highway
Back of Beyond
Three Weeks to Say Goodbye
Blue Heaven

SHORT FICTION

Shots Fired: Stories from Joe Pickett Country

OFF THE GRID

A JOE PICKETT NOVEL

C. J. BOX

G. P. PUTNAM'S SONS
NEW YORK

PUTNAM

G. P. PUTNAM'S SONS
Publishers Since 1838
An imprint of Penguin Random House LLC
375 Hudson Street
New York, New York 10014

ISBN 978-0-399-17660-9
International edition ISBN 978-0-399-57480-1

Printed in the United States of America
1   3   5   7   9   10   8   6   4   2

BOOK DESIGN BY MEIGHAN CAVANAUGH

To Laurie, always

All progressions from a higher to a lower order are marked by ruins and mystery and a residue of nameless rage.

—CORMAC MCCARTHY, *Blood Meridian*

PART ONE

ENCAMPMENT

To live outside the law, you must be honest.

—Bob Dylan, "Absolutely Sweet Marie"

1

NATE ROMANOWSKI KNEW TROUBLE WAS ON THE WAY WHEN HE saw the falcon's wings suddenly flare in the distance. Something beyond his eyesight was coming fast. It was cool and crisp in the desert and the light dawn breeze smelled of dust and the rotting carcasses of dead wild horses who had drunk at a poisoned spring.

The rising sun bathed the eastern sky ocher and silhouetted the rock haystacks and hoodoos into a dark snaggletoothed horizon. It was the best time of day, he thought: the anticipatory moment before the morning light lifted the curtain on the landscape to reveal the reds, pinks, oranges, and beiges of the striations in the bone-dry rock formations and revealed the rugged, broken terrain. The desert was made up of canyons, arroyos, and vast sheets of hard-packed clay that had been sculpted through history first by magma, then water, now wind.

Nate had learned that in the morning the desert didn't wake up. Instead, it shut down. Herds of pronghorns moved from the sparse grassy bottoms where they'd been grazing through the night to the high-desert plateaus where they could be seen for miles—and they could be on the lookout for predators. Herds of wild horses, with their cracked hooves and woolly jug heads, trotted across openings, headed for the shade of wind-formed rock oddities that looked in the right light like Doric columns that remained from ancient ruins.

It was the early-morning hours when cottontails retreated to their dens and upland game birds moved from feeding on seeds and grass to structure and safety.

That was why Nate chose this time to hunt.

But he wasn't the only predator in the area.

THE GYRFALCON, the largest and most formidable of the species, was a horizontal hunter. Unlike the prairie falcon, which struck its prey fast and low from a perch or promontory, or the peregrine, which screamed down from the heavens at two hundred miles an hour with balled talons and intercepted its target in a midflight explosion of meat and feathers, the huge gyr cruised silent and white above the desert floor. When the gyrfalcon sighted its prey—a rabbit, sage grouse, or gopher—it maneuvered its profile into the sun, then simply dropped down on it as if from the sun itself and pinned its prey to the ground. The gyr then used its weight and the powerful grip of its talons to crush the life out of its meal. If the prey continued to struggle or wouldn't die fast enough, the gyr bent over and severed the spinal cord with its hooked, razor-sharp beak.

NATE WASN'T SURE how long he'd been hunting with the new gyrfalcon. There were gaps in his memory. All he knew was that the big bird was his partner and had arrived as some kind of gift from the Arctic, where it thrived, and now he was hunting with it.

The falcon was stocky and thick the first time Nate lifted it up on his glove, and it weighed more than any raptor he'd ever flown. It was smaller than a golden or bald eagle but not by much, maybe a pound or two less. When it was in the air, its five-foot wingspan and mottled white coloring reminded Nate of a flying white wolf. In the dawn of the desert, when the first shafts of the sun lit up the gyrfalcon in flight, its coloring made it look twice as big as it actually was. The gyrfalcon was a formidable weapon. If a peregrine was a cruise missile, Nate thought, then the gyr was a stealth bomber.

In ancient times, gyrfalcons had been reserved for royalty. Commoners couldn't fly them. It was a miracle that the big white bird had shown up. She was a big female, almost silver in color, and females of the species were larger than the males. He enjoyed simply staring at her when she was on the glove, and she seemed to enjoy— and expect—his admiration.

Because his new bird had no natural predators except the occasional golden eagle, it flew and hunted with impunity.

So when it flared sharply upward a mile and a half away and immediately started climbing, when its long wings blurred with effort as they worked hard and fast to ascend from the threat, Nate knew the raptor had encountered something deadly and unusual.

WHATEVER WAS APPROACHING also attracted the attention of a small herd of pronghorns to his right. He hadn't previously seen the creatures in the dark, but there they were. As one, the animals froze and turned their heads to the north where the falcon had flared.

After a beat, a secret signal was given and the herd came alive and took off to the south. Small puffs of dust rose in their wake from hooves. The pronghorns moved away, like molten liquid flowing across the desert, until they were gone.

Then Nate felt a vibration through the ground itself. It was remarkable in the desert how he could feel something coming before he could see or hear it.

A motley herd of twelve or thirteen shaggy horses thundered over the wide northern horizon. One by one they appeared, manes flying and nostrils flared. The rhythm of their hoofbeats increased in volume and they were far enough away that the sound was disconnected from their movement.

Something was driving them, he knew. Something had spooked them into running straight at him.

The horses came toward Nate over the hardpan, kicking up a spoor of dust that hung in the air behind them. They were getting close enough now—maybe a hundred and fifty yards away—so that the sound of their pounding hooves started to sync with their movement.

He wondered if the herd was going to run right over the top of him.

Nate raised both of his hands in the air and waved his arms. The herd kept coming.

Not until they were twenty-five yards away did the animals part and run by him on both sides. The ground shook. Before he closed his eyes against the dust, he caught glimpses of white-tinged eyes, matted manes, and scabbed-over wounds on their flanks. They were sorrels, mostly, but the lead stallion was black with a single white sock. Their smell lingered after they'd gone, a heavy musk that was part dried sweat, part caked mud.

They continued to thunder south.

WHEN NATE OPENED HIS EYES, he saw a pair of headlights, like pinpricks, poke through the hanging dust where the horses had appeared on the horizon.

Nate squinted, trying to see better. The vehicle, like the horses, was coming right at him.

He turned and scanned the cloudless sky. The gyrfalcon was a tiny white speck against the powder blue. Nate knew the difference between a falcon rising in a thermal current for a better hunting lane or circling for an angle of attack and when it was flying away.

The gyrfalcon was flying away. He knew in his heart he'd never see it again.

He'd had the experience before. Sometimes falcons that he'd spent years feeding, training, and hunting with simply flew away. Each time it happened, it opened a hole inside of him that could only be filled by a new raptor. But this time he didn't feel loss as much as a sense of betrayal. His thought was:

The bitch set me up.

NATE TURNED to the oncoming vehicle and was surprised to find it had divided into three parts. What he'd initially assumed to be a single four-wheel-drive unit was now three, and he realized that what he'd first seen was the lead truck in a small convoy of pickups. The two trucks behind the lead vehicle had flared out to its flanks and they were coming at Nate in an arrowhead formation trailed by plumes of dust that lit up orange in the morning sun.

Three pickups coming fast.

He could now hear the sounds of their motors revving and their tires crunching volcanic silica on the desert surface.

Within a minute, he could see that, in addition to the drivers, there were men in the backs of the trucks. As the vehicles approached, the men in back rose warily, trying to keep their balance as the trucks got closer. They steadied themselves one-handed on the side-walls or roofs of the pickups and held long guns in their other hand.

The lead pickup had something large, black, and bloody attached to the top of the hood. Nate caught a glimpse of long yellow teeth and blood-matted hair . . .

He glanced down. There were revolvers holstered under each of his arms, curved grips out. The weapon under his right arm was a five-shot single-action .454 Casull. The weapon under his left was a .500 Wyoming Express, also a single-action manufactured by Freedom Arms, and with five big rounds in the chamber.

He couldn't remember when he'd started sporting two guns, but he didn't question his decision. Just like he couldn't recall the circumstances of the gyrfalcon making itself available to him.

Or why he was in the desert.

He looked over his shoulder. He thought he'd driven there in his Yarak, Inc., white panel van, but he was surprised to find out it had turned into his ancient Jeep CJ-5. The Jeep was parked a quarter of a mile away, under a rock formation that resembled an umbrella: a ten-ton slab of sandstone balanced somehow on a single narrow column of rock.

He scanned the outcropping for a sign of his friend Joe Pickett.

Nate wasn't sure why, but he thought Joe would be there backing him up. Not that Joe could hit anything, but he meant well and he could be surprisingly ferocious when he thought he was in the right.

But was he in the right? Were *either* of them? It was confusing.

Nate doubted he could turn and run to the Jeep and get it started before the three pickups converged on him. Plus, he refused to be run down like a dog or shot in the back.

So he set his feet into a shooting stance and squared his shoulders. Tiny beads of volcanic silica crunched under his boots as he got ready.

He knew what he had to do. He had no choice.

NATE DID THE MATH. Three drivers, three or four armed passengers in the back of each pickup. Actually, the lead truck had four in the back and two in the cab, he now saw. So as many as eighteen armed men.

He had ten live rounds before he had to reload. And by then, they'd be on top of him.

He reached across his body with both hands and pulled his weapons. With the muzzles pointed down, he thumbed back the hammers.

The trucks were now fifty yards away and closing fast. The morning air was filled with the sound of shouting men—Nate recognized the language and what they were yelling—and the snapping metal-on-metal *snicks* of semiautomatic rifles being armed.

The sun lit up their olive-colored faces and electrified the barrels of their weapons. Most wore black beards. He knew the driver of the lead pickup, and he thought he shouldn't have been surprised it was *him*.

2

NATE AWOKE WITH A START AND A SHOUT AND SAT BOLT UP-
right in bed. His eyes were wide and his bare skin was beaded with
sweat. Strands of his long blond hair stuck to his neck and shoulders.

Olivia Brannan turned around from where she'd been packing a
suitcase that was sitting on an old pine dresser. She'd chosen not to
turn on the light so as not to disturb him while he slept, and she'd
been using the ambient light from the hallway to see.

"Are you okay, babe?" she asked, arching her eyebrows.

"I had a bad dream," Nate said, his heart still racing. He realized
that both of his fists were clenched around imaginary pistol grips
under the covers. He stretched his fingers out and placed his hands
on his knees.

"Obviously. Are you better now?"

"Dandy," he lied.

"Doesn't sound like it," she said.

Liv Brannan spoke with a soft Louisiana cadence that always
seemed to wrap him in a warm blanket. Sometimes he asked her

questions to which he knew the answers. She was the only woman he'd ever been with whom he encouraged to keep speaking.

"What was it that happened in your dream?" she asked. "You really yelled there. It about scared me half to death."

"What did I yell?"

Her smile was bright in the dark room. It contrasted with her mocha-colored skin. "Something about *'Now you're going to die!'* You know, your usual morning pleasantry."

Nate rubbed his face with both hands and grunted.

"You haven't done that for a few months," she said, concerned. "I thought you were getting past all that."

"This wasn't the usual," Nate said. "It wasn't about getting ambushed or anything else that happened in the past. This one was completely new and I don't know where it came from."

She turned and put her hands on her slim hips and said, "Tell me about it."

WHEN HE WAS THROUGH recounting the dream, she said, "Damn. That's crazy."

"I know."

"What were they shouting at you? The men in the pickups?"

"Allahu Akbar."

She paused. "'God is great.' So this dream of yours took place in the Middle East?"

"Seems like it," Nate said. They'd discussed his experiences in Afghanistan when he was a special operator and had been sent to a falconry hunting camp in the desert in 1999. She'd been fascinated to hear about the time he'd had a throwaway discussion with a man in the desert he later learned was Osama bin Laden. Osama was an aficionado of American Western movies and television series. He'd apparently grown up watching them. Nate told her they'd talked about several specific episodes of the Western television show *Gunsmoke* that they'd both seen in their youth.

"What brought all that back, I wonder?" Liv asked.

Nate shook his head. "It looked and felt like Afghanistan, but it *wasn't* Afghanistan. There aren't any pronghorn antelope or wild horses running around in Afghanistan that I know of. The only wildlife I saw when I was over there were the bustards we were hunting with the royal falcons."

Bustards are large terrestrial game birds that thrive in the high desert. There's no similar species in North America. The elaborate desert camp was set up with Bedouin-style tents, luxury SUVs, electric generators, and in the distance a fleet of custom 737s that had delivered the falconers from Saudi Arabia and other Arab countries. Outside each tent were several tall perches for hooded birds. Although Osama bin Laden wasn't a falconer himself, he had business with the members of the Saudi royal family who were camped there.

"Maybe you imported a little of Wyoming," she said. "No one ever claimed dreams had to make perfect sense."

"This one sure as hell didn't," Nate said, swinging his feet out from beneath the covers. The floor was cold.

"And if Joe was there, it couldn't have been Afghanistan. Joe never goes anywhere, as far as I know."

It was true. Nate's friend Joe was a Wyoming game warden. He rarely took time off, and when he did, it was to go fishing, camping, or hunting . . . in Wyoming. Joe had once told Nate he felt no need to visit anywhere else until he knew every square inch of the state. Since

Wyoming was nearly a hundred thousand square miles, the statement was akin to Joe admitting he would never travel anywhere ever.

Nate stood and stretched. He still felt lingering pain from his wounds, especially in the morning. Nate was tall and broad-shouldered and his flesh was marked by two dozen comma-shaped scars on the front of his thighs as well as across his abdomen, chest, and neck. That's where the doctors had dug out the double-ought buckshot pellets that were slightly larger than the size of a .22 round. The previous spring, he'd been hit in an ambush by two men with shotguns. Nate was unarmed at the time.

While he'd been in critical condition in a hospital in Billings after the assault, Liv had been imprisoned in an underground root cellar on a compound owned by a family of savages. Rest, exercise, stretching, and reclaiming his life as a falconer had led to his recovery. Liv had recovered as well, although her injuries had been psychological. She'd healed, but not to the point where she could sleep yet without a light on.

After they'd reunited, he and Liv had gone off the grid and had stayed in a remote cabin they'd been offered by a friendly rancher in southern Wyoming.

His peregrine and red-tailed hawk—released from his van by the family of white-trash miscreants named Cates—had both somehow located him and returned. It was a small miracle, and the reunification had astounded Liz Brannan. Nate, who had become accustomed to small miracles he couldn't explain, had simply shrugged.

"THERE WERE SO MANY strange things in that dream," he said to Liv. "I've never flown a gyrfalcon, for one thing. I don't know where I got it. And I was wearing two guns strapped across my chest like some kind of Western outlaw. I've never packed two guns."

"Maybe you should put some clothes on," she said.

Nate slept naked and he didn't mind walking around the cabin unclothed. Sometimes he perched on the branch of a cottonwood tree overlooking the Encampment River and simply watched it flow by for hours with his legs dangling. Occasionally, a raft filled with fly fishermen would float by underneath him. They never looked up.

He retrieved a light blanket from the bed and draped it over his shoulders. "I wish I could shake that dream," he mumbled.

"Have some coffee. I made a pot while you were threatening bad guys."

"I'd rather have you."

"Nate, we don't have the time." She said it with less finality than he'd expected.

IN THE SMALL KITCHEN, Nate poured coffee into a mug and took it to the front window and parted the curtains. It was not quite daylight.

A carpet of light fog haunted the late-fall grass and it hung low in the trees. A mule deer fawn and doe picked their way through the close-packed trees to the river.

It was October—seven months after he'd been attacked and nearly killed—and it was his favorite month of the year. The temperature was cool at night, even cold, but it warmed during the day. It was a *serious* month in the mountains, he thought. At seven thousand feet above sea level, it was time to get things done before winter roared in. Veins of aspens in the folds of the mountains had turned a brilliant yellow and red. Clouds scudded across the sky as if looking over their shoulders. Summer frivolity was over. The elk bugled at night in their mating ritual, beaver finished their lodges, and the river rose and flowed with true muscle as the upstream trees stopped drinking from it.

BECAUSE THE DREAM had been so remarkably vivid and real, Nate reached up on top of the bookshelf to assure himself that his .500 was up there where he put it every night. It was, and there was no second weapon.

The house had been built of logs not long after World War II for cowboys who worked the farthest sections of the vast ranch. It had fallen into disrepair in the 1970s, and was no longer used as a line shack but as a hunting lodge for guests. Despite an extensive remodeling five years previously that had sealed the gaps in the logs and updated the electric and plumbing, it still seemed populated with the ghosts of postwar cowboys who, in their isolation, had carved local cattle brands and their own names—*Wiley, Buck, Slim*—into the doorframes. Liv had tried to brighten up the place with new curtains and rugs on the floor, but she'd declared defeat. There was no landline telephone inside, no television, and no Internet access. The shortwave radio on the counter was their only connection to the outside world.

Nate wouldn't have it any other way.

He heard Liv zip her suitcase closed in the bedroom and he turned to see her wheel it out behind her.

It had been a long time since he'd seen her wearing her professional clothes: charcoal-gray slacks, a white blouse, a jacket, her pearls. She looked stunning.

"I'm going to miss you," he said.

It stopped her and she tilted her head slightly to the side. Her expression was one of bemusement, but tears filled her eyes.

"You aren't turning into goo, now, are you?" she asked.

He said, "I've never spent so much time with anyone on a day-to-day basis in my life. I think I love you more now than ever."

"You *think*?"

"I know."

"Stop it," she said, although her expression belied her words. "I love you, too."

He wanted to grab her, throw her over his shoulder, and march back into the bedroom. She sensed it and said, "Be good while I'm gone, now. I don't want to hear any reports of a naked, wild-haired white man running through the trees."

He grinned. "I can't promise that. But it is getting cold in the mornings now."

She let go of her suitcase handle and approached him, reaching up to wrap her hands around his neck. She rose on her toes so they could kiss. It was a warm kiss but it wasn't going anywhere, because outside they could hear the sound of an approaching ranch pickup.

"Damn him for being on time," Nate said.

"I know," she said, stepping back and smoothing her blouse.

As Nate wheeled the suitcase outside the cabin, he said to her, "I know I don't need to say it again, but be careful. Never forget for a minute that they're trying to find us. Stay off the grid as much as you can, and only communicate with me the way we discussed."

"You don't need to tell me that," she said. "Believe me, I've got it."

"I know you do," he said, swinging her bag into the bed of the pickup. In the back, there were stray hay stalks, a few empty beer cans, a haunch from a mule deer, and errant coils of baling twine.

"I'd be lying if I said I didn't look forward to vegging out in front of a television and ordering in pizza," she said. "Maybe a movie, you know? It's been a long time, and I'm amazed how you can miss those kinds of things when you don't have them."

"I understand."

The pickup was driven by a ranch hand named Rodrigo Ramirez. He was dark and short and wore the same misshapen straw cowboy hat in both the summer and winter. But the rancher, and Nate, trusted him to do his job and keep quiet about it.

"What time is your flight?" Nate asked as he opened the passenger door for her.

"One-thirty. I'll be in New Orleans by four-thirty this afternoon."

Four and a half hours south to Denver, an hour and a half to check in and get through security. That was why Rodrigo was there at six-thirty in the morning.

"Give your mother my best," Nate said, leaning in to give Liv another kiss good-bye. "I hope she can get through this."

"You'd like her," Liv said. "But she won't be around much longer. She knows that, and she's prepared for it. I can't say the same about me. That's why I need to be there."

He shut the door and Rodrigo rumbled away. Before the pickup vanished into the copse of aspen on the old two-track road that led to the highway, Liv turned and smiled sadly at Nate through the back window.

NATE WRAPPED THE BLANKET tightly around himself and waited until he could no longer hear Rodrigo's truck. Then he stood and listened to the hush.

In the Upper North Platte River Valley of southern Wyoming, every day had its own personality, he'd learned. Often it was subtle, a combination of temperature, low humidity, cloud cover, and the ancient, ritual movement of big-game animals, as well as the location of cattle and ranch horses. Even the trout in the Encampment and North Platte rivers had their own rhythms and routines, and he was just learning them.

More often, though, the days differentiated wildly. It was a land of extremes: extreme winds, heat, and cold. He'd awakened to snow flurries in July and August, and he was learning that it wasn't unusual for a fall or winter day to reach sixty degrees. Just the day before, for example, it had been so warm that a midmorning hatch of Trico flies on the river had sent the trout into a feeding frenzy that sounded like cupped hands being slapped down hard on the water.

There was something different about this morning, he noticed. What it was, he couldn't yet discern. It was extremely quiet: no wildlife since the two mulies, no birds flapping from tree to tree, no squirrels chattering, no fish hitting the surface of the river.

He was anxious and a little paranoid. It was the feeling he used to get before a special operation. It was more intuitive than pragmatic.

And it was more than Liv departing to be with her dying mother in Louisiana or the desert dream he'd had.

Nate felt like he was on the edge of something big.

Whether it was the beginning or the end, he didn't know. But later, when he heard another vehicle coming, he knew he would find out.

3

After a breakfast of elk steak and eggs, Nate pulled on his jeans and hooded sweatshirt and laced up his boots. He had the cabin to himself, but he had no desire to do anything different with Liv gone than what he normally did. There was no sense of freedom or liberation at all. He wished she'd just come back, although the reason for her to come back quickly—the death of her mother—made him feel selfish and small.

Because the feeling of dread from his dream still lingered, he threaded his arms through his shoulder holster and hung the .500 beneath his left armpit before going out.

He thought that, later in the morning, after he'd fed his birds, he'd climb up the tree that overhung the river and recall the desert dream he'd had. He'd run it back frame by frame, as if watching a surveillance tape. Maybe he could get more meaning from it.

But even as he opened the metal latch of an outdoor cage and reached inside for a pigeon, he wondered what the gyrfalcon meant. The questions mounted up.

Why two guns?

Where was he in the dream? Afghanistan? Some other country?

If he knew who was driving the lead truck, how did he know the man? What was his name?

Why did he think Joe Pickett was there somewhere, either hiding or backing him up?

And most of all, how was he going to defend himself against eighteen screaming jihadis?

THE MEWS WHERE THE FALCONS were kept was tucked into a pro-tected alcove between the cabin and the riverbank. He'd sunk the posts, framed it, and covered it with three-quarter-inch plywood that he'd painted camouflage green. The roof was peaked and cov-ered with steel sheeting that would withstand the snow. Inside were three birds balanced on stoops—a peregrine falcon, a prairie falcon, and a red-tailed hawk. Each had a tasseled leather hood covering its eyes and had turned its head toward him when he entered the mews. It smelled strongly of nitrogen from the white hawk excrement that was practically cemented to the stoops.

Nate pulled an eighteen-inch-long welder's glove onto his left hand and gripped the shaft of the glove with his teeth to make it snug. He held the pigeon tight to his body with his right elbow.

As quickly and humanely as possible, he gripped the pigeon's head and swung the bird through the air with a sharp rotation to snap its neck and kill it. The pigeon's wings flapped crazily in its death throes and he held it out away from him until it was still. The flapping got the raptors' attention and they all stood stock-still in anticipation.

Then he pulled the pigeon apart. The blood of the bird spilled on the dust of the floor and smelled hot and metallic.

One by one, he took the hood off each falcon and untied its jess, a long leather string, from the stoop. With the jess fitted into the palm of his welding glove so the falcon couldn't fly, he lifted each bird up and fed it.

The raptors ate with cold efficiency, breaking bones with their beaks and swallowing chunks of the pigeon whole—including the feathers. Nate watched as each bird's crop swelled to the size of a golf ball on its breast. He often engaged in staring contests with the falcons while they fed. Their sharp black eyes were bottomless, and even after years of concentration he still couldn't locate their soul. He always thought that if the raptors could talk they might say the same thing about him.

When he was done, he replaced the hoods and retied the jesses to small metal rings on the stoop.

Nate spent several hours a day gathering food for his falcons. He preferred pigeons for their high protein and fat content, followed by ducks, quail, and rabbits. He'd fed each of his birds tiny BB-sized rangle stones hidden in the meat that would lodge in their gullet and help them grind and digest the morning meal.

They'd be ready for more food by evening, which was when he'd take one of them hunting. The other two would eat pigeon or duck in the mews. He rotated the birds each day because he didn't yet trust flying them all at once. Since the prairie falcon was his newest bird, he wouldn't hunt her with the others quite yet.

When he hunted, Nate was more the bird dog than the hunter. His job was to release the falcon and try to kick up targets, whether on the ground or in the air.

Nate looked forward to the day when he could launch his little air force together to see what kind of havoc they would create.

HE WAS TYING the jesses of the red tail to the stoop when he heard the distant rumbling sound of a motor wash over the mews. It was coming from the direction of the ranch house, which was three and a half miles away to the north.

It was so rare that Nate and Liv saw visitors that he immediately tensed up. He was glad he'd strapped his weapon on before going out to feed the falcons that morning.

Then he heard a distinctive clatter, and his shoulders relaxed.

Ranch pickups always had loose trash, tools, and other objects in the back, just like Rodrigo's truck that morning. As the vehicles navigated old two-track roads or washboard gravel trails, the objects in the back rattled around. Each truck had a different array of items, so each had its own unique clatter. Because of this characteristic, it was impossible for a rancher or cowboy to sneak up on anything, Nate thought.

He closed the mews door behind him and waited. The pickup rattled closer.

A maroon new-model Ford F-250 Super Cab nosed through the cottonwood trees. Nate recognized the truck as belonging to Dr. Kurt Bucholz, the rancher himself.

NATE SAW IMMEDIATELY that Dr. Bucholz wasn't alone in the cab of his pickup—there were two other men with him. That fact alone meant something was hinky. Dr. Bucholz had *never* brought others to the cabin. Plus, he looked stricken. It was obvious by the set of his mouth that he'd been coerced into delivering the two men.

Bucholz had grown up on the place as a boy before going to medical school and becoming a successful surgeon in Omaha. He'd returned to the ranch after his father died and still worked at the Carbon County hospital part-time. He'd explained to Nate that he still practiced in order to keep the ranch afloat financially. As with most family operations, the owners were land-rich but cash-poor. Even with beef prices up, the cattle and hay operation barely made a profit from year to year. The only way Dr. Bucholz and his wife would make any money from the ranch, he said, was to sell it or to parcel it off to developers. And damned if he was ever going to do that, he insisted.

Dr. Bucholz was wiry and spry, with a sharp long nose and silver-white hair. He was taller than he looked at first because he had a habit of bending over at the waist and looking up through his thick white eyebrows. He was well read and brusque, and he'd never hidden his view that "the country was going to hell in a handbasket." Which was why he provided aid and comfort to people like Nate who'd been deemed outlaws.

There was a small network of men like Dr. Bucholz across the nation and it was growing by the month. These were men who'd all but given up on society writ large but still contributed and participated in their local communities. They were a step up from doomsday preppers or survivalists, although in a crisis they were more than prepared to take care of themselves, their families, and their friends. To them, the federal government and the coastal elites were practically foreign enemies. Nate felt comfortable with men like Dr. Bucholz, and they in turn offered him shelter and privacy.

Dr. Bucholz occasionally ventured over to the cabin he'd lent to Nate and Olivia to share a few drinks. He always brought good bourbon. He'd once told Nate, "This country was built by righteous rebels. Not by corporatists or elitists, and sure as hell not by politicians. If I can help keep that spirit alive, then count me in!"

INSTINCTIVELY, NATE TOOK a step back behind the trunk of an ancient river cottonwood and drew his weapon. The *snick-snick* sound of the hammer cocking back and the cylinder rotating was an audible signal that put all of his senses on hyperalert. Suddenly, he could hear the sound of the river flow increase in volume, and the clatter of Bucholz's pickup became a cacophony. The bitter, dusty smell of the cottonwood tree stung his nose. And the faces of the two men sitting next to the doctor in the cab zoomed into high focus.

Both passengers were in their late forties or early fifties. The man next to the doctor, in the middle, was clean-cut and serious. He had short-cropped FBI hair, a jutting jaw, and black horn-rimmed glasses.

The other man, next to the passenger door, had a heavy brow, a shaved head, a broad nose, and sharp eyes. His face looked like a fist cocked back, ready to strike.

Nate placed the front sight of his weapon squarely between the bald man's eyes. He could take him out first and kill the man in the middle with a snap second shot. He'd long ago perfected the technique of rapid-firing the single-action revolver: recocking it in a single smooth motion as he pulled it back to level from its massive recoil. He could fire all five rounds nearly as fast as a semiauto, but with more accuracy. It would take two-point-five seconds.

But what if the man in the middle had a gun jammed into the ribs of the doctor?

Nate hesitated, but didn't lower his weapon.

Dr. Bucholz slowed to a stop and killed the motor. He was twenty yards away.

Slowly, the man in the middle raised his hands, palms out, so that Nate could see them. He said something to the bald man, and the passenger raised his hands as well.

Without moving the .500, Nate surveyed the brush and trees on both sides of the pickup for movement or sound. Had the men come alone?

He could hear nothing but the ticking of the rancher's truck as the engine cooled.

The man in the middle said something again and a moment later both the driver's-side and passenger-side windows whirred down.

"We're going to come out now," the man in the middle said. "We're unarmed, so there's no need for fireworks. We're well aware of what you can do with that gun of yours. Dr. Bucholz and his wife have not been harmed in any way, have you, Doctor?"

Nate looked hard at Dr. Bucholz. He seemed concerned but not terrified. If the men in the doctor's pickup had come to take him out, Nate thought, they wouldn't have chosen to do it this way. They wouldn't have driven right up to the cabin and made themselves targets.

"I'm sorry, Nate," Dr. Bucholz said through his open window. "They didn't give me much of a choice."

The man in the middle gestured to the bald man to open his door.

"No need to get excited," the bald man said to Nate as he stepped out.

"I'm not excitable," Nate said. He kept his gun on the bald man's forehead. "Now step around the door and come to the front of the vehicle. Keep your hands where I can see them."

The bald man nodded and did what he'd been asked. He was tall and solid. He wore a canvas safari-like jacket over a button-down shirt and jeans that looked straight off the rack. The jacket had a lot of bulging pockets, Nate observed. He didn't like that.

Nate said, "Let your coat slide off to the ground."

"It'll get dirty," the man protested. But after a glance at the man still in the truck, he shimmied his shoulders so the jacket slid down his arms and fell into a heap at his feet.

The second man slid across the bench seat and took his place next to the bald man. He was taller but thinner and he looked fit and professional. He wore a North Face down shell over a crisp plaid shirt. Like the bald man's, his blue jeans looked pristine. Both men, Nate thought, looked out of place because they had tried too hard not to. And both had a distinctive military bearing about them that Nate recognized from the first moment he'd seen them.

The man in the glasses said, "Nate Romanowski, you're a hard man to find."

Nate nodded. "That's the point."

"I'm Brian Tyrell and this is Keith Volk. We've been looking for you for months."

"Why?" Although he had a good idea.

Tyrell said, "I'd like to say that we're from the government and we're here to help you, but I have a feeling that wouldn't go over so well."

Nate didn't respond.

"Let me get straight to the point," Tyrell said. "You're a wanted man. You're an outlaw. I've seen the charging documents that will be used to indict you and Olivia Brannan in federal court. As usual, they've overcharged you. But even if they can prove half of the crimes in the indictment, they could put you away for the rest of your life."

Nate nodded.

"So you're not here to arrest me?"

"I'm here to offer you a proposal and a deal. If you accept it, we can make all the charges go away for both you and Ms. Brannan. You won't have to live off the grid anymore."

"I kind of like being off the grid," Nate said.

"I know you do. That's why you were so damned hard to find and why you should be very interested in what we plan to offer, if for no other reason than to get Ms. Brannan off the hook. From what I've read, her biggest crime comes from aiding and abetting you."

Tyrell seemed very sure of himself, Nate thought. And he was right about Liv. Nate couldn't stand to see her go to federal prison.

"If you'll come with us to Dr. Bucholz's house, I can explain further," Tyrell said.

Nate didn't lower his gun. "Why can't you just lay it out right here?"

"Look," Volk said, unsuccessfully trying to hide his impatience. "If we wanted to kill you, you'd already be dead. If we wanted to arrest you, you'd be in custody right now. But we drove out here because Mr. Tyrell said he thought he could reason with you. That wouldn't have been the way I would have played it, but he's in charge."

"In charge of what?" Nate asked.

"That's part of our discussion," Tyrell said. Then to Dr. Bucholz: "Would you please drive us all back to your lovely home?"

4

THERE WAS A BLACK YUKON XL WITH U.S. GOVERNMENT plates parked in front of the Bucholz ranch house and another man—younger, with a buzz cut and sunglasses—standing on the front porch. His loose jacket and the way he set his feet when the pickup neared told Nate the man was armed and wary. Despite his casual clothing, Nate thought, he looked tightly wrapped.

The ranch house itself was a modest, white two-story clapboard that served as the hub to barns, sheds, and outbuildings. And, except for modernized electric and plumbing, the house was virtually the same as when Bucholz was growing up. The home was shaded in the summer by hundred-year-old cottonwoods that looked stark and skeleton-like in the fall. The ground was carpeted with cupped yellow leaves, and a flock of teardrop-shaped wild turkeys strutted in slow motion at the tree line.

As he neared his home, Dr. Bucholz found Nate's eyes in the rearview mirror and said, "Again, I'm sorry the way this worked out."

"Don't be," Nate said from the backseat. More than anything, he was intrigued. Tyrell and Volk were the type of men who could exude menace in certain situations, but they seemed to have everything under control. If they feared Nate's reaction to whatever it was they were doing or planned to propose, they didn't show it. Both sat in the front seat with their backs to him. He assumed they had concealed weapons, but they'd not shown them. They hadn't asked Nate to leave his weapon back at the cabin and the .500 was holstered under his arm.

They were either sure of themselves, Nate thought, or profoundly foolish. He guessed the former.

Tyrell, Volk, and the man on the porch all looked familiar to Nate. Although he'd never seen or met any of them before, he felt that he knew them. They were the kind of men he'd worked with, and for, as a special operator.

"Is he one of yours?" Nate asked Tyrell, gesturing to the younger man on the front porch.

"Yes, of course. And we've got another colleague inside."

"So, four of you?"

"Yes."

"Dr. Bucholz, did you see any others?" Nate asked.

"No. These four showed up about an hour after Rodrigo left this morning. Laura and I were just finishing breakfast."

Dr. Bucholz pulled in next to the Yukon. Tyrell said to him, "When we go inside, you can get your wife and go to a different part of the house if you like, or the two of you can go out and do ranch things. You know, buildin' fence or pullin' calves or whatever it is you people do. But under no circumstances should you sit in on or overhear the discussion I'm going to have with Mr. Romanowski."

"You expect me to leave you all alone in my home?" Bucholz asked, affronted.

"That's exactly what I hope you'll do. Believe me when I tell you that for the safety of you and your wife, the less you know about this, the better. And when we're gone, which we will be soon, I hope you'll keep the fact that you met us confidential."

It wasn't exactly a threat, Nate observed. It was said with a tone of compassion. But he wasn't sure there wasn't a double meaning.

"What if I call the sheriff?" Bucholz asked. "After all, you're trespassing on my ranch and you're keeping my wife inside with one of your men."

Tyrell took a deep breath and expelled it in a sigh. "Dr. Bucholz, you can do whatever you want. Go ahead and call your sheriff. Explain to him why we're here and why you've harbored two federal fugitives on your ranch for the last seven months. If your wish is to get Mr. Romanowski here arrested and taken to federal lockup, that's the way to proceed. I can make one call and the four of us out-of-towners will be released without charges. It's up to you."

Dr. Bucholz shook his head.

"And please," Tyrell said, "don't imply that we've threatened you or your wife in any way, because we haven't. You invited us in when we showed up. Your wife offered us coffee. She's been free to get up and leave anytime she wanted to. If you don't believe me, just ask her."

Volk said, "We're all on the same side here."

"Really?" Bucholz asked.

"Really."

The doctor said, "All right, all right. Nate, are you okay with this?"

Both Tyrell and Volk turned their heads to him.

"I'll hear what they have to say."

"That was a good answer," Volk said.

ON THE FRONT PORCH, the younger man with the buzz cut strode across the planks toward Nate while he mounted the steps.

The man raised his sunglasses to his forehead and his eyes blazed with an intensity that stopped Nate short. Buzz Cut held out his hand.

"Nate Romanowski, it's a real honor to meet you. I've followed your career for a long time."

"I don't have a career," Nate said, shaking the man's hand.

"I should have said 'cause.'" Buzz Cut grinned.

"I don't have one of those, either," Nate said.

"Can we end the lovefest and go inside?" Volk asked.

TYRELL, VOLK, AND NATE sat at the kitchen table while Doctor and Laura Bucholz left the room for the upstairs library. Before climbing the stairs, Bucholz turned and looked over his shoulder at Nate, as if it were the last time he'd ever see him.

Nate wasn't sure that he was wrong. "It's okay," he said to Bucholz.

When the couple was upstairs with their door shut, Tyrell said, "Shall we get to it?" It was more of a statement than a question.

Nate nodded.

Tyrell reached out and opened a laptop sitting in the middle of the table.

"We had to talk here because I needed a secure Wi-Fi connection," Tyrell said. "I know you don't have one at your place."

"You've got that right."

"Or a landline, or a cell phone, or for that matter anything that will link you to the outside world," Tyrell continued. "No credit cards, loans, subscriptions, licenses, tax forms . . ."

"I have a Social Security number," Nate said with a wry smile.

"That you never use," Tyrell said. "We know the number, believe me."

Volk said, "Five-one-six, three-three, three-one-one-eight. Montana prefix."

Nate arched his eyebrows at that. Volk was correct.

"We probably know as much about you as anyone could," Tyrell said. "And like our colleague out there on the porch, we think there is much to admire. Your years in special ops were . . . special. The men you worked with all speak highly of you, if we can persuade them to speak. The black ops reports of your missions are impressive."

He hesitated a moment. "But you've certainly gone your own way since you were a special operator for the Peregrines, haven't you?"

Nate didn't answer.

The Peregrines were an off-the-books strike team that had operated on behalf of the government without any official sanction. If the team failed on a mission, there weren't any officials who could take responsibility, because the command structure was top secret.

Nate and his colleagues knew at the time that the existence of the Peregrines was known to fewer than five people in Washington and he didn't know the names of any of them. But the team rarely failed.

The special status of the Peregrines had led to hubris in the commander, John Nemecek, and resulted in a wholesale dissolution of the strike team. Nate didn't disapprove of the action, because he'd been betrayed by Nemecek. Later, he'd taken his old ranking officer down.

Tyrell said, "You've done a hell of a job staying off our radar the last seven months, and that's a pretty hard thing to do these days for anyone, as you know. That's how long we've been trying to find you. As far as we can tell, you never made a phone call, logged on to the Internet, or sent an email or a text. Not to mention no use of credit cards or anything else. You don't have a bank account. Obviously, you've paid no federal income taxes."

"I haven't had income," Nate said.

"You still have to file and you know that. But we're not here on behalf of the IRS. What I'm saying is, you've done as good a job of hiding in plain sight as anyone we've ever tracked domestically. We have access to surveillance video nationwide and there's never been a hit. We find it nearly incomprehensible that you've never shown up in a public or private place with cameras."

Nate said, "Public *or* private?"

Tyrell grinned. "We have access to it all. If you walked into the local convenience store for a quart of milk, we'd know it."

"Face recognition software," Volk added.

"So how did you find me?" Nate asked.

"Alas," Tyrell said with what appeared to be sincerity. "Olivia Brannan had to make a few calls in the last month, didn't she?"

Nate got it. When Liv learned that her mother had a terminal illness, she'd driven into town to call her, as well as the doctors in Louisiana. She'd done it from the only pay phone remaining in the little Wyoming community of Saratoga, and from borrowed telephones in the grocery store and convenience store.

Nate said, "You monitored every outgoing call from the Platte River Valley?"

Tyrell said, "Mr. Romanowski, we monitor every call in the United States. We didn't have to focus our efforts here. We can see and hear everywhere. You should know that."

"Who are you with, the NSA?" Nate asked.

Tyrell and Volk exchanged glances.

"Not exactly," Tyrell said.

"Then who? You guys have 'fed' written all over you."

Volk said, "Are we that obvious?"

"Yes."

"Maybe we ought to grow our hair into ponytails and start hanging around hawks?" Volk said to Tyrell. "Then we wouldn't look like G-men?"

"Maybe," Tyrell said. Then to Nate: "Let me give you some background on us. I'm telling you more than I want to because it's important to establish credibility. I have the feeling you won't cooperate with us unless you have more background."

Nate nodded and tried to fight back his anger toward both of them.

"Do you love your country, Nate Romanowski?" Tyrell asked. It was a serious question.

"I do." It was a serious answer.

"Do you love your government?"

"That's different," Nate said.

"I've read the agreement you signed earlier this year with Special Agent Stan Dudley of the FBI," Tyrell said, tapping his screen with his finger. "You agreed to quite a few conditions that led to your release from federal custody. You made an agreement with the U.S. government, in effect."

Tyrell swept his fingertip across the screen as he read.

"Let's see. You agreed to wear a digital monitor so your movements could be tracked at all times." Tyrell's eyes rose from the screen to Nate.

"I wore it until they cut it off at the hospital. There's nothing in that document that requires me to get a new one."

"A technicality, but okay, I'll buy that," Tyrell said. "Next, you agreed to check in every day with Agent Dudley via smartphone."

Nate said, "The phone was damaged when I was ambushed by two men with shotguns. The FBI never provided another one."

Tyrell smiled at that. "Another technicality, but legally you have a leg to stand on, according to our lawyers. How about 'Subject agrees to cooperate with all ongoing federal investigations concerning one Wolfgang Templeton and his criminal network. Subject agrees to provide testimony in court if requested by the DOJ. Subject agrees to participate in any local operations, if asked by the DOJ, involving Wolfgang Templeton, and to serve as an agent of the prosecution during said investigation'?"

"There has been no trial I'm aware of," Nate said.

Prior to the agreement, Nate had been persuaded by his friend Joe Pickett to provide state's evidence against Templeton, who had successfully run a high-powered murder-for-hire operation out of his ranch in the Wyoming Black Hills. Nate had been hired by

Templeton to do what he considered honorable work that turned out not to be. After Nate turned, Templeton fled in a private plane and had not been located or arrested, as yet.

"Does this have to do with Templeton?" Nate asked.

"No," Tyrell said. "The FBI would love to catch him, and there's some political heat to get that done, but no, we're not here about Wolfgang Templeton. In fact, if you ask me personally, I approve of most of the murders he committed. He took out some real dirtballs we couldn't touch through legal means."

Nate shook his head. He said, "You're an unusual fed, that's for sure."

Tyrell shrugged and continued scrolling through the document. "It says here you signed away your right to carry a gun."

"That was my mistake," Nate said. "I didn't realize at the time that Dudley was offering me up as bait. He wanted me unarmed so that if Templeton came after me he would show himself and they could go after him. It was a trap set by Dudley. Only, the wrong people took advantage of it. I was ambushed without a way to fight back. The agreement violated my Second Amendment rights and it nearly got me killed. I wasn't a convicted felon. That's not right."

Tyrell said, "I agree that it was an unusual provision in an agreement of this kind, but the fact is, you signed it."

"I did, and I shouldn't have. It's not something I'm proud of. But I would have signed just about anything to get out of federal lockup."

"So what you're saying is, you feel you have the right to decide which provisions of the agreement you'll actually follow? That you'll only abide by the terms you agree with?"

Nate said, "I know the difference between right and wrong. Offering me up as a target with no way to defend myself was wrong."

———

Tyrell moved his finger from the screen and stubbed the tabletop with it to emphasize a point. "So, Mr. Romanowski, do you think that your own personal code about what's right and wrong supersedes anything else?"

"In this case, yes."

"I see," Tyrell said, sitting back.

"You left two things out," Nate said. "In that same document, I agreed to Governor Rulon's request that I not commit any crimes in the state of Wyoming while he was still governor, and I haven't."

Volk looked to Tyrell with surprise. "Can a governor actually make that kind of deal?"

Tyrell rolled his eyes. "You don't know Governor Spencer Rulon. He's a loose cannon, and apparently he found out the same deal was given to Butch Cassidy back in the day. Supposedly, it's an offer made to 'honorable outlaws.'"

"And I've stuck to that," Nate interjected. "Dudley also made me promise not to be in contact with Joe Pickett or his family. I've stuck to that, too."

Left unsaid was the incident that had happened the last time Nate had encountered the Pickett family, when he'd thwarted a threat to the then-comatose April Pickett in Billings, Montana. But they'd not really been in "contact" . . .

Nate said, "I'm tired of talking. You said you were here to make a proposal of some kind. Either do it or cut me loose. I don't even know what kind of federal people you really are."

"There are hundreds of us from every federal department and agency in Washington," Tyrell said. "We're part of a shadow government devoted to national security. We call ourselves the Wolverines, after that band of rebels in the movie *Red Dawn*. You know, the kids that rose up to defend our democracy using guerrilla tactics. We're trying to protect the country from the political ruling class who care only about themselves and are too timid to look up and see the dangers we're facing. We hope you'll help us."

Nate said, "I'm not your man. I'm not political. I just want to live my life and be left alone."

"Then you're political," Volk said. "Welcome aboard."

"THE WOLVERINES AREN'T about any particular political party," Tyrell said. "It might surprise you to find out I'm a registered Democrat and Volk here is a die-hard Tea Party Republican. We don't agree on much, but the one thing we do agree on is maintaining national security. We know that our country is in danger from internal and external enemies. There are people out there who want either to subjugate us or kill us, and our so-called leaders think they have to play by the rules when there aren't any rules."

"I don't see what this has to do with me," Nate said.

Volk leaned forward. "What Brian meant when he said we've got people in every agency and department is that we can make things happen . . . and we can make things go away. The government is so huge and unmanageable that no one will ever know either way. The Wolverines realize we have to win this thing on our own without the 'leadership' of Washington. If and when we win it, we can go back to arguing about domestic policies. But if we don't win it, it's over."

"Again," Nate said, "I don't see what it has to do with me."

"The FBI and several other law enforcement agencies have been after you for years," Tyrell said. "We can now deliver you to them if we choose to. We can deliver Olivia Brannan as well. But we don't want to do that. We want to make all the federal charges against you go *poof.* There are prominent Wolverines within the NSA, the CIA, the Pentagon, and the Department of Justice, including the FBI. We even have a couple of secret members on the president's cabinet and within his national security team. Between them all, we know how to get things done.

"You'll no longer be a target. In fact, you won't even exist in any federal law enforcement databases. Agent Stan Dudley will go to pull your file and find out it's been digitally deleted from the server."

"And I should believe you why?" Nate asked.

Tyrell sighed while he tapped the laptop's screen several times. Then he spun it around so Nate could see the screen.

At first, he wasn't sure what he was looking at other than a kind of Google Maps–type overhead image of a paved two-lane road through a vast sagebrush plain. It looked like a still photo.

"I'll zoom in," Tyrell said.

In seconds, Nate could see the roof of a pickup as well as the contents in its bed as the vehicle moved down the highway. There was no other traffic. The shot reminded him of many he'd seen before of an enemy vehicle or convoy moments before it was struck with a missile. Then Nate recognized the truck as belonging to Rodrigo.

"Olivia is in that truck," Nate said, feeling his anger rise.

"On her way to the Denver airport, no doubt," Tyrell said. "We'll have eyes on her all the way there. We'll have an image of her checking in. And we'll have an image of her entering and departing the New Orleans airport."

"So this is a threat," Nate said.

"Not at all," Tyrell said, seemingly offended. "I'm just showing you this to prove that we've got access to the best surveillance systems our government has to offer. We're showing you this so you know we're not blowing smoke."

Smoke or not, Nate was furious. He sat back and glared at Tyrell. He wanted to launch himself across the table and tear their heads off. A few months ago, he would have. Nate had never liked hardasses like Tyrell and Volk, no matter who they were with. But it wasn't just about him anymore. He had Olivia to think about. She didn't deserve to be collateral damage for his past deeds. He owed it to her to find out what they wanted.

In fact, he didn't see how he had any choice. Gritting his teeth, he said, "What are you asking me to do in exchange for clearing Liv and me?"

"That's more like it," Tyrell said with a warm smile.

Volk said, "Don't expect a written agreement from us like you got from Dudley. We don't do written. Written means a record. We don't do records, either."

"It probably won't surprise you," Tyrell said, "to find out that my name isn't really Brian Tyrell and he's not really Keith Volk. Our real names aren't relevant here, and neither are our agencies. But our offer is rock solid: You accomplish your mission and we will guarantee that you will be left alone to live your life. The files created to build up an indictment against you will be expunged. Plus, you'll be helping save the country you love and you can help preserve our freedoms and our way of life."

Both men paused. It was Nate's move.

After a full silent minute, he said, "Why me, if you have all these people available throughout the government?"

"Many reasons," Tyrell said. He counted them off by tapping the tabletop with his index finger. "One, you have a unique special ops background. Two, the stakes are high enough on both sides that a deal can be struck. Three, you know the Mountain West and you're comfortable here. You'll never be mistaken as an outsider, like us. Plus, you're not exactly an unknown entity. Certain people like Dr. Bucholz know you by your reputation. There is no way we could establish anyone with an identity like that in a credible way."

"You're kind of a homicidal libertarian folk hero," Volk said with a grin.

"I'm not sure I like that description," Nate said. Then to Tyrell: "Is that all?"

"No. We've left out the most critical attribute: You're a master falconer. Believe it or not, there isn't a Wolverine in any position anywhere who knows and practices falconry."

"Why is that important?" Nate asked.

"We'll get to that," Tyrell said, spinning the laptop around so he could access another file. "But first, have you ever hunted with your falcons in the Red Desert?"

"The Red Desert? Here in Wyoming?"

"Where else?"

"Wyoming?"

"We're tracking potential terrorist activity in all fifty states."

Tyrell reached forward and drummed his fingers on the tabletop to punctuate each word as he said again, *"All. Fifty. States."*

Nate had absolutely no desire to have anything to do with these men. But they had him, and he knew it.

5

LATER, AT DUSK, AS NATE BALANCED HIMSELF ON THE COTTON-
wood branch that reached over the bank of the Encampment River,
a cloud of tiny Trico flies rolled over the water below him. The
bugs were so tightly packed together they looked like a spoor of
light-colored smoke. A pod of brown trout beneath the surface
noted the Tricos as well; they broke up and rose one by one to sip
the bugs that were caught in the film of the surface. The trout
barely rippled the water as they fed, but from Nate's vantage point,
he could see them clearly as they emerged from the depths with
a slight upward tilt of their open mouths. They looked like slow-
motion pistons working in a natural engine as they sucked in bugs.

A herd of seven mule deer—three does, three fawns, and a big
but wary buck—ghosted through the trees and brush on the other
side of the river until they all stood side by side and drank. They
never looked up at Nate and he didn't move or make a sound. He
could hear them slurping.

He thought, as he often did, how even a small river like the

Encampment provided the absolute lifeblood to a dry mountain state like Wyoming. Find the water, he thought, and you'll find life.

The deer raised their heads when an upstream beaver slapped the water with its tail. The sound startled Nate as well, and he realized how jumpy he was.

And no wonder. The day had started off with a nightmare and it had only gotten stranger with the arrival of Tyrell and Volk. Nate half expected to wake up and realize it had all been some kind of interconnected fever dream.

But it wasn't. It had happened.

And the next morning, he'd transport his birds and his gear less than a hundred miles to the west beyond the Sierra Madre mountains.

To the nine-thousand-square-mile anomaly filled with dunes, mesas, hoodoos, canyons, and harsh vistas known as the Red Desert. Where there was very little water at all.

"His given name is Muhammad Ibraaheem," Tyrell had said, gesturing to the screen of his laptop. "He's twenty-nine years old next month. He grew up in Georgetown as the oldest son of the ambassador to the U.S. from the Kingdom. He was born in Jeddah, but his father brought him to this country when he was five. He went to private schools in Virginia, where he excelled. As a senior in high school, he was rated the number-one placekicker in the country and he was offered dozens of scholarships. Unfortunately, the summer before he went to college, he was in a car accident with his mother and their driver that trashed his knee.

"Instead of playing football," Tyrell went on, "Ibraaheem got his bachelor's degree at the University of Michigan and his master's at the University of Southern California's Annenberg School for Communication and Journalism. At both universities, he wrote for the college newspapers and participated in student government. From everything we can find, he was popular, well liked, and considered a brilliant student. He's fluent in four languages: English, French, Spanish, and Arabic. He was known as 'Ibby,' not Muhammad. Although he is certainly considered a devout Muslim—with his dad being who he is, he *better* be—he wasn't known to be strident and certainly not extreme in his religious views. He's what we'd call a moderate or even secular Muslim, like the great majority within that religion.

"He wrote a lot of articles and op-eds at USC and there isn't a hint of Islamic extremism in any of them. Believe me, we've read them all. If anything, he went out of his way to avoid religious or political subjects. And he was a hell of a good sportswriter."

"An all-American boy," Volk said with a barely suppressed sneer.

The photo of Ibraaheem confirmed everything Tyrell had said so far, Nate observed. He was dark, good-looking, and had a jaunty but confident smile. His eyes were warm and intelligent. In the photo, he wore a USC hoodie and was surrounded by a dozen students who looked like they were on their way to, or from, a football game. It was a beautiful Southern California day with palm trees in the background and a perfect blue sky. Two blond and pleasant-looking female students were draped on him, and Ibraaheem looked at the camera like he couldn't believe his luck, either. Black curls reflected the sun.

"He got hired straight out of J-school by an international wire service to be a foreign correspondent," Tyrell said. "You can guess that his connections and language skills helped in that regard, and he traveled all over the world filing stories. Europe, Russia, Argentina, China. If you do a Google search you can find his byline on hundreds of stories over the last six years. His last ports of call were Saudi, Yemen, and Syria. Then . . . nothing.

"For six years he was the hardest-working journalist in the world," Tyrell added. "Then he dropped off the map."

"No calls, emails, texts, nothing."

Nate raised his eyebrows.

"Exactly," Volk said. "You can see how that aroused our interest. And then this came up." Volk tapped on the screen and spun the computer back around. On the screen was a pixelated black-and-white photo of five men huddled in conversation outside of what looked like a mosque. Four of the men wore robes, but one didn't.

"These guys are high-value al-Qaeda militants in Yemen. It was taken two years ago by a drone, but initially overlooked," Volk said. "Look at the figure on the right."

The slim man in Western dress had his back to the camera but there was a quarter view of his face as he turned his head toward the others. Nate shook his head. The photo was too blurry to make a positive identification.

Volk said, "I know it isn't definitive, but it *could* be him. The build is the same, at least. We know he was in Yemen at the time."

Tyrell took over. "There's an unofficial-slash-official policy to check up on every citizen with a U.S. passport who has returned here after spending time in an ISIS-controlled territory: Syria, Iraq, Yemen, et cetera.

"So a couple of special agents went to visit the Ibraaheem family. It didn't go well," Tyrell said. "In fact, the ambassador filed an official complaint against the two FBI guys who showed up at his house to check on the well-being of his oldest son. It wasn't just any complaint—it went straight to the president. It turns out our administration is working closely with people in the Kingdom to implement a super-secret antiterrorism strategy within the Middle East. The ambassador—Ibby's dad—is the primary conduit. He said the FBI agents harassed him, and they both lost their jobs because of it. The ambassador is apparently a *very* special diplomat."

Volk snorted and sat back. He said, "Those poor FBI guys never knew what hit them."

Nate asked, "Was Ibby there?"

Tyrell and Volk again exchanged glances.

"No, he wasn't," Tyrell said. "His family claims they don't know where he is. There's a reason why Ibby has gone completely off the grid. He doesn't want to be found."

"I sympathize," Nate said. "But what does any of this have to do with me, and why is it so important that you had to hunt me down?"

"Because," Tyrell said, "there's been chatter intercepted overseas about an upcoming terror event. We don't know who's involved or when it's supposed to happen, but our people think it's going to be huge. It's supposed to take place out here in the Mountain West, where no one expects it. They want to show us that no one anywhere is safe."

"Isn't there always chatter?" Nate asked skeptically.

"Yes. Sorting it out is like trying to get a drink from a fire hose, but we believe this to be credible."

Tyrell stopped speaking while he opened another file on his laptop.

Volk used the opening to cut in. "And it's more than just the

---

chatter. Other things have happened in this sector. A couple of tractor-trailers were stolen from truck stops along I-80 while the drivers were away from their vehicles. There have been at least three large-scale thefts of oil field equipment and copper tubing. Someone broke into the warehouse of a huge sporting goods company and hauled out survival gear and weapons, and they were very specific about what they took: tents, generators, high-powered rifles and ammunition, freeze-dried food, camouflage clothing."

"So?"

"The crimes and what was taken cross-check with certain words and phrases our spooks picked up in the chatter stream at the same time. Bad guys in Europe and the Middle East were talking about semitrucks and electronic gear hours after they were stolen over here. We don't have enough intel to connect the dots—but we know there are dots to connect. And *that's* why we're here, and here's why *you're* here."

Tyrell spun the laptop around to him again. On the screen was another photo taken from a satellite or drone of what was obviously a falconer flying a bird in the desert. Nate leaned forward as Tyrell clicked to zoom it in.

The man in the photo was in the act of swinging a lure around his head. A lure was a piece of bird wing tied to a line that would draw the attention of a raptor in the air and entice it back in from the sky. At the top of the photo was a blurred image of a falcon in a stoop.

The falconer looked a lot like Ibby.

"This was taken two months ago, less than a hundred miles from here."

Nate had guessed this part. "So Ibby's a falconer."

"He has been since he was a child," Tyrell said, scrolling through photo after photo of a young Ibraaheem with a succession of falcons: kestrels, red tails, prairie falcons, peregrines, goshawks. "You know all about this, don't you? The thing Middle Eastern royals have for falconry."

Nate nodded.

"You have a unique opportunity to be able to check him out," Volk said, "one falconer to another. Try to figure out what his deal is, what he's been doing these past two years. And, of course, let us know if he appears to be a part of this impending threat."

Nate closed his eyes briefly, and when he opened them he was angry again. He said, *You people are out of your minds.*"

"What do you mean?" Tyrell asked. His neck was flushed red.

"Falconers are loners," Nate said. "That's a big part of the appeal. If you're a dedicated falconer, you devote your life to falconry. Everything you do is structured around your birds and hunting. We aren't a bunch of sociable guys who hang out together. That goes against everything we believe in."

"Oh, come on," Tyrell said with some heat. "We've got files upon files on falconry conclaves overseas. Sheiks and their royal family members fly their 737s to the desert, put up tents, and hunt together."

Nate nodded. "They do. And they'll pay thousands for a raptor that they'll use only once or twice a year. But other than falconry itself, there is no similarity between their brand of falconry and ours.

"Over here, we're outlaws and loners. We don't get together like a social club. When we do get together on occasion, all we do is argue and fight. We're like a bunch of farmers and ranchers and we don't agree on much. We're independent. We're *American*," he said.

"Ibby is about as unlikely to want to talk to me as I would be to talk to him. He's doing his thing with his birds in the desert and he doesn't want to be encroached on by another falconer. He'd resent the hell out of me moving into his turf.

"Why is it so incomprehensible to you two," Nate asked, "that maybe Ibby had a bellyful of politics, religion, and war and he's dropped out to fly his falcons for a while? Nature is a powerful narcotic, boys. Once you step into it and accept how beautiful and cruel it is, you want to stay there. How do you know Ibby doesn't just want to be left alone to practice falconry?"

Tyrell said, "We don't. That's why you're here. You're going to find out."

"Either that," Volk said with a harsh grin, "or you can go on and on for years about 'beautiful nature' to federal correctional officers in prison, and you'll likely never see Olivia Brannan again. Your choice."

"I would have stated it with a little more diplomacy," Tyrell said. "But he's right."

Nate felt a black gloom settle over him.

"One more thing," Volk said, "and this is important. If you're caught or exposed, we've never heard of you and you can't expect us to use any influence to get you out of your predicament. If either of those things happen, you're dead to us. No one will believe you were recruited by the Wolverines because no one knows the Wolverines exist. You can't point to us"—he gestured to Tyrell and himself—"because the names we gave you don't exist, either. We're phantoms.

"We need you, because if you're caught or exposed, it won't lead back to us or the administration. Things are so out of control around the world right now that we can't risk the Kingdom thinking we're targeting the son of their highest official. That would be a disaster, and we can't afford disasters. Got that?"

"Got it," Nate said bitterly.

NATE SHINNIED DOWN the tree in the dark. He still had to feed his falcons in their mews.

Could he believe or even trust Tyrell and Volk? He wasn't sure.

But they'd found him and they were tracking Liv. He didn't see that he had a choice but to do what they wanted. Nate wished Joe Pickett was around to talk to. Joe often had wisdom that surprised them both.

They'd given Nate an advanced compact satellite phone. He was to keep the phone hidden away and it was to be used only for communicating directly with Tyrell and Volk. Their two private numbers were already programmed into the display. The phone had encryption technology in it, Tyrell said, that not only prevented anyone from listening in but also instantly wiped out any record that a call was made and to whom.

Nate assumed the device also had a GPS chip that would keep them informed as to his exact location even when the telephone was powered down.

HE NARROWED HIS EYES when he sensed something out of place near the cabin. It was too dark to see the grounds clearly, though, and the moon fused through the trees at an angle that cast everything in half-light. It was not yet dark enough that the stars could illuminate the ground. Nate drew his weapon and held it down at his side as he slipped from tree to tree.

It was the white smudge on top of the roof of the mews that had caught his eye, he realized.

When he got closer he saw the gyrfalcon. It was the one from his dream.

The bird turned its head and their eyes locked.

He realized that perhaps it had not been a bad dream that morning, but a premonition.

PART TWO

RUNAWAY BEAR

The closer you get to Canada, the more things'll eat your horse.

—THOMAS McGUANE, *The Missouri Breaks*

6

IN THE LATE AFTERNOON OF HIS FORTY-SEVENTH BIRTHDAY, Wyoming game warden Joe Pickett was headed off the eastern slope of the Bighorn Mountains toward home in his green departmental pickup when he got the call urging him to turn around and go back.

He had just made a tight turn on the switchback road from the dark timber into the light when his phone lit up. He squinted against the setting sun and checked the screen on his phone. The call was from Jessica Nicol White, one of three large-carnivore biologists doing a study in the area.

Joe eased his truck and horse trailer onto a pull-out barely big enough to accommodate both units. He could feel Rojo, his saddled sorrel gelding, shift his weight for balance in the trailer behind him. He'd probably been sleeping, Joe guessed, after a full day of trail riding in the mountains. Rojo was ready to go home and get turned out, and Joe was ready to get home as well. He'd been up since four-thirty a.m., because it was the first week of hunting season.

It had been a long day that started with Joe saddling Rojo in the dark by the headlights of his truck. His fingers had been as stiff as the leather on the saddle from the cold, and his breath billowed around his head. He rode for a quarter mile and dismounted to walk so his joints would loosen up and he could warm up through exercise. Joe had to do more and more of that kind of thing as he got older, he'd found. He didn't really feel comfortable until the sun rose and penetrated the dark lodgepole pine forest.

At the first camp, he'd shared a bacon-and-egg breakfast over a campfire with a trio of elk hunters from West Virginia, and then rode in a huge loop through the trees for the rest of the day, checking licenses, conservation stamps, and making sure game laws had been obeyed.

Joe preferred riding from camp to camp on horseback rather than using his pickup or four-wheel ATV. There were few good roads in the forest, and on Rojo he could cut through stands of trees and enter the camps fairly silent. There was no reason to make a splashy entrance and possibly alert poachers or spook elk being stalked. The department *wanted* hunters in the area to have a big harvest, because the elk population was getting out of control.

The risk of riding, though, was the possibility of a hunter mistaking Joe's horse for an elk or a moose in the trees and firing away. That, and getting thrown if Rojo acted up. More hunters were injured by horse accidents, Joe knew, than any other reason.

The day had gone smoothly with no drama. The hunters he met were serious sportsmen and he'd found no violations and had issued no citations. Of the twenty-three hunters he'd checked, seven had already killed their elk. The big animals had been field-dressed and hung from game poles.

Throughout the day, the hunters swapped stories and asked Joe where the elk were, what the weather would be like, and if there had been bears or wolves spotted recently in the area. The reintroduction of wolves and the growing population of grizzly bears had thrown a new curve into the elk-hunting experience. Decades before, the biggest fear that hunters had had was being mistaken for a game animal by another hunter or getting injured while on the hunt. Now they worried about being attacked and eaten by grizzly bears, or harassed by wolves—as improbable as the latter might be.

FROM JOE'S VANTAGE POINT at the pull-out, the Twelve Sleep River Valley sprawled out below him, the town of Saddlestring a smattering of buildings and streets in the far distance. Eight miles beyond Saddlestring was the dark blue hump of Wolf Mountain and his home, where his wife, Marybeth, and two of his daughters were waiting for him. He hoped they hadn't baked a cake, and for once— after years of pleading his case—were placing dozens of candles on a peach or apple "birthday pie" instead.

His yellow Labrador, Daisy, was curled up on the passenger seat beside him and she lifted her head and yawned. She was tired, too.

"Joe Pickett," he answered.

"Joe, this is Jessica White. We've got a situation with GB-53."

GB-53 (which stood for "Grizzly Bear Number Fifty-three") was a 550-pound male grizzly bear that had wandered into the Bighorns from Grand Teton National Park the summer before. The GPS collar had tracked its meandering route through the Bridger-Teton Forest, over the Absaroka Range, across the Powder River Basin, and over the top of the Bighorns near Burgess Junction. It seemed to have found a home on the game-rich eastern slope of the mountains and had been there for the last three months.

"What kind of situation?"

"There may have been an interaction with a hunter."

"An interaction? Speak English, not bureaucrat."

There was panic in her voice. She said, "A hunter we met this morning agreed to carry a transmitter with him. We've been watching his movements all day and the movements of GB-53. About fifteen minutes ago, their locations merged into one."

"Did you hear any shots?" Joe asked.

"No, no shots."

"Can you see anything?"

"Not from where we are. We're about two miles away from . . . the interaction. We need your help. We don't want this to be what we think it is."

Joe didn't, either. He said, "I'll get turned around. You're still at the meadow where I saw you last?"

"Yes, Joe."

"Hang tight. I'll be there in thirty minutes. In the meantime, call dispatch and Sheriff Reed in Saddlestring. Ask him to get the search-and-rescue team assembled. Tell them to arm up, since we may have a killer bear on the loose."

"Oh my God," she said. "This is what we didn't want to happen."

"Don't panic," Joe said. "Keep your eyes on your screen so we know where the bear goes. Do you have a way to contact the hunter?"

"We've tried," she said. He could hear a sob catch in her throat. "We've tried his cell number a dozen times, but service is terrible up here."

"You didn't give him a handheld?" Joe asked. "So you could communicate with him directly?"

"We meant to . . ." she said, her voice trailing off.

Joe closed his eyes and reopened them. The interagency grizzly bear team had been asking hunters to be volunteers in its study. Most of the hunters asked had agreed to participate. In addition to the GPS transmitter, hunters were supposed to be given a two-way radio as part of the protocol. That way, the study team could alert the volunteer if a grizzly was nearby. Apparently, the study team had forgotten to give the man a radio.

"GB-53 is still there," she said. "He's not moving at all."

"Has the hunter moved?"

A long beat. "No."

Joe thought of, but didn't say, the maxim he'd heard countless times over the years: *A fed bear is a dead bear.*

As Joe turned his rig around from the pull-out, he speed-dialed Marybeth.

She answered on the second ring.

"Yes, Joe?" she asked. Her voice was flat. She knew what it meant when he called her close to dusk and he was expected home.

"I'm going to be late," he said.

"Of course you are."

Marybeth ran the Twelve Sleep County Library. She'd been working long days because the library board was pushing a one-cent sales tax to expand the old Carnegie building and modernize the facility. The local election was two weeks away. She'd obviously left work early to get home to prepare for Joe's birthday party. Even though he really didn't care about his birthday anymore, he always looked forward to seeing his family together.

"I'm sorry," he said. "We may have an injured elk hunter. A grizzly bear may have gotten him."

"Is it anyone we know?"

"I don't know yet," Joe said. "I'll call as soon as I can."

"Any idea when you might get home?"

He looked in his rearview mirror. Rojo was peering through the slider of the horse trailer and seemed to be asking him the same question. So was Daisy from the passenger seat.

"Not sure," he said.

"We have birthday pie," she said.

"Finally!"

"I hope it isn't all gone by the time you get home."

Joe chuckled at that.

"Be safe," she said. "Don't get eaten by a bear."

"Not to worry. I'm stringy."

THERE WERE FIFTY GAME WARDENS in the state of Wyoming and their badge numbers reflected their seniority. Joe was now badge number twenty because Bill Haley, badge number one, had retired that summer. As usual, Joe was wearing Wrangler jeans, lace-up outfitter boots, a sweat-stained Stetson, and a red uniform shirt with the pronghorn antelope shoulder patch. His pickup was his business office, and it was crammed with maps, notebooks, gear, and weapons.

He had a special designation no other game warden shared, that of "Special Liaison to the Executive Branch," which meant that he sometimes was called upon by Governor Spencer Rulon to take on assignments outside his normal duties. Rulon liked to call Joe his "range rider," much to the chagrin of the agency's director, Lisa Greene-Dempsey, who didn't like sharing her employees with anyone. Rulon didn't really care about that.

Governor Rulon was in the final months of his second and last term and Joe hadn't heard from him recently. Joe wondered what Rulon, a charismatic but at times erratic go-getter, would do with his free time. He also wondered if the next governor would maintain the special designation with Joe, who, frankly, wasn't sure he wanted to work for anyone other than Rulon.

The governor-to-be was Colter Allen, a Big Piney–area lawyer and rancher. Since Allen had won a hard-fought Republican primary in August against three other candidates, there was no doubt he'd be the next governor. His campaign slogan was "Stick it to the feds," which was pretty much the theme of all the Republican candidates in the race.

Joe didn't even know the name of the Democratic candidate, whom Independent Democrat Rulon had not endorsed or campaigned for. All Joe knew was that the candidate was a college professor. He didn't have a chance. In the strange tableau of Wyoming politics that was unique to the state, Rulon seemed to favor Allen and had publicly offered to assist with the transition before the general election even took place.

As far as Joe was concerned, the jury was still out on Colter Allen. The game warden in Big Piney had had several run-ins with Allen and he didn't have many good things to say about him. The game warden suspected that Allen was anti–Game and Fish Department and anti–state employee. Joe wasn't so sure that Wyoming voters didn't just seem to like Allen's very Wyoming-sounding name, as well as the fact that he'd been a U.S. Marine and a high school rodeo champion.

Marybeth had told Joe they were going to meet Colter Allen when he visited Saddlestring the next week. She wanted to try and get his endorsement for the library tax and Allen's people had sent a request through Joe's director that Colter looked forward to meeting him. Joe, as usual, didn't want to go to a political event of any kind, but he felt obligated to show up and support his wife. It was up to Colter Allen, Joe thought, to prove himself. The state had such a small population that all politics were personal and conducted one-on-one. Democrats often sneaked through, like Rulon had, because the governor had a way of connecting with people. He remembered names, and he didn't govern as a partisan. Joe had no doubt that if the state constitution allowed three terms, Rulon would win again in a landslide in a state that was seventy percent Republican.

Allen would be Joe's third governor since he had become the game warden for his 5,000-square-mile district. He'd arrested the first governor, Bill Budd, for fishing without a license, and he'd worked directly for Rulon. He wondered how many more governors he had left in him.

THE LARGE-CARNIVORE research team had set up on the edge of a mountain meadow less than a half mile from Crazy Woman Creek. They had two vehicles, an SUV with state plates and a panel van topped with a satellite dish and antennae and filled with electronics equipment. The team consisted of team leader Jessica Nicol White, state biologist Marcia Mead, and technician Tyler Frink. Joe had seen and talked with them several times that week while he was on patrol, and they'd filled him in on their objectives.

Because of the marked increase in human and grizzly bear "interactions" in the past few years, the states of Idaho, Montana, and Wyoming had all agreed to conduct studies in cooperation with the U.S. Fish and Wildlife Service to try to determine what was going on. In that year alone, Joe knew, a fisherman in Yellowstone Park and a hiker in Grand Teton National Park had been attacked and killed by separate grizzlies. There had been three deaths in Montana and two others in Idaho. With the exception of a photographer who foolishly got too close to a grizzly sow and her cubs in Idaho, the remaining six deaths all appeared unprovoked.

Hunting season brought a whole new set of problems because the mountains were flooded with human beings actively encroaching on grizzly bear country—which was growing in size by the year. That many humans meant that many more potential encounters, and that many more bloody deaths. The three states and the federal wildlife agency hoped that the simultaneous studies of the bears would provide new insight into grizzly bear behavior.

Some of the early findings, Jessica White told Joe, had startled the researchers. Because collars with GPS technology had replaced simple but reliable radio transmitters, researchers were able to track the movement of collared grizzlies as never before. Instead of tracking bears in close proximity to them, the researchers could use satellite technology to track the bears from any computer and location. They'd learned, for example, that one female bear named Ethyl had covered 2,800 miles over three years—a distance and range never before imagined by bear researchers. Ethyl had traveled throughout Montana and Idaho, over mountain ranges, across rivers, and through the sleeping downtowns of small villages. Ethyl had raided dumpsters behind motels and grocery stores, and had holed up in the brush next to a rural grade-school playground for two nights and had not been detected by locals.

Other findings were even more ominous, she said, and they involved hunters. The research teams asked men to volunteer in the study by carrying GPS devices of their own. That way, the biologists could track both grizzlies and humans at the same time and chart their movements. What they found in some instances was that grizzlies stalked hunters without ever being seen as the men moved through the trees. In some cases, the bears got within fifty yards of unsuspecting hunters. In other cases, it appeared the bears were scouting the humans the way they'd stalk other prey.

The new findings created a good deal of debate and the controversy was getting bigger. Factions were lining up on different sides: animal rights advocates, outdoor groups, biologists, environmentalists, anti- and pro-hunting groups, guides and outfitters, sportsmen's clubs. A recent article about the findings in the *New York Times* had stirred nationwide media interest and questions Joe couldn't begin to answer:

Had grizzly bears always behaved this way or was it something new?

If the behavior was new, what had triggered it?

Had something evolved in the genetics of bears that caused them to think of humans as a food source?

Had studying the bears itself led to breaking down the natural wall between humans and the large carnivores?

Should people just stay out of the forests altogether to lessen the chances of bear-human encounters?

Jessica Nicol White and Marcia Mead were obviously distraught when Joe arrived at their camp in the meadow. Both worked for the department out of the Jackson Hole office, and they looked it, Joe thought. There was a veneer of resort town chic in their dress and manner.

White was in her late twenties and wore a fleece vest, heavy jeans, and glasses designed to make her look smart. She had her brown hair tied back in a ponytail. Mead was a cowgirl in boots, an untucked shirt with snap buttons, and a King Ropes cap that held her hair out of her eyes. Both women were smart, schooled, and professional. They were also a little naive, Joe thought. He'd strongly suggested that, in addition to the bear spray they both had within easy reach, they should have a large-caliber gun in their camp in case one of their study subjects got too close. They didn't like that idea.

Although it had warmed to the low fifties during the day, it was cooling fast as the sun chinned the western peaks. The aroma of pine and sage hung in the air. It was not yet deep enough into the fall that the grass crunched under his boot soles.

White motioned to him from the open van door as Joe pulled up and parked between the tree line and the meadow.

"You have to come look at this," she said.

Mead stood off to the side of the van, her face blank. She looked to be in shock.

As Joe approached and clamped on his hat, he saw Tyler Frink, the tech guy, roll back in his chair inside the van so that Joe could get his shoulders in.

"Did you call Sheriff Reed?" Joe asked.

"Yes. He says he can't get up here for at least an *hour*." White sounded annoyed.

"It's thirty-five miles. It takes an hour to get here from town," Joe said. "That's actually pretty quick."

"It'll be almost dark by then," she said, her voice rising in pitch.

"Yup," Joe said. "Show me what you've got."

He leaned inside and Frink pointed at a computer monitor on a small inset desk. Tyler Frink had mussed hair, an oversized flannel shirt, and hipster glasses that looked as out of place in the Bighorns as the panel van itself. When Joe had first met him, Frink had said he liked to be called "T-Frink." Joe said, "Okay, Tyler."

On the background of the screen was a high-altitude satellite view of the Crazy Woman Creek drainage with two lines going through it.

"The red line is GB-53," Frink said, pressing his fingertip against the screen. "You can see him moving through the heavy timber from west to east."

"How often does the collar transmit?" Joe asked.

"We've got it set to transmit every twenty minutes."

"Isn't that a lot?" Joe asked skeptically. He knew that one of the big issues with the new GPS tracking collars was battery power. The more the collar transmitted, the faster the charge was depleted. Joe knew it because he'd heard researchers over the radio complaining about "lost" bears.

"It is a lot," White said defensively over Joe's shoulder. "But we increase the transmissions if we think there's a greater likelihood of a human encounter."

"Got it," Joe said.

"The blue line is our hunter," Frink said, clicking to another screen and moving his finger.

"Does he have a name?" Joe asked.

"Bub-something," Frink said. "Really: *Bub*." He had a slight smirk.

"Bub Beeman," Joe said. "I know him. Good guy."

Bub Beeman was actually a no-account roofer from Winchester who was in and out of the county jail on possession charges. On September 1, Joe had cited him for killing too many mourning doves. He really wasn't known around the county as a model citizen, but Joe wanted to impress upon the researchers that Bub wasn't just a test subject—he was an actual human being. Joe's experience with biologists was that they sometimes saw the world through the point of view of the creatures they were studying and they discounted the citizens who paid their salaries.

Frink exchanged looks with Jessica White. They were thinking that over.

"Go on," Joe prompted.

"So Bub is moving from west to east as well, kind of following this drainage as it curves around. What we're looking at here is about ten this morning."

"Where's your bear?" Joe asked.

"Way up here," he said, widening the scope.

"How far apart are they at this point?"

"A mile and a half, I think. There's a high ridge and lots of trees between them. Now watch this," Frink said, and clicked to the next image. "This is about ten-forty."

Joe narrowed his eyes. The red line had turned sharply toward the blue line.

"Now the bear is about a quarter of a mile away from Bub."

"Could a grizzly smell a man from a mile and a half away?" Joe asked.

"It's unlikely but possible," White said from behind Joe. "Their sense of smell is amazing. We've watched a grizzly make a beeline toward a dying moose from three miles away and all we can guess is that he was using his olfactory assets."

"His nose," Joe said.

"Yes."

"Tell me," Joe said, "did you hear any shots around then?"

White turned to Marcia Mead. "Remember when you said you heard a couple of gunshots? When was that?"

"Around ten-thirty," Mead said. "I didn't look at my watch."

Joe said, "Don't these grizzlies like to feed on gut piles?"

A gut pile was made up of organs and viscera after a big-game animal was dressed in the field. Birds circling around gut piles was the way he found where most hunters had made their kills.

"They do," White said.

"So a couple of shots might be just like a dinner bell to your grizzly."

"It's possible," White said. "I hope that's not the case."

"Anyway," Joe said, turning back to Frink, "if it was Bub who took a couple of shots, he must have missed. He wouldn't leave a dead animal, and it doesn't look like he's tracking one he hit. It looks like he just moved on after he shot."

———

"That works," Frink said. "I'll advance the screenshots hour by hour."

Joe felt his stomach clench as he watched. At eleven, the bear was less than a hundred yards from Bub. Bub apparently couldn't see it, though, because he stopped at a single location from noon to two. Joe guessed Bub stopped at a vantage point where he could see out into the creek drainage below him. Bub probably looked for elk and ate some lunch. Maybe he even took a nap. The whole time Bub was there, GB-53 had stopped as well. Keeping close to Bub.

At three, Bub moved again. The grizzly tracked him, and on the screen the lines were a quarter inch apart. On the ground, Frink said, it was probably seventy to eighty yards. Joe knew the timber was thick where Bub hunted, and he probably couldn't have seen the bear even if he'd known it was there and was looking for it.

"Is this when you tried to call him?" Joe asked.

"Yes," White said. "We couldn't get any response."

"And what happened to the handheld you forgot to give him?" Joe asked.

"We didn't forget," White said. "But somebody forgot to put it on the charger overnight." She looked accusingly at Frink.

"Dude, since when is that my job?" he asked back heatedly. "I man the tracking equipment and download the data. Where in my job description does it say I have to keep your radios charged up at all times, too? Are you going to pay me overtime for that when I'm off the clock?"

"It's implied," White said.

"Implied," Frink repeated under his breath, as if it were the most outlandish thing he had ever heard. "Look, we didn't cause this to

happen. We're not liable for any of this. We didn't know GB-53 would go after Bub. How could we?"

Joe wanted to smack him.

"We can talk about this later, T-Frink," White said.

"Okay," Frink said after a deep sigh. He looked over at Joe and gestured to the monitor. "Here's where things went bad."

The lines merged sometime between three-ten and three-thirty. The tracking devices continued to send out signals every twenty minutes, but they didn't move.

"How far is that from here?" Joe asked.

"Three miles," White said.

Joe leaned out of the van and scanned the terrain to the west where Bub had stopped moving. Across the open meadow was a wall of trees that continued as far as he could see.

"There's no way to drive there," Joe said. "But if we take my horse, we can get there in less than an hour, if we go now."

Frink quickly sat back in his chair with his hands up in a *Not me* gesture.

"I don't want you along anyway," Joe said. To Jessica White and Marcia Mead, he said, "One of you should stay here to direct the sheriff. The other one can come with Rojo and me."

"I'll go," White said, instinctively reaching back for the can of bear spray on her belt to make sure it was there.

"Bet you wish you had that gun now," Joe said, grim.

"We're here to save bears, not to kill them," White said.

"Best not let Bub's family hear you say that."

7

"GB-53 IS ON THE MOVE," JESSICA WHITE REPORTED TO JOE, even though he'd just clearly heard Marcia Mead say exactly that on the handheld radio White had looped around her neck.

"Which way?" Joe asked, which White repeated.

"South," Mead said.

"South," White said, looking up.

"Away from us," Joe said. "That makes me feel a little more secure."

"Me too," White said.

They were on foot in the black timber. Joe was leading Rojo with a loose rope as they shinnied through closely spaced trees and stepped over downed logs. He'd thought about trying to ride double with Jessica White, but because Rojo was worn out from the day and the close timber was all around them, he'd decided against it. Too many low-hanging branches to navigate with two riders. The reason for walking Rojo in was in case Joe had to transport a body out.

Much to Daisy's dismay, Joe had closed her in the cab of his truck with the windows cracked. He didn't want to risk losing his Labrador.

IT WAS NOT YET DUSK above the crown of the trees, but inside the forest it was already twilight and muted. The only sounds were from unseen squirrels, announcing their encroachment up the line to other squirrels, and the heavy footfalls of Rojo in the pine needle mulch.

Jessica White had a battery-powered GPS tracking device hanging from around her neck, as well as the radio. She'd said she preferred to be in contact with Marcia Mead and Tyler Frink back in the van rather than use the unit. Their electronics had better capability than the portable unit, she'd told Joe.

He thought it an odd decision at first until he realized that she was scared and she needed to maintain constant contact with her colleagues. She was used to doing research by staring at computer monitors and analyzing what she saw, not taking off across mountains as the sun slipped behind the western peaks. Otherwise, he thought, what they were doing and what they might encounter would seem too *real*.

BEFORE THEY'D LEFT, she'd asked T-Frink to increase the rapidity of the transmission rate on GB-53's collar to fifteen-second pulses. She'd said, "Too much can happen if we can only track him in twenty-minute increments." At the time, Joe saw the sense in that, even though he knew it meant it would draw down further on the battery capability of the collar.

In addition to his .40 Glock semiauto, Joe carried his Remington Wingmaster 12-gauge shotgun. He'd replaced the buckshot shells with slugs for close-in lethality. An M14 carbine chambered in .308 Winchester was in the saddle scabbard on Rojo. A fresh canister of bear spray was clipped to his belt.

"I've done this before, you know," he said to White. "We had a rogue grizzly bear about ten years ago in the Bighorns. I saw him attack a man from behind. I still can't get that image out of my mind—how fast and how powerful that bear was."

"Did you kill it?" she asked, sure of his answer.

"I was too slow," he said, surprising her. "It ran off."

"Did you ever see it again?"

"Nope."

"Good for both of you, I guess," she said. "What are you going to do if we walk into GB-53?"

Joe hesitated a moment and said, "Whatever I have to."

"That's what I was afraid of," she said.

GB-53 WAS YOUNGER and bigger than the grizzly Joe had encountered ten years before. At that time, a terrific drought had caused some bears in Yellowstone to wander out of the park in search of food. The reintroduction of gray wolves into the park by the federal government had skewed the balance, and there was terrific competition for carrion and other staples. The rogue bear was four hundred pounds of desperation.

This five-year-old, 550-pound male grizzly was another matter. Some males, known as silvertips because their heavy coats eventually looked frosted, reached eight hundred to a thousand pounds and could be eight to nine feet tall when standing up. A single swipe from their three-inch razor-sharp claws could disembowel a horse. They had no natural predators. Jessica White or Marcia Mead couldn't provide a good reason why it had left Grand Teton Park on its own and had subsequently covered so much ground. That it had apparently stalked and attacked Bub Beeman would make it—and them—infamous. *A fed bear is a dead bear,* Joe thought again.

"*Ursus horribilis,*" Joe said, citing the scientific name for the grizzly.

"We don't use that name," White said.

"Of course you don't," Joe said. "If you don't say it out loud, it can't mean 'horrible bear.' Right?"

"I HEARD A THEORY about why the grizzly bears are acting the way they are," Joe said as they probed deeper into the forest. "I heard it from an old hunting guide. He wasn't a biologist and I don't think he even finished high school, but he'd spent his life hunting elk and bighorn sheep in the most rugged country in Wyoming. Want to hear it?"

White sighed and said, "Sure. I love these old unscientific mountain-man theories."

Joe smiled and said, "His theory was that by overstudying grizzly bears we're creating a whole new and more dangerous strain of them."

She rolled her eyes. "That makes absolutely no sense."

Joe continued anyway. "His theory was that the bears are constantly being tranquilized, transported, measured, weighed, and tracked. From when they're cubs there are people knocking them out and checking their teeth, then buckling tracking collars on them. These bears, which maybe a hundred years ago stayed as far away from humans as they could get because they might get shot on sight, now grow up with people sticking their hands in their mouths and crowding everything they do. They no longer have a built-in fear of humans, and why should they? Besides, maybe we taste good and we're easy to kill because we no longer think of them as 'horrible bears.'"

"That's ridiculous," White said with heat. "Are you saying people should go back to killing them on sight? That's probably what your old mountain man would want to do."

"I'm not sure what his solution was," Joe said. "I just thought it was an interesting theory."

"He never told you his solution?" she asked, arching her eyebrows.

"He died before he could," Joe said. "A grizzly bear killed him in his hunting camp last fall."

"Oh, very funny," she said. Then she thought about it and her tone changed. "Last fall? Was it up near Dubois?"

"Yup."

"GB-38. I wasn't tracking him, but the other research team said that the old man hadn't hung his camp meat in the trees far enough away from his tent. They said GB-38 must have been drawn to that elk camp because of that man's bad practices."

"That must have been it, all right," Joe said.

"If you're being sarcastic . . ." she began, but stopped speaking in midsentence because she noticed Joe had dropped the subject and was pointing off to the side of the skinny game trail they were on.

THE GROUND WAS CHURNED UP between the bases of a half-dozen pine trees as if someone had brought in a piece of heavy machinery. At the edge of the disturbance was a large mound of fresh dirt, dry branches, and turned-up mulch.

Twenty feet from the mound, a scoped hunting rifle was leaned carefully against a tree trunk, as if someone had taken the rifle from his shoulder, propped it against the tree, and started to relieve himself or light a cigarette.

Joe whispered, "You know that sometimes they bury their meat in a cache for later."

White nodded, her eyes wide. "Do you think he's in there?" she asked, gesturing to the mound.

"Yup," Joe said. He could see glimpses of bloody flesh and clothing through the crosshatched branches.

To confirm that they were where they should be, she asked Mead, back at the van, to read the coordinates.

"Yes," Mead said. "You're right on top of the volunteer location."

Joe bent over and dug a GPS tracking unit from the upturned soil.

"Is this the one you gave to Bub?" he asked quietly.

She nodded that it was.

Her radio crackled alive. "Jess, GB-53 is coming back. Can you hear me?"

She raised the radio. "Yes, I can hear you. Are you sure about GB-53?"

"I'm sure. He's coming fast."

Joe said, "He knows we found his cache . . ."

ROJO TUGGED BACK on the lead rope in Joe's hand and snorted through his nostrils. The gelding could either hear the grizzly coming or smell its scent. Rojo's eyes showed white as they rolled back in his head.

"Whoa, whoa," Joe said, trying to calm his horse.

"What do we do?" White asked with pleading eyes.

"Get ready," Joe said. He managed to coax Rojo to the side of the trail and he quickly tied him off around the trunk of a spruce.

"I can hear him coming," White said, fumbling for the bear spray she had clipped to her belt. She mishandled the canister and it fell to the ground. "Oh my God . . ."

Joe could hear him, too. GB-53 was coming up the trail like a freight train, snapping branches and shouldering through dense brush. There was a guttural *woof-woof-woof* that sent Rojo into a kicking fit. Joe wasn't sure his horse wouldn't break the lead rope or pull the tree down on top of them all. Needles in the pine tree rained down. Out of the corner of his eye, he saw White scramble for the canister and inadvertently kick it farther away from herself.

Joe had his bear spray canister in his right hand and his shotgun in his left. The bear was coming so fast he didn't know which one to toss aside. He could feel the ground vibrate through the soles of his boots.

Glimpses of a heavy, low-to-the-ground dark brown form strobed through the trees to the south. The speed of the bear was incredible, and Joe recalled that a grizzly at full speed could run down and catch a quarter horse in full gallop.

There was no way they could get away before the bear was on them.

What happened next took place in seconds.

The grizzly crashed through the brush less than fifteen yards away and stopped. Joe could see the bear's tiny eyes set in its hubcap face and the nascent hump on its back. The short fur around its mouth was tinged pink with dried blood—Bub Beeman's blood. The plastic GPS collar was partially visible on the bear's thick neck. The grizzly rocked back and looked like a five-hundred-pound fist ready to strike a fatal blow.

Joe sensed confusion from the bear. The grizzly had three targets in front of it—Jessica White, Rojo, and Joe—and it wasn't sure which one to attack. Jessica White screamed and flailed her arms in the air, one of two methods that supposedly worked to spook a bear. The other was playing dead. No one seemed certain of the correct method. Joe glanced over to see the dropped can of bear spray was still beyond White's reach.

GB-53 hunched its front shoulders and leaned its head back and roared, a sound Joe knew would haunt him in his dreams, if he ever dreamed again. His heart raced and he could barely get a breath.

Without thinking, Joe raised his own canister of bear spray, thumbed off the safety catch, and pulled the red trigger. It hissed and blew out a cone-shaped fountain of red mist toward the grizzly. He knew that the canister supposedly worked at thirty feet for nine seconds and that the spray itself was packed with capsaicinoids— superconcentrated red pepper.

———

The cloud of red spray enveloped the bear and it roared again, then yelped like a kicked dog while it spun a hundred and eighty degrees and rocketed back down the trail to the south.

It was gone.

PINE NEEDLES STILL RAINED around Joe as Rojo flung himself back and the rope snapped with a crack like a pistol shot. Joe realized, when the sound jarred him, that he was still pressing the trigger of the bear spray even though it was empty. The spray can continued to hiss.

Branches snapped in the forest as Rojo ran north and the grizzly stormed south.

Joe took a deep breath now and closed his eyes for a moment. His heart pounded and his limbs burned with adrenaline. He lowered the canister and let it drop to the ground.

"I thought we were going to die," White said.

"So did I," Joe said. His voice was thin and reedy.

"I dropped my bear spray and I think I need a change of pants." Joe grunted.

"I also thought you were going to use your shotgun."

"Spray seemed like it would work better," Joe said. "What if I missed or wounded him? He might have kept coming."

"You made the right call," she said, hunkering down until she was in a squatting position. She was feeling the aftereffects of pure terror as well. He could tell by the way her hands shook as she tried to clip her bear spray canister back on her belt.

"Maybe," Joe replied, turning and squinting to the north. "I wonder where my horse went."

. . .

BUB BEEMAN'S MUTILATED BODY was under the mulch and branches. Joe could smell blood and viscera as he got close to the mound, and he photographed the crime scene with his phone before he disturbed it. To be sure that Beeman wasn't still somehow alive, Joe leaned down and reached into a gap in the cover to see if he could find the hunter's throat to check for a pulse. Jessica White stayed on the trail as if it somehow provided a safe haven. She obviously had no desire to see up close what a grizzly bear could do to a man.

"Can you track it?" she asked Mead over her radio with a panic-tight voice. *"Is it coming back?"*

"No, it's still going south. What happened?"

"GB-53 was right in front of us . . . I could literally look into his eyes . . ."

Joe overheard from her radio conversation with Mead that Sheriff Reed and his search-and-rescue team had arrived. So had Rojo, who had come running from the forest with empty stirrups flapping against his sides. One of Reed's deputies who had horses of his own caught Rojo and led the sweat-soaked gelding into Joe's horse trailer.

"WE'VE GOT A PROBLEM," White said after a muted but intense conversation with either Mead or Frink.

"Another one?" Joe said, still feeling around inside the pile. His fingers were sticky with warm blood. He'd located one of Beeman's wrists, but he couldn't detect a pulse. Now he was working his way up the body toward the head. He tried to step outside himself and not think about what he was doing.

"GB-53's GPS unit is about to run out of power," she said. "We had it set on high output so we could follow it in real time, but it's getting so we can hardly detect a signal."

Joe half heard what she was saying. His fingertips had found the sharp ridge of Beeman's collarbone.

"The power supply is so low we can't choke it back remotely. It will keep sending out that high-frequency signal until it just . . . stops. We've got to find that bear fast and replace the batteries," she said with alarm. "If the collar goes dead, we won't have any idea where he is."

Joe closed his eyes and tuned her out completely in order to concentrate. He thought he'd felt something faint, a kind of rhythmic flutter, in Beeman's neck.

And there it was again.

He said, "Forget all that right now. Tell Sheriff Reed that Bub's alive—barely. He needs to get his team here so we can get Bub to the clinic before we lose all of our light."

"But—"

Joe spoke sharply. "Forget about your bear for now. No one's going to tranquilize that bear so you can put new batteries in the collar. If they find it, they'll kill it. Right now, we need to try and save a man's life."

8

Joe returned to his small house on Bighorn Road after midnight. He was exhausted and it took another fifteen minutes after parking his pickup and trailer in the front to unload and unsaddle Rojo and lead him to the corral out back, where he threw him some hay. The only occupant of the house still awake, it seemed, was their Corgi/Lab mix, Tube, who rushed from window to window to watch Joe's progress. The mixed-breed dog could barely lift his snout over the windowsill.

When Joe got to the front door, he let Daisy in ahead of him and the two dogs bumped noses. Daisy was exhausted as well and collapsed in a heap a few feet out of the mudroom, where Joe left his boots and jacket.

The house was quiet except for the murmur of the television in the living room. He hadn't expected anyone to wait up for him that late, but he still felt a mixture of both guilt and loneliness when he crossed through the room toward the kitchen in his stocking feet.

He'd been thinking about a double bourbon for hours and, by God, he was going to have one.

Marybeth sat up on the couch with a start and her sudden movement made *him* jump. He hadn't seen her there.

"Finally," she said, brushing blond hair out of her eyes. She was attractive without makeup, Joe thought, but her eyes were wild for a moment until she seemed to realize where she was.

"Are you all right?" he asked. She usually woke up slowly.

"Bad dream is all," she said. "What time is it?"

Joe looked at his watch. "One."

"One," she echoed. Then, with disappointed finality: "Your birthday is over."

"Yup."

She started to speak, but something caught her eye and made her stop short. "Joe, is that blood on your clothes?"

He looked down. His red sleeves were stained black and his Wranglers were crusty and stiff with it. "I guess it is."

She was used to him coming home in clothes covered with mud, grease, and sometimes animal blood, fat, and hair. But this was *human* blood. Bub Beeman's blood.

"Take all that off in the mudroom," she said. "I'll bring you a robe."

He turned on his heel as instructed while she peeled off the blanket she'd slept under and headed up the stairs to their bedroom.

THEY SAT AT THE KITCHEN TABLE, Joe with his bourbon and Marybeth with a glass of wine.

"Good birthday pie," he said. "Thanks for baking it. Peach is my favorite."

"It's also a little weird, but the girls liked it."

"Maybe we can start a new tradition."

"Maybe." She smiled.

April, nineteen years old, had come home for the night for Joe's birthday party that never happened. She'd stayed over and was asleep in her old bed. She now shared an apartment in Saddlestring with another girl her age and was saving up money to attend community college starting the spring semester. She had gotten her old job back at Welton's Western Wear after fully recovering from injuries she'd received the previous spring. Both Joe and Marybeth were cautiously thrilled to observe that she was once again on track. The good April was back.

Lucy, seventeen, was a junior in high school and had just been voted homecoming queen, although she seemed strangely ambivalent about it. Lucy was hardwired to be sunny and caring and blond. She was a social butterfly and not very concerned about college or what would come next, which frustrated Marybeth. The challenge of paying for more daughters in college concerned her.

Sheridan, twenty-two, was a senior at the University of Wyoming and she'd decided to change her major to criminal justice. Because of that change, she'd need to attend a fifth year to nail down all the right credit hours. She couldn't make it home for Joe's birthday, which was just as well, he thought, since he hadn't, either. He'd been meaning to pin her down and ask her what her plans were post-college, since she was always very vague about them. Her offhand comments to Marybeth about "taking a year off to travel or really get into falconry" had not been enthusiastically received.

Joe hadn't yet wrapped his mind around what it would be like in a year not to have daughters in the house during school. He was pretty sure Marybeth couldn't quite imagine it either, although she'd surely thought about it more than he had. It had been years, Joe thought, since he'd actually been able to use the downstairs bathroom, because it seemed there was always a daughter or two in it.

"So the grizzly bear is where?" Marybeth asked. Joe had kept her informed of what he was doing throughout the evening and night.

He shrugged. "No one knows. They lost his signal."

"That can't be good."

"It isn't. We have to wait to see if someone reports him."

"How could a battery just run out like that?"

Joe explained the situation and the circumstances.

He told her he'd overheard a couple of members of the sheriff's search-and-rescue team opining that he should have killed the grizzly instead of hitting it with the bear spray.

"Did you explain yourself to them?" Marybeth asked.

"Nope. They're young and gung ho. They don't realize I've had a few go-rounds with grizzly bears that don't die easy. They have no idea what kind of havoc a wounded griz can create."

She sighed with frustration. He knew it annoyed her when he didn't explain his actions well to others.

"Is there more pie?" he asked.

. . .

"AND BUB BEEMAN?"

Joe sat back and sighed. "He died on the way to the clinic. I honestly don't know how he even survived the attack. His wounds were awful," he said, involuntarily shivering when he recalled them. "People don't realize what kind of damage those claws and teeth can do."

"Don't describe it," Marybeth said quickly.

"I won't."

"You went to his house?"

Joe said he had. "Bub's wife, Tracy, knew before we got there. She'd seen it posted on the Twitter feed of a department tech guy named Tyler Frink. He apparently live-tweeted the whole search and rescue. Next time I see him I'm going to pop him right in the mouth."

"What an awful way to find out," Marybeth said, taken aback.

Joe said, "I don't know why she happened to be following Frink on Twitter, but she was. Sometimes these researchers get so focused on what they're doing, they can't see the forest for the trees. They forget real people are involved."

"April went to school with Bub's son. She said he was a pretty nice guy. There's a Beeman in middle school also. Now they've lost their dad. I'll see tomorrow if there is a fund set up for them or anything we can do. Maybe I can set up a fund from the library."

Joe nodded. He appreciated how pragmatic Marybeth could be and how quickly she moved past emotion to action.

"Of course, we won't be able to contribute much," she said.

The massive hospital bills racked up by April's injury and medically induced coma were staggering. Marybeth spent several hours each week battling with their health insurance company, which seemed to be just as confused about their coverage as Marybeth was. If it couldn't be sorted out, the Picketts owed the hospital in Billings hundreds of thousands of dollars they didn't have. It could bankrupt them, and it was something that kept both Joe and Marybeth awake nights. She'd even suggested reaching out to her mother, Missy Vankueren, who had last been seen on the run with Wolfgang Templeton. Missy was worth millions due to "trading up" over a series of seven husbands, each wealthier than the last.

That Marybeth would even consider contacting her mother told Joe what desperate financial shape they were in. He wished he had a solution, or someone who could help.

In the meantime, all he could hope for was that the insurance company would get its act together.

"I CAN'T BELIEVE how late we're up," Marybeth said, looking at the clock above the stove. Joe finished his pie and poured a little more bourbon over his ice. "We're *never* up this late," she said.

"My fault."

"Of course it is. And don't forget we're going to that thing with Colter Allen tomorrow."

He moaned.

"Governor Rulon is coming up with him," she said. "That's kind of unusual, don't you think?"

Joe shook his head. Even he knew that it didn't make much sense for an outgoing Democratic governor to campaign with a Republican front-runner.

"Rulon wants to see you," she said. "I nearly forgot to tell you."

"How do you know that?"

"His office called. Apparently, they couldn't reach you on your cell. Do you want to hear the message he left for you?"

Joe indicated he did.

Marybeth retrieved the phone from the wall and punched in the code for saved messages. A staffer in the governor's office said, "Hold for Governor Rulon." After an electronic click came Rulon's distinctive growl: *"Hope you're ready for one last roundup, range rider."*

The message ended.

"That's it?" Joe asked.

"That's it. Do you have any idea what he's talking about?"

Joe shook his head, puzzled. "Something to do with that bear? Maybe he heard about it and he doesn't want any more hunters getting killed. But I just don't know."

"You're gonna miss him, aren't you?" she said slyly.

"Not when he does things like this," Joe said.

LATER, IN BED, Joe turned to Marybeth a few minutes after they'd shut off their lights.

"When I came in, you said you'd had a bad dream. What was it about?"

"Oh, nothing."

"It must have been something. You looked a little spooked."

After a beat, Marybeth said, "It was a dream about Nate."

"Nate?" Joe said, propping up on an elbow.

"I know. It doesn't make sense that after not hearing a word from him for months, I'd have a crazy dream about him."

"Funny, I never dream about him myself," Joe chided her.

"It wasn't *that* kind of dream," she said defensively.

"Then what kind was it?"

She was quiet for a moment. "It was just strange, but it was very realistic. It was like I was there. In my dream, Nate was standing in the middle of a desert somewhere. You were there, too, but I couldn't see you. I just knew somehow you were there."

"Hmmm."

"And there were three pickups driving right toward him. In the back of the trucks were a lot of men with guns. They were screaming . . ."

9

"So, Joe," Governor Spencer Rulon said the next day as he leaned in closely at the back of the room in the Twelve Sleep County Library, "are you ready for your last roundup, range rider?"

"Maybe if I knew what it meant," Joe said, easing back a little. Rulon had a habit of moving into personal space when he meant to persuade. The idea was to get so close that whomever he was talking to would agree with him just to break up the situation.

Rulon chuckled at Joe and looked around furtively. He had a politician's ability to always be checking out the room around him to note who was talking to whom, who might be conspiring against him with a rival, or who might break away any second and approach him.

Governor Rulon was a burly, red-faced man who walked with a forward tilt, as if he planned to open every door by butting it down with his head. He had a sly smile and a wink for everyone he met that seemed to suggest they shared a secret. *Formidable* and *unpredictable* were two adjectives often attributed to him.

"I've got a couple of minutes because no one expected me here and I'm not speaking—Colter is," Rulon said, nodding toward the candidate, who was working the room. Marybeth was in front, near the podium, reviewing the notes she'd made for the introduction in a few minutes.

Joe wore a jacket and tie, and the minute he'd put them on that morning he was reminded why he didn't like either. But because the event was political and he was a state employee, he didn't want to show up in uniform. Without his red shirt, Stetson, and gun and badge, he realized, most of the people at the event didn't even recognize him. Governor Rulon had, though, and cornered him at the back.

As Joe looked over the small crowd, Allen was leaning over and grasping the hand of Sheriff Reed in his wheelchair. Allen looked sincere and affable. Joe picked up a few words of the conversation and decided that Allen was asking Reed about the dead hunter and the rogue bear. The story had made the wire services and had appeared everywhere, mainly due to Tyler Frink's live tweets.

Colter Allen was a tall man with wide shoulders, longish silver hair, a movie star jawline, and bushy eyebrows. He wore a yoked camel hair jacket, a string tie, and scuffed cowboy boots—practically a Wyoming uniform, Joe thought.

Allen was being trailed through the crowd by the new managing editor of the Saddlestring *Roundup*, T. Cletus Glatt. Glatt was tall and stooped, his face and neck forested with skin tags, his glasses pushed far down on his nose. His reporter's notebook was out in front of him, poised to jot down any comments by Allen that might prove to be controversial. It was a topic of conversation among the morning coffee drinkers at the Burg-O-Pardner restaurant why the out-of-state publisher who owned the *Roundup* had hired T. Cletus Glatt as the new editor. Glatt's résumé included stints as the editor of a large metropolitan newspaper in the Deep South, then as a columnist for a Chicago daily before he was fired along with most of the newsroom during staff reduction.

After that, Glatt had moved across the country to smaller and smaller newspapers, getting more and more bitter, until he ended up, literally, at the Saddlestring *Roundup*.

Since his first weeks helming the small weekly, Glatt had made it clear that he despised both Saddlestring and Wyoming in general. Also on his hate list were politicians (especially Governor Rulon), teachers, law enforcement, the Mountain West, and anyone who pushed back against the imperial and acerbic viewpoints he espoused in weekly editorials. His most recent diatribe, aimed at paraplegic sheriff (and Joe's friend) Mike Reed, was titled "Rolling Toward Incompetence?"

Rulon turned to Joe and leaned back in. "I see Cletus Glatt over there. I used to get mad when I read his editorials, but now I just feel sorry for the guy. It must be tough when no one who reads what you write takes you as seriously as you take yourself," he said, dismissing Glatt with a shake of his head. "He doesn't realize people only subscribe to his rag for the obituaries, the police blotter, and high school sports. It's pathetic, really."

Then: "Anyway, when I heard from Allen's people that he was making a campaign swing through the Bighorns, I asked if I could come along. Hell, he has a better plane than I do and I wanted to ride in it. He's going to miss it when he gets in office and has to use the state plane."

Rulon's state airplane was a small Cessna jet with the state bucking-horse logo on the tail. It was known as *Rulon One.*

"Sometimes, the best way to get your message across is to say nothing at all," Rulon said. "I don't need to speak, or to endorse him, or to do any damn thing. All I have to do is show up here with him and the message is clear. Anybody who cares will hear it. Even Cletus Glatt might get the message. I hope Colter appreciates it, and I think he does." After a brief pause, he said, "We'll see when I'm out of office."

Joe simply nodded. Rulon often said things that turned out to have several interpretations when heard from different angles. It was one of his gifts.

"Look," Rulon said, "remember when I sent you up to Medicine Wheel County to poke around for me? How we figured a game warden wouldn't be suspicious in a county filled with paranoid lunatics who didn't have the sense to vote for me either time I ran?"

Joe said, "Of course I remember."

"Well, we know it didn't work worth shit, but you still got the job done in the end. You possess special skills. Your talent for bumbling around until the situation explodes into a bloodbath or a debacle is uncanny. I don't know how you manage to do it."

"Me either," Joe said, flushing red.

"I need you to do it again," Rulon said. "Don't worry, I'll clear it with your director. Or better yet, you'll go off and do it and I'll just let her know later. That way, she'll have something to remember me by."

Joe said, "Elk-hunting season just opened here and we've got a grizzly bear on the loose that killed a hunter. I'm sure you've heard about that. Are you sure this is the best time?"

Rulon looked at Joe as if he couldn't believe the naivety of the statement. "Who is to say that your hunt for the rogue killer grizzly bear might not take you out of your district to another part of the state? Would it be so unusual for you to show up in an unfamiliar place looking for your lost bear?"

"I guess not, but it might be a waste of time."

"In all these years, you haven't learned to be a state employee, have you?" Rulon asked, rolling his eyes. "Wasting time is part of the deal. But look, Joe, it's two weeks until the election. After that, I'll be in transition mode until Allen's inauguration party. I don't have that much time left."

"I see," Joe said, not seeing at all.

"It's strange when you're a short-timer in politics," Rulon said. "Staff that used to snap to now kind of roll their eyes and grudgingly do what I tell them. All the sudden, people forget to stand up when I enter the room. It's like they've already moved on to the next guy, who of course will be Colter. But I've still got juice and there are still a couple of things I want to get straightened out before I go.

"I got this call from a donor of mine, Dr. Kurt Bucholz. Do you know him?"

"No."

"He's a good man, a straight shooter. He hosted a couple of fund-raisers for me on his ranch even though he's a dyed-in-the-wool Tea Party guy. You know, your typical Wyoming rancher. He lives down in the Upper North Platte River Valley between Saratoga and Encampment. You know that country?"

"Well enough," Joe said. He'd assisted the game warden down there on a poaching case. Joe thought the high-altitude valley with mountains on three sides was one of the most beautiful parts of the

state. He'd always thought that if the Saratoga District warden retired, he might apply for it.

"Do you know who was living on Bucholz's ranch the last few
months?"

"No."

"Seriously, you don't?"

"I don't."

"Your old pal Nate Romanowski and that hot little number
of his."

Joe stepped back, startled. "Nate?"

"The good doctor was hiding him from the feds. I didn't know it
either until he told me. Apparently, Romanowski didn't let you know
because of that stupid federal agreement he was forced to sign."

Joe rubbed his jaw, and while he did, he noticed Marybeth looking hard at him from across the room. At first he thought she was
trying to figure out what Rulon was telling him. Then he realized
she'd likely lip-read him saying *Nate Romanowski*.

"So where is Nate now?" Joe asked.

"That's what I want you to find out."

Joe shook his head, confused. Why did the governor care about
Nate Romanowski? As far as Joe knew, Nate had abided by his
agreement not to commit any more crimes in Wyoming.

Rulon leaned in even closer so no one could overhear him. Joe
noticed in his peripheral vision that Allen and his small entourage
were getting closer. The candidate was working his way to the back
of the room one handshake at a time. He'd already mastered the
politician's skill of seeming to devote his entire attention to whomever he was meeting and then using the grasped hand to push away
to the next person. His entourage consisted of a man and a woman

in business clothes holding clipboards and with benevolent expressions on their faces.

"It's not just about your buddy," Rulon said. "Bucholz told me he was visited by four mysterious federal agents who gave him false names and business cards. They were there for Romanowski. The agents sent the doctor away and spent a couple of hours with your guy. They sent the doctor out of the room *in his own home.* Think about the arrogance of that. The next day, Romanowski was gone. All he left was a thank-you note to Kurt for helping him and saying he hoped someday to return and repay the favor. The doctor said Romanowski had cleared out of his cabin and taken his falcons with him."

"What about Olivia Brannan?" Joe asked.

Rulon shrugged. "He didn't say anything about anyone else, so I assume she wasn't there."

"But the feds didn't arrest him?" Joe asked, surprised.

"No. The doctor was taken by that, too. Lord knows they want Romanowski back in custody after what he pulled. We get inquiries from the FBI and the DOJ all the time asking if we know his whereabouts. No, the doctor thinks these guys recruited him to do something."

"Any idea what or where?" Joe asked.

"Again, that's what I want you to find out. You know how I am against the goddamned feds coming into my state and acting like they own the place. I've told them time and time again I want to be notified of what those spooks are up to. When I heard a team of them harassed a local rancher and called out one of my constituents it made my blood boil."

———

As Rulon spoke, his neck and cheeks reddened. Joe had heard versions of this rant before.

"I had some of my people check with Chuck Coon at the FBI," he said, mentioning the name of the special agent in charge, whom Joe had come to like and trust, "and Coon honestly knew nothing about this. So that means an agency outside the FBI is strutting around my state, throwing its weight around. It's just common courtesy and professional protocol to advise the local authorities when you come to town—you know that. And I've warned them time and time again not to bigfoot within our borders."

Joe agreed. Rulon had once threatened loudly to have federal employees arrested, but he'd never followed through with it.

Rulon said, "We think we have a general idea where Romanowski went. It's based on an uptick of unrelated crimes over the last few months along I-80. Missing eighteen-wheelers taken from truck stops, big-equipment thefts from the energy companies, things like that. The feds won't say what they're looking for and they've kept my guys frozen out of the investigation. When they act like that, I can't help but think it's terrorism-related."

"Really?" Joe asked. "Where on I-80?"

Interstate 80 ran across southern Wyoming from border to border. It started in San Francisco and ended in Teaneck, New Jersey. Cities on the interstate included Sacramento, Oakland, Reno, Salt Lake City, Cheyenne, Omaha, Des Moines, Chicago, and Toledo. The Wyoming stretch included the highest elevation and the most brutal terrain, and it was often closed by blizzards in the winter. In the state, it connected Cheyenne with Laramie, Rawlins, and Rock Springs. Between those towns were thousands of miles of high-country desert and rough country. Joe always did his best to avoid it, but there were times it couldn't be helped.

Rulon said, "My DCI agents have heard through some of their CIs that there is unusual activity going on in the Red Desert."

"Really?"

"I know—there's not much there but sand and wind. But it's right on the Colorado border, Joe. My first thought was that they were using the desert as a staging area for reselling legal weed from Colorado. But whatever it is seems to be more than that. I think that's where you should start looking for Romanowski.

"So, in my last days in office, I'm using my authority to order you to find Romanowski and figure out what those feds are up to. Go down there and start poking around. Play game warden. If I send my Division of Criminal Investigation suits, the feds will hear about it and know what I'm up to. I don't want them to know I'm onto the bastards. Keep my chief of staff informed of what you learn, and if it's something big, I want you to call me direct. You can run your expenses through my discretionary fund, but don't go crazy buying new vehicles or anything like that. When you find Romanowski and figure out what those feds put him up to, get in touch with me for your report. Then I'm going after them like a rabid wolverine."

It was a lot to grasp, and Joe had a hundred questions. But Colter Allen was getting closer. He was working his way toward them and would be there any minute. There were only about a dozen more hands to shake.

Joe said, "But what if I can't find Nate by the time you're out of office?"

"You too, eh?" Rulon said, acting hurt. Then he grinned and

punched Joe playfully in the shoulder. "I've already got a desk in a powerhouse law firm waiting for me. The partners understand I'm going to devote my first few years to suing all the bastards who gave me a hard time while I was in office, and that mainly consists of people in Washington, D.C., and certain federal agencies. I was going to start with the EPA, the IRS, and the Department of Health and Human Services, but these new clowns who harassed the doctor and recruited your friend are going to the top of the list."

"Will the new governor keep me on this special assignment?" Joe asked.

"I'll have to ask him," Rulon said with a tone that brushed aside the question. "But there's something you should know. I know what kind of shit you're in over those hospital bills. I know that the problem comes in because the federal government kept changing the rules for health care right at the time your daughter was injured, so nobody quite knows what the law is or what your state health insurance covers. She—and you—shouldn't suffer because our government is incompetent and running scared.

"This sounds like a groundbreaking case to me, and I want to break some ground. If you do this last thing for me, Joe, I'll take a hard look at your situation and start suing those bastards. If nothing else, we'll get a settlement so you don't go bankrupt for no good reason."

Joe was taken aback.

"Thank you."

Allen's man with the clipboard was now standing three feet away. He wanted Rulon's attention. Rulon refused to look over.

"You're a good man, Joe. You've got a great wife and a wonderful family. You've worked hard for me and you've taken on risks you didn't need to take. This is the least I can do. We'll get those political hacks to squeal."

"Governor Rulon, a moment of your time?" the man with the clipboard insisted.

Rulon patted Joe on the shoulder, meaning they were done talking. Joe's questions would have to wait, like *Where in the Red Desert?* The area was huge.

"What?" Rulon asked the campaign staffer.

Colter Allen shouldered past his man. He didn't even acknowledge Joe. "Spencer, I was wondering if you wanted to say a few words before my speech?"

Rulon squinted up his face with distaste. "Hell no."

"Will you at least come up there and stand with me? You know, for pictures?"

Joe looked back and forth, to the governor and future governor, as if watching a tennis match.

"Absolutely not."

Allen's face fell.

"I'm here," Rulon said. "That's enough."

"Are you sure?"

"If you keep asking, I might accept and end up saying something you don't want said."

Allen seemed at a loss for words.

At that moment in the front of the room, Joe heard Marybeth's familiar voice say, "I'm Marybeth Pickett, the director of the Twelve Sleep County Library. Today we'd like to welcome Mr. Colter Allen, who is running for governor and who has enthusiastically endorsed our local one-cent tax for a new expansion of the library . . ."

Joe watched as Allen put his game face on and turned and strode toward the podium as if the conversation he'd had with Rulon hadn't taken place.

"I'm not sure what he's going to be like," Rulon said sotto voce to Joe. "Everybody thinks it's an easy job until they get behind that desk. He might have been happier just strutting around Big Piney country thinking he knew all the answers. I just hope he doesn't listen too much to his donors and screw things up in this state."

Joe barely heard what Rulon said. He was already thinking about going south to find Nate Romanowski.

He had a guilt-ridden feeling of excitement about a new assignment outside of his normal duties. He knew he was always at his best—and sometimes his worst—when he was forced out of his district and comfort zone.

What, he wondered, did the feds suspect was going on down there? It had to be more than reselling marijuana purchased legally in Colorado, although that was certainly starting to become a problem.

And what had Nate been recruited to do?

10

THAT EVENING IN LARAMIE, UNDER THE LIGHT OF A USED BANK-er's lamp she'd found at a flea market, twenty-two-year-old Sheridan Pickett sealed the envelope containing a belated birthday card. She needed a stamp to send it. She wasn't sure she even had one.

She'd texted her father on his birthday and he'd replied *Thanks!* the next day. He wasn't much for texting. She hoped he'd appreciate the card. On the cover it said:

> *There was a dad who had a daughter,*
>
> *Swung her,*
>
> *Chased her,*
>
> *Caught her.*

And on the inside it read:

> *Oh, what happiness he brought her!*

Except that she'd messed up the rhyme by penning *Not to mention teaching her how to fish, drive, and stand up for herself* before the *Oh, what happiness he brought her* line.

She liked it, although he really wasn't one for cards, either.

She rooted through her drawer looking for stamps and piled the items she found in it on top of the desk: rubber bands, ticket stubs, several old thumb drives, her freshman student ID when she'd lived in the dorms, a can of pepper spray her dad had given her . . .

"Knock-knock."

It was Kira Harden, one of two roommates who shared the off-campus rental house on Steele Street with her. Erin was the other. Sheridan hadn't seen Erin in three weeks, even though Erin was the reason she'd moved there. They were both seniors and both from Twelve Sleep County in northern Wyoming. Erin had all but moved in with her boyfriend, Lars, a blond exchange student from Norway who lived on the other side of town.

Kira had come with the deal. She was small and pixieish with dark eyes, hair shaved to her scalp, gold rings in her nose and lower lip, and paisley full-sleeve tattoos. Not that Sheridan could see them. Kira was always cold, and she moved through the rental in baggy sweatpants and an oversized hoodie with sleeves so long they covered her hands to her fingertips.

"Got a minute, Church Mouse?"

"I do, Lisbeth," Sheridan said.

Kira smirked at the nickname.

KIRA HAD GROWN UP in the Bay Area and was perpetually bemused by all things Wyoming: the weather, the students, cowgirls, the culture (or lack of it). She was a first-year law student with a husky voice who described herself on social media as "Dilettante/ Activist." She invited Sheridan to LGBTQ (Lesbian, Gay, Bisexual, Transgender, Queer) campus awareness events and had hosted a meatless reception for members of the organization at the house. It hadn't been well attended, but Kira hadn't seemed disappointed. She'd shrugged and gone on. And she'd appreciated Sheridan offering to help clean up afterward.

Sheridan was fascinated with her, and Kira seemed oddly fascinated with Sheridan. They'd become friends, even though they had nothing in common except Erin, who wasn't even there anymore. She'd started calling Sheridan "Church Mouse" after the LGBTQ reception, because she said her roommate stood wide-eyed at the back of the room the whole time, studying the attendees as if they were an exotic species.

To Sheridan, they were. And she'd responded with her own nickname for Kira—Lisbeth Salander, after the character in *The Girl with the Dragon Tattoo*. Kira liked that.

SHERIDAN'S ON-AGAIN, off-again boyfriend, Jason, who was convinced that Sheridan would wind up with him in the end because he was tall, good-looking, and came from a prominent Cheyenne family, refused to come by the house on Steele Street if Kira's trail bike was out front. Sheridan realized it didn't bother her at all, because the less she saw of Jason these days, the better she liked it. The qualities she'd seen in him—his loyalty, easy laugh, and good manners—were being eclipsed by jealousy and neediness, attributes she hadn't detected before. The relationship was going nowhere, even if Jason refused to believe it. He was smothering, and she didn't agree, even though he insisted, that they were "inevitable" (although he'd pronounced it "invitable" the first time).

"What's up?" Sheridan asked Kira, who still hovered in the shadows just outside the doorframe. She was big on personal privacy, which Sheridan appreciated. "You can come in, you know."

"Thanks."

Kira padded across the floor and passed through the pool of light from Sheridan's banker's lamp to sit cross-legged, yoga-style, on Sheridan's bed. Kira liked to keep the lights off in the house to save energy, she said. That she was constantly turning up the thermostat was apparently another matter.

"Do you have a stamp I could borrow?" Sheridan asked.

"I have one on my back."

Sheridan laughed and held up the envelope. "You know what I mean."

"Who has stamps? Who even sends things in the mail?"

"It's a birthday card for my dad. It's late, but . . . I need a stamp."

"I read about them once. Little square sticky things, right? Pictures of dead white males on the front of them?"

"Right."

"Actually, I have some in my room. My mom gave them to me, thinking I would write her a letter, I guess. They're called 'Forever Stamps' because she knows it'll take forever for me to use them. You can have one, though."

"Cool, thanks. I appreciate it."

. . .

KIRA LIKED TO QUESTION Sheridan about where she came from. Sheridan told her stories of growing up outside the small town of Saddlestring, riding horses with her mother, apprenticing in falconry with a master falconer named Nate Romanowski, going on ride-alongs with her father the game warden. Kira regarded Sheridan as if she were some kind of throwback to another age. At one point, she'd said, "You really like your mom and dad, don't you?"

Sheridan had said yes.

"That must be nice," Kira said dreamily. Then she asked if Sheridan had grown up with indoor plumbing and the Internet.

To confound Kira, Sheridan said she hadn't experienced either before she got to college. It took several weeks for Kira to figure out that Sheridan had been putting her on.

Sheridan wondered what her family would think of Kira, and toyed with the idea of inviting her north some weekend. She guessed that her mom would kind of enjoy Kira once she got to know her and she'd managed to get her on a horse. Sheridan's mom thought all differences melted away and that anyone could be pleasant company once they were on horseback. Her dad would be silently confounded by Kira and worry about his daughter a little, and her sisters would act like they had Kiras in their lives, too, which maybe they did.

"SO THE REAL REASON I'm here. Do you have anything going on next weekend?" Kira asked. "Going to the big football game with that dreamy Jason?"

Sheridan smiled at Kira's sarcasm. "Probably not."

Kira beheld Sheridan and a conspiratorial grin formed on her mouth. "Are you up for a little adventure?"

"It depends on what you mean, I guess. If it's marching with signs and chanting, I'll have to pass."

"Don't worry," Kira said, waving her arm dismissively so the end of her sleeve flapped. "It's not another LGBTQ shindig. I've given up trying to expand your horizons and I can see that isn't your thing. Besides, the people in the club spend too much time fighting amongst themselves. No, this is actually an *outdoor* adventure."

"You, outdoors?" Sheridan said. "Ha!"

"Yeah, I know, believe me. I had to look up 's'mores' on Google to find out what they were. And they sound *disgusting*."

"Everything tastes better outdoors," Sheridan said. "You'll believe me when you try it."

"I'll try anything, I guess." Then: "You've got, like, camping stuff in your closet, right?" Kira asked.

Sheridan nodded.

"You've done all that stuff like camping, hiking, sleeping in tents, and things like that?"

"Yes, with my dad."

Kira leaped up from the bed and walked over to a corkboard that Sheridan had pinned with photos. There were shots of horse pack trips, fly-fishing excursions, and falconry kills. Her roommate shook her head. "So you really know how to do that kind of thing? These aren't, like, Photoshopped?"

Sheridan didn't need to answer.

"You see," Kira said, "I'm Internet friends with some really cool people, and they need volunteers to help out on a project."

———

Sheridan leaned back, suspicious. "Are they on Facebook? I'd like to see them."

"Not exactly Facebook," Kira said. "Facebook is too lame for what we talk about."

"Then what's this project?"

"I don't know. They're doing this thing out in the . . . wilderness, I guess. That's all hush-hush. I don't even know where it is yet and they won't tell me until I commit. But the thing is, it involves camping, I guess. I don't know the first thing about that shit."

"So you want to borrow my gear?" Sheridan said. "Sure, no problem. I'll lend it to you for the price of a stamp."

Kira laughed and shook her head. "No, dude, I don't want to just borrow it. I want you to go with me."

"What? I don't even know these people. Why would I go with you?"

"Oh, Sheridan, you'll love them. They're passionate about this country, they're passionate about the earth. And you get to get away for a couple of days! Don't tell me you aren't sick of studying! Come on! Church Mouse, it'll be a blast." Sheridan didn't want to say no outright before she even knew what it was. She wasn't crazy about being called Church Mouse. Besides, she found herself more than a little intrigued.

"If you come with us, you've got to promise me you won't tell anyone about it, right?" Kira said. "You can't tell anyone where we're going or what we do, okay? If you do, my ass is on the line with these people."

"You still haven't told me what it is," Sheridan said.

Kira sat back down and thumped the bedspread with her hands and laughed. "That's because I don't know myself! They won't tell me online. But I know it's something righteous—something you'll tell your grandkids about, because I probably won't have any. But they won't tell me what exactly is going on yet until I"—she hesitated for a moment—"I mean *we*, commit."

"Boy," Sheridan said. "I'm just not sure I want to . . ."

"Please," Kira said. "All you do is study and work and play around with that Ken doll. Isn't this what college is supposed to be about? A time to try things and have new experiences?"

When Sheridan didn't respond, Kira begged, *"Please-please-please.* I know I can't do it on my own, and from what I understand this might be the last weekend they need volunteers. Come on, help out your friend here."

Sheridan wavered. She'd never seen Kira beg before, and she felt sorry for her.

And Kira was right. She could use a break from studying and from the drama surrounding Jason.

Despite herself, she found herself asking, "All you know is that it involves a couple of nights of tent camping?"

"Yeah. I'll bring the food."

"We can shop together," Sheridan said. "Not everything can be cooked over a campfire or a stove. Tofu might slip through a grate."

"Very funny."

"The weather is still decent," Sheridan mused. "It won't last all that much longer."

"Exactly! Come on, say yes!"

"How many people will be there?" Sheridan asked.

"I don't know. I just know a couple of them. But they seem like really great human beings, at least online."

"I'm bringing my pepper spray," Sheridan said.

————

"I think that'll be cool with them, but I'll check."

"I'm bringing my pepper spray."

Kira's eyes widened. She'd never heard her roommate use that tone before.

"You cowgirls," she said.

"That's right."

PART THREE

THE RED DESERT

Man has emerged from the shadows of antiquity
with a peregrine on his wrist.

—Roger Tory Peterson, *Birds over America*

11

IT TOOK FOUR DAYS IN THE DESERT BEFORE SOMEONE MADE contact with him. When it happened, Nate Romanowski was standing naked over a small murky cisternlike spring, washing the red out of his clothing. He knew his movements had been tracked for the past forty-eight hours, ever since he'd found the discarded leather jess.

That meant he was getting close.

The length of leather had been curled up on the hard silica surface like a dead angleworm on concrete. He could see that it had frayed where it had once been attached to the falcon's leg and that it had come loose and dropped to the ground. The leather was still pliable—it hadn't been exposed very long to the sun and wind. Nate guessed it had been there for no more than a week.

He also guessed that anyone else who found the jess wouldn't know it for what it was.

Whoever was tracking him had kept their distance until now.

Nate had glimpsed the reflection of the sun off a vehicle window a few miles away the day before, and he'd seen the spoor of dust from the tires rise like a slow-motion plume as it moved from place to place. The night before, he'd heard footfalls and the scrape of a hard boot sole against sandstone in a nearby arroyo.

BEFORE TAKING THE EXIT from the interstate at Bitter Creek and driving seventy-three miles on unpaved roads into the Red Desert, Nate had geared up in Rawlins at Walmart. He'd topped five-gallon containers with gasoline and water, bought and packed a Yeti cooler with ice and food that would last for days, and filled up both a duffel bag and a daypack with camping essentials: cookstove, fuel, one-man dome tent, pots, pans, utensils. The encrypted phone Volk and Tyrell had given him came with a solar-powered battery charger that also worked for the handheld GPS and topo map software he'd bought. He knew of a gun store that sold .50-caliber cartridges for his revolver and he added three boxes of 6.8 SPC shells for his Ruger All-Weather Ranch Rifle. He paid for it all with cash so there would be no record of the transactions.

Once he left the pavement of the highway behind he pulled over and removed the battery from the satellite phone Tyrell and Volk had given him in order to track his movements. Nate knew that by doing so he would infuriate them, but he didn't care. He would reinstall the battery when the time was right. Until then, though, they'd have to guess at his exact location and he could operate with the freedom that came from not being watched.

In his left front jeans pocket was a braided strand of Alisha Whiteplume's hair. It was all he still had of her, besides his memories. Although Liv had turned out to be all he had ever wanted, he couldn't make himself discard all that remained of Alisha.

In his right front pocket was a laminated photo of Liv from just the month before. She was holding up the first rainbow trout she had ever caught on a fly rod, and she was beaming.

He wondered if he'd ever see her again.

EVEN THOUGH NATE KNEW he was being tracked by someone in the desert other than Tyrell and Volk, he hadn't acknowledged his observer or called out. He'd learned from decades of hunting that often it was best to let his prey come to him and not to pursue it outright. It took patience, silence, and the ability not to look directly at what he was after. He'd killed dozens of elk that way, and he knew that the best method of attracting pronghorn antelope was to tie a scrap of cloth to a tree or pole and wait for the curious animals to come in close and check it out.

Plus, the first reaction of prey being aggressively pursued was to either fight or run. So if he let it come to him . . .

In this instance, his scrap of cloth turned out to be his falcons, with whom he hunted every time he stopped. The birds in the air could be seen for miles if someone knew to look for them and was aware of what they were looking at. Master falconers could see a speck in the sky no one else even noticed and identify the species. Every falcon had a distinct profile in the air.

THE RED DESERT was some of the roughest and most inhospitable terrain he'd ever encountered. There were no paved roads and many of the eroded two-tracks led to nowhere. He saw dry red buttes, slot canyons, and sheets of tilted slick rock that, if climbed, would rim-rock and abandon the climber. Rock formations—haystacks, hoo-doos, columns shaped like giant mushrooms—were scattered across the landscape like headstones.

The place identified on the map north of Skull Creek Rim as "Adobe Town" was a particular concentration of buttes, spires, and rock formations molded by the wind into something resembling an abandoned cathedral or castle more than a town made of adobe, Nate thought. Walking through the formations was akin to explor-ing ancient Roman ruins, but these ruins were natural. Monument Valley, a miniaturized version of the famous Western movie land-scape in the Southwest, was north of that.

There was just enough vegetation, juniper, and prickly pear to hold the sand dunes to the east in place so they wouldn't blow away. To the north, he'd driven up to the rim of a 180,000-acre canyon formed millions of years before with no river or stream at the bot-tom of it. Whenever he found a good place to hunt, he'd stop his Jeep and fly one of his birds. They'd killed several rabbits thus far, and two sage grouse.

Despite the seeming lack of water for wildlife, Nate had spotted hundreds of pronghorns, wild horses, bighorn sheep, and a large herd of desert elk.

But no people, except for whoever was tracking him. No ranch-ers, sheepherders, or oil exploration vehicles despite the fact that the desert had been identified and targeted for future drilling. There were no power lines, fences, buildings, or ubiquitous wind towers on the horizon. Just a vast treeless expanse with deep blue sky on top and a hard volcanic surface on the bottom.

It was an unseasonably warm day for October, and heat waves undulated in the distance. It was still and there was no sound, except for a distant moaning of wind through the canyon near Adobe Town several miles away.

That's when he saw them.

The two men were in silhouette on the top of an escarpment to the west. They'd deliberately, he thought, chosen to appear with the sun in back of them so they were harder to see.

One of them had a falcon on his fist.

The other carried a rifle.

As they approached him, Nate glanced over at his mud-splattered Jeep. The Ranch Rifle was wedged between the seats. Inside, the still forms of three hooded falcons perched in the back could be seen through the plastic window.

He stepped away from the water and bent over. His revolver was in its coiled holster on top of his dirty clothing, but he didn't reach for it. Instead, he fished out a pair of shorts that were, like everything else, pink-tinged from the red soil. Then he tossed his dirty hooded sweatshirt over the top of the weapon so it couldn't be seen but was in easy reach.

He stepped into the shorts and waited for them to come.

"Damned red dirt gets in everything, doesn't it?" Muhammad Ibraaheem said with a friendly grin. Nate recognized him from the photos that Tyrell and Volk had shown him, but he looked thinner and more wiry and he moved like an athlete. He was unshaved and his black curls flowed over his collar. He wore a beige fatigue jacket tinged pink by dust, and black cargo pants. There was a bulging falconry bag strapped across his chest.

"It does," Nate said. "You caught me cleaning up."

"Don't let us stop you. We saw you out here and thought it would be rude not to stop by and say hello."

His voice was crisp and a little high-pitched, but there was absolutely no accent. He sounded like he was from Virginia.

"Hello," Nate said.

The man with the rifle was taller and older than Ibby, and he didn't seem to feel a need to smile. He wore aviator sunglasses and had black short-cropped hair and a pockmarked face. Like Ibby, he looked Middle Eastern. The rifle was slung over his shoulder, but Nate could see the barrel and muzzle. It looked like an AR-15 or similar semiauto. Unless the man turned, Nate couldn't tell if it was scoped or had a high-capacity magazine. The man didn't turn. Instead, he tipped his chin up a little and looked to be silently sizing up Nate, the pile of clothes, and the Jeep.

Tyrell and Volk hadn't said there would be two of them. He wondered if they even knew.

"Mind if we filter some water?" Ibby asked. "We've covered a lot of miles today, and if you know this area, you know how far it is between springs. A man could go days without finding water if he didn't know where it was."

"It's not very good water," Nate said. "It's bitter with alkali."

"You get used to it," Ibby said.

Nate stepped aside so they would have a clear path to the cistern. Ibby gently lowered his hooded falcon to the ground and slid a rock over the jess to keep the peregrine in place.

"How did *you* find it?" Ibby asked.

Nate gestured to the dents in the hard ground near the edge of the hole. "A herd of wild horses ran from here when I drove up. Find the animals and you find water."

"Smart," he said, unscrewing the plastic filter cap of a well-used Nalgene quart bottle. He looked over to his companion and asked, "You too?"

"I'm fine," the man said. No accent there, either.

"You need to hydrate more," Ibby said to him as he dropped to his haunches and filled up. The man didn't respond.

After screwing the cap back on, Ibby raised the bottle over his head and squeezed. A thin stream of filtered water squirted into his mouth.

"I've got to ask you," Ibby said to Nate, "are you flying a gyrfalcon?"

"I am."

Ibby shook his head and grinned. He looked over at his colleague. "See, man, I *told* you that was a gyrfalcon. You need to learn never to doubt me. I know my falcons, even from miles away."

To Nate, he said, "I've never flown a gyr, but I've always wanted one. I've flown golden eagles and used them to take down small deer. But I've always wondered how cool it would be to have a gyr."

"I'm getting used to her," Nate said. "I still haven't quite figured her out."

"Did you trap her?"

"No. She just showed up."

Ibby shook his head doubtfully. "She just showed up? And allowed you to hood and jess her?"

"That's what I thought, too," Nate said truthfully.

He was talking to Ibby, but he kept the man with the rifle in mind the whole time. Nate put odds on the fact that he could drop to the ground, roll over to his weapon, and fire before the man could take the rifle off his shoulder and aim.

If it came to that. And if Ibby didn't have a weapon of his own in his falconry bag.

As if suddenly remembering his manners, Ibby said, "I'm Ibby, and this is Ghazi Saeed, my apprentice."

"I'm Nate Romanowski."

Nate noticed the tic of recognition in Ibby's eyes.

"*The* Nate Romanowski?" he asked. Then: "I'd heard you were a master falconer. You've made some news in your life, haven't you?"

"Not on purpose," Nate said. For a brief moment, he considered dropping and rolling. But when he thought about it, he realized that some of the things he'd done in the past might work more to his advantage than to his disadvantage, if what Tyrell and Volk suspected of Ibby was true.

"Mr. Romanowski here is kind of a legend," Ibby said to Saeed over his shoulder. "He is suspected of 'disappearing' some rogue *federales* a few years back. Not that I'm saying he did it, but his name came up in some of the material I was researching for a story once. You see," he said to Nate, "I used to be a journalist."

"Sorry to hear that."

Ibby laughed. He had a pleasant laugh that came from his belly. "I've recovered nicely, thank you. These big skies and this fine hunting out here has helped me get my head on straight. Right, Saeed?"

Saeed grunted. Nate couldn't tell if it was a yes or a no.

"That's what I'm trying to impress on Saeed," Ibby said. "Falconry is more than getting your bird to kill something. It's more than even hunting. It's experiencing a partnership with a wild creature so that in the end both of you remain true and free. Would you agree with that, Mr. Romanowski?"

"I would. Here," Nate said, handing the jess he'd found to Ibby. "I think this is probably yours."

Ibby took it and looked it over. "I recognize it, yes. I lost it the other day. Thank you."

"I didn't mean to encroach on your hunting area," Nate said. "I didn't realize there was another falconer out here until I found that. I'll be moving on as soon as I finish up here. There's plenty of country in the Red Desert for both of us."

Saeed nodded his approval, but Ibby didn't reply. Instead, he studied Nate. His dark eyes were piercing. It was as if he was trying to decide an internal question right there and then, Nate thought.

"This is a magnificent place, isn't it?" Ibby asked. He seemed to be playing for time with pleasantries while he thought about something else. "It's amazing to me that in a country this big and crowded there are still places like this. You can go days and never see another person. There aren't any cell towers, or Internet. You can't check your Twitter feed or Facebook page even if you wanted to. Instead of everybody staring at their phones every waking minute, you can look up and see this brutal and beautiful landscape. Have you been to Adobe Town?"

"I have."

"If it weren't so remote, it should be a national park or monument, don't you think? Of course, that would ruin it. It would attract tourists and we wouldn't have the place to ourselves, would we?"

Nate nodded. He was getting annoyed that Ibby spoke in a way that almost forced him to agree with him.

Ibby said, "Some people—most people, in fact—would probably call this a wasteland. They wouldn't be caught dead here, because they couldn't check email or even make a call. But I find that to be one of the most beautiful features of the Red Desert. It's like they can't get to us here even if they try. We're out of the system and we're off the map. It's like we can be human again, and free."

Saeed shifted his weight from one foot to the other in either frustration or boredom. He said, "Maybe we should get going."

It was spoken in a guttural tone.

"Saeed's getting antsy," Ibby said to Nate. "He wants to kill something, whether with my bird or with his rifle. While I see beauty, Saeed sees targets. He gets bloodlust out here."

It was said in a half-mocking way, Nate thought, but he didn't doubt for a second there was some truth in it.

"Before we go, can I ask a favor?" Ibby said.

Nate nodded.

"Can I see your gyrfalcon up close?"

"She's not really mine," Nate said. "She's a free agent, like all my birds. They can fly away at any time. But yes, I'll go get her."

Ibby joined Nate as he walked toward the Jeep. Nate would have preferred to bring the bird over, so Ibby or Saeed wouldn't be familiar with the contents of his Jeep, but Ibby gave him no choice.

"Yes," Ibby said, "I've read about falconers like you who don't even name their birds and they let the falcons come and go as they please. It's a different kind of falconry than I grew up with."

Nate nodded that he heard him.

"That's not our way," Ibby said. "We feel that the raptor exists to serve us, to feed us. I think that even though we've been practicing falconry for thousands of years, your way is more . . . enlightened. But if you ever told my uncles or any of the royal falconers I said that, well, I'd have to deny it."

"Royal falconers?" Nate asked. "Are you royalty?"

Ibby gestured with his hands as if to dismiss the question. "I'm related to royalty, but it's complicated."

NATE SHOWED Ibby the hooded pale bird and let the other falconer look it over closely on his fist. Ibby smiled at the weight of the gyr. Meanwhile, Saeed stayed by the spring without even feigning interest. Nate didn't observe Ibby looking into the Jeep at all. He was entranced with the gyrfalcon.

"Thank you," Ibby said, handing it back. "It was an honor to hold that bird. I'd be lying if I didn't say that someday I would love to own one—" He caught himself and grinned. "I should say that I would love to *fly* one and *hunt* with it. That is more your way."

Nate put the falcon back inside his Jeep. Ibby skipped away.

When Nate returned to the spring, Ibby was once again topping off his Nalgene bottle.

"Tell me," he asked. "Why did you find the need to hide your famous gun from us?"

The question surprised Nate. His .500 was still hidden away beneath his sweatshirt.

"I didn't want Saeed to overreact, because then I'd have to kill you both," he said.

Ibby threw back his head and laughed again. He seemed genuinely delighted with the response. Saeed's face darkened, however.

123

"Anyone who has heard about Nate Romanowski has heard about his famous big gun," Ibby said. "Is it true the weapon is accurate at over a mile away?"

"It's not the gun that's accurate," Nate said. "It's the shooter."

"Well said." Ibby grinned.

He stood, capped his bottle, and extended his hand. "Maybe we'll run into each other again."

Nate shook it and said, "Tell me where you'll be hunting tomorrow and I'll stay out of the way so we don't crowd each other."

"I'll be up by Adobe Town," Ibby said. "Our camp isn't far from there."

Saeed glared at Ibby, his face a mask.

"Good to know," Nate said.

AFTER THEY'D LEFT, Nate rinsed out the rest of his clothing and hung it on prickly pears and the bumpers of his Jeep to dry. There was no humidity in the air and he knew the pieces would dry very quickly.

The sharp silica crystals on the desert floor hurt his feet as he walked, and they crunched under his weight.

Just like in the dream.

AT DUSK, he pitched the dome tent and rolled out his sleeping bag inside. Although it had been a warm day, the Red Desert straddled the Continental Divide and the high elevation made it cool quickly.

Before eating, he checked his three falcons to make sure their gullets were still swelled with the meat they had caught and eaten earlier. The sheet he'd spread across the back was spattered with excrement, and he made a note to himself to wash it in the spring the next morning.

Instead of digging into the cooler for the food he'd bought in Rawlins, Nate grilled the backstrap of a pronghorn antelope over a campfire. It was delicious and it felt right harvesting his meat from where he hunted and slept. He'd killed it earlier in the day with a single shot at a hundred and fifty yards.

Whenever he poached a game animal without a license he was reminded of how angry Joe Pickett would be if he were there, and it made Nate smile. Joe was a straight arrow and it was one of the qualities he liked about the man.

NATE STOOD AND STRETCHED and let the fire burn itself out after he'd eaten. He hoped he'd be able to find more wood to burn for future campfires. Wood was as scarce as water. He waited until it was dark before he returned to his Jeep for the encrypted phone. Even though there was just the thinnest slice of moon in the sky, the surface of the desert was lit up in a very light blue.

Because he was so far from a town or any other source of ambient electric light, the stars appeared roiling, endless and deep, like cream poured into an upside-down cup of coffee.

Instead of opening the door to trigger the interior light, Nate reached in through the open window for the phone. He clipped it to his belt so it was out of the way. Then, one by one, he retrieved his three hooded birds from inside. They didn't like being disturbed, but they settled down quickly. With the peregrine and red tail on his left fist and the gyrfalcon on his right, he walked about a hundred and fifty yards from his camp and the spring to a small shallow cave that had been carved out of the sandstone ridge by the wind. The cave was located on a rise, so his camp was below him.

He sat with his back to the rock wall with his legs stretched out and his revolver alongside his thigh. From there, he could see the last of the fire and the light blue smudge that was his dome tent. The three birds stood like little stone statues in a wind hollow at the base of the cave.

He opened the back of the phone and snapped the battery in before powering it up. While it searched for the satellite, he cupped the face of the phone with his free hand so it wouldn't leak out any light.

Tyrell answered without a greeting of any kind. "What the hell are you doing disabling your phone, goddamnit?"

Nate ignored him. "I've made contact. He's with a guy named Ghazi Saeed."

There was a beat. Then: "Spell that."

"Figure it out."

Tyrell sighed, and said, "Do you have a location where he's staying?"

"Not yet."

"Has he done or said anything that gives you an idea what he's up to?"

"He's hunting with his falcon. He's a serious falconer."

"Besides that."

"One thing," Nate said. "I'm being watched."

"What do you mean?"

"Someone is out there right now. I'm waiting for them to move in."

"Is it Ibby?"

"Don't know."

"Whatever you do, keep that battery in your phone on so we can get an exact location on you at all times."

In response, Nate powered down the phone, removed the battery, and shoved it in his pocket. He didn't want to talk or listen anymore and he needed all of his senses on high alert.

12

NATE'S EYES SHOT OPEN AND HE SAT UP AND LEANED FORWARD in the cave while silently cursing himself for falling asleep. He checked his watch. It was one-eighteen a.m. Cold from the ground had penetrated his legs and buttocks and made him momentarily numb. He rocked forward onto his knees and looked out but he didn't see anything suspicious. No doubt, though, something had awakened him. He closed his eyes and listened.

Then he heard it again: the distant and very muffled sound of a vehicle door closing.

The sound came from somewhere beyond the south rim of a toothy vertical wall of sandstone. The top of the rim prevented him from seeing what was up there behind it. There was no light splash from headlights and no sound of a motor running. He'd not heard them approach. But he knew that at least two doors had been shut, and not silently.

He thought: *Sloppy*.

. . .

FOR THE NEXT FIFTEEN MINUTES, Nate sat as still as his falcons beside him. He concentrated on the south rim, and his eyes adjusted to the starlight. There were three openings in the rock wall, three cracks wide enough for a man to come through toward his camp. Whether or not the openings were as wide on the top where the vehicle was, he didn't know. There was also the possibility, he thought, that the intruder or intruders might skirt the rock formations entirely and flank the camp on the right or left.

He tensed when a single mountain plover chirped and flew out of the third opening like a shot. The plover was a ground bird and something or somebody had disturbed its nesting area. The little bird looked like a light blue spark as it flew through the starlight.

Nate swiveled slightly and raised his scoped revolver with both hands to steady it. A good scope like the one he had mounted on his .500 gathered a little more light than the naked eye. He trained the crosshairs on the third opening.

There were three of them. He could see their heads bobbing slowly as they crept one after the other through the crack in the wall. He couldn't see their features yet, just glimpses of the crowns of their heads in a thin bar of starlight that penetrated the crack through a fissure. They moved like ghosts.

They paused at the mouth of the opening, which was unfortunately where the shadow was the deepest. He guessed they were observing his camping spot and going over last-minute plans. Although there was a slight cold breeze, he could hear the faint murmur of whispered voices.

Two of the three emerged from the mouth and moved toward the camp. They were bent over, walking, not running. He couldn't see if they were armed. Man Number One crab-walked toward the tent. Man Number Two angled toward Nate's Jeep.

Man Number Three hung back, not letting himself be seen.

Come on out with your buddies, Nate mouthed to himself.

As Man Number One got within ten feet of Nate's dome tent, he straightened up and closed the distance swiftly. As he did, he raised his arms above his head. When he reached the tent, he brought his hands down and snorted with effort and the sword he held sliced through the fabric and thudded into something inside. Nate saw the blade flash in the starlight.

Then, with energy surely fueled by fear and a release of tension, Man Number One raised the sword again and again and hacked into the tent. The sound of the blade hitting home was a solid *thunk*. The dome collapsed as its frame was destroyed and down feathers from the sliced-up sleeping bag rose from the fabric. Nate could hear the sound of bones crunching and the edge of the sword cutting deeply into flesh and hide. Chunks of the pronghorn antelope carcass Nate had laid down beside his sleeping bag flew into the air as Man Number One hacked away.

"Got him!" Man Number One said, excited but out of breath. "Holy shit! He wasn't so tough. I chopped him into fucking *pieces*."

"Stand back," Man Number Two said. "Get out of my line of fire."

Man Number One skipped away from the tent, circling the sword through the air over his head as Man Number Two shouldered a long gun and aimed it at what was left of the tent. The

burst of automatic gunfire split the night open and the long orange tongue of flame strobed the camp. Nate saw the walls of his
tent dance as bullets struck it and more pieces of antelope flesh
flew from the wreckage, including a long broken bone slick with
blood.

"Woo-hoo!" Man Number One sang when the gunfire stopped.
"Ain't nothing left of that guy, that's for sure."

Nate squinted at the opening, imploring Man Number Three to
come out. He didn't.

Man Number Two said, "Keep back," and a flashlight blinked
on and bathed the smoking tent in light. Nate looked away because
he didn't want the sudden illumination to blot out his night vision.
Besides, he knew what they would see.

"Oh shit," Man Number Two said. "What's *that*? It has hair and
a fucking *horn* on its head."

"A what?" Man Number One said.

Nate raised his weapon and squeezed the trigger and blew Man
Number Two's heart out of his back. Two dropped straight down
into a heap.

Nate recocked the revolver with his thumb as he brought it back
level from the massive recoil and then fired at One as he tried to
flee. The shots were barely a second apart. The impact of a bullet
knocked One sidewise to the ground like a mule kick. The sword
clattered on the hard surface.

The two orange fireballs from the muzzle of Nate's gun turned
slowly in the lingering afterimage of his field of vision. He waited
impatiently to get his sight back before rising and charging across
the flat toward the third opening.

. . .

MAN NUMBER ONE WRITHED on the ground as Nate loped past him toward the sandstone wall. Number Two was stock-still. The dry desert air smelled of dust, gunpowder, and blood.

Man Number Three was gone from the mouth of the opening.

Nate followed his outstretched weapon as he powered up the trail created by the crack in the rim. Periodically, he passed through short stretches where starlight found the sandy path. It was pocked with three sets of boot prints going toward his camp and one set heading back up. Man Number Three had a good lead on him, Nate thought, and he was a long strider.

Before he could emerge from the crevice, Nate heard a motor start up on the rim above him. The driver gunned it and the spinning back tires threw a spray of gravel into the crack. Nate didn't see it coming and the dirt hit him in the face and temporarily blinded him.

By the time he was able to clean most of the grit from his right eye and see again, Nate knew, the vehicle would be too far away to hit or catch. Nevertheless, he climbed to the top of the rim and carefully raised his head over the lip of the crevice. In the distance, muted by kicked-up dust, were the two tiny pink taillights of fleeing Man Number Three.

He was headed south.

USING HIS OLD HEADLAMP TO SEE, Nate approached his camp from the direction the invaders had come. He could hear a high whistling sound from one of the victims.

Man Number Two, whom Nate renamed "Heartless," was a stocky Caucasian in his mid-twenties. He wore a hipster stocking cap, a full beard, cargo pants, and a flannel shirt. His pink face had been daubed with soot or grease so it would be harder to see him in the dark. Beside his body was an AK-47 modified to fire full-auto. An extra magazine of 7.62x39mm ammo was jammed in his belt. He had no wallet or identification on him, which Nate found interesting.

Nate turned Heartless's pockets inside out. There were only a few coins, a lighter, and two joints of weed. Nate could smell marijuana smoke on the man's clothing as well.

The whistling sound turned out to be from Man Number One. He'd apparently turned at the last second when Nate aimed and he'd altered the hit a few inches from a heart shot into a lung shot. Frothy bright red blood foamed from the man's mouth and nose and pooled around his body. He was unconscious and nearly bled out and he clearly wouldn't make it.

Number One was also a Caucasian male, young and lean to the point of malnourishment, with long hair over his shoulders and a scraggly beard that flowed halfway down his chest. He wore a kind of trendy porkpie hat and a dirty North Face sweatshirt. His clothing also smelled of weed. Perhaps that explained, Nate thought, why the two of them had so carelessly slammed their car doors shut.

The sword the man had used looked like a replica of a pirate's cutlass—heavy, long, and brutal. The blade was covered with blood, bone chips, and bristly antelope hair.

No ID, either, so Nate gave him the name "Hipster."

He stood and said, "I'm sorry"—not to Hipster but to the mutilated antelope carcass inside his tent. He hated to take the life of a magnificent creature like that and to then use the bulk of the meat and carcass not to eat but as a decoy. He vowed to pass up the next clean shot he had at a similar animal—even if he was hungry.

He'd thought that intruders might shoot into his tent and hear the unmistakable sound of bullets hitting flesh. But he never thought they'd come at him with a sword and try to hack him to death in his sleep.

Hipster whistled again.

Nate stood over him. "Are you conscious? Can you hear me?"

Gurgling.

"Who are you with? Can you talk?"

Choking.

Nate ended it with a point-blank head shot.

In his death throes, Hipster's legs windmilled as if he were doing an air jig. Then they went still.

NATE DRAGGED THE BODIES TOGETHER until they lay shoulder to shoulder on the desert floor. He placed the sword and the AK-47 across their chests as he reassembled the satellite phone and took a photo of them and sent it. As he did, he was reminded of the grisly photos of dead outlaws from the Wild West days who were posed for viewing by tourists.

He kept his phone on just long enough to send the image to Tyrell with the text message *Who are these guys?* Then he turned it off again and pulled out the battery.

AS HE RETREATED to his cave in the rim where his birds were, Nate pocketed the three spent casings and replaced them with fresh rounds. He wondered about Man Number Three, who was clearly hanging back for a reason. It was either because he'd lost his nerve or because he was directing the operation. Nate was inclined to believe the latter.

He left the bodies of Heartless and Hipster where he'd arranged them in order to be found by Man Number Three. He'd get the message.

He thought of Man Number Three as Ghazi Saeed.

Or possibly Muhammad Ibraaheem, or "Ibby."

No reason to make up a name in this case, Nate thought.

13

Earlier that day, Joe Pickett parked his pickup in the gravel lot in front of the Mustang Café to wait for the game warden of the Red Desert district, Phil Parker, to meet him for lunch. Joe was fifteen minutes early. Parker had suggested the meeting place.

The Mustang Café was a run-down structure within sight of I-80, ten miles west of Wamsutter. It had once been painted white, but it was now tinged pink from windstorms filled with Red Desert grit that had sandblasted the north side of it bare. There was a Coors sign in one window that simply spelled COO, and a brash WE ARE OPEN sign in the other window that looked cheerily out of place.

There was a single muddy pickup with Sweetwater County plates parked in front of the place and an ancient panel van in gray primer in the back.

Joe looked over the Mustang Café and planned to chide Parker about meeting there. He'd noticed over the years that shabby retail buildings on the fringes of society were never torn down—they were repurposed. That had certainly happened with this building.

Joe remembered the Mustang Café from fifteen years before when it had first been put up to serve coal-bed methane energy workers in southwest Wyoming. At the time, it was a notorious strip club, where patrons could eat biscuits and gravy for breakfast on the lip of the stage while women danced during the shift change in the oil patch. The place was shut down after it had gone to seed in a few years and it had become a hub for workers to buy drugs. A sting operation by the Division of Criminal Investigation had led to the arrest and conviction of the original owner.

After a bankruptcy auction, new owners took over and turned the building into a convenience store, again to appeal to the energy workers in the county. It was a place where they could fill up coffee thermoses or their sixty-four-ounce soft drink containers and heat up soggy bacon, egg, and cheese sandwiches for breakfast or pre-packaged green chili burritos for lunch. When the market for methane tanked, so did the convenience store.

It was then turned into a porn shop that stocked videos and magazines. But the Internet killed it.

Now it was once again the Mustang Café, but without the dancers. Joe had only been inside when it was a convenience store, but the sign out front said it was now a bar and grill.

Rather than wait outside for Parker to show up, Joe decided to get a table and wait.

JOE KEPT HIS HAT ON when he stepped inside and he waited a moment for his eyes to adjust to the darkness. When he could see, his first impression was that it wasn't really worth the wait. The décor was haphazard—signed dollar bills stapled to the wall, a few dented license plates nailed up, beer posters with long-legged women, a silent jukebox, and deer and elk antlers that needed dusting. A skinny man with deep-set eyes and stringy hair wearing an untucked, short-sleeved retro-western shirt with snap buttons stood behind the bar, while a put-together young woman with long dark hair and tight jeans, who kept her back to Joe, sat on a barstool.

"Anyplace?" Joe asked the bartender. There hadn't been a sign to wait for seating.

"Anyplace you'd like," the man said. He gave Joe a furtive glance and busied himself washing glasses. It was the behavior of someone who felt guilty about something who didn't want to show it in the presence of a law enforcement officer, even if it was a game warden. Joe looked the bartender over and thought: *Drugs*. Buying for sure, but maybe dealing as well.

Joe could care less. In fact, he found himself fighting back a grin. It came from the realization that he *loved* this.

He loved being on assignment. He got a thrill out of walking into a microculture with a mission when no one knew him or why he was really there. Joe liked getting the lay of the land, listening to the conversations of locals to try and discern their backstories, motivations, and agendas. For a brief period of time, he didn't have to answer callouts from dispatch or solve disputes between hunters and landowners or locate the remains of a game animal someone had poached on a back road. And when he showed up wearing his uniform, no one could ever see past it to guess what he was doing.

But not only did he want to complete this last job as Governor Rulon's range rider, he wanted to find Nate Romanowski. He *missed* Nate. So did Marybeth, but she'd never admit it to Joe.

As if she could read his thoughts, the woman at the bar rotated a slow quarter turn on her stool and looked at him over her shoulder in a sidelong stare. She was striking, he thought: alabaster skin, long black bangs, big brown eyes, a bee-sting mouth. Her expression was both bold and amused.

She doesn't belong here, he thought, *but she acts like she owns the place.*

After making eye contact for a beat too long, she swiveled back around. He felt unjustly dismissed. And he immediately felt guilty about his reaction.

HE TOOK A SEAT in a booth so he could face both the door and the bar. The tabletop was sticky and punctuated with cigarette burns.

"Would you like to see a menu?" the bartender asked.

"Sure. Bring two. I'm meeting Phil Parker. Do you know him?"

"He's the game warden around here?" the man asked.

"Yup."

"Yeah," the man sighed. "He comes by here every once in a while. He's a character."

"That's him," Joe said.

Phil Parker had a reputation within the department as a game warden who worked hard, played hard, and liked the ladies. He'd been married and divorced twice and he'd gotten into trouble in his former district in Star Valley when he was accused by a local Mormon bishop (who was also a Game and Fish commissioner) of sneaking around with the man's wife. Thus, he was reassigned to the Red Desert country.

Joe didn't know Parker well, because their districts were hundreds of miles apart, but he had once bunked with him at a mountain tactics workshop in the Wyoming Range near Afton. Parker had snuck out of the room to go to town when Joe went to bed, but he'd shown up for breakfast the next morning with everyone else. Joe didn't ask, and Parker didn't tell. The only indication of what Parker had been up to all night was a wink over scrambled eggs and bacon.

The bartender came out from behind the bar with two laminated sheets—the menus. He placed one in front of Joe and the other where Phil Parker would sit.

"I'm Cooter," he said.

"Of course you are."

Cooter looked at Joe quizzically.

"Nice to meet you, Cooter. I'm Joe. Are you the owner of the Mustang Café?"

"Part owner," Cooter said. "I've got a few silent partners who live in the area. They like to have a place to go at night, you know? As you can see, there aren't a lot of other options here."

Joe nodded. "Must be tough at times."

"It's not so bad," Cooter said. "We do okay." Which surprised Joe a little, considering he was the only customer in the place besides the woman at the bar.

"Should I wait to take your order when Phil gets here?"

"Please," Joe said, noting that Parker had already gone from a good guy who stopped by once in a while to being on a first-name basis. Maybe the Mustang Café was back to its old tricks after all, he thought.

Joe checked out the menu. It read:

> *Hamburger*
> *Cheeseburger*
> *Bacon Cheeseburger*

Chiliburger
Double Chiliburger
Hot Dog
Chili Dog

"Quite a variety," Joe said.

Cooter shrugged. He said, "We pared it down to what everybody orders all the time."

"Gotcha."

Cooter hesitated for a moment, then said, "We got some other things, too. On the other side."

Joe flipped the menu over. It read:

Vegan Chunky Chili
Al Kabsa

He said, "Really?"

"Them's a couple of local specialties," Cooter said.

"Vegan chunky chili?"

"Kidney beans, white beans, brown lentils, tomatoes, celery, onion, red onion, extra-firm tofu. Jan over there orders it every time," he said, chinning toward the bar. She didn't turn back around.

Joe paused, looking closely at Cooter to see if it was a joke.

"No meat in the chili?"

"No, sir."

"And what is *al kabsa*?"

Cooter rubbed his hands together. He said, "It's really pretty good. Chicken over rice. Lots of spices, including one called *shattah* that'll blow your mind."

Joe waited a beat, then said, *"Why?"*

Cooter laughed. "Ah, a local guy around here showed me how to make it and he orders it every time he comes in. Sometimes he brings his friends and they all eat it. I thought I'd never get it down, but he says he thinks it's great now. He scored me some Maggi cubes I put in it that really makes it go *zing*."

"It just seems strange, is all," Joe said.

"Oh," Cooter said, widening his eyes and nodding his head emphatically, "this is a strange place! Stranger than hell! You never know who will show up and what they'll want, but I am smart enough to cater to the few folks who really get a jones on for a particular item, you know?"

In his peripheral vision, Joe noticed Jan had turned and was looking over at them with a slightly annoyed expression on her face, as if silently imploring Cooter to shut up.

Before Joe could ask about these locals, the door pushed open and Phil Parker entered and said, "Cooter, you should have poured me a beer by now."

"On it, Phil," Cooter said, raising one finger and scuttling back behind the bar.

"Jan, how's my favorite little rock hound?" Parker asked with a big smile.

"I'm fine, Phil. Thanks for asking." She had a sultry voice, Joe thought, with articulate phrasing.

He thought: *Rock hound?*

Parker strode over to Jan and gave her a hello hug. Joe could tell the difference between a woman who wanted to be embraced and a woman putting up with it. In Jan's case, it was the latter.

. . .

PARKER WAGGLED HIS EYEBROWS conspiratorially as he left Jan and approached Joe, who had started to scoot out of his booth seat.

"Naw, don't get up," Parker said.

They shook hands and Parker sat down across from Joe. Tall and broad-shouldered with large hands and a sweeping gunfighter's mustache, an angular face, and weathered skin under a black cowboy hat with a sharply upturned rodeo brim, Phil Parker looked like a walking Marlboro ad.

"I hate to sit with my back to her," he whispered with a sly smile. "I'm missing the scenery. Tell me if she looks around."

"She's not looking around."

Parker leaned across the table closer to Joe. "She's something else, ain't she? Who would think you'd find a trust-fund beauty who likes to collect rocks way out here in the middle of nowhere?"

"It does seem odd," Joe said.

"Jan Stalkup," he said. "I run across her out in the desert every once in a while, but usually in here. She likes that vegan crap Cooter has learned to cook up. Sometimes her friends show up here and she takes them south to look around, I guess. Maybe they go camping or whatever. She seems to know a lot of people and they seem to know where to find her."

Joe sat back and cocked his head.

"I know what you're thinking, but as far as I know she isn't a prostitute," Parker said. "I *wish* she was," he added with a guffaw.

They made small talk for a few minutes, discussing the latest policy initiatives sent down from the agency's director, Lisa Greene-Dempsey, whom Parker despised. "What do you think about that GPS deal?" he asked.

Cheyenne had recently required all state vehicles, whether pool cars for bureaucrats or pickups for game wardens, to have installed GPS transmitters that would track and record every mile they took on the roads. While it made sense for state employees from the Department of Family Services and other personnel, game wardens across the state instantly rose up in arms. That's because much of the time they spent watching hunters and fishers was done from their parked trucks. They didn't want bureaucrats in Cheyenne asking them why they had just sat there on a certain hill for hours the previous week, or why they were in a neighboring county when dispatch called them to respond to an emergency.

"You know what I did after they installed that GPS on my truck?" Parker asked.

"I can guess."

"I took it off and threw it in a ditch. Since I don't plan to go to Cheyenne again in the future, I don't know when they'll get a chance to install another one," he said with sly sidewise smile.

"My truck still doesn't have one," Joe said. "I missed the appointment."

"Clever," Parker said with a wink. "I thought they'd probably made a cost-benefit decision not to put one on your truck because it would just get damaged anyway."

"Very funny," Joe said.

"The rest of us game wardens like it when you waste another truck out in the field," Parker said. "It makes us all look good by comparison."

Joe changed the subject. "How come Cooter acted like he barely knew who you were when I asked about you?"

Parker shrugged. "You know the type. He's got a suspicious mind-set like a criminal. His default mode is to obfuscate and deflect. I don't even know if he's aware of it."

"Cooter's a bad guy?"

"Most folks around here are . . . colorful," Parker said with a laugh. "Including me."

Parker had a devil-may-care manner and an infectious laugh that made Joe want to laugh along with him.

"So how in the hell are you, Joe?"

"Keeping up."

"It's been a while."

"It has."

"You have many run-ins with LGD?" he asked, meaning Lisa Greene-Dempsey.

"A few."

"Is she as annoying as everyone says?" he asked. "Whenever she comes through, I'm conveniently out in the field or assisting another game warden somewhere. I've never actually met the woman."

"She's not as bad as all that," Joe said.

"I have a feeling she wouldn't like me very much," Parker said.

"I have a feeling you're right."

Parker threw back his hands and laughed again, nearly knocking a glass of draft beer out of Cooter's hand before it could be placed in front of the game warden.

"Sorry about that, Cooter," he said.

Joe thought there was no reason to remind Parker that drinking on duty was against the rules.

"Do you gentlemen know what you want?"

"I do, but she won't agree to it," Parker said.

Joe rolled his eyes and Cooter stifled a laugh.

They both ordered cheeseburgers.

WHILE COOTER WAS IN BACK frying the patties, Parker said, "So do you really think that grizzly bear came all the way down here? It's a hell of a long way."

Joe said, "Honestly, I doubt it. There's two hundred and fifty-five miles between where we sit and where we last tracked that bear. But let me show you what we know," he said, pulling a weathered Wyoming highway map out of his back pocket and spreading it across the table.

With his index finger, he jabbed an *X* he'd made with a pen in the Bighorn Mountains.

"This is where he jumped and killed that hunter," Joe said.

Another jab to the south on a second mark: "This is where we last got a signal from him immediately afterward."

Parker said, "I don't mean to interrupt, but that bear nearly attacked you, right?"

"Yup," Joe said.

"I want to hear that story."

"In a minute. Now back to the map. The day after we thought we'd lost the signal completely, there were two more pings. Apparently, the battery wasn't completely worn out and it rallied back and sent out a couple of transmissions before it died for good."

Joe indicated a third mark south of the second. The closest town was Mayoworth. Then a fourth mark north of Waltman.

He reached over and retrieved the laminated menu and used its edge to line up all four ink marks.

"I'll be damned," Parker said. "It looks like that grizzly is making a beeline to the Red Desert, don't it?"

Parker reached out and tapped the map. "He'll have to cross a whole lot of country, including the Rattlesnake Range and the Green Mountains. But he doesn't have to worry about too many roads, does he?"

There were only two paved roads between the Bighorns and where they sat waiting for lunch: U.S. Highway 20 between Casper and Shoshoni and U.S. Highway 287 between Muddy Gap and Lander.

"We contracted with a couple of pilots to fly the route," Joe said. "Obviously, they didn't spot the grizzly. There's just too much terrain to cover."

Joe wasn't lying, because he didn't lie. The unexpected transmissions from the GPS collar were marked exactly where they had occurred. And LGD had authorized several flyovers by a single-engine aircraft.

That the route of the grizzly happened to be headed to where Joe had to go anyway was fortuitous. He tried not to factor in Nate and Nate's strange way with wild creatures as part of the explanation for why the bear might be acting the way it had. Over the years, Joe had seen Nate do things that defied rational explanation. Like the way he hunted by letting game animals come to him. And that time he was telling Joe a story and reached out with a pointed index finger and a wild meadowlark lit on it. Nate hadn't even hesitated while he continued talking, but Joe lost the thread of the story because he couldn't stop marveling at the bird.

. . .

"So, where are you staying?" Parker asked after Cooter delivered the food.

"I'm not sure yet," Joe said. "There aren't a lot of options, are there? I'll probably camp out for a couple of nights in the desert while the weather holds."

"Bring water," Parker warned. "And send me the coordinates of where you're camped. I might be able to stop by and join you for a while, if you don't mind."

Joe did, but he didn't say that. He didn't want Parker to know about his assignment, or to get into the middle of his investigation. Joe had no reason not to trust the local game warden, but he'd been burned before.

"If I see GB-53, I know I could use some help," Joe said. "This time I'm afraid we need to put him down. He's too unpredictable and he's already killed one hunter."

"Just let me know," Parker said, acting a little distant. He'd picked up on the vibe that Joe didn't really want him around, Joe guessed. Joe felt bad about that because this was, after all, Parker's jurisdiction.

Joe changed the subject by asking questions about Parker's district—about the desert elk herd, the growing wild horse herd, the sage grouse population. Parker knew his district well and seemed to be on top of everything. Despite his reputation and the beer for lunch, Joe thought, Parker was serious about his job and his responsibilities.

When Parker mentioned issuing two falconry permits recently, Joe's ears perked up.

To become a legal falconer in Wyoming, the applicant had to pass an exam based on the California Hawking Club guidelines, unless he or she was a certified master falconer. In that case, the nonresident master falconer could obtain a hunting permit from the local game warden for sixteen dollars.

"Two of them at once?" Joe asked.

"Yeah, a master falconer and his apprentice. They said they wanted to hunt rabbits and sage grouse. Middle Eastern–looking guys."

"Do you remember the master falconer's name?"

Parker thought for a moment. He said, "I'd have to go check my records. The master falconer was named Abraham Muhammad, I think. I can't remember the other guy's name. Maybe Saeed or some such nonsense. He didn't say much, but Abraham was a really good guy, very friendly. He was a master falconer out of Virginia and very personable, very knowledgeable. I don't worry much about guys like that who know what they're doing."

"Interesting," Joe said. "I've probably not issued more than a half-dozen falconry permits in my career." He could have added: *None to Nate*. Nate didn't believe in government-issued permits.

"Middle Eastern, you say?" Joe asked.

"They spoke perfect English."

Parker paused for a minute and said, "As you can imagine, being so close to the interstate, we get all kinds down here. The desert seems to attract people who just sort of wash up like they have no-place else to go.

"You should come back *here* at night," Parker added, meaning the Mustang Café. "There's nobody here now but us, but if you come at night you'll see the strangest collection of people you'll ever meet. Survivalist types, dead-enders, computer geeks I would swear are probably anarchist hackers, trappers, and trust-fund babies like Jan. There's no place in Wyoming where you'll find an odder group of folks."

Joe took that in and wasn't sure what to make of it.

"I'd suggest Adobe Town," Parker said.

"What?"

"If you're camping out, I'd suggest camping around Adobe Town. There aren't any developed sites, but it's an amazing place if you haven't seen it. There's no water, but if I were camping, that's where I'd go."

Joe thanked him for the advice.

Cooter brought the check over and handed it to Parker, who handed it to Joe. "Visiting game warden pays," he said with a smile.

"Glad to."

Parker said that if Joe was headed south to Adobe Town, he might want to get going before it got too late. "Fire up your GPS," Parker said. "There aren't any good roads and the ones you find likely won't be marked. I don't want to hear about a guest getting lost out there and getting into trouble."

Joe wasn't sure what to make of that last statement, but he shook Parker's hand good-bye and watched as the game warden thanked Cooter and pecked Jan's cheek on his way out. She didn't react.

BEFORE HE WENT to the counter to pay, Joe pulled his cell phone out of his pocket to check messages and email. There were none of either, and he discovered the screen said: NO SERVICE.

He opened his settings to find out that the Mustang Café didn't have Wi-Fi available.

"No Wi-Fi?" Joe asked Cooter as he handed him the bill and a credit card that Governor Rulon's office had made available to him for expenses.

"Nope. No cell phone reception, either. Sorry," Cooter said. Then he pointed to a sign Joe had missed that read CASH ONLY.

Joe handed over a twenty and a ten and asked for a receipt.

As he waited for change, he glanced down the bar at Jan, who eyed him back. She was sipping hot tea and cupping something in her hands that she'd lowered and buried in her lap.

"I feel like it's 1964 around here," he said to her.

"I prefer 1968," she said with a sly smile. "Ain't it grand?"

He smiled back like he knew what that meant.

Then she withdrew her hands from her lap and put them on the bar. She was holding a paperback.

"It's odd seeing someone sitting on a stool not checking their phone," he said. He realized he'd assumed that's what she'd been doing with her back to them.

"It's known as a book," she said.

"I remember them."

"Edward Abbey," she said. "*Desert Solitaire.* I just finished *The Monkey Wrench Gang.*"

"This does seem like a place where George Washington Hayduke might show up." He'd read the novel in college.

Her eyes widened with recognition and surprise.

"I guess all game wardens aren't the same," she said.

When Cooter came back with change, Joe gave him a tip out of it. "Is there an ATM around?" he asked. "I'll need to get more cash if I come back here."

"Rawlins," Cooter said. Rawlins was forty-eight miles away.

"*Are* you coming back?" Jan asked while raising her eyebrows.

"Maybe."

She said, "I think I'd like that."

In response, he held up his left hand with his palm facing him so she could clearly see the gold wedding band. It had been there so long it had formed a groove in his finger.

She grinned, said, "It's never stopped me before," and then turned back to her book.

Again he thought: *She doesn't belong here.*

IN HIS PICKUP, Joe located Adobe Town on the topo screen of his GPS and keyed it in. Daisy watched him as if it were the most fascinating thing she'd ever seen.

As he did, he thought, *She doesn't belong here unless she's one of Cooter's silent partners.* Next time he saw Phil Parker, he thought, he'd ask him about that.

A dust devil swirled out on the Red Desert across the highway in the distance: rising, undulating, and dispersing until it was gone. Unlike his home country, the horizon wasn't edged with blue mountains, but instead the terrain seemed to fade out into nothing. Far away on the desert floor, he could see dozens of tiny puffs of dust that confused him for a moment until he realized they were being kicked up by a small herd of pronghorn antelope running east to west at full speed. Their natural coloration blended almost perfectly with the beige-and-white topsoil, rendering them almost invisible.

A lone coyote loped along in their wake. In the sky, a golden eagle was being dive-bombed and driven away by a much-smaller falcon guarding its hunting ground.

He doubted that the drivers hurtling down the interstate even noticed the herd, the coyote, or the dogfight in the clouds. Like so many vistas in the state, Joe thought, it looked like a whole lot of nothing at first. But if one stopped and observed, really sat still for a few minutes and *observed*, there was a lot going on. The high-steppe desert was alive and complex.

HUGE EIGHTEEN-WHEELERS roared down I-80 and Joe joined their flow.

As soon as he did, his cell phone vibrated while it loaded with messages and texts. When he looked at the screen, he saw the signal was strong.

It was as if the Mustang Café was a bizarre step back in time and he had returned to modernity.

Ain't it grand, she'd said.

14

JOE RUMBLED HIS PICKUP DOWN UNGRADED TWO-TRACK DIRT roads for the rest of the afternoon. After the roar of I-80 ceased, he continued another hour until he lost cell phone reception. Shortly after, the truck's radio emitted only static and stray squawks of language, so he shut it off.

The terrain was open, but not as flat and featureless as it had appeared to be from a distance. He drove through dry washes and arroyos, around huge red boulders, and for a while down the middle of a riverbed that only went live, it appeared, during flash floods. Through his open window, it smelled of dust and sage and the sunlight seemed raw, harsh, and unfiltered by trees.

While he negotiated the back roads, he kept his eye out for Nate's Jeep, a camp where he might be staying, or a falcon hunting in the sky. He knew that the Red Desert had a few hikers in the summer months, but there appeared to be no other humans in the fall despite the mild weather. Not even an energy exploration truck or seismograph crew.

The wildlife he encountered—pronghorn antelope, coyotes, rabbits, a flock of sage grouse walking down the middle of the road that he had to brake for so he wouldn't run them over—seemed surprised to see him but not necessarily skittish.

THE DEEPER HE DROVE into the desert, the closer he felt he was getting to Nate, although he had no good reason to feel that way. He'd found no tire tracks, no cold camps, no remains of falcon-killed prey. Nate had always had an uncanny ability to find *him* in the past, Joe thought, whether it was in the Bighorns or Yellowstone Park or the Teton Wilderness. Maybe this time it could work in reverse.

His relationship with Nate Romanowski had changed and morphed over the years and Joe found himself reliving it as he drove in desert silence. He'd met Nate nearly a decade before, when the outlaw falconer had been arrested for a murder he didn't commit. Joe had worked to free him, and after that Nate had pledged that he'd always be there to protect Joe's family. It was a mixed blessing, and, over the years, the cumulative body count that had derived from that pledge was something Joe didn't like to think about.

Marybeth had a blind spot where Nate was concerned.

No other man could rip the ears off other men and tear them limb from limb with his bare hands and still keep a specially reserved place in her heart, Joe knew. Nate was woven through the Pickett family history in a wild and unpredictable way. Sheridan had once been Nate's apprentice in falconry. And he'd been there for Joe when Joe needed him.

And Joe had been there for Nate when his friend went off the rails after he'd lost two lovers to violence and when he'd worked briefly for Wolfgang Templeton to "kill people who needed killing." After that, Joe had urged his friend to turn himself in and testify against Templeton. Nate had also found Olivia Brannan, and she him.

Maybe, Joe thought, Nate would need his help again. If so, he hoped he could be there.

"Come on, buddy," Joe said out loud. "Show yourself."

Daisy raised her head and looked at him.

"Not you," Joe said.

JOE HAD NEVER BEEN to the area known as Adobe Town, but he recognized it when he saw the spires, rock formations, and columns of stone balancing ten-ton rocks on their tops. In the late-afternoon light the feature was dramatic and looked as if it were on fire. Long shadows from the promontories striped the red sand and scrub.

Getting closer on the two-track, he noted another dirt road, running north–south through the sage, that intersected the road he was on. As he drove over the crossroad, he leaned out his open window and saw the fresh tire tracks in the sandy soil.

Joe stopped his pickup and got out. Daisy bounded behind him. He knelt down on the crossroad and studied the tracks carefully. They were fresh, made that morning, he thought. There had been no moisture or wind to degrade them and he could clearly see sharp tread marks in the loose sand. There were two and possibly three sets of individual tracks.

He walked along the road, keeping to the side of it, and stepping over tightly coiled sagebrush and prickly-pear cactus. At a wide spot fifty yards from where he started, he could see the tracks diverge slightly.

He said to Daisy, "A vehicle came from the south and the same vehicle went back. You can see that, right? And another unit with thinner, balder tires came from the north and went right over the top of them."

Daisy stood looking up at him and wagging her tail. She wanted him to throw something for her to retrieve.

"My guess," he said, "is that the first vehicle came up this road and then went back. Someone followed it in a second car. Jeeps have narrow tires, you know."

He put his hands on his hips and scanned the horizon in every direction. There was perhaps an hour left of sunlight. There was no way to know how far the vehicles that had made the tracks had gone or where they were headed. He knew he was close to the Colorado border to the south, and to the Utah border to the south and west. And he knew he was a long way from a paved road where he could make up time.

Joe photographed the tracks with his cell phone and jotted down the coordinates in his notebook.

"We can follow these tracks or set up camp before it gets dark. What do you think?"

Daisy thought he should throw something for her to retrieve.

So she'd quit staring at him and wagging her tail, he walked back to his pickup and dug a plastic dummy out from behind the seat and tossed it out into the desert.

After ten minutes, he said to his panting dog, "Okay, get back in.

We'll follow them for a while, but we'll get back here before it gets too late."

MINUTES BEFORE he'd have to switch on his headlamps or his under-the-bumper "sneak lights" to see the road, Joe topped a long, gradual rise where he could look down into the big swale in front of him.

There, a mile and a half away on the desert floor, was what looked like a long-abandoned ranch: a cluster of old buildings in the fading light in different stages of decline. He was surprised there was an old ranch at all, since all around him was federally owned Bureau of Land Management land, but there it was. Perhaps, he thought, the landowner had had some special deal at one time with the feds or the property had been grandfathered in after the BLM imposed their will.

He was studying the layout of the property when he realized he was about to drive into a four-strand barbed-wire-fence gate that crossed the road, and he stopped short. He saw the chain and heavy combination lock on the gate when he got out to open it. Joe grasped the lock and gave it a yank. Sometimes landowners only appeared to lock up behind them. But no luck.

He studied the road and he could see that two—not three— of the tracks had proceeded through the gate during the day. The vehicle had come and gone through it. But the set of thinner tracks he'd observed earlier was nowhere to be seen. He scanned the fence both ways and saw that, in fact, the driver or occupants of the second vehicle had driven about a hundred yards to the east and had pulled the staples out of two posts that held up the barbed wire. They'd probably lowered the strands, weighted them down with something heavy, and driven over them to continue pursuit. He couldn't see anyplace where the second vehicle had come out.

But when he looked over the old ranch complex, he saw no vehicles, no people, and no sign of occupancy. The buildings that still stood were dark and there were no power lines stretching across the desert to them.

Joe didn't want to trespass and follow. Not tonight, anyway. Instead, he attached his spotting scope to a tripod and opened it up on the hood of his pickup. Leaning into the eyepiece, he focused and moved his field of vision from building to building.

There was no doubt the ranch was no longer in operation. What was left of a main house was a burned-out shell with a missing roof and broken windows. He could make out smoke stains above the window frames on the outside walls.

An ancient outhouse behind the main house leaned hard to the left, and a small shed near it had collapsed in on itself.

Four dead trees flanked the ruins. Trees couldn't grow where there wasn't any rain, he thought.

Three very long sheds were parallel to each other across the ranch yard from the burned-out house. They were much bigger and longer than Joe had seen on other ranches, and he guessed they were used not only for equipment but for livestock. Probably, he guessed, the ranch had been a huge but failed sheep operation back when millions of sheep were raised in the state.

So who had driven in and out of the abandoned ranch and locked the gate behind them? And who had followed and not come back?

· · ·

IN THE FADING LIGHT, he moved the spotting scope slowly over the three sheds, hoping to spot the nose of a truck poking out of one of the openings or the driver moving about. A battered pre-1960s pickup with broken windows was all he saw.

Then, barely in his field of vision, he thought he saw a flicker of light from behind a broken window from inside the middle shed. He leaned against the fender of his truck and tried to steady himself further so he could zoom the focus of the spotting scope down on the open window. He saw it again: a flicker of orange-red, as if someone had struck a match. A man's face—dark features, hooked nose—was illuminated in pink for a few seconds while he lit a cigarette. It wasn't Nate. Then the match was blown out, leaving a tiny red dot that was the lit end of the cigarette.

The dot moved from window to window for a quarter length of the long shed and then vanished altogether.

Joe kept the scope still and focused for ten minutes, trained on the distant windows. He didn't see it again.

WHEN JOE CLIMBED back inside his pickup it was full dark. There wasn't a single artificial light as far as he could see, and not even a wash of it on the horizon. The stars were creamy and deep and endless, and the old ranch buildings were no more than black shapes on a dark blue tableau.

He kept his lights off as he backed up the hill and didn't turn them on until he was a hundred yards down the other side. There was no good reason to reveal to the man in the shed that he'd been observed, Joe thought.

THE SMALL GREASEWOOD FIRE popped and smoked and made a sharp, bitter smell that Joe didn't particularly like. But the few old twisted branches were the only fuel he could find at Adobe Town and he'd ranged the perimeter of his camp by headlamp.

The fire was primarily for heat and light and it didn't do a very good job of either. For dinner, he'd warmed a can of beef stew over his gas stove and it tasted much better than it should have, like everything did under the stars. Daisy was curled up a few feet away on the other side of the fire. Since he'd forgotten to pack dog food, she'd had a can of stew as well. Unheated.

Joe knew that with Daisy's hardwired bouts of Labrador flatulence, he'd likely pay for forgetting dog food later in the night.

He'd pitched his one-man tent on the desert floor with the opening aimed at the fire and he'd unrolled his sleeping bag inside. The temperature had dropped twenty degrees since the sun had gone down, but it didn't feel like it would freeze during the night. Still, he wore his jacket over his Filson vest and had set up his Crazy Creek camp chair so he didn't have to sit directly on the cold desert ground.

Joe grabbed a handful of ice from his Yeti cooler and sipped from a tin cup of bourbon and water. He thought about the sheep ranch. He came to no conclusions.

His shotgun was across his knees.

. . .

IT FELT LIKE MIDNIGHT, but it was only eight-thirty when Joe powered up the satellite phone and called Marybeth at home.

She answered tentatively. "Hello?"

"It's me," he said.

"Oh, good. I didn't recognize the number."

"It's a sat phone. Where I'm at, there's no radio or cell signal."

"Sometimes I wish I could be in that place," she said. Then: "No, I don't. It would drive me crazy."

She told him about her day and the editorial in the Saddlestring *Roundup* written by managing editor T. Cletus Glatt, who opposed the library bond issue and urged residents to vote against it.

"He actually said, and I quote, 'Why do we even need libraries since we have the Internet? Libraries are only good for employing people who can't get a real job.' Can you believe that?" she asked angrily.

"Unfortunately, I can," Joe said.

She said she'd fed the horses and walked Tube, and the weather was so nice she planned to ride in the morning.

"So what are you doing now?" he asked.

"I'm home alone. Lucy is at the high school football game . . ."

He'd forgotten it was Friday night.

". . . and April is out on a date, although she didn't call it that."

"A *date*?"

It didn't need to be said that this was the first time she'd gone out with a boy since her injuries and hospitalization.

"I think it's a good thing," Marybeth said. "She's finally starting to get past all of that."

"Who is the boy?"

"His name is Bo Simmons. He seems nice. He even came to the house to pick her up. He works at the western wear store with her. He's nothing like Dallas Cates."

"He better not be," Joe said.

Dallas Cates was in the Wyoming penitentiary in Rawlins serving two to four years for wanton destruction of big-game animals, taking game animals without a license, using an unregistered snowmobile to harass wildlife, and several other misdemeanors that Joe and County Attorney Dulcie Schalk had cobbled together to put him away. The sentence by Judge Hewitt had been unusually harsh and Joe surmised the judge had wanted to put Dallas away also. Joe only wished they could have come up with more to charge him with. Dallas Cates was a time bomb who would likely go off after he was released. Every night he spent in prison was a good night for Joe and his family.

T. Cletus Glatt had further inflamed the situation when he wrote an editorial several months before titled "Will Dallas Cates Come Back for Revenge?"

Dallas's mother, Brenda Cates, was a paraplegic in the Wyoming Women's Center in Lusk, where she was going to spend the rest of her life after being convicted of kidnapping, conspiracy, assault with a deadly weapon, accessory to murder, and ten other felony charges. It was a good place for her to be, Joe thought. Even though Dallas might be a threat when he got out, Brenda scared Joe even more.

"And I got a text from your daughter Sheridan," Marybeth continued. Joe knew when Marybeth said *your daughter* that bad news would follow. "She said since the weather is so nice she's going camping with friends this weekend. She didn't say where or how many friends, but I'm guessing it isn't all girls."

Joe moaned and closed his eyes.

"I know she's twenty-one and she can do what she wants, but, well, you know . . ." she said, trailing off.

"I know. But I don't think you should worry. She's smart and tough like her mom."

"Her mom was twenty-one once," Marybeth said.

"Lucky I saved you," Joe said.

"Very funny. So what are you up to?"

"I'm sitting by myself in the dark next to a stinky campfire in a desert in the middle of nowhere," Joe said. "I ate beef stew for dinner out of the can."

"Oh, Joe. Aren't you getting a little old for that?"

"Yup. The ground gets harder to sleep on every year."

"I'll think of you tonight in my empty nest," she said, flirting with him.

"Now you're piling it on."

She laughed. He liked to make her laugh.

He said, "I haven't found Nate, but I may have a lead on him. I'll let you know tomorrow."

"Be careful."

"I always am."

"Ha!"

AT TWO-THIRTY IN THE MORNING, Joe woke up suddenly and for a moment he didn't know where he was. Daisy was crowding him in the little tent and she was up because she'd been awakened by something, too.

He rolled to his side and unzipped the front tent flap. Cold seeped in. The campfire had burned down to embers.

It was still outside and the stars were hard and white. There were so many of them it seemed they were pressing down on his tent from above.

He thought he'd heard two distant shots in rapid succession, but he couldn't be sure of it. Gunshots in the middle of nowhere weren't that unusual anyplace in Wyoming, he knew, but he'd not seen a single other human all day except for the cigarette-smoking man in the shed. Perhaps, he thought, instead of gunshots it was one of those balanced rocks finally toppling over.

Then there was a third.

He sat up and simply listened.

Silence.

Then there was something else: a high whining sound in the distance. It sounded like motorcycles or snowmobiles, and it didn't make sense.

The whine came from the south where the old sheep ranch was.

HE LEFT HIS CAMP as it was and he drove back down the two-track. It was too cold to leave his windows open to listen, but every few minutes he'd stop and power one down to confirm that the sound was getting louder.

Joe parked short of the top of the rise he'd been on earlier and he made Daisy stay in the cab. He kept low and crab-walked over the top until he could see into the swale again.

He eased down so he could lie flat, but a dozen cactus needles stung his belly. He cursed and moved to the side, then fitted binoculars to his eyes.

Small vehicles that he now identified as four-wheel ATVs were streaming across the desert floor toward the sheep ranch from the east. He counted five, then six. Their engines were loud in the still night, and their headlights pointed all over the ground. They were driving erratically.

He heard someone whoop, and he thought: *They're drunk or high. That's why they're driving like idiots.*

The ATVs got to the ranch and the first one vanished inside the outer shed. The rest of the caravan followed, and finally all the motors were shut off. He heard someone laugh and there was loud drunken chatter—both male and female voices.

It took five minutes for them to quiet down.

They'd come from the northeast, he thought. They hadn't used established roads but had gone cross-country.

From the direction of the Mustang Café.

Joe watched the sheds for a while, looking for lights being switched on or for people emerging from the shed where the ATVs had gone. Nothing. It was as if the riders had vanished into a black hole.

Then he saw figures in the shadows between the sheds. They were busy doing something: pitching small dome tents. They climbed inside the tents and it was silent.

It seemed like an odd place to camp, he thought.

Grunting, he pushed himself to his feet and he let the binoculars dangle from their strap on his chest. He brushed himself off, and as he started back for his truck he saw a flash of lights in his peripheral vision.

Headlights, two of them, coming out of the middle shed. The vehicle appeared to be coming up the access road beyond the locked gate.

Toward *him*.

Although he couldn't believe anyone had seen him up there in the dark, Joe double-timed it over the top of the hill and threw himself into the cab of his truck and drove away quickly.

WHEN HE RETURNED to his camp, his headlights revealed that someone, or something, had been there in his absence. His tent was flattened, his sleeping bag balled up in the dirt, his cooking kit and stove smashed flat.

He said, "What have we gotten ourselves into, Daisy?"

IT HAD BEEN a stampeding herd of wild horses. Dozens, maybe as many as thirty or forty, had run through the camp in a tight enough bunch that they'd demolished everything in it. He could see their hoof tracks on the surface. Some of the horses had been so heavy, their hooves had broken through the hard silica into the dry clay below.

As he surveyed what was left of his camp in the headlights of his pickup, he thanked God he had taken Daisy and they hadn't been there when the herd thundered through. He cursed under his breath and kicked at the shredded tent with the tip of his boot.

Then he heard the sound of an oncoming vehicle out in the

darkness. He guessed it was the same one that had left the middle shed, coming his way.

JOE QUICKLY GATHERED UP his smashed cooking gear and threw it into a pile in the middle of the tent fabric, then carried the bundle back to his truck. He heaved the bundle into the bed and scrambled in.

Since he'd left the truck running, it took seconds to throw it into reverse to get out of there. The starlight was bright enough that he thought he could navigate his way out of Adobe Town by his sneak lights alone.

As he started a three-point turn, he saw the nose of a dark pickup truck appear on the southern horizon about two hundred feet away. The occupants had also shut off their headlights. Since they'd arrived so quickly, Joe assumed they'd deliberately followed him and he thought, *Okay, let's see what they want.* He put the truck into park and didn't begin his maneuver.

"Get ready, Daisy," he said. He wasn't sure if a confrontation was coming or if he'd feel compelled to race away. He could feel his throat constrict with fear.

Joe reached down and touched the receiver of his shotgun, which was wedged muzzle-down between the seats. He'd reloaded it with double-ought buckshot that was devastating at close range.

The truck on the horizon revved its motor and reversed, then appeared again with its rear end pointed at Joe. There was a camper shell of some kind on the bed of the vehicle.

Had they not seen him down there? Or had they decided to go back?

Then he saw the figures of two men get out of the truck and run to the back. One crawled inside and the other returned to the cab. Odd.

What did they have in the back of the truck? Scenarios raced through his mind—a heavy weapon of some kind, a machine gun, artillery—and he reached for the gearshift again and shoved it into reverse and stomped on the accelerator while at the same time keeping his eyes on the black maw of the back of the pickup.

But there was no flash of gunfire, no projectile. Just a loud clicking sound, like an angry electrical short. He felt his cell phone vibrate in his breast pocket as if he were receiving a call, even though he knew there was no signal out there.

Then his truck went silent and died, although it still rolled back a few feet before clumps of sagebrush slowed the tires to a complete stop. The steering wheel became stiff. Somehow, he'd killed the engine.

He looked up at the open back of the pickup in a panic as he turned the ignition key. Nothing, not even the grinding of the starter. In fact, the interior lights and the instrument panel were dead as well.

His first thought was that they'd fired something into his engine block and disabled it. But that didn't make sense: there had been no physical impact to the front of his truck.

As he twisted uselessly on the key, he saw a figure emerge from the pickup, close up the back, and return to the cab. With that, the truck drove away in the direction it had come.

WHEN JOE CLIMBED OUT of his vehicle, the silence and darkness were overwhelming. He noticed that the interior lights of the cab hadn't come on when he opened the door. He also noted a bitter and slightly burned odor in the air, like ozone just before a lightning storm. But the sky was absolutely cloudless.

He shook his head. Although he was no expert mechanic, he'd been forced, over the years, to do minor engine repairs to his trucks, snowmobiles, and ATVs out in the field. On several occasions, he'd been in remote locations where it would have taken days for a mechanic to arrive. Usually, though, the problem was something he could handle: a flat tire, battery cables shaken loose by rough roads, getting his axle high-centered on a rock. But when it came to getting a motor started without a spare battery or computer diagnosis, he was lost.

Then he remembered the strange vibration he'd felt in his breast pocket. For a split second after it happened, he'd thought he'd been shot. But now when he reached up and patted his breast pocket, he felt only the solid square form of his iPhone beneath the fabric. Even though he knew he didn't have cell reception, he dug it out. It was dead as well. He spent several minutes trying to reboot it. He *knew* there had been plenty of charge left in it, but it wouldn't turn on.

Feeling panic start to rise, he tested his satellite phone, both the portable and dash-mounted GPS systems, and his digital camera. His wristwatch was frozen at three-eighteen in the morning. Everything was dead, dead, dead.

And he was at least thirty-eight miles from the highway.

Daisy sat down at his feet and looked up at the sky, no doubt wondering what Joe was searching for up there.

PART FOUR

THE RANCH

A conspiracy is everything that ordinary life
is not.

—Don DeLillo, *Libra*

15

EARLIER THE NIGHT BEFORE, NATE ROMANOWSKI HAD FOL-
lowed the tire tracks of the fleeing vehicle driven by Man Number
Three until he reached the locked gate with the sprawling old ranch
below. He drove a short distance up the hill and pulled the staples
from the fence post and lowered the rusted strands of barbed wire
so he could drive over them in his Jeep. He'd decided not to approach the old ranch compound head-on, where he assumed Man
Number Three had gone. There was too much open ground between the fence and the buildings, and therefore no possibility of
getting down there unobserved.

Instead, he'd driven along inside the fence line to the west in
four-wheel-drive low with his lights out, using the starlight to navigate by. While the structures in the far-off swale were in view, he
nervously looked over his shoulder for lights or any sign of activity.
He didn't breathe easily until he'd driven four miles from the gate
and had dropped over a large hill that obscured him from the buildings or anyone in them who might be watching.

The fence had been built decades before, and the farther he got from the locked gate, the more it deteriorated in condition. Rusted metal T-posts gave way to gnarled posts made of greasewood and long stretches where the wire had fallen to the ground. It had been a long time since the fence had been maintained, and whoever had built it in the first place appeared to have lost their enthusiasm the farther they got from the gate in the road. Eventually, the fence was no more than broken or leaning sticks of wood with barbed wire looped around them.

Nate assumed there was a story there somewhere, either a ranch hand who started slacking off once he got out of view of the ranch, or the rancher himself who realized the futility of fencing a desert.

HIS PROGRESS WAS STOPPED by a deep dry wash that had walls too steep to descend or to drive out of in his vehicle, so he killed the motor and climbed out to reconnoiter.

The wash fed an ancient, dry streambed that curled out into the valley and meandered east on the valley floor. The dry creek looked substantial, although there was sand on the bed of it instead of flowing water. It was likely, Nate thought, that the only time it functioned as a creek was during flash floods. Judging by the contours of the valley out in front of him, he surmised that it eventually passed through the old ranch compound. Whoever had owned the place, he thought, had probably hoped at one time that the stream would provide reliable water for the inhabitants and the stock.

Nope.

. . .

THE DRY STREAM was a good place to hole up, though, he thought. He was able to drive the Jeep down along the edge of the steep wash until it flattened out near the valley floor, then drive back up until the walls narrowed and closed around it. That way, his vehicle couldn't be seen from either the valley floor to the south or from the north above where he'd come. Anyone peering across the broken treeless country from either the east or the west would look right over the top of it. The tattered beige canvas cover on the top of his Jeep was approximately the same color as the terrain, so it was unlikely it'd be spotted even from above by an aircraft or one of Tyrell and Volk's spy satellites.

Nate wasn't sure why he got so much pleasure out of confounding Tyrell and Volk and keeping them guessing as to his location and actions until he was ready to reveal both—but he did.

HE MOVED HIS HOODED BIRDS under a rock overhang in the wash and secured them by tying their jesses to ancient roots that curled out of the wall face like exposed steel cables. Then he sat with his boots on the sandy gravel of the streambed with his back to the wall. He covered himself with a ratty wool blanket he kept under his seat that smelled faintly of gasoline and falcon excrement. Then he closed his eyes and tried to get some sleep.

AT TWO-THIRTY HE HEARD the far-off sounds of whining ATVs in the distance. The sounds were coming from the east—from the direction of the old ranch compound where the tire tracks had led.

He sat up, placed his .500 across his thighs, and waited to see if the vehicles would show up.

They didn't, and fifteen minutes later it was quiet again.

Something, he thought, was going on at that old ranch. And whatever it might be was important enough to someone to dispatch two thugs, one with a sword and one with an automatic weapon, to rub him out.

He thought, *I've got you right where I want you.*

TWO HOURS BEFORE DAWN, Nate awoke to find himself face-to-face with a pair of pale yellow canine eyes.

The skinny coyote had been patrolling the length of the dry streambed, tail swishing from side to side, when it realized there was a vehicle blocking its route and the sharp, unfamiliar smell of a man and three birds in the air.

Nate opened his eyes when the coyote was two feet away to his right side, cautiously making its way up the wash wall toward the hooded birds.

He grasped the grip of his revolver and swung it in a tight arc through the air. The barrel struck the coyote between the eyes and the animal yelped like a domestic dog and tumbled down the incline to the dry streambed, where it scrambled unsteadily to its feet and loped away as if drunk.

"Hey, coyote," Nate growled. "Leave my birds alone."

He kept the coyote in his sights until it vanished among the scrub on the dark valley floor, but he didn't cock his weapon or pull the trigger. There had been enough of that already, he thought. Coyotes did coyote things. No reason to kill it.

BUT THERE *WAS* REASON to secure his birds to their makeshift perches inside his Jeep so no more predators could get at them.

That's how he left them in the predawn, when he set out on foot in the dry streambed with his .500 under his arm in its shoulder holster. He left the Ranch Rifle in his Jeep. He wore a small day-pack containing two quarts of water, binoculars, ammunition, and the satellite phone.

The morning was dry with a slight northern wind that made it seem even cooler than it was. High noctilucent clouds caught the still-hidden sun and looked like bands of scalloped orange lace on the eastern horizon. The early-fall air smelled of dust and sage.

It was a good day to go hunting, he thought.

Before setting out, he'd installed the battery to the phone, but he kept the power off. Tyrell and Volk couldn't call him or grill him or give him instructions, which was the way he wanted it. But they could track his progress to the ancient ranch.

And they'd know if his movement suddenly stopped.

16

It stopped two and a half hours later.

Nate had worked his way silently toward the old ranch compound, keeping to the sandy, dry streambed and grateful for the high rocky banks that kept him out of view. Every twenty minutes or so, he'd crawl up to the lip of the eastern edge and carefully peer over to mark his progress. Because the dry stream wound through the valley floor in a loopy serpentine pattern, it sometimes seemed like he'd trudge for half a mile but not get any closer, like the buildings were a figment of his imagination and would forever be just out of reach.

When he picked his way through an old ranch graveyard of abandoned rusty pickups, discarded manual washing machines, and tangles of old barbed wire, he knew he was getting close.

Although it was very early, he assumed he'd hear something as he got closer: the ATVs, vehicles moving around, chatter. But it was just as silent when he got within two hundred yards as it had been when he set out. It was as if the large collection of falling-down buildings had absorbed whoever had gotten close to it.

THE DRY STREAM DID, in fact, halve the collection of structures. He stopped short of walking through the heart of the ranch compound and instead shinnied up the side of the cut until he could push his binoculars through thorny brush. That way, he could see the compound clearly without showing himself.

There wasn't much to see. The three large sheds were gray and weather-beaten with sagging rooflines and whole panels of corrugated roofing gone. All of the windows he could see had been broken out, leaving toothy shards of discolored glass in the frames.

The two-story residence still stood but barely, and it was obvious a fire had long ago gutted it.

The only sign of activity he could see were tire tracks around the sheds and a packed set of them near the closed garage-like doors on the ends of the sheds. Someone had driven around, into, and possibly through the buildings recently. But there were no working vehicles in or around the ranch yard.

That was one thing about high desert, Nate thought. Any movement, whether by machine or animal, left a record on the surface for a long time. Only wind or rain—the first common and the latter rare—could eventually remove it.

WHEN HE MOVED farther down the creek bed and looked again at a different angle, he saw something that startled him: multihued dome tents pitched haphazardly between sheds two and three. He counted six. It was early in the morning yet and no campers had emerged from them.

It didn't make sense. Although he'd been trained in special operations always to expect the unexpected . . . *Campers?* he thought.

If nothing else, he questioned their judgment. Wyoming was a state filled with parks, forests, vistas, and wilderness. With all of that available, these people had chosen to camp *here?*

He recalled the sound of the ATVs the night before, and thought that perhaps a swarm of them had ended up in the shelter of the old ranch.

NATE SLID DOWN THE SLOPE to regroup. He needed to puzzle out this new development.

That's when he noticed the small oblong camo-colored plastic item sitting on a rock shelf on the other side of the cut. It was partially hidden behind stalks of brittle yellow cheatgrass, but there was no mistaking the perfectly black round eye and the short antenna on the side of it.

A wireless motion-detection security device. He recognized the make and model. It was a Spypoint, powered by a single nine-volt battery, and it was capable of sending the detection of a security breach up to a thousand feet—well within the distance between Nate and the ranch compound.

He cursed, and reached for the device to turn it off, when he heard the squeak of rusty hinges and heavy footfalls from the direction of the third shed, the one closest to him.

Then nothing. No voices, no more movements.

He drew his revolver. After stashing the satellite phone in a gopher hole and plugging the opening with a rock, he turned and took a step to climb back up the bank where he'd glassed the compound. The .500 was held loosely at his side. He could sense men out in the open, but he couldn't yet see or hear them. By keeping his weapon out of sight, he'd give them no reason to fire at him.

As if they needed a reason, he thought. He had, after all, trespassed on the old ranch property.

With each step up the bank of the cut, he got closer to being exposed. In his field of vision, he saw the roofs of the sheds followed by the broken windows of the second level. Then, as he cleared the lip of the embankment, three men. They'd obviously come out of the second shed, likely alerted by the remote motion detector. The two on the wings stood among the dome tents. They were Middle Eastern–looking and each carried a modified AK-47 with a banana magazine.

The man in the middle was Ghazi Saeed.

Nate thought: *He goes first.*

It took a moment for Saeed to see him over the cutbank, but when he did there was a twitch of recognition in his eyes. The two men on the wings had yet to realize he was there.

Nate said nothing, and Saeed just stared.

Showdown.

After Saeed went down, Nate thought, he'd take out the one on the left before swinging on the man on the right, because that first man had the muzzle of his rifle slightly higher and therefore could react more quickly. Nate was already visualizing the movements it would take.

He had a fleeting advantage on them, he figured, because they were in the open and he could drop back down into the cut, and out of sight, in a heartbeat.

Without turning his head, Saeed hissed something Nate couldn't make out. That got the attention of the two men by the tents, and they turned to him. When they did, Saeed simply nodded silently toward Nate until both men saw him. The man on the right started to raise his weapon and Nate started to raise his when Saeed hissed again. This time the hiss contained several words in Arabic that Nate didn't understand.

But the men on the wings did, and instead of pointing their weapons at Nate, each picked out a dome tent and aimed at it. They did it in a frighteningly casual way, Nate thought, like they'd done this kind of thing before, like it meant nothing to them. He had no doubt they'd carry through with the threat.

Nate was puzzled for a second until Saeed nodded toward him, then gestured to the right and left.

It was an unusual play, Nate thought, but he instantly understood Saeed's move. Saeed was willing to bet that Nate would be less likely to gun them down if there was more of a chance that one of the men would fire into a tent than if the three of them aimed simultaneously at Nate. It was the play of a man who knew his adversary valued innocent human life more than he did.

So who was in the tents?

As if to answer Nate's thought, a zipper on a yellow North Face dome slowly opened and the groggy face of a slight and wiry college-age girl poked out. Her nose and ears were pierced and her head was shaved to the scalp. Her skin was so pale it was almost translucent. Nate got the impression of a girl who wanted to look tough but was uncomfortable and wholly out of place. She rubbed her eyes and stared out at the dawn with a grimace. She seemed to have no idea what was happening around her: that behind her tent a few feet away a man with an AK-47 was poised to chew her up in a hail of 7.62x39mm rounds that would perforate the nylon tent walls as if they didn't exist. The camper wasn't alone, either, because she turned her head and said a few words to whoever else was in the tent.

She never looked Nate's way, or over her shoulder where Saeed stood.

The camper, after apparently seeing it was still too early to rise from her sleeping bag, withdrew back into her tent. A moment later, a thin arm fully inked with tattoos reached up and the front tent flap was clumsily zipped closed.

Nate noted that the man on the right was silently mouthing a mantra of some kind.

Was it *Allahu Akbar*?

Nate looked at Saeed, who nodded at him and mouthed the word *You*.

Nate nodded back. *Me*.

The message was clear. *Come out unarmed*, Saeed communicated with a grim smile, *or the people in the tents will die*.

17

The holstered .500 thumped to the ground on the edge of the wash and Nate followed with his hands up, palms out. The man on the right stepped forward to retrieve the gun. He walked sideways toward it with his AK-47 across his body pointed behind him so he was still capable of firing into the tents if Nate made a threatening move.

When the man had picked up the holster, Saeed locked eyes with Nate and chinned over his shoulder to the left. He wanted Nate to follow them out of the tents and toward the front of the closest shed. Nate nodded and followed.

Implicit in everything Saeed did, Nate thought, was his wish to get all of them out of the gathering of the tents to someplace else. For whatever reason, Saeed didn't want the sleepers inside the tents to know what had just transpired around them. Nate saw no advantage in breaking the silence, either, and possibly endangering the lives of the people inside the tents.

Not until he knew more.

·   ·   ·

SAEED LED THE WAY and Nate followed. The two gunmen held back a few feet and flanked him on either side. He could feel rather than see the muzzles aimed at his back.

Once they cleared the corner of the first shed, Saeed turned and held out his hand and motioned to Nate to stop. Then he twirled his finger, indicating that Nate should turn around so his back was to him.

Nate waited a beat, then hissed, "That's not a good idea."

Saeed said something with his eyes to the men behind Nate, and Nate braced himself for a blow. Would they club him in the head with a rifle, or kick out his feet?

Instead, he heard a footfall and felt a twin bite of cold metal on the side of his neck before eleven million volts from a Stun Master stun gun blasted through his body and made his eyes seem to explode out of their sockets. Nate's legs went limp and he involuntarily dropped to his knees while his ears roared from inside.

Although he'd been hit with both a stun gun and a Taser in special ops training, he'd known at the time it was coming. This was devastating because it was so unexpected. His muscles convulsed as if inhabited by electric snakes and he cramped up at the same time. He had no control of his arms and legs or neck and his head lolled forward as if his neck were the stalk of a dying sunflower.

He caught a glimpse of Saeed bending down with a long plastic zip tie in his hands. Although groggy, Nate had the presence of mind to clench his fists behind him and resist just enough so that the first knuckles of his thumbs butted together rather than letting them force his wrists on top of each other. Then he heard the *zzzzzzzzzz* sound of the mechanism of the zip tie sing as it was pulled tight.

It took a full minute for him to recover enough to raise his head. When he did, Saeed was looking him over to see if he'd voided himself. After noting that he hadn't, Saeed said, "Listen the next time."

Nate shook his head to try and clear it. A smoky metallic taste filled his mouth from where the fillings in his teeth had arced with electricity.

His voice was a croak. "I'll remember that."

The two men on his flanks reached under his arms and helped him to his feet. His legs trembled but he managed to stay upright.

"Thank you for not screaming," Saeed said.

THEY WALKED PAST the closed barn doors of the first shed. As they passed it, Nate took a quick peek through a broken window and saw, just a few feet inside, a pie-plate-sized headlight covered with dead insects and a glimpse of a chrome grille.

"Keep your eyes straight ahead," Saeed hissed at him from over his shoulder.

But he'd seen it: the toothy, grinning front of a Peterbilt semi-tractor. He wondered if the rest of the trailer was attached behind it. The shed was certainly long enough for a full-sized eighteen-wheeler. And it was wide enough for two.

"We go to the third building," Saeed said aloud. They were far enough away from the tents that he spoke in a normal, though hushed, tone.

As they walked past the second shed, Nate again stole a look through the window. It was too dark to see well inside, but he thought he could make out the shapes of haphazardly parked vehicles: pickups, a tractor, ATVs. He also caught a whiff of spilled gasoline.

"I want to talk to Ibby," Nate said as they approached the side door of the third shed.

"You will."

"I want to know what's going on around here. Aren't you guys in the wrong desert in the wrong country?"

No response from Saeed.

"Who is sleeping in those tents?"

Saeed turned. "Why do you even care? What does it have to do with flying your falcons out in the desert?"

"It has nothing to do with that," Nate said. "It has to do with three men who came to my camp to try and kill me in my sleep. I thought maybe you knew something about that."

There was no reaction on Saeed's face. He said, "Who were they?"

"No IDs."

"Where are they now?"

"Two of them didn't come back," Nate said. "The third came here."

Saeed arched his eyebrows and shook his head. "It's not possible. No one here would do something like that."

"Then give me my gun back and let me go on my way."

Nate thought it telling that Saeed didn't ask about why the two men hadn't come back, or what had happened out in the desert. Or why Nate thought the third man had returned to the old ranch.

"We talk first," Saeed said.

He said something in Arabic to the two men with the AK-47s. Nate didn't understand the words but it was obvious Saeed had told them both to stay and to keep an eye on him.

Unlike the other two sheds, the one they entered had been partitioned off inside. From the outside door they entered a room with low ceilings and cheap wood-paneled walls that looked like it had once been an office of some kind. There was a dusty metal desk, three hard-backed chairs, and an ancient cork bulletin board still showing the silhouettes of papers and business cards that had once been pinned to its surface. There was no overhead lamp and the only light was natural and filtered through the discolored and sandblasted window. Mouse droppings covered the floor like errant punctuation.

"Have a sit," Saeed told Nate.

Instead, Nate walked across the ancient, curling linoleum and leaned back against the desk.

The two men with the AKs slid chairs from the middle of the room to the two corners opposite Nate and sat down, but kept their rifles ready. *They've had training,* Nate thought. By choosing the corners, they'd eliminated any chance of him taking them out at the same time. If he went after one, the other would cut him in two.

"Do either of you speak English?" he asked.

It was obvious they understood his question by the way they looked up. But neither spoke.

The man on the left had a close-cropped beard, a long nose that had been broken a few times, and thin, almost translucent lips. His fingers were long and spidery. He wore a loose-fitting oversized shirt and cargo pants made out of rough green canvas. A spare magazine for the AK-47 jutted out from a side pocket on his right thigh.

The man on the right, the one who had been silently chanting while he aimed at the tent, was shorter and stockier, with a black bandana covering the top of his head. His beard was wispy and thin and came to a point under his chin. He wore a faded Batman T-shirt under a light desert camo jacket. Nate saw the strap of his portable Stun Master protruding from the breast pocket of his military surplus jacket. He noted it for later.

Both men were hard-looking and inscrutable, and both had been obviously instructed not to speak. They looked like jihadis Nate had encountered in the Middle East: devout, earnest, humorless fanatics who were also deadly. They were the kind of men, he guessed, who grinned only when someone's face was beneath their boot, begging for mercy.

Saeed studied Nate for a few moments with his eyes narrowed. Then he asked, "Where are your hawks?"

"Falcons," Nate corrected. "All falcons are hawks, but not all hawks are falcons."

"These are the kinds of things I don't understand."

"You don't have to."

"Did you let them go?"

Not *Did they get killed when someone attacked your camp?*

"They're in my Jeep about three and a half miles away," Nate said, nodding toward the west. "Let me go and I'll bring them here. I haven't fed them or hunted them yet today. Since you spend time with Ibby, you know that with falconers our birds come first."

Saeed said, "I'll go get him."

"Ibby?"

"Of course Ibby."

"And you'll leave me here with your goons Ahmed and Ahmed? Or is it Muhammad and Muhammad?"

At the mention of the last name, the stocky man who'd used the stun gun on Nate started to get up angrily and come after him until Saeed said something in Arabic that stopped him.

To Nate, Saeed said, "Don't provoke them. And don't forget the reason you're here is that you're a trespasser. You entered our camp armed and without an invitation."

"So call the county sheriff," Nate said.

Saeed almost smiled.

18

Ten minutes later, Nate heard Saeed's and Ibby's angry voices increase in volume as they neared the third shed from outside. He couldn't understand a word they were saying because they were speaking Arabic.

The door flew open and Ibby strode inside. His face was flushed red and his eyes sparkled with emotion. He looked embarrassed. Saeed came in after him and closed the door behind them. The room suddenly seemed much smaller.

"I'm so sorry this happened," Ibby said to Nate. "Are you hurt in any way?"

"No."

"Good, good. Is it true that your camp was attacked by someone last night?"

"Yes."

"Do you have any idea who it was?"

Nate nodded toward Saeed. "Ask him."

Ibby stared at Saeed, who held his glare. In Arabic, Ibby fired off a flurry of angry questions. Saeed continued to shake his head no. Saeed's face was impenetrable, Nate thought. He couldn't tell if the man was lying.

Then, calmly, Saeed explained himself. Ibby listened with his hands on his hips and his head bowed. Saeed's voice rose until the last sentence was almost shouted.

Ibby appeared to be contemplating what he'd heard, then he said to Nate, "Saeed says he doesn't know for sure who came after you, but he has an idea who it could have been. Unfortunately, we can't always control everyone who comes here to help with our project. What did these men look like?"

Nate described Heartless and Hipster, and as he did, Ibby and Saeed looked at each other in a way that indicated they were thinking the same thing.

"They were here," Ibby said. "Sometimes losers show up and we have to send them away. The two you describe were sent away two days ago. We don't know who the third man could have been. Are you sure you tracked him to here?"

Nate nodded.

"Then we've got a big problem," Ibby said. "A number of new volunteers showed up last night and your man might have been one of them, or mixed up with them. It'll be difficult to figure out who it was."

He turned to Saeed and said, "You should start questioning everybody. Don't tell them what we know, but try and figure out if a lone man arrived last night when those others did. And ask the team, too. Find out if someone went missing last night and showed up later. He—or she—could have recruited those two losers and driven them to his camp."

Saeed nodded once. But he didn't move.

"I'd suggest you start now," Ibby said.

"No. Not until we are sure this is a safe situation," Saeed said, nodding toward Nate.

Ibby said to Nate, "I'm sorry, but Saeed looks out for me even when I don't want him to. He protects me and this camp, and he protects our work here. He's like my own private Secret Service agent: a pain in the ass ninety-nine-point-nine percent of the time, but worth his weight in diamonds if I'm threatened or our project is threatened. It's the same with his men here," he said, gesturing to the two guards with the AK-47s. "They were surprised when you showed up on foot today and they assumed you came here with some other purpose in mind. So please tell me it was a misunderstanding."

Nate said, "It was a misunderstanding."

"You're not working for someone who sent you here? I have to ask."

"I'm on no one's payroll," Nate said. It was true enough.

Ibby assessed him for a half minute, then said, "I believe you. Remember that I told you that your reputation precedes you. We have two things in common—falconry and contempt for the overreach of the U.S. government."

Little alarm bells rang deep inside Nate's chest. Tyrell and Volk hadn't characterized Muhammad Ibraaheem as one who had open contempt for the government. Nate wondered if they, or the other Wolverines, expected as much. He guessed that they probably did but had no proof. He recalled Tyrell and Volk saying Ibby's reporting wasn't strident in any kind of advocacy.

Ibby said, "Saeed said you have your famous big gun, but no communication devices. Does anyone know you're here?"

Nate said, "You mean on this old ranch? No. I don't even know for sure where I am. I was surprised to find all of these old buildings so far out here in the Red Desert."

Ibby chuckled. "Me too. I came upon them when I was hunting. This was a sheep ranch at one time, but no one has lived here in decades."

"So you don't own it?"

Ibby shook his head. "We're just borrowing it for a while."

"What is this project you mentioned? The one that needs to be protected by Saeed and his thugs?"

Ibby paused for a moment and looked at his shoes. When he raised his head, his face was utterly sincere. He said, "We're doing something good here."

Then to Saeed: "Please unlock his handcuffs."

"It's a zip tie," Saeed said.

"Then cut him loose and go start questioning the team and the volunteers after you've retrieved Nate's falcons. Drive his Jeep back here. In the meantime, Nate and I have a lot to talk about."

Saeed's face betrayed him and he said, "You're going to tell him everything?"

"Not just that," Ibby said, "I'm going to show him. Nate is one of us. When he sees what we're doing here, I'm confident he'll join us. Believe me when I tell you we can use someone like him."

Saeed was obviously skeptical. He again spoke in Arabic to Ibby in flat, declarative sentences that had just a note of pleading in them.

Ibby answered in a tone that was soft and low and ended in English: "Nate Romanowski has been the scourge of the powerful elites for some time now. He is my brother in falconry and I know I can trust him."

Nate didn't know what to think about that, but it was obvious Saeed didn't like it at all. Nate wished he hadn't started to like Ibby.

Reluctantly, Saeed unsheathed a stubby fixed-blade knife and stepped over to Nate.

"Turn around," he said.

"No need," Nate said while unclenching his fists and pressing the palms of his hands together so the zip tie slid off. He handed the plastic loop to Saeed, whose eyes flashed with both anger and surprise.

"How did you do that?" Saeed asked.

"I was trained to be a Peregrine. We don't willingly let ourselves be caught."

Nate turned to the man with the stun gun. "And for my next trick, I rip the ears off Ahmed over there."

The man's eyes got big and he sat up straight with the AK-47 pointed at Nate.

Ibby nodded approvingly. He said to Saeed: "This is why I want him on our team."

WHEN SAEED and his two men were gone, Ibby said, "We'll find out who is responsible for attacking your camp. Saeed can be very persuasive."

"I'm not surprised."

"So, I bet you have a million questions."

"I do."

"Go ahead."

"What do you mean when you say you're doing something good here?"

They were seated in the chairs in the small room and Ibby scooted his over until their knees were nearly touching. He placed his hands on his thighs and leaned forward.

"I used to be a journalist," Ibby said. "In my job I traveled all over the world, but I spent a good deal of time in the Middle East. I saw what was happening over there firsthand, and I spoke constantly with American military and intelligence officials. I learned what this government, and specifically the National Security Agency, was capable of. At first I thought, 'Okay, every government has to spy on other regimes.' Then I learned more and I started to get very, very alarmed. It's one thing to spy to keep your people safe. I would expect that—anyone would expect that. But it's another thing to build an apparatus that can spy on each and every citizen in the country."

Nate nodded for him to go on.

"What if I were to tell you that there is a government facility that is storing every electronic communication made by every American citizen? I'm talking phone calls, emails, texts, social media posts— *everything*—all in blatant violation of the Fourth Amendment of the Bill of Rights in the U.S. Constitution?"

Ibby closed his eyes and recited: "'The right of the people to be secure in their persons, houses, papers, and effects, against unreasonable searches and seizures, shall not be violated, and no Warrants shall issue, but upon probable cause, supported by Oath or affirmation, and particularly describing the place to be searched, and the persons or things to be seized.' That's verbatim because I've memorized it.

"What would you say?" he asked.

"I'd say that is a problem."

"It's not hypothetical," Ibby said. "It's not something they might do or they could do. It's something they're doing *right now*. When I heard about it from a disillusioned NSA agent, I couldn't believe it at first, and I'm not a technical wizard, so it took a while to wrap my mind around it.

"Here's how it works: Metadata—meaning phone calls, phone numbers, emails, texts, satellite spying data, *everything*—that is generated by or intercepted by the NSA has to go somewhere. It's a gigantic river of information that comes from multiple places: satellites that are routed through the Aerospace Data Facility at Buckley Air Force Base in Colorado; NSA facilities at Fort Gordon, Georgia; NSA Texas in San Antonio; NSA Hawaii in Oahu; plus domestic and overseas 'listening posts,' as they call them. All of that data now goes to *one place*"—he emphasized the words by thrusting a single finger in the air—"one place with the server capacity to store and analyze it all. Think of it as the NSA's own personal taxpayer-funded cloud.

"So, after it gets to that *one place*, the data is analyzed by supersophisticated supercomputers that have computing power beyond our imagination. They can do billions of algorithms per second. The results are funneled to the Multiprogam Research Facility in Oak Ridge, Tennessee; the NSA headquarters at Fort Meade, Maryland; and eventually to the CIA, the Pentagon, and the White House."

"I'd say it's a big operation," Nate said. "But isn't the purpose to identify bad guys?"

Ibby laughed. "That was the original premise. That by gathering all this information, the people in charge could figure out who the bad guys were and who they were talking to or communicating with. But it's gone beyond that and we both know it. It's gotten so out of hand it's unrecognizable. That's why you and I have chosen to stay off the grid, isn't it?"

Nate nodded. He recalled how Tyrell and Volk had located him only when Liv placed two calls to her dying mother in Louisiana.

"I come from a totalitarian country," Ibby said. "The people are controlled because the government spies on them and denies them human rights. The government keeps the lid on domestic uprisings by thwarting them before they get started. They do this by spying on people. I grew up a beneficiary of that system but it took me a long time to realize what it was. That's not supposed to happen here, is it? Spying on three hundred and fifty million people sounds impossible. But that capability now exists."

Nate said, "I thought they shut down the program last year."

Ibby paused and stared at Nate as if he had grown a second nose. He said, "Do you *really* think they'd spend four billion dollars on the facility and stop using it just because Congress told them to? They've lied about it before. Do you *really* trust your government to pull back on data-gathering? When was the last time you heard of a government program that got smaller?"

"I see your point," Nate conceded.

"I thought you would."

"So what are you going to do about it?"

"You mean *we*, don't you?"

Nate suppressed a smile.

"We're designing something right here, under the roofs of these sheds and in plain view of satellite imagery, that will restore the Fourth Amendment to all Americans."

Ibby grinned. His passion for the subject was evident. Even bordering on obsessive, Nate thought.

"We're building something that will fuck up all the data within that facility."

"You're building it here?" Nate asked, incredulous.

"Yes."

"Please tell me it's not a bomb."

"Of course not," Ibby said, taken aback. "Our target is illegal data: ones and zeros, lots of them. Trillions of them. But not people. Absolutely not."

"So how are you going to do this?"

"You'll understand when I show you our team and our facilities."

"I've seen them," Nate said. "This place is a dump."

Ibby laughed again. "That's what we want them to see."

Then he turned serious. "Early on, a couple of years ago, some chatter got out about what we wanted to do. That was before I found this place and imposed standards and practices here: absolutely no Internet access, no cell phones, not even hardwired phones. I knew we had to be completely self-sufficient . . . primitive, even. I communicate with other people with handwritten messages and by courier only, and I make sure I trust the courier with my life— which I literally do."

He leaned forward again. "We are right under their noses, but they don't know it."

"What do you mean?"

Ibby paused. "You know the *one place* I mentioned earlier? The *one place* where all the data goes to be stored and analyzed?"

"Yes?"

"It's two hundred and seventy-seven miles from here on I-80, outside a little town called Bluffdale, Utah. Population about ten thousand people. It's called the Utah Data Center but it's owned by the NSA."

"You're kidding," Nate said.

"I wish I was," Ibby said. "It's over a million square feet and cost more than four billion dollars to build. They finished it a couple of years ago. We're talking four twenty-five-thousand-square-foot facilities filled with rows and rows of servers and over nine hundred thousand square feet of technical support. It's got its own power substation to generate sixty-five-megawatt demand—that's about forty million dollars a year in electricity alone. And the security is mind-blowing. Cameras everywhere, and a fence that'll stop a fifteen-thousand-pound vehicle going fifty miles an hour."

"How are you going to get in?" Nate asked.

Ibby smiled. "That's the thing. We don't have to."

"How do you know if your plan will work?" Nate asked.

Ibby shook his head. "Nothing is certain and anything can go wrong."

He paused a moment and a grin formed. "But I heard some very encouraging news this morning.

"Someone was spying on us from the top of the ridge up there. Saeed's guys saw him and he sent out a small prototype of our device, one small enough that it fits into the back of a pickup truck. We located the spy out in the desert and—*poof*—put his truck out of commission. It worked perfectly, and the spy, whoever he was, just walked away."

Nate frowned. "A man on foot in the Red Desert . . ."

Ibby shrugged. "I thought about that, but then again, he was spying on us. Hopefully, he can walk to safety. And by the time he's found and they recover his vehicle, we will have left this place. Our mission will be complete."

"You're that close?"

"Yes."

Nate crossed his arms over his chest. The million questions allotted to him by Ibby, he thought, might not be enough.

For the first time, Nate was glad he didn't have the satellite phone with him. If Tyrell and Volk had an inkling of what was going on, he thought, they'd have already flattened the place—probably with him in it.

Before he could ask, *Who is paying for all of this?* there was a cacophony of voices passing by the door of the shed. They were young voices, laughing, talking, someone repeating a snippet from a hip-hop song.

"Volunteers going to breakfast," Ibby explained with a smile. "They're so cheerful the first couple of days here that it kind of rubs off on you. But in a way, they're here to remind us that we are saving this country for them. It makes me feel, well, like we're doing a very noble thing.

"You know what Thomas Jefferson wrote, don't you?" Ibby asked. "He said, 'I hold it that a little rebellion now and then is a good thing, and as necessary in the political world as storms in the physical.'"

A half-dozen heads passed by the grubby window. They *did* seem cheerful.

Nate tried hard to keep the look off his face.

"Something wrong?" Ibby asked.

"No. I thought I recognized someone, but I was wrong."

And he thought, *What in the hell are you doing here, Sheridan?*

PART FIVE

A HORSE WITH NO NAME

Even today you can get into trouble easily out in
the Red Desert. Marooned with a broken car . . .
People still get lost out there.

—Annie Proulx interview,
The Paris Review, 2009

19

The next morning, Marybeth Pickett filled a small thermos with coffee from the pot to take to work at the library while Lucy finished her breakfast and scrolled through her Twitter feed and Facebook page on her phone.

"Guess who changed their status to 'In a Relationship' at two-thirty in the morning?" Lucy asked.

Marybeth had other things on her mind, so even though she heard her youngest daughter talking, the words didn't register.

After a pause, Lucy said, "Mom, are you with us this morning?"

"What?"

"I said, guess who changed their status to 'In a Relationship' at two-thirty in the morning."

"Who?"

Lucy sighed, rolled her eyes, and lowered her phone. "Who do you think? April. Your daughter. One date, and . . . *boom*."

Now Marybeth understood and she winced.

"You know what happened the last time she fell so hard so quick," Lucy said.

"You don't have to remind me." *Dallas Cates.*

Lucy said, "Let's hope she has more sense now. Nobody wants to go through something like that again."

Marybeth placed her hand on Lucy's shoulder and nodded her head.

"I kind of thought there would be a bigger reaction from you," Lucy said.

"She's nineteen. She's old enough to make her own decisions."

"But they're nearly always wrong."

"She's older now. Wiser."

"If you say so," Lucy said with an unconvinced sigh. She placed her phone on the table and rose to take her dish to the sink.

As she rinsed it, she said, "So what's going on?"

Marybeth knew she'd need to answer. Lucy was intuitive and rarely wrong. She'd spent her life as the youngest, carefully observing every member of the family. She was the holding tank of her siblings' emotions and aspirations. If Marybeth wanted to know what was going on with either Sheridan or April, she asked Lucy. Lucy also had a special understanding of her mother.

"When I talked to your dad last night, he sounded so . . . forlorn. He was by himself in the middle of the Red Desert. I know he tried to sound cheery for me, but I could tell he had a lot on his mind." Marybeth sighed. "I know he's often in the field by himself, so I guess I shouldn't worry."

"But . . ." Lucy interjected.

"But he sounded lonely, I guess. I tried to give him a call this morning on his cell phone, but he must be out of cell tower range.

When I called the satellite phone, I got an error message. Then I contacted dispatch in Cheyenne and they haven't been able to reach him. The thing is, he promised to keep his phone on."

"Hasn't this happened before?" Lucy asked.

"Only a hundred times," Marybeth said.

"So why is this different?" Lucy asked sincerely.

"I'm really not sure, but it is," Marybeth said. "I've just got a bad feeling and I'm not sure I can say why."

Lucy seemed to understand. "I hope he's okay," she said.

Marybeth said quickly, "Oh, I'm sure he is. I didn't mean to upset you for no good reason. It's just that being the wife of Joe Pickett is sometimes . . . trying."

"Imagine being his daughter," Lucy said.

WHILE DRIVING toward Saddlestring after Lucy had left for play practice at school, Marybeth flipped through the contacts on her cell phone and placed the call.

"Governor Rulon's office, this is Lisa."

Lisa Casper was Rulon's administrative assistant, but she was more than that, Marybeth knew. Casper was Rulon's gatekeeper and quasi-bodyguard. She looked out for the governor when he refused to look out for himself, and she diverted problem people away from him before he knew they were even around, and therefore he couldn't engage with them and get himself in trouble. She probably knew more about Rulon than he knew about himself. Mrs. Rulon trusted Casper to keep her husband in line and out of the newspapers. Mostly, Casper succeeded.

"Lisa, this is Marybeth Pickett, Joe Pickett's wife."

"Hello, Mrs. Pickett."

They'd met once at a reception, but Marybeth couldn't be sure Lisa actually recalled her.

"And how are the girls?" Lisa asked.

So she did.

"They're fine. Thanks for asking."

"And Joe?"

"That's what I'm calling about. I was hoping I might be able to speak to the governor."

Casper paused. "I'm afraid the governor is in a meeting with some federal officials right now. I can take a message and get it to him when he's through. And this is regarding?"

Marybeth said, "This is regarding the fact that Governor Rulon sent Joe on an assignment and now I can't reach him."

"I see," she said. Marybeth could hear a keyboard clacking gently in the background. She hoped Casper was messaging Rulon and not simply typing up a request.

Marybeth found it telling that Rulon had chosen to keep Casper unaware of Joe's special assignment. That meant something. Rulon was a superior political practitioner when it came to preemptively establishing deniability if something he'd ordered—or suggested with emphasis—went horribly wrong. Because Lisa Casper was a straight arrow, he wouldn't want her implicated in something sensitive where she'd be forced to choose between loyalty to him and honesty.

Before Marybeth could give Casper any more information, Rulon broke into the call.

"Thanks for the distraction," he said in his booming voice. Then to someone else in his office: "I've got to take this call. It's important state business and I'm still the governor. It doesn't concern you people"—he was now addressing someone else in his office—"even though you think everything concerns you. So why don't you folks go out and wander around town and target some people to fine and regulate? There should be some honest, hardworking citizens you can find to shake down. Maybe someone has an oversized toilet tank or they're using the wrong kind of dishwasher soap. That's what you do, right?"

Marybeth heard grumbling, then a door shut harder than it probably needed to be.

Rulon came back on the line and said, "It's the fetching Mrs. Pickett. I hope you're doing well. I will never understand how a guy like Joe married so above his station."

"Oh, please."

"So what is the nature of this very pleasant interruption?"

She paused for a moment, then said, "Right now, I'm worried about my husband and his friend. They're very important men in my life."

20

THE WORST ASPECT OF THE LONG TREK FOR JOE WASN'T HIS sore feet and burning calves or the sheen of cold sweat that bathed his entire body or the heavy daypack on his back as he walked in a northerly direction toward the interstate highway, it was that damned song that kept running through his head like an earworm:

I've been through the desert on a horse with no name . . .

His breath pounded out the melody and his cadence supplemented it, and the most miserable aspect of the whole experience was he'd never liked that old song by America in the first place. He'd thought it too clever and morose.

So why was it there?

It felt good to be out of the rain . . .

THIRTY-EIGHT MILES. At four miles an hour by foot, that meant he might reach the highway in nine and a half hours. If he could hitch a ride with a trucker into Rawlins or use the driver's cell phone, he might be able to convince a tow-truck operator or Phil Parker to drive out into the middle of the Red Desert to retrieve his vehicle. And he could touch base with Marybeth and Governor Rulon to let them both know that he was alive and well and what was going on.

As if he knew what was going on or what had happened, he thought.

He replayed the incident over and over as he walked. Joe could still hear the crackle in the air and he could still feel the truck—and his cell phone—go dead. Whatever had been in the back of that other pickup had caused it to happen, he was sure.

But was it? What kind of weapon could do such a thing?

And how many damaged trucks was he up to now, he thought. How many state vehicles he was responsible for had been burned, wrecked, shot up, or destroyed in his career? He knew he held the record within the state government agencies in Wyoming for the number of ruined trucks, although a bulldozer operator near Cody still claimed the largest monetary loss after he'd accidentally driven his heavy equipment over the Buffalo Bill Reservoir dam. Still, Joe's record was an embarrassing and dubious honor. He knew there was a pool of Game and Fish administrative employees at the headquarters in Cheyenne who actually bet real money on how long each truck assigned to him would last. This one: four months, assuming they couldn't get it going again.

Most of them *had not been his fault*, a point he'd made in futility to the agency's director when she'd shown him a list someone had compiled. How could he be blamed for the fact that once, while he was in Yellowstone Park on an assignment from the governor, the asphalt melted away under his parked vehicle and a hot new geyser had erupted through the undercarriage?

But he'd never had to walk this far out of anyplace he'd been stranded.

HE DECIDED TO CARRY his .308 M14 carbine with a peep sight instead of his shotgun, which was a hard choice for him to make. The rifle had a shoulder sling while the shotgun did not, plus he figured if he had to further defend himself it would be better to have long-distance capability. After all, he could see for miles in every direction. He doubted that if he got into another situation, he'd be close enough to the bad guy to use his shotgun.

The pack he carried contained two gallon jugs of water, a water filter he hoped he'd have the opportunity to use if he found a source, Steiner binoculars, flex-cuffs, year-old energy bars, a first-aid kit, a length of parachute cord, his Filson vest, matches, bear spray, and his .40 Glock. The cooler was too large and heavy to carry, so he reluctantly left it behind. There was no reason to bring essential gear like a radio, GPS, digital camera, phone, or digital recorder. None of them worked anymore anyway.

He already wished he'd left his handgun behind. It was heavy and he preferred his shotgun or carbine.

AT FIRST, Daisy had enjoyed the hike. She caromed around in the predawn, in front and back of him like a cream-colored ghost. He told her to calm down, to save her energy, but she didn't obey. For a quarter of a mile, she loped a circle around him, the leathery remains of a dead mouse she had found sticking out of her mouth like a half-smoked cigar.

About three hours from the truck, Joe realized Daisy was lagging farther and farther behind and her tongue hung out of her mouth. Her gait was labored, so he paused to let her catch up.

While waiting, he looked around, scanning the horizon in all four directions. If he hadn't been so miserable and worried, he thought, he would enjoy the view. The sun brought out the colors of the orange and yellow rocks, and it lit up the spikes and needles of the mean and stingy desert scrub into something almost benign. In the western distance, soaring turkey vultures rode thermal currents and tracked across the front of wispy clouds.

Deserts held a particular kind of cold, distant beauty he knew was there but had never been able to fully appreciate. He doubted his trek would bring out that appreciation. Joe much preferred the foothills country leading up to his Bighorn Mountains, and even the dark and tangled timber itself to desert landscape. It had always bothered him that tracks in the desert stayed there for years and that the terrain was so bereft of moisture that something that was dropped carelessly—like a gum wrapper or a beer bottle cap— would remain where it fell for seasons. The desert, he decided, was *dirty*.

Of course, there were advantages as well. He could see and hear forever. No one could sneak up on him or spring from behind a tree. If his situation got desperate, there was game to kill and eat, and water—somewhere—to drink.

Joe took off his hat and bent down to one knee. Inside his stained and weather-beaten Stetson was a satin depiction of a 1940s cowboy giving his horse a drink out of the upside-down crown. He mimicked the scene by pouring half a gallon of water into his hat and putting it down for Daisy. She eagerly and sloppily lapped at it, almost as if she were eating it, until her belly was full. All that remained when she was done was a frothy viscous stew that he poured out into the dirt.

Joe stood and drank from the jug, nearly emptying it. He tried to remember how long the water jugs had sloshed around in the back of his gearbox and decided it had been more than a year. Despite that fact, and the mild taste of plastic, he couldn't recall drinking anything better.

His wet hat felt wonderfully cool on his head when he clamped it back on. His pack was lighter because a gallon of the water was gone, but that was a mixed blessing.

Although it was nice to stop and rest, he could feel his muscles start to stiffen and the chill set in from the early-morning cold, so he turned and continued on. The water brought Daisy back to life, and she padded along beside him, her tail wagging in the air from side to side like a metronome.

A metronome keeping the beat of . . .

I've been through the desert on a horse with no name . . .

AN HOUR LATER, as Joe labored up a long sandy rise toward the northern horizon, he heard gunfire in the distance. Instinctively, he dropped to his haunches and pulled his carbine off his shoulder. Daisy was alarmed by his reaction and huddled with him.

It sounded like popcorn popping. Twenty, thirty rapid-fire shots, then a long automatic burst that ripped through the morning like fabric being torn into strips. Obviously, there were multiple shooters and multiple weapons.

And whatever they were shooting at was being hit, at least occasionally. He could tell by the way some gunshots ended abruptly in a closed-off way and didn't sing or echo over the landscape.

Pow-THUNK. Pow-THUNK.

There was no doubt the fire was coming from the north, from somewhere over the top of the sandy hill. It was impossible to discern the distance, but he knew it wasn't close. At least a mile away, maybe two.

With the carbine in his right hand, Joe scrambled the rest of the way up the hill. He kept low, bending at the waist. The footing was loose and his boots kept slipping in the sand as he climbed. He avoided clumps of cactus.

As he approached the top, he hunkered down lower until he was on his hands and knees. His destination was a gnarled ancient one-foot-high greasewood shrub that clung stubbornly to the sand. He would use it to peer through toward the flat below. Although whoever was shooting might be friendly, he thought, he didn't want to show his head or his hat. Yet.

Not to someone—or a group of people—with automatic weapons.

It wasn't unusual, he knew, to hear shots at any time of the year or in any place away from towns or roads. It could be target shooters, sportsmen sighting in their rifles, locals with illegal automatic firearms testing them out where there was no law enforcement presence, or predator hunters going after coyotes.

"Daisy, get away," he ordered when she assumed that because he was on all fours he'd like to have his face licked. She shrunk away.

THE SHOOTING HAD STOPPED by the time Joe parted the thick dry shrub with the barrel of his carbine so he could see through it.

The fabric of his red shirt clung to his back from sweat, and he felt a trickle of it through his scalp. The morning was heating up in more ways than one.

What he could view through the opening would determine whether he would stand and wave for rescue or stay put, as miserable as that sounded.

There, over a mile and a half away on the desert floor, were four parked white pickup trucks in a tight circle surrounding something of great interest to the people inside the cabs and in the back of the vehicles. None of the pickups had a topper on it like the truck he'd encountered the night before that knocked out all of his electronics, so he assumed the men below weren't involved in that event. He was too far away to hear voices or see clearly, but he guessed there were at least ten figures milling around, maybe eleven.

Eleven men with automatic weapons?

He opted to stay where he was.

Then he heard two point-blank kill shots, which justified his decision even more.

JOE SHINNIED A FEW FEET back down the rise and dug the binoculars out of the pack he'd dropped. When he returned to the brush, he jammed the barrels of the lenses through the scrub and focused.

It was still too far to make out any faces or the license plates of the pickups, but he could see that the figures all appeared to be men in dark clothing. Most of them were bent over an object in the middle of where the trucks were parked. A couple of them pranced about in a kind of celebratory dance. He noted that the doors of the pickups had been left hanging open, as if the drivers had stopped to jump out in a hurry.

He speculated as to what they had shot up. A lost cow? A wild horse? A desert elk? He hoped it wasn't a human being.

Joe lowered the field glasses and scanned the desert floor as far as he could see. If their target had been a horse or elk, he thought he would see signs of a retreating herd. But he saw nothing.

And when he pressed the lenses to his eyes again, he could see that the figures were climbing back into the cabs and beds of the trucks. The doors closed and the men in the truck beds settled in with their backs to the walls. He could see the glint of the sun from rifle barrels of weapons that were pointed upward.

They were finished with whatever it was they had done.

One by one, the pickups left the scene in a southeasterly direction. He could hear snatches of engines as they departed. The trailing vehicles hung back from the dust kicked up by the first.

Joe kept his focus on the trucks as they drove away, hoping he could make out a license plate or at least a distinctive color or design of one. Joe was a student of out-of-state plates.

Before the last rear bumper vanished in a roll of dust, he thought he caught a glimpse of black lettering on a pure white background without colored highlights or a colored border. So, not Wyoming with its iconic bucking-horse logo. Maybe Texas?

Texas trucks were common in the energy-producing parts of the state. But four of them with armed men in the back? Not even in the Red Desert . . .

He swung his field of vision back to where the pickups had gathered. There was a huge brown-black lump of some kind that looked like a furry rock. The shape was too rounded to have been an elk or a horse, but he couldn't be sure what it was.

Joe waited until the pickups were long out of sight before getting up, dusting off the thighs of his Wranglers, and shouldering his carbine.

It would be a long walk in the wrong direction, but he had to see what they'd left behind.

A cold black ball of dread filled his stomach, and as he descended down the sandy hill, he kept his senses on alert for the possibility that the trucks might return. He scanned the terrain out in front of him for boulders or brush he could hide behind, if needed, but saw nothing of note.

Once he committed himself to being in the open, he thought, he'd made a decision he couldn't take back.

21

Joe shook his head with disbelief as he got closer to the dark lump. He no longer doubted what he was going to find. Daisy's reaction confirmed it. She was hiding behind his legs, skittering from side to side to look around, and whining. She did *not* want to get closer. The smell of blood and musk hung low in the air.

Two black ravens had already discovered the carnage. They'd landed on the carcass and didn't leave until Joe hissed at them.

His boots were crunching on silica sand and spent shell casings—7.62×39mm, and a lot of them—when he identified the dead and mutilated grizzly bear. It had taken a lot of rounds to kill it, and the targeting had been sloppy, indiscriminate, but deadly. Throw enough lead at any living thing and some of the rounds would hit vital organs or break bones. The bear's back leg had been nearly severed from its body by bullets, and its thick fur was matted with blood.

Joe circled the carcass. The head had been sawn off and all four paws had been removed. What was left oozed strong-smelling black blood that was pooling beneath the body.

The collar reading GB-53 had been tossed aside in a bog of mud and blood.

He recalled GB-53 rising to a standing position right in front of him and the roar he could still hear. Now this.

Joe took a deep breath and closed his eyes. He was astonished that the bear had traveled this far this quickly. He was also astonished that the story he'd told Phil Parker about the path of the grizzly had played out so accurately.

He was sickened and angry, though, by what the men in the trucks had done. They'd slaughtered the creature and beheaded it, and they'd taken his massive head and paws for trophies.

Joe *hated* the wanton destruction of wildlife. The bear had been no threat to the men in the trucks out there in the open, and they'd chased it down like modern-day hunters slaughtering the last bison. No meat had been taken or even the hide. And for reasons he couldn't explain fully to himself, Joe felt responsible. Like he'd *willed* the bear there somehow.

He gathered up a dozen spent shells with distinct firing-pin strikes and put them in the side pocket of his pack. He cut a bolt of thick hair from the hump of the carcass. The DNA within the hair could be matched up to the paws and head if they were found. Then, in his notebook, he noted the time of day and the approximate location of the body, but he knew it was unlikely he could locate it again.

Joe also dropped the bloody GPS collar into his backpack. Proof of what he'd found.

He longed for the tools of his profession: digital camera, GPS, radio, his pickup to pursue the killers.

He thought that if he ever saw them again, there would be hell to pay.

"I'm just sorry about this," he said to what was left of the bear. "I really am."

Then to Daisy: "What kind of savages are we dealing with?"

THE SUN WAS STRAIGHT overhead and relentless when Joe peered out from beneath the brim of his hat and saw a glimpse of white far ahead of him in the desert to the north. His first thought was *The trucks are back*. He again dropped to a squat.

There was no place to conceal himself, but he thought that if the trucks were far enough away he might be able to find a dry wash or arroyo to flatten into before they arrived.

His face was hot with sunburn, even though the temperature was barely seventy degrees. The wide brim of his Stetson protected him from above, but the high-altitude sun bounced off the surface of the desert and darkened his face, hands, and neck. It was the same thing that happened when he was fly-fishing in a drift boat on a mountain river: the sun's rays got him on the bounce.

Daisy stood by, panting, her tongue lolling out of the side of her mouth. He could feel her hot breath on his neck.

He raised the binoculars and focused the wheel. It wasn't a white truck. It was a white shirt.

The person wearing the white shirt was on foot as well and coming slowly—very slowly—in his direction.

"What kind of fool would be on foot out here?" he asked Daisy aloud. "Besides us, I mean?"

He sat back and rested his elbows on his bent knees so he could steady the glasses. Despite the magnification, it took five minutes before he could identify the walker. It was the woman from the Mustang Café, the attractive woman who hadn't belonged there, Jan-something. It turned out she wasn't walking slowly at all, but with great will and determination. Her arms swung back and forth at her sides and her head was bent forward.

She had no hat, no backpack, no walking staff. She was at least fifteen miles from the highway and maybe twenty from the café, with no vehicle of any kind in sight.

Obviously, judging by her body language, she wanted to get somewhere as quickly as she could.

JOE WAS CONTENT with letting her come to him. He wondered how long it would take for her to break her stride to see him sitting there. She was less than a hundred yards out when she looked up and froze for a moment.

He watched her face through the binoculars, although at that close range it seemed faintly voyeuristic. She didn't look as young and clever as she had the first time he saw her. What remained of her makeup had streamed down her skin and her hair hung moist and stringy.

Jan stood back and placed her hands on her hips, a visual conflict of emotions. She seemed both angry and anxious, and she shook her head and looked at him again to see if she'd imagined him.

When he was still there, she sighed, turned slightly, and walked directly toward him.

Joe groaned as he stood up. His muscles were stiffening already, and the soles of his feet burned within his boots. Why couldn't she have brought a bucket of ice water he could soak them in?

But she not only didn't have ice water, she had no water, period. And nothing else besides the shirt on her back, dusty but tight jeans, and a strong will to get somewhere fast.

When she got closer, he could see that her lips were swollen.

"Jan, right?"

"Yes."

"Want some water?" he asked.

"Oh God, yes," she said. "Thank you, I'm a mess."

He dropped his pack and dug out his last remaining half-gallon of water and handed it to her. She twisted off the cap and raised it, drinking hard.

"Not too fast," Joe said. "Take it easy so you don't get sick."

Joe had grown up with the fact that at this elevation in the Rocky Mountains, despite the desert terrain and the fairly cool temperature, dehydration happened at warp speed. Visitors to the region often experienced early symptoms of it and usually blamed it on "altitude sickness." But it was lack of water.

He averted his eyes while she drank—it seemed rude to watch her—and he waited for her to finish and return the jug. Maybe two pints left, he thought, but he didn't make that point out loud. She wasn't quick to hand over the rest of the water.

"I've never been so thirsty," she said, wiping her mouth with the back of her hand.

"You didn't bring water, huh?"

"I didn't get a chance to bring any."

He looked her over. Before he could speak, she said, "You're that game warden I met with Phil Parker yesterday, aren't you? I forgot your name as soon as I noticed the wedding ring."

"Yup," he said, raising his hand and showing it to her again.

"And now you're out here all by yourself with your dog."

"Meet Daisy."

"Hi, Daisy."

At the sound of her name, Daisy padded over to Jan so the woman would have the privilege of stroking the top of her head. Daisy was shameless, Joe thought.

Then Jan asked, "Didn't you have a truck?"

"I did."

"But now you're walking," she said. "Did you break down or something?"

"Something."

Now that hydration was taking place within her, Joe noted, her color was back and her eyes were sharper. He was amazed how quickly it happened.

She said, "Don't you find it kind of weird that we're both here? That we ran across each other like this? I mean, two people on foot in the middle of the Red Desert—what are the odds of that?"

"Slim."

"If I weren't an atheist, I'd thank God you're here. You saved my life, I think."

Almost reluctantly, she handed over the jug and he dropped it into his backpack.

"I'm a believer myself," Joe said.

She nodded, and the look of confusion he'd seen on her face earlier returned. She said, "You're a game warden. Are you out here doing game warden things?"

"Right now, my only goal is to make it to the highway and catch a ride before Daisy and I keel over."

She didn't ask why he didn't have a phone or a radio with him. He found that interesting.

"I'm doing the same, sort of," she said.

"But you're walking in the opposite direction."

Her eyes slid off him toward the south and she nodded grimly.

"What's out there you're in such a hurry to get to?" Joe asked.

She paused for a long moment before saying, "I've got to warn Ibby."

"Who's Ibby?"

"He's a guy I know. He's a great guy. He's in danger and he doesn't even know it."

"So Ibby lives in the desert?"

Jan eyed him warily. "Yes."

"And you decided to walk out there from the café and tell him?" Joe asked, skeptical.

"No, I didn't decide to walk," she said, flashing anger. "That's just how it turned out."

She dug an old-fashioned pocket compass out of her jeans pocket, opened it, and let it settle on the palm of her hand. The compass had no electronic parts.

When the arrow was on true north, she looked over Joe's shoulder. He followed her gaze to a south-southeasterly direction.

Joe said, "That's the direction of the old sheep ranch."

"So you've seen it?"

"Yup. Kind of some suspicious activity around that place."

"Suspicious to you. Inspiring to me."

"So inspiring you decided to walk there," Joe said.

She looked up at him with a puzzled squint. "No. Something happened back at the café and I got out of there through the back door as fast as I could. I was able to get into Cooter's van before they could hurt me, and I took off cross-country to find Ibby and warn him.

"But Cooter's gas gauge doesn't work," she said, her voice rising. "It reads three-quarters full when apparently there's less than two gallons of gas in it. So I ran out of gas back there a few miles and I've been walking ever since."

Jan looked down at her hiking shoes. "Something has gone horribly wrong."

"Does it involve four white pickups filled with yay-hoos?"

She was surprised. "How did you know about them?"

"I ran across them a couple of hours ago. They didn't see me."

"If they had, you wouldn't be here." Despite the heat she shivered. "What they did to Cooter . . ."

She let the sentence trail off into nothing. She hugged herself as if she were recalling a recent trauma. A trauma so significant, he thought, that it propelled her out of an empty van to continue her journey on foot without food, water, or anything else.

"What happened to Cooter?" Joe asked.

"Can't you see? I can't waste time talking with you right now. I appreciate the water, but I've got to get going. I've got to warn Ibby."

She shouldered past Joe and regained the stride he'd noted earlier.

He called after her, "When I get to the highway, I can call for help. What do I tell them?"

Instead of answering, she waved good-bye to him over her shoulder without turning her head.

When she was fifty yards away, she stopped and slowly turned around.

"Joe Pickett?"

"Yup."

"Do you know someone named Sheridan?"

"I've got a daughter named Sheridan."

"Blond, green-eyed, maybe twenty-one or twenty-two? Student at the University of Wyoming?"

"That's her."

Jan gestured vaguely south. "She's with Ibby."

He felt a yank in his gut. He recalled Marybeth saying their daughter was going camping this weekend. But . . .

"Hold up," he said. "I'm going with you."

"What if I don't want company?"

"You're getting it anyway," he said. "Besides, that will give us a chance to talk. We can start with why Sheridan would be out here with this guy Ibby."

AFTER FORTY-FIVE MINUTES of bearing south-southeast and covering some of the same terrain Joe had tracked earlier, they paused to drink the last of the water at the scene of the grizzly bear carcass. Joe's head was spinning with Jan's revelations. She'd seemed comfortable talking to him and he was a good listener. It was one of his gifts.

But after what he'd heard, he was anxious to find Sheridan and get her out of there.

———

He questioned some of the things Jan said Ibby was up to, but he didn't doubt she believed them. He kept his own doubts to himself—how Ibby had managed to keep his mission a secret, for example, and how he had managed to provide an engineering facility without apparent water, power, or other infrastructure—to keep her talking.

It seemed too otherworldly to Joe, this mix of conspiracy, technology, and politics out there in the high desert.

But he had to admit to himself that some of what she said made sense: the fund-raising, the activism, the ideology. It could only be done off the grid, he knew, or officials would learn about it.

Jan didn't know how everything fit together, though. She worshipped Ibby and she believed in his idealism, and she knew her part in the whole scheme extremely well. What she didn't understand, *couldn't* understand, she said, was what had happened that morning.

And while she'd heard Ibby mention seeing another falconer in the desert, she didn't have a description of the man and she didn't know the name Nate Romanowski.

The more Joe learned, the more he thought it likely Nate would be involved in one way or the other. Nate thrived past the edges and beyond the margins.

Joe could never exist out there, he'd decided. He'd already experienced what it was like to be off the grid, even for a few hours.

He didn't like it.

FOR ONCE, Joe was glad not to be in direct contact with Marybeth, because she'd be both horrified and worried sick about what he'd learned. At the same time, though, he could use her counsel because she usually had a clearer head than he did. And he could *certainly* use her sense of urgency and the network of law enforcement and government contacts she had at her fingertips in order to send in the cavalry.

Jan cringed when she saw the bear carcass up close and she quickly turned away. The flies had found it and they kept up a steady hum.

"It was them," she said to Joe. "That's what they did to Cooter."

"They cut off his head?"

She nodded. "I would have been next if I hadn't run out the back door. And that would have been *after* they humiliated me. I could see it in their eyes. I've never been looked at like that before."

Joe pondered that. He thought of the last time he'd seen Sheridan, a month before, on her weekend visit home. She was fresh-faced, intelligent, attractive, and independent, just like her mother.

He said, "Let's get going, then."

PART SIX

THE NEW MONKEY WRENCH GANG

Somewhere in the depths of solitude, beyond
wilderness and freedom, lay the trap of madness.

—Edward Abbey, *The Monkey Wrench Gang*

22

As Ibby got up from his chair he asked Nate, "Do you know what an EMP—an electromagnetic pulse—can do?"

"Vaguely."

"An EMP can literally kill every electronic device in the vicinity of the pulse itself. We're talking phones, computers, cars—anything running on an electric current, which is just about everything there is. A powerful EMP could take down the electrical grid in this country. And it doesn't just shut things down. An EMP corrupts all the processors and circuitry so they can't be used again. It can fuse the insides of a power plant together so it wouldn't work again."

Nate sat back. "You're making a bomb here to do that?"

"No, no, not a bomb," Ibby said, insulted that Nate would even use the word. "Sure, that's one way a massive EMP could be delivered, by a nuclear device on the tip of a missile. A device like that could take out the electrical grid and shut the country down, except for a few isolated pockets and the facilities that had backup power supplies and generators. It would cause massive destruction and death. I can't even imagine how many people would die if the grid went out for a long time. But I said that no one will get hurt here."

"So if not a bomb . . ."

"Not a bomb."

Nate was skeptical.

"Look," Ibby said, "all you need in order to build a small EMP device, say small enough to kill a smartphone forever from two feet away, is a simple circuit board, a nine-volt battery, a high-voltage capacitor, a voltmeter, a switch, and copper wire to coil around a post. These are all things you can buy at any hardware or electronics store; they're not state secrets. When it's completed, it's about the size of a paperback novel. I'm no engineer, but even I can put a small one together now. It's not brain surgery or nuclear science."

"So who is building this thing?"

"Some of our team members who *are* engineers. They're as upset at the government as you and I are for what it's doing. I gave them the task of building a larger version of the EMP device I just described. A *much* larger one."

Nate said, "I saw the eighteen-wheeler in the first shed."

"There's two of them in there, side by side, actually," Ibby said. "We're putting the giant EMP devices into the trailers of both trucks so they can fire a highly concentrated pulse out the back. We're just days away from deploying them."

Ibby opened the shed door to the outside and gestured to Nate to follow him. He said, "By this time next week, there will be no more illegal surveillance of Americans. The government won't know what hit them."

. . .

NATE TRAILED IBBY to the second shed. As he did, he glanced over his shoulder. The "volunteers"—including Sheridan—had apparently gone around the third shed and entered a makeshift dining area. He caught snatches of distant conversation in the still morning.

"I need my weapons back," Nate said.

"Sorry, but we've got a strict 'no firearms' policy here. When you leave the premises, you'll get your guns back."

"I've had bad experiences without my guns."

"Yes, I heard."

"The policy doesn't seem to be in effect for Saeed and his goons, I noticed."

"They're *security*, Nate. Of course they're armed."

Nate shook his head. Ibby ignored him.

"When I found this ranch, I was amazed to discover that the former owner had apparently prepared for the coming nuclear war by building one hell of an underground bomb shelter," Ibby said. "Keep in mind that this place was built in the early 1960s. I wasn't around then, but I've read all about the paranoia. Apparently, the owner thought the Russians might drop one on him way out here in the middle of nowhere. It doesn't make sense to me, but the fact that he built it sure has been useful. If the team and the volunteers operate out of sight at all times, there's no way the spy satellites can figure out what we're up to."

Ibby stopped and looked up. He said, "This is my dream, that someday soon I'll be able to stand here and look up and see the sky, the clouds, and maybe my falcons without someone up there looking back at me, wondering what I'm doing and making an electronic record of it. Or me calling my family without knowing some spook is listening in. I don't think that's too much to ask, do you?"

Ibby looked down, but not before Nate caught a wink of moisture in his eyes.

"Not that my family has any idea where I am or what I'm doing," he said. "If my father knew . . . God help me."

THEY ENTERED THE SECOND SHED, the one filled with parked vehicles and equipment. It smelled of decades-old sheep manure, dust, and spilled fuel. The floor was hard-packed dirt, and since there were no rooms partitioned inside like the third shed, it was cavernous. Swallows had built hundreds of bulbous nests in the rafters, and the small birds swirled high above their heads.

"There are still some pigeons I haven't yet trapped to feed my falcons," Ibby pointed out. "You're welcome to them if you need them."

"Thanks."

Nate could feel a slight thrumming vibration through his boot soles as he stood on the floor of the shed.

"Generators," Ibby said in explanation. "As you might imagine, we're entirely self-contained. We get our electricity from our own source and water from a well. It gets pretty lonely at times for everybody, so I allow weekend breaks, but only at night."

He smiled and said, "Not that there are many places to go from here. Wamsutter or Rawlins . . . well, you get my drift. There's a little café on the interstate I have an interest in. It's not much, but most of us go there when we need a break."

Nate knew the place. It used to be a strip club.

Ibby approached what looked like the entrance to a storm cellar in the corner of the shed. The cinder-block base had slanted horizontal double doors on it. Before grasping the door handles, Ibby spoke into a rusty Schlitz beer can sitting on a windowsill over the entrance.

"It's me."

Nate heard a dull click from the other side of the double doors. Apparently, the beer can hid a microphone.

Ibby grinned at Nate. He was obviously very proud of this place, Nate thought.

"Watch your step," Ibby said.

THE BOMB SHELTER was constructed of thick concrete and it ran nearly the entire length of the shed. Bare bulbs were strung along electrical wires attached to the ceiling, bathing the space in harsh white light and creating deep shadows in the corners. As they descended from the entrance on a stout ladder, Nate looked over his shoulder to see four or five curious faces looking up from crude desks and workstations.

Ibby waited for Nate to climb down and join him, then said to the others, "This is Nate Romanowski, folks. He's a brother of mine from the world of falconry. More important, he's a brother to all of us when it comes to our mission here."

A fiftyish man wearing a dark jumpsuit said, "Welcome to our world."

Nate nodded to him. The man *looked* like an engineer; half-glasses, disheveled hair, bulbous nose, rough hands, grease-smeared tool handles sticking out from every pocket of his overalls.

"This is Bill Henn," Ibby said. "He's our chief designer. Bill helped build the Utah Data Center and he was there when it opened. But Bill was under the impression the facility would be used only to find and target terrorists. When he objected to its actual use, Bill found himself suddenly unemployed."

"I'd rather be doing the Lord's work," Henn said. "Which is what I'm doing now. My wife, Donna, came with me and she does most of the cooking."

"Bill can answer any technical questions," Ibby said. "This is his baby from start to finish."

Henn nodded quickly, then went back to soldering on a circuit board of some kind on his desk.

A young, hard-looking woman with frizzed black hair and a feline cast to her eyes approached them. She was tall, slim, and fit. She wore a suede vest over a long-sleeved T-shirt and tight gray slacks.

"Suzy Gudenkauf," she said. "Pleased to meet you."

Nate shook her hand.

"Suzy's our outreach director," Ibby said. "She's been with us as long as Bill."

"Outreach?" Nate asked. "I thought you used couriers?"

"We do," Gudenkauf said. "But that's just part of what I do. Maybe the smallest part."

Nate found himself mesmerized by her deep brown eyes, and she didn't look away.

Ibby said, "Suzy's talent is in networking. She's incredibly well connected with people who share our outlook. She identified funding sources and distribution paths that keep us in business. As you can imagine, it's really super-expensive to buy all the parts and equipment we need and to do it all under the radar so it isn't tracked. Suzy has people on both coasts who trust her and our mission to the point that they'll send hard, untraceable cash through the couriers."

Gudenkauf said, "If Bill over there needs a half ton of copper wire to get delivered to a pickup point along I-80, I make sure it gets handled. If he needs industrial batteries or two big-ass Caterpillar generators, I find sources who can deliver them. If Ibby here just has to have his chai tea latte in the afternoon, I make sure he gets it."

Ibby nodded at that.

"So if there's anything at all you need . . ." She let the sentence end in a slight smile.

Nate ignored the implication.

"WANT A TOUR?" Ibby asked Nate.

"Sure, but first I have a question."

"Is it technical?"

"Sort of."

"Then ask Bill."

Henn looked up expectantly.

Nate said, "I've been at facilities overseas that were prepped to withstand an EMP attack. I saw copper-mesh cages over the top of the electronics that could absorb a pulse and divert it into the ground. I can't imagine the NSA hasn't built screens around the hardware at the data center. Or is your device so powerful it can cut through the shield somehow?"

Henn nodded. "They've got a shield around the supercomputer that my EMP device probably can't penetrate. The pulse *may* be powerful enough to leak inside and screw up a few things, but there's no way it would create the massive failure we hope for."

Nate looked over to Ibby.

Ibby said, "We've thought of that. Actually, Bill thought of it early on. So we've got a work-around."

"I know you said no one will get hurt," Nate said. "But having done special operations, I know that something unexpected always happens. What if there's someone walking around in there with a pacemaker in his chest? Wouldn't an EMP kill him?"

"It's possible," Ibby said. "We pray that won't happen, or anything like it. Believe me, that kind of thing has kept me up at night. But in the end I have to accept the possibility of unintentional collateral damage. It sounds harsh, but it's true."

"Kind of like disabling the vehicle of that spy you told me about?" Nate said. "You hope he can walk to the highway without dying of exposure."

Nate and Ibby stared at each other for a moment before Ibby looked away. Ibby said, "It would be unfortunate. We're doing everything we can to minimize casualties. You've got to believe me on that. There are so many other ways we could've taken out the data center—bombs, a frontal assault—and we think we've chosen the one that will do the least human damage. I hope at least you'll give us credit for that."

Nate grunted. Neither a yes nor a no.

To Henn, Ibby said, "Let's walk him through."

"Mind if I tag along?" Suzy Gudenkauf asked while linking her arm through Nate's.

"I COULD BORE YOU with the jargon associated with supercomputers," Bill Henn said as he slowly led Nate and Ibby through a concrete hallway that connected the workroom to another space directly beneath the first shed.

"Petaflops, nodes, processors, how many quadrillion floating points per second, chiller plants—all that—but it's simpler for a non-engineer to simply understand if you think of a supercomputer as a giant brain and everything built around it as organs that exist to keep the brain healthy and functioning. If the organs fail completely or blood stops circulating, the brain will die rather quickly."

Henn stopped and turned around so he could use his hands to gesture while he talked.

"A supercomputer is millions of dollars' worth of interconnected hardware and software running at maximum capacity doing billions of calculations of ones and zeros every second. For every watt of electricity used, a watt of heat is generated by the machine. There's no way around it. Those computers get hot fast, and in order to function they must be kept cool. Think of the fans they used to have in old desktop computers. Those fans were there for a reason.

"So the supercomputer must be kept cool at all times—sixty-five degrees, to be exact—or the nodes inside will delaminate, meaning they'll fall apart and fail. What you need to keep in mind about a supercomputer facility is that for every foot of space occupied by the brain there needs to be an additional four feet of space devoted to keeping the brain cool. It's all about keeping the brain cool at all times. There can be no fluctuation at all. If the temperature fluctuates, the nodes delaminate and the data goes kablooey.

"That's why there are so many cloud server centers out here in the West," Henn said. "High elevations, dry air, and long winters mean cooler temperatures. That's why they built the Utah Data Center where they did.

"So, how do you keep the brain cool? Water and air, but mostly water. You circulate cool water over, under, and through the super-computer itself. They haven't come up with anything more efficient than just plain cool water, and believe me, they've tried. That's why every supercomputer facility has water storage, chiller plants so water heated by the machines can be cooled down again, and a shit-load of cooling towers outside. Think of water as blood to the brain.

"In order to keep that water flowing at all times, there's a power substation plugged into the electrical grid. But of course they have backups to their backups. Remember: it's *all* about cooling. If the power goes out for some reason, there is massive battery backup in one of the buildings that keeps the power going so the water can continue to circulate. But batteries don't last forever, either, and if the power is out for hours there are sophisticated backup generators on site that fire up. They'll power the electricity and water supply as long as fuel can be delivered to them."

Gudenkauf squeezed Nate's arm. "I love this part," she said. "Now Bill is going to tell you how we'll kill the evil, diseased brain of the U.S. government."

"We're going to act like a smart boxer," Henn said. "Instead of head shots, we're going to do a series of body shots. We're going to knock out all the infrastructure that keeps the brain cool. Kill the body . . ."

". . . and the head will die," Nate finished.

"Exactly."

"Bill knows everything about the data center," Ibby said. "He knows where the cooling towers are most vulnerable, where the power plant can be breached, and where to hit the water plant and the chiller plants. Once they're all shut down, the brain will fry it-self into a silicon block that can never be used again."

Nate shook his head, still skeptical. He said, "I just can't buy it that the people inside that facility would stand around and let the super-computer and the storage of all those records just burn up. Aren't there manual ways of just shutting it all down before it seizes up?"

"Sure," Henn said. "It's not easily done, and there's no doubt some of the data would be corrupted before they could get it all shut down, but *sure*, they could do it."

"And that would preserve what they'd already collected, right?" Nate said. "So after they get everything repaired that you knocked out, they'd still have all those records stored away. It might take a while, but once they've got the place running again, they wouldn't even have to start over."

"Look," Ibby said, interrupting. "We really don't want to reveal everything to you right now, but what you need to know is we've got it figured out."

Henn smiled slowly. Nate could tell that he really wanted to let him in on the whole plan because he was very, very proud of it.

Nate pressed on. "The head may die, but they can bring it back to life once they get the body repaired, right?"

"Right," Henn said. "Unless, hypothetically, there was a bug in the overall facility's computer programming that is so masked and hidden away no one could ever find it. Let's say, again hypotheti-cally, that the bug is designed to come to life only upon *a reboot of the entire system*. And playing this out, let's say the bug would infect the system so rapidly that it would corrupt all of the remaining rec-ords before they could be searchable."

"Which means," Ibby said, sharing Henn's enthusiasm, "if they bring that facility back to life, they'll find it's filled with gibberish. No phone records, no metadata they can use. If they want, really want, to pursue this illegal data collection, they'll have to totally rebuild from the ground up. That will take years and billions more dollars. By then, I hope, the citizens of the nation will stand up and say, 'No, damn you. Not again.'"

"KNOWING YOUR BACKGROUND, I've got a question for you," Ibby said to Nate.

Nate responded with raised eyebrows.

Ibby moved to the doorway so he could click on a set of lights that illuminated the previously darkened corner of the room. Nate noted a large schematic map headed UTAH DATA CENTER taped to a whiteboard. Next to the map were aerial photos of the facility shown in context to the landscape surrounding it.

"Here it is," Ibby said, approaching the map. The huge facility itself was peanut-shaped and ran north to south. It was outlined by high fences. The largest buildings within the compound were dead center and were labeled DATA HALLS 1 & 2 and DATA HALLS 3 & 4. Between them was an oblong administration building.

Flanking the data halls to the north and south sides were power buildings, chiller plants, water storage, fuel tanks, and six cooling towers built cheek by jowl.

A power substation and power line coming from Bluffdale to the north sat outside the perimeter of the fence. On the southeast bend of the perimeter was a visitor center.

Ibby said, "If you were to hit this facility with two trailer-mounted EMP pulses, where would you set up?"

Nate approached the map and studied the aerial photographs. The UDC sat on a huge flat swale beneath some foothills to the east. There was no residential housing in the area outside the perimeter. Only sagebrush.

Nate jabbed his index finger on the image. "It looks like there's a series of checkpoints along the road before you can even get to the visitor center, so unless you plan to crash through them, that's not an option. The north end, toward Bluffdale, looks level, but there are no paved roads to get near it."

He looked over at Ibby, to find him nodding.

Nate gestured to a set of foothills to the west of the facility that appeared to overlook it.

"Here," Nate said, indicating the foothills. "You'd be above the buildings just outside the perimeter fence. If you stationed one device to the northeast and the other to the southeast, you could fire down in a pincer design."

He bent over and studied the image closely. "There are no paved roads up there, either, but it looks like there are some old Jeep roads and two-tracks. It doesn't look too steep for a vehicle.

"And when the attack is over," he said, "you could take I-15 north to I-80 and get the hell out of there."

He looked up to find Ibby and Henn nodding in agreement.

"It's good to get a second opinion from someone who has actually conducted a raid in the real world," Ibby said. "And that's exactly what Henn and I thought."

Nate said, "How you'd ever get two big EMP weapons up there without being detected is another matter."

"Yes, it is," Ibby said with a grin.

———

23

HENN LED THE PROCESSION UP ANOTHER LADDER AND NATE found himself in the first shed. Two huge eighteen-wheelers were parked next to each other. Electronics gear and thick coils of wire littered the floor space between them. The inside walls of the shed were papered with technical schematics.

"Let's see the EMP devices before the volunteers get here," Ibby said to Henn. "That'll be any minute."

To Nate, Ibby said, "Bill works them like dogs, I'm happy to say. He's had a crew every weekend for two months helping out. Suzy used her courier network to get the word out, and they just started showing up like magic. A few of them do technical stuff, and one guy is a really good welder. But for the most part, they do mundane work like janitorial and cleanup, schlepping tools and gear—that kind of thing. They completely donate their time and all we do is feed them and show them a good party at the café when they're done. This is the last weekend we'll need them, so I don't want us to distract them while they work."

Nate nodded. He didn't want the volunteers, especially Sheridan Pickett, to wander in, either.

The presence of Sheridan surprised him. Although he knew her to be smart and daring, he'd never thought of her as a radical.

Of course, she *had* been in college for four years.

AS THEY WALKED DOWN the length of the vehicles, Nate noticed that one trailer was emblazoned with the logo for a heavy-duty industrial battery company and the other had the name of a familiar over-the-road commercial carrier.

He barely listened as Henn explained how the battery truck had arrived filled to the brim and how they'd off-loaded only half of the units and placed the remainder in the other trailer.

They walked to the wide-open back ends of the two trucks. Reinforced steel ramps stretched from the dirt floor to the bottom lip of the trailer box.

The EMP devices filled the long fifty-two-foot trailers. Nate had expected them to look high-tech, but what he saw seemed almost medieval: glimpses of large yellow Caterpillar generators in the back wired into walls of batteries, huge slabs of discolored steel welded together, a massive spool of copper wire the size of a pickup, a spoked snout that protruded from it all aiming out the back-door opening. Nate caught the gist of how the EMP worked: the generators charged the batteries, industrial capacitors and copper wire amplified the power, and the burst was fired through the snout.

In theory, Henn said, each EMP device had two full-power blasts in it before the generators had to be used to recharge the batteries. That would take several hours.

"How many times do you plan to fire it?" Nate asked.

Henn and Ibby looked at each other.

"Let's just say that we hope we won't have to recharge the batteries at all," Henn said.

"So what do you think?" Ibby asked, moving his eyes from Nate toward the entrance door as the voices of the volunteers increased in volume.

"I don't know *what* to think," Nate said. But he was impressed. *Very* impressed. Cobbling together a high-tech weapons system in the middle of a desert without outside power was a magnificent technical achievement. Plus, Ibby seemed to have his heart in the right place. Nate was nagged by the thought that perhaps he was on the wrong side in this adventure.

"We'll talk about it in a minute," Ibby said. "I need to give our volunteers a pep talk when they come in. It's important they're motivated to finish up today.

"I wish I could attract a higher class of volunteers," Ibby added, "but this is the hand I was dealt. We've learned we can't keep them longer than a weekend at a time. They get bored easily and they aren't exactly hard workers, I'm afraid. It's important to keep them motivated."

"We'll meet you afterward," Gudenkauf said, tugging on Nate's arm. Henn stayed with Ibby.

Nate went with her willingly, and he heard the volunteers pour into the third shed just as they climbed down the ladder into the dark hallway.

Sheridan hadn't seen him.

. . .

BEFORE THEY REACHED the control room, Suzy Gudenkauf pulled Nate aside and grasped his hands in hers.

"Look," she said, "Ibby's motivating the volunteers and Saeed should be back any minute with your Jeep and your falcons. We don't have much time, so I need you to listen up.

"I don't know you, but Ibby obviously trusts you. What I'm asking you, what I'm begging you right now, is to watch out for him. Protect him. He's in over his head and he refuses to believe it."

"What do you mean?" Nate asked.

She gripped his hands harder. She was strong.

"Ibby is a charismatic leader. He's a great guy and a true believer in this. He's been able to pull us all together here to work in these conditions for months, and we do it because we believe in it and we believe in him. It takes someone really special to lure me out of Palo Alto into the middle of fucking nowhere just to help him out. He's an American patriot and I believe in him, just like everyone here does. Who would have thought that a Muslim not even born in this country would have the guts and the courage to do what the sheeple out here won't do? But I think right now he's in terrible danger, and maybe we all are."

"From the NSA?"

"Probably, if they knew what we were doing," she said. "But no, he's in danger from within."

She pressed closer and Nate felt the wall at his back. She looked both ways to make sure no one was coming down the hallway.

"When Saeed showed up, it made some sense to me," she continued. "Bill Henn and the rest of them are a bunch of tech geeks, and we needed security. I came because of my connections with the billionaire tech people who wanted to help fund this. We aren't soldiers—we're activists. We welcomed Saeed because he seemed devoted to Ibby.

"Although it might not look like it, Saeed has gradually taken over. Even Ibby doesn't seem to realize it. Saeed's impatient, and he keeps pushing. When our cash flow slowed down, Saeed gave me some contacts for more funding and they came through, but it was all real sketchy. I know they came from shell corporations that I'm guessing were set up to launder money for some other purpose. What I do know is that the funds came from overseas in the Middle East and Europe.

"I was willing to overlook that, but Saeed kept moving in. While I was working on a deal to *buy* all the batteries we needed, Saeed used his contacts to go out and hijack a truck on I-80 and drive it here. God knows what happened to the driver," she said with a shiver.

"Ibby seems to trust him," she stated, "but I don't. Not after he brought in those other two guys. Do you know how they got here?"

Before Nate could answer, she said, "They came over the border from Mexico. One's Yemeni, the other Syrian."

"Which is which?" Nate asked.

"The tall skinny one with the beard is from Yemen. The nasty fat one is Syrian."

"He hit me with a stun gun," Nate said, reaching up and touching his fingertips to the burn marks on his neck.

"Not surprising," she said. "Late last night, I saw the Syrian drive out of here a couple of hours after Ibby sent those two loser volunteers away. I just had this feeling he was going to pick them up and take them somewhere."

"I know where that was," Nate said. "Did Ibby know about it?"

"No," she said. "He was hunkered down with Henn working out a few last details. The Syrian was back here a couple of hours later and he was alone."

"Did you tell Ibby?"

"He won't listen when I complain about Saeed or his men," she said quickly. "He thinks I'm trying to guard my territory. Plus, the closer we get to deploying the EMPs, the more focused he is on the mission. He ignores distractions . . . like me."

Nate could tell by the way she said it that there was history between Ibby and Suzy Gudenkauf that went beyond the team. They'd been romantically involved, and for one reason or another they no longer were.

She took a deep breath and said, "I think they're connected to ISIS or al-Qaeda, and I think they're going to use our EMPs for terror attacks."

"*What?*"

"Think of what terrorists could do beyond the destruction of the UDC. I think Saeed just wants these EMPs. Imagine what a terrorist could do with them—they can go after government buildings, hospitals, stadiums, senior centers, power substations, you name it."

Nate's mind spun. The legitimate purpose of the NSA facility was to gather electronic records so they could drill down into the metadata to detect terrorists talking to each other. If the entire facility was off-line, bad guys all over the world would have free rein. Plus, he *could* imagine purposes for EMP devices hidden in the back of eighteen-wheelers moving across America's highway system. The devices could be used to bring down airplanes as they took off or landed at airports, to derail trains, to disrupt the electrical grid, or to take out radar installations that could warn about impending missile attacks.

She paused. "We've built an awesome weapon."

"Yes, you have," he said.

"This thing is getting way out of control," Suzy said. "If Saeed takes those EMP devices from Ibby . . ." She shivered again. "You've got to stay close to him and make sure they don't hurt him. Please don't let them hurt Ibby—or any of us.

"Maybe you can talk with them," she said. "For whatever reason, they've let you inside their circle, so they must respect you. Maybe you can take them aside and explain in a calm and rational way that they need to leave Ibby alone, and they need to let us do our work."

Nate grinned.

"Why is that funny?" she asked.

He said, "Might as well ask me to reason with a snake. Snakes are snakes. Tigers are tigers. You can't *reason* them out of what they are. The only thing you can do is kill them."

She cringed at that.

Nate said, "There's only three of them. I need to get my weapons back. Do you know where they keep them?"

She shrugged. "There's an armory room underneath shed number three. I'd guess that's where they are, but it's locked up.

"One more thing," she said. Her eyes were wide. "I think there may be more of Saeed's men on the way."

"Why do you say that?"

"The volunteers used to stay in kind of crappy dorm rooms we built in the first shed. Even though it turned out to be more of a party atmosphere than we really wanted around here—as you can imagine—we didn't want them out wandering around where an eye in the sky could spot them. But as you can see, this weekend they were asked to bring camping gear so they could stay outside in tents. It's a breach of security, but I didn't give it much thought at first. But if Saeed needs those rooms . . ." She trailed off.

She said, "Saeed sends messages via my courier network. I don't look at them, and I don't know who they go to. But in the last month, he's been sending *a lot* of messages."

Nate, once again, recalled the dream he'd had back on the Bucholz ranch. In the dream, there had been more of the enemy than he had bullets.

He'd had plenty of time to play the dream over again in his head. Each time, he couldn't conjure up a way where it would end well for him. What he never could have guessed from his dream, though, was that there would be other lives at stake as well.

And he thought: *I've got to recover that phone and get Sheridan out of here.*

NATE THANKED SUZY GUDENKAUF and strode through the control room. He ignored the curious looks of Ibby's team as he passed them, although he nodded toward a rumpled man who stood near the ladder. Nate walked with such purpose, he thought, that the man stepped aside for him and didn't ask where he was going.

After scrambling up through the entrance and across the shed, he closed the door behind him and looked around. No one but him, it seemed, was outside.

He'd made his decision quickly. Ibby had, perhaps, noble intentions. In another circumstance, Nate knew he might have thrown in with him. But what Suzy had told him had poisoned the well.

He duckwalked below the windows of the first shed so he couldn't be seen. As he did, he could hear snatches of a speech Ibby was giving to the volunteers.

"*. . . The Founders were brave and honorable patriots who put their best interests aside to stand up for the ideals of liberty and freedom . . .*"

Nate paused at the corner of the first shed when he could see the expanse of the desert swale to the west. The empty tents were between him and the dry streambed he'd used to get there.

"*. . . Thomas Jefferson, in a letter to James Madison, said, 'I hold it that a little rebellion now and then is a good thing, and as necessary in the political world as storms in the physical.'*"

Far in the distance, miles away, were two tiny dots. Vehicles coming: Saeed's and his own Jeep. He'd have maybe a minute or two to retrieve the satellite phone, install the battery, and scramble back before they arrived. If he hurried, he thought, he could make it to the third shed and find the armory . . .

"*Someday, folks, you'll look back at this time and you'll know that your efforts helped usher in a renewal of our founding principles. You'll know that you did your part to take America back . . .*"

AT FIRST, Nate thought he was at the wrong gopher hole because, when he reached inside, there was no phone.

He cursed, and scanned the stream bank, wondering how he'd gotten turned around. No, he concluded, he was in the right place.

Then he realized someone had gotten there before him and had taken it.

Saeed, the Syrian, and the Yemeni were getting closer and he could hear their distant motors.

This wasn't his dream yet, though, he thought. In his dream he was armed and doomed.

Now he just felt doomed.

24

———

SHERIDAN LOOKED AROUND AT THE OTHER EIGHT VOLUNTEERS in the shed while the man named Ibby addressed them, and she thought: *I don't think I like any of these people and I want to go home.*

She fought the feeling, tried to tamp it down. Just because she was uncomfortable, she thought, she shouldn't just pack up and leave. Plus, given the circumstances of their arrival the night before, it might be difficult and embarrassing.

She'd been quiet at breakfast while the others talked, making do with a gentle nodding of her head if someone addressed her. There were discussions about inequality, racism, oppression, trigger warnings, but most of all about the fact that their government was spying on them without their permission and it must be stopped. Sheridan was mildly sympathetic with that topic, but she questioned herself. Why had she agreed to come and what was she going to do there? She assumed it would be illegal just by the way the other volunteers talked to one another.

These were the kinds of long-into-the-night discussions she'd heard and participated in on campus and off, where the answers to all of the problems were simple and easy if the idiots in authority would *just listen to the students who had it all figured out.*

At the time, she thought, the talk was exhilarating. It was wonderful to be in the company of bright, articulate people who knew more about the world than she did and never missed an opportunity to remind her of that. But something about the endless "salons" had worn off over the years. She couldn't decide if she'd moved past them, or if they'd left her behind, dog-paddling in her shallow pool of small-town ignorance.

Even Kira, who was usually quite vocal on just about everything, had kept her head down and spooned tiny bits of watery scrambled eggs into her mouth. There was no bacon or ham, and the coffee was weak.

A male with a wispy growth of beard and a stocking cap pulled down over his ears for style but not warmth had stabbed a fork at Sheridan and asked, "This your first time?"

"My first time what?"

"Your first time here. I don't remember seeing you before and . . . I think I'd remember." He smiled and she realized he intended it as a compliment.

"It's my first time," she said.

"How'd you find out about what we're doing here?"

Sheridan indicated Kira, who seemed to be in a world of her own. In her pickup on I-80, Kira had told her that she'd learned about the deep web through some other campus activists. The deep web, Sheridan learned, was a hidden category of the Internet filled with content that couldn't be found by normal search engines. That's where she'd located the secret site devoted to stopping government spying and saw the call for volunteers. Kira had completed a questionnaire and submitted an application, and three weeks later, the approval arrived.

"Haven't seen her, either," the man said, as if Kira couldn't hear him.

"I'm Seth," he said.

"Sheridan," she replied, deadpan. She didn't want this to go anywhere.

"I've been here most of the volunteer weekends, although I have to say our living situation kind of sucks now. We used to sleep indoors on bunks. I'm not much of a tent guy."

Neither is Kira, Sheridan thought.

Kira, who was normally as pale as a blank sheet of white paper, looked almost translucent as she sat slumped, barely eating. Sleeping in the tent in a sleeping bag had apparently taken a lot out of her.

Seth asked, "Are you two, you know, together?"

"Not like that," Sheridan said.

He warmed to the response. "So you're . . ."

"No."

"That was fast," he said. A note of distaste entered his voice. "You know, we're all here for the same thing. We're here to further the cause. Sometimes, you know, people bond together."

He chuckled, but his eyes weren't laughing along. She realized she had answered so quickly she had offended him. She imagined that he enjoyed the bunks and the camaraderie. And whatever else he could get from girls like her.

"You kind of look like you're not sure you're into all of this," he said, leaning forward.

"I'm keeping an open mind."

"Good, that's good," he said. "You don't want to be 'Lindsey'd.'"

"Lindsey'd?"

"I'll tell you later," he said, looking around to see if he'd been overheard and keeping his voice low.

SHERIDAN TRIED not to be so judgmental about the other volunteers, but they looked like losers to her. They were made up of sixth-year seniors and off-campus lifers from colleges in Colorado, Utah, Montana, and Wyoming majoring in fields that ended with the word *studies*. Rather than complete their degrees, they lived in an alternate world of activism, conspiracy, and the elusive quest for social justice.

She realized as she stood there that she really wanted no part of them and she resented Kira for inviting her along because she had camping gear. And she was angry at herself for accepting.

The only bright spot, she decided, was listening to this guy Ibby. He was impressive: caring, impassioned, charismatic. He was a born leader, and he could inspire others to his cause, including her. She felt herself being swept up in his patriotic fervor.

Plus, he was a falconer. Just like Nate.

Still, though, she planned to leave at the first opportunity.

THE NIGHT BEFORE *had* been an adventure, but the feeling was wearing off fast.

They'd arrived at the Mustang Café on I-80 promptly at seven in the evening, as per the instructions Kira had received. One by one, other volunteers had arrived and Sheridan could tell from their interaction that they obviously knew one another. A bartender named Cooter poured draft Coors Lights and served deep-fried cheese and vegetables on plates. Potent marijuana smoke hung in the air. The guys who had brought it said they had just bought it legally across the border in Colorado.

Sheridan instantly regretted that she'd arrived wearing her day-to-day clothes: jeans, cowboy boots, hooded University of Wyoming sweatshirt. She stood out among the others who, like Kira, wore primarily black.

The volunteers had brought in their backpacks and duffel bags and stacked them in a pile near the door. They milled around the small dance floor, smoking and drinking and trading stories about what they'd done since they'd last seen each other.

Sheridan leaned in close to Kira and asked, "What happens now?"

Kira barely shrugged. She didn't look back at Sheridan when she said, "We'll find out, I guess."

"I'm really not sure about this."

"Come on. Don't chicken out now."

"Where are we going? Do we all drive somewhere in a pack?"

"I don't know."

"Why did they bring all their gear in here?"

"Why do you keep asking me questions I can't answer?" Kira said, annoyed. Sheridan got the impression Kira didn't want to be perceived as anxious or uncool—like her friend in the University of Wyoming hoodie.

"Can I help?" came a female voice from behind them.

Sheridan had turned and was face-to-face with an attractive woman in her late twenties or early thirties who had clever eyes and a sly smile. Although the woman was dressed in jeans, a fleece vest, and hiking boots, she looked out of place.

"I'm Jan," the woman said. She thumbed through a sheaf of papers on a clipboard. "Which one of you is Kira?"

"I'm Kira," her friend said.

Jan nodded, and said to Sheridan, "I'm sorry, but you have to go."

"Why?" Sheridan asked. "Go where?"

"Wherever you came from," Jan said. "You haven't been vetted. We've got a strict policy about that."

Even though Sheridan was having second thoughts, she felt embarrassed. Kira looked crestfallen.

"Look," Kira said, "I asked online if she could come. Whoever was on the other end didn't say no, so I thought it was cool."

"It isn't," Jan said.

"She's my friend," Kira pleaded. "She's my *ride*. I can vouch for her."

She gestured to the outdoor gear. "This is all her stuff. I don't have any of my own. I'm not an outdoors person. I don't even drive. Come on, *please*?"

Kira was pitiful and looked to be near tears. She was also persuasive.

Jan stood there looking at them for a long moment. "I'll make an exception only because we desperately need people and she's vouching for you," she finally said to Sheridan. "Several of our longtime volunteers got themselves in trouble at a protest in Boulder, so we're shorthanded. I'll need you to fill out an application. It has a confidentiality clause that says you can't reveal the nature of our work or your part in it. Among other things."

Sheridan was of two minds. She didn't like to be singled out and rejected, but at the same time her enthusiasm for this experience had rapidly waned. But she couldn't simply abandon Kira.

"I'll do it," Sheridan said. Kira was relieved.

After completing the form and grudgingly listing all of her personal information as well as agreeing to the confidentiality and legal liability release requirements, she handed it back to Jan.

Jan looked it over and was apparently okay with it. She read from the form and said, "Sheridan Pickett and Kira Harden. Both of you are first-timers, so welcome. As you can imagine, we've got to be careful how we do things. But first, I'd like to officially thank you both for coming. You don't realize how much we appreciate your help."

Sheridan nodded.

Jan looked at her wristwatch and said, "Now that it's getting dark out, we'll get started soon."

"Doing what?" Sheridan asked tentatively. She felt Kira glare at her, but she didn't look over.

"First, does anyone know you're here or what you're doing this weekend? Any friends, relatives, acquaintances?"

Sheridan and Kira both shook their heads.

"Good. Second, you'll both have to leave your cell phones here. Don't worry, they'll be safe. Did you bring any other devices? Laptops, iPads, anything like that? Anything that can transmit or receive data?"

"No," Sheridan said. Kira shook her head.

"No weapons or anything like that, either?" Jan said.

Sheridan handed over her pepper spray.

"And no intoxicants of any kind. We have a zero tolerance policy about that—for your own safety. You'll be around heavy machinery and equipment and we don't want anyone getting hurt. I hope you understand."

"What about the weed?" Sheridan asked, chinning over her shoulder toward the smokers.

"They know the rules. They'll leave it here."

"Kind of harsh," Kira said. Sheridan knew that Kira liked to light up before breakfast every morning.

"Harsh but safe," Jan said breezily. "If you can't do it, you know where the door is."

Kira looked down at her heavy boots and said, "No, that's not what I meant. I'm cool with it."

Jan continued. "In a few minutes, some of our team members will arrive from the desert. You'll leave your car here and they'll take you to our location. Can either of you drive a four-wheeler?"

Kira looked to Sheridan with a blank face.

"I can," Sheridan said. "I learned to drive an ATV with my dad."

"You look like you could," Jan said with an appreciative smile. "You two can go together, then. Just don't lose sight of the team leader out there in the desert. If you get lost, you might stay lost. Do you understand?"

"Yes," Sheridan said.

"Okay then," Jan said, patting them both on their shoulders as she slid past them toward the other volunteers, who greeted her like a long-lost friend.

"What in the *hell* have you gotten me into?" Sheridan asked Kira.

Kira shrugged. Then: "Thank you for coming. You're much cooler than I thought."

Sheridan almost said, *No, I'm much dumber than you thought.*

. . .

SHERIDAN LOVED THE RIDE across the desert in the dark. The wind whipped her hair and the air smelled dry and foreign. Kira was behind her on the seat with her arms around Sheridan's waist.

Once they left the café and the distant interstate, it was a dark and lonely world: no lights, no roads, no power lines or other signs of human encroachment. The ATV tires kicked up dust and at times Sheridan chose to hang back far enough so that she could see and breathe better. But she never lost sight of the twin taillights of the lead four-wheeler. Her roommate's head was buried into Sheridan's back, and at times Kira squeezed so hard Sheridan had trouble breathing.

An hour out, she was surprised to find that she was second in the pack and the other volunteers were behind her. She'd noticed before they'd left that a few of the "team members" who delivered the four-wheelers had stayed back at the café, presumably to help load gear and return to the "location" in the truck. And presumably to have a few beers with Cooter as well.

PUTTING UP THE TENTS in the dark produced a lot of grumbling. Sheridan had brought a headlamp and she used it to set up hers. Kira was worthless with that kind of chore. She simply stood there, shifting on her feet from side to side, holding her sleeping bag until the tent was tight. Once Kira was inside, Sheridan lent her lamp to a couple of volunteers who were still struggling with their tents.

When she climbed inside and zipped the flap closed, Kira was deep into her bag. Her voice was muffled when she said, "I'm covered in dust. My eyes are full of grit. I forgot my toothbrush."

"You'll live."

"I know I won't sleep. All I'll think about is that I have to pee, and when I do, a wolf will eat me."

"There are no wolves down here."

"A bear, then."

"There might be a bear," Sheridan said.

"Oh, great. Did I ever tell you I *fucking hate camping*?"

"I would have guessed that."

Sheridan fell asleep with a smirk on her lips.

BUT NOW, AS SHE LISTENED to the one named Ibby say that this should be the last weekend they would ever be needed and that by this time next week what they'd done would be known around the world, Sheridan briefly closed her eyes.

She didn't want to be famous, and she didn't want to get into trouble. She judged the nature of the work by the volunteers who were there to do it and it left a sour taste in her mouth.

Although she didn't doubt Ibby's sincerity for a moment, in her mind's eye she kept seeing the disapproving squint of her dad's face, and the voice of her mother asking her *what was she thinking*.

Sheridan didn't like the idea of the government collecting metadata from innocent people. It was wrong, she thought. But she also knew that she'd never sent a text or email or said anything over her cell phone that could be construed as dangerous. Boring, yes. But not dangerous to anyone.

She wasn't surprised that Seth had positioned himself next to her while Ibby talked. He eagerly turned his head to her when she leaned toward him.

"What does it mean to be 'Lindsey'd'?" she asked in a whisper.

He looked around again and lowered his lips to her ear.

"Lindsey was a pain in the ass," he said. "She got here and made all kinds of demands about the living conditions, and basically announced that if she wasn't allowed to leave here, she'd blow the whistle on the whole project. She bitched and moaned about everything and she was a goddamned prima donna, and she should never have been preapproved to come here. She got on everyone's nerves real fast."

Sheridan nodded for him to go on.

"There's this security guy named Saeed," Seth said. "He said he'd take her back to her car so we could get back to work. We all stood up and applauded when he drove her away and we never saw her again. That's the worst thing that can happen here, that you get Lindsey'd."

"So did she keep quiet?" Sheridan asked.

Seth shrugged.

"What happened to her?"

"I don't know and I don't care," he said. "All I know is that when we got back to the Mustang Café two days later, her car was still there."

Sheridan felt a cold chill tremble down her spine.

"So don't get Lindsey'd," Seth said.

PART SEVEN

UTAH DATA CENTER

This is the place!

—BRIGHAM YOUNG, 1847

25

"IS THAT A SPRING?" JAN STALKUP ASKED WITH A SQUINT. SHE pointed to a distant smudge of blue-green beneath a rock formation to the southeast.

Joe raised his binoculars to his eyes and focused. Although he couldn't see standing water or an outlet stream, the ground was churned up and dark. Mud.

"Yup," he said. "Good eye."

He'd obviously missed the spring that morning when he came through, but he'd been farther west and the angle would have been back and over his shoulder.

It was good timing, he thought, since they'd run out of water the hour before. He realized how desperate they were when he'd barked at Daisy for spilling too much. He still felt guilty for it.

"Just when we really, really need to find water, we find water," Jan said, ebullient. She reached out and grasped his arm. "Maybe I need to spend more time with believers."

.   .   .

JOE FILLED BOTH PLASTIC JUGS after filtering the water through his old camping pump filter. The spring wasn't so much a spring as a seep. Tepid water filled a foot-wide depression and swirled like coffee and cream in smaller holes. He couldn't remember the last time he changed out the filter unit and he hoped it was still functioning, even though he'd decided to drink the water either way. There was no choice.

The water was murky and warm and it tasked like alkali, but they didn't complain. Jan drank her fill, followed by Joe and Daisy. Then Joe sank to his muddy knees again to replenish the jug.

While he pumped, he surveyed the ground around the spring. It told a story.

When he stood and capped the second full jug, he said, "He's here, all right."

Jan looked at him, puzzled.

"My friend Nate. Plus another falconer and a third unknown guy."

"You can see all this how?" she asked.

"Looking around."

"Looking around where?" she asked, puzzled.

He gestured toward the ground itself, which had been churned up by visiting wild horses, desert elk, and other wildlife. He identified the tracks of bobcat, fox, and a variety of birds.

"And look here," he said, pointing out the boot prints in and outside of the muddy area and the tire tracks beyond them.

"Three men," he said. "Two came from the south on foot, one arrived in a vehicle."

Then he pointed out a large splash of what looked like white paint on the side of a deep hoofprint.

"That's falcon excrement," he said.

He walked out of the bog and pointed to a smaller splash among the two sets of boot prints. "And here is another one. So we've got a large bird and a smaller bird."

"Where did they go?" Jan asked.

"Probably the same place we're going," he said.

"SO YOU'RE MARRIED," she said.

They were walking side by side to the south. He almost welcomed the question, because it distracted him from the opening bars of "A Horse with No Name," which had again entered his head.

"Yup. A lot of years."

"But is it a happy marriage?"

"Yes, it is."

"I'm often attracted to happily married men," she said. "There aren't many of them. Maybe it's the fact that they're so rare. Maybe it's the challenge . . ."

She was baiting him and he refused to acknowledge it. Finally, she chuckled.

"You don't like this topic?"

"No."

"Then let's change the subject. You've got three daughters, Sheridan being the oldest."

He nodded.

"Really," she said, "you probably don't even realize it, but I can count on one hand the number of people I know who were raised in a family where the mom and dad liked each other, stayed married, and raised semi-normal kids. It's a rarity."

"You're like a prehistoric throwback," Jan said. "You should be on display in the Museum of Natural History."

"Thank you."

"I hardly saw my dad," she said. "Of course, he was nice enough to me, considering he was right of Attila the Hun. He bought me nice things, but he was a lot more devoted to his new wife and his second family in Orange County than he ever was to ours. In fact, his wife was only five years older than I was when I met her. She insisted that I call her Athena, like we were sisters. She was nice enough, I guess."

Joe had no response.

"I get my commitment to activism from my mother," Jan said. "I grew up going to rallies with her. There was even a front-page photo in the *Los Angeles Times* of us being dragged out of an antiwar hearing by the cops. I was seven at the time and I had a pink ribbon in my hair. I was crying, but I looked *really cute!*"

The way she said it made Joe smile.

"The only thing my dad ever did for me, really, was establish a trust fund," Jan said. "He wanted me to use it for college, which I did. He wanted me to use the rest for seed money to start a business like he did. Instead, I used it to help fund people like Ibby who could really use the money. If my dad knew what I did with his money, he'd have a heart attack. Which is sort of the point, you know."

"I figured," Joe said.

"I'm glad to know Sheridan was raised with a social conscience."
Joe eyed her.

"You don't approve of what she's doing," Jan said.

"She's twenty-one. She was raised right, thanks to her mother.
She's old enough to make her own decisions."

"That's a surprisingly enlightened view," Jan said with a hint of
sarcasm.

"Even if they're stupid decisions," Joe finished. "Because look
where she is now."

"We can agree to disagree," Jan said. "I admire her. I admire all
of our volunteers. Most of them just want freedom and social justice. They want to take our country back."

Joe shrugged. He said, "Right now, I just want to take my daughter back."

"And I want to warn Ibby."

They each settled into their own thoughts for a quarter of a mile
before Joe asked, "How many men were in those pickups this
morning?"

Her face darkened. "I think I counted eleven. They just kept
coming into the café. I couldn't believe it."

"Where were they from?"

"Didn't say, but not this country originally. That I would swear
to. They were all of Middle Eastern origin."

"Were you scared?"

She hesitated. "I hate to say that I was scared by their ethnicity—
and certainly not by their religious beliefs," she said. "It goes against
everything I am. I hate it when people judge others by what they
look like, or what color they are, or what god they believe in. I just
hate that kind of intolerance."

After a long pause, she said, "But all that aside, they looked menacing and they had guns. So yes, damn you, I was scared."

"How did they get here?"

"They came in four pickup trucks."

"I mean, where did they come from?"

"I think Mexico," she said. "They looked like they'd been driving all night. From what I could understand, they had no problem crossing the border at all, and they drove straight here. I know this only because Cooter speaks—I mean, spoke—a little Arabic. Ibby taught him some words. Cooter was asking them questions while he made them all orders of *al kabsa*."

"Were they in communication with anyone?" Joe asked.

"They all had cell phones," she said. "A couple had the latest iPhone. But no, they were pretty pissed off when they realized there was no signal. It really put them in a bad mood."

"Did any of them talk to you?"

"They just *glared* at me. It was disgusting."

"What did Cooter do to get himself killed?" Joe asked.

"Nothing. Cooter was just being Cooter." She shivered, then continued. "I can still see it like it's happening right in front of my eyes. A couple of them who acted like the leaders were in the kitchen watching him cook. He was still trying to talk to them in Arabic, you know, just typical Cooter small talk. He wasn't interrogating them or anything. But they kept getting closer and closer to him like they were really interested in his technique.

"Then, when he ladled the last order into a bowl and it was served, one of them in the kitchen just casually stepped behind him. I saw that he had a big knife. He grabbed Cooter's head with one arm and cut his throat with the other hand. It was really quick, I mean *really* quick. There wasn't a moment of hesitation, either. Blood shot out everywhere, like a hose. Then the killer started sawing at Cooter's neck, back and forth. The sound was horrible. I'll never forget it."

She said, "The others were so mesmerized they weren't paying attention to me. They were just eating their food and watching like it was something on television. One of them stood up and filmed it on his cell phone. A couple of them said something in Arabic, like a chant or something."

Joe stopped. He looked Jan over closely.

"How did you get away?"

"I walked toward the back of the place like I was going to get sick in the bathroom. I heard one of them laugh at me. Then I busted out through the back door and took Cooter's van. I knew he always left his keys in the ashtray. I was out of there before they could catch me."

"Why do you suppose they killed him?" Joe asked.

"I think they wanted to eliminate any witnesses," she said. "They didn't want Cooter telling anyone they'd shown up, is my guess. And they were going to do the same thing to me."

"They didn't chase you?" Joe asked.

"They did, but it took a while for them to get organized. I drove east on I-80, and I'm sure they saw me get on the highway. What they didn't know at the time was that, as soon as I was out of sight from them over a hill, I drove across the median and the other lane into the desert. I'm guessing they drove down the interstate for a long time looking for me before they realized that."

"I'm glad you made it," Joe said.

"I am, too," she said.

"What makes you think they're going after this Ibby guy?"

Jan paused and shook her head in disbelief. "Why *else* would they be here?"

AN HOUR LATER, they arrived at Joe's green Ford Game and Fish pickup. It looked exactly like how he'd left it, he thought, and why shouldn't it? Although it seemed like he'd been hiking for days, it had only been hours.

Daisy was ecstatic, and she hopped up and down by the passenger door, waiting to be let in.

Joe dropped his pack and climbed in the driver's side, Daisy beside him.

Before he turned the key, he said to Jan through the open window, "I know this is stupid, but . . ."

Nothing.

"I had to try," he said, climbing out. Daisy remained inside, her head cocked expectantly.

"How much do you know about these EMP pulses you told me about?" Joe asked. "Do the effects wear off? Will this truck ever run again?"

She shook her head. "From what Ibby told me, they pretty much make electronics dead forever. But I'm no expert on this stuff. Remember, I'm just the facilitator and a fund-raiser for the cause."

Joe grunted. He removed the battery from the grizzly bear collar and used it to replace the old battery in the satellite phone. Although the collar batteries no longer had enough juice left to power the transmitter, he hoped the phone required less voltage. His shoulders slumped when it didn't work.

"Maybe you should just give up," Jan said, sitting down in the shade of the pickup.

"Maybe I should," Joe conceded, pulling the batteries from the phone and putting them back into the collar.

When he did, he saw the light on the collar's GPS unit flicker and he heard two dull clicks. He realized he had put the batteries back into the unit in a different configuration than when he'd pulled them out. Somehow, the new setup had pulled some power. His heart swelled.

"Hear that?" he whispered to Jan. The collar clicked again. "It's sending a signal."

"How long will it last?" she asked.

"I don't know."

"Who will see it?"

"I'm not sure anyone will."

After a few beats, she said, "If someone notices the signal, won't it just mean they'll think they found the bear? Not us?"

Joe sighed. "Yup."

He thought that the possibility of Jessica White, Marcia Mead, or Tyler Frink seeing the pings was remote at best. Why would they be sitting at their console days after they'd lost contact? Even if they were seeing it, he thought, they'd probably chalk it up to a technical anomaly.

Especially when the clicks stopped, which they just had.

"That's all she wrote," he said. "I got my hopes up there for a second."

"Oh well," she said, standing and forcing a smile meant to be encouraging. "We're just in the same boat as we were before."

He conceded that.

———

. . .

JOE ROOTED THROUGH HIS CAB, behind his seat, and through his gearbox for additional gear or food that might help them further. He valued a second chance at adding to their equipment, but he was hampered by the fact that whatever he gathered they had to carry on their backs. He slid a .22 revolver loaded with cracker shells into his pack, as well as a flare gun and two extra shells. He couldn't conceive of their future usefulness, but he wanted to be well prepared, and now that they were back at his truck he got a second bite at the apple.

The cracker loads were used to fire small explosives over the backs of game animals—elk, usually—who were eating a rancher's hay. The flare pistol was supposed to be used to signal search-and-rescue aircraft or to mark his location.

He gave Jan an old military daypack he'd found in the bottom of his gearbox that smelled of gasoline and elk blood. He'd discovered it in the woods a long time ago and had forgotten about it. Before he handed it down, he filled it with a coil of parachute cord, a fire-starter, a box of 12-gauge shells, and a thick roll of duct tape.

"You always need duct tape," he said.

"If you say so," she grumped as she reached up and took the pack. "This thing stinks."

He located a faded King Ropes ball cap and a pair of old polarized fishing sunglasses and handed them to her as well. She reluctantly put them on.

"And this," he said, handing her his carbine. "I'll take my shotgun along."

"I've never fired a gun in my life," she said, holding the rifle as if it were a live snake.

"High time to start, then," he said.

"Great," she said in a mocking faux drawl. *"Let's go kill us some A-rabs."*

"They might be Persians."

"Whatever."

THEY WEREN'T A HUNDRED YARDS south of his dead pickup when they heard trucks rumbling across the desert. The sound came in waves carried by northeasterly breezes.

They turned as one. Joe raised his binoculars.

"Four white trucks," he said. He lowered the glasses and scanned the horizon. The ridge where the pickup with the EMP had been was straight south.

He gripped her elbow and said, "Run. Let's get to those rocks before they see us."

"THEY'RE APPROACHING my pickup cautiously," he said to Jan. "The guys in the back of the trucks have their rifles up."

Joe watched them with his binoculars through the crack of an ancient yellow boulder that was one of several on the ridgeline about two hundred yards from his pickup. Jan kept hidden behind him.

"I think they're worried about the Game and Fish logo on the side of my truck," he said. "They're looking around, wondering where I am."

Three minutes later, Joe said, "They've decided I'm not there. Now they're looting the cab and the gearbox. They're throwing everything out on the ground."

Joe tried to think of anything of value he'd left behind, something the armed men might be able to use to their advantage. He couldn't think of anything.

"Crap," Joe said. "One of them found one of my red uniform shirts behind the seat. He's holding it up for the others. They're getting a good laugh out of it."

"Is he putting it on?" Jan asked.

"Nope. He threw it down and stomped on it."

"Subtle," she said.

As he watched them, he panned the lenses from the first truck to the third, looking closely at the vehicles. Texas plates, all right. He could make out a few numbers and letters, but he couldn't see the entirety of a single plate. What he did see, though, made him gasp.

"What?" she asked.

"I'm not sure you want to know."

"Now I do," she said, annoyed.

He took a breath. He said, "They've got the head of the grizzly bear mounted on the grille of the first truck. And they've got the bear paws wired to the hoods of the second and third trucks. Man, that makes me mad."

The severed paws were the size of catcher's mitts.

"That's disgusting," she said. "And don't forget poor Cooter."

"Poor Cooter," Joe echoed. But he was thinking about GB-53.

JOE WATCHED IN SILENCE for a minute or two before he said, "Oh, great."

"What now?"

"Listen."

There was a six-count before the *whump*.

The smell of burning tires, fuel, and interior fabric would take moments to reach them.

"They're just fools," Joe said.

"Why?"

"They're burning my truck to the ground to prevent me from getting into it and driving off. They're fools because they don't know *I can't even start it.*"

"So the joke's on them, I guess," she said.

"Yup," he said with a heavy sigh.

Joe didn't stand up until the four trucks and all the men in them were gone, but he could see their dust trails clearly. They were headed south.

Toward the old sheep ranch.

26

Nate stayed out of the sight lines of the oncoming vehicles—including his Jeep, which was being driven by the Yemeni—and slipped back into the office in the third shed, assuming the armory would be there.

It was: behind a sliding door made of cheap paneling like the rest of the room.

When he saw the huge steel gun safe, he said, "Shit."

The full-sized steel Liberty safe had a high-gloss finish and a five-spoke handle mounted next to a combination dial. He knew that a safe of that size cost north of five thousand dollars, which meant Ibby was serious about keeping weapons out of the hands of everybody except Saeed and his men.

Nate had some experience cracking small combination locks by placing downward pressure on the lock itself, clearing the tumblers, and then starting at 0, but there was no way he could attempt to open a safe of this size and complexity. Judging by how heavy and stout it was, he doubted he could open it with power tools or even explosives.

Would Suzy Gudenkauf know the combination? Probably not, but it was worth running her down and asking her. Ibby certainly knew, and so did Saeed.

Nate was flummoxed and he felt something in his chest that was unfamiliar: a stab of panic. He needed to contact Tyrell and Volk and tell them where he was and what was going on. Despite Ibby's careful planning and blithe assurances that the EMPs would minimize casualties, Nate knew better. Plans like that *never* worked out as envisioned.

Plus, the presence of Saeed and his men—and the possible new additions Suzy had warned of—meant that the likelihood of them concluding their operations after the Utah Data Center was unlikely at best. With weapons like those, Nate thought, the incentive to keep going would be mighty. Extremely powerful mobile EMP devices rolling anonymously across the nation's highway system could be a disaster, and something Ibby couldn't control—provided he actually intended to stop with the UDC. The devices, if they worked as Ibby had described them, could wreak havoc beyond belief.

Plus, he needed to get Sheridan off the ranch without creating a situation that drew attention to the act.

And most of all, he needed his weapon back.

Nate stepped back and closed the door. He could hear the two vehicles enter the ranch compound and drive into the second shed just beyond the office wall. Both motors were turned off and doors slammed shut. There was a muffled conversation in Arabic.

How would he explain being inside the office when they arrived?

. . .

"So how are my birds?" Nate asked Saeed while he strode through the shed door toward his parked Jeep.

Saeed looked up in surprise. The Yemeni and the Syrian both squared up, the Yemeni reaching across his body and touching the grip of his weapon. They looked to Saeed for guidance on how to proceed. There was something going on between the three of them, Nate thought, and his presence was interfering with it. Both gunmen looked eager and ready to unsling the rifles from their shoulders and take him out of the picture.

He ignored them while he pulled on a heavy welder's glove he'd taken from the bed of his Jeep and lifted the gyrfalcon to inspect it.

"I need to feed my guys," Nate said to Saeed. "I've been waiting for you to get back so that I could."

"I don't understand this devotion you and Ibby have to your falcons," Saeed said. "It's childish."

"Maybe so," Nate said.

Saeed simply watched Nate, his face implacable. Out of the corner of his eye, Nate saw Saeed check his wristwatch. It was a tell, he thought. Something was going to happen soon and Saeed was tracking the time.

"I need my gun back," Nate said.

"That's not possible right now," Saeed said. "Go play with your birds. Why do you need a gun to play with your birds?"

The Yemeni smirked. He obviously understood English better than the Syrian, who remained stone-faced.

"Because," Nate said, "I may have to kill you all."

He let it linger for a second, then grinned.

Saeed did not smile back.

THE OUTSIDE DOOR flew open and Henn filled the doorframe. The light of day streamed around him and turned him into a silhouette. He seemed exercised. "Is Ibby in here?"

His arrival broke the tension slightly. Saeed said, "No."

"I need to talk to him right away."

Nate noticed that Henn had something in his hand. An oblong instrument of some kind.

"Why?" Saeed asked.

"One of the volunteers snuck out into the ditch. He said he went out to pee, but I think he might have stashed some weed out there. You know how they are."

Saeed raised his eyebrows, as if to say *Why is this my problem?*

"He found this," Henn said, coming in. As he left the bright white doorframe, Nate could see what he had in his hand: the satellite phone Nate had stashed in the gopher hole.

Saeed took it from Henn and looked it over.

"It's an advanced piece of equipment," Henn said. "Somebody must have smuggled it in here and hidden it. I'm thinking one of the volunteers, but why? Maybe I'm paranoid and there's an explanation, but it looks like somebody was going to use this phone to call out when we're literally hours away from deployment."

Saeed turned the phone over in his hand. "Where was it found?"

"In the dry wash," Henn said. "Less than a hundred yards from the third shed."

Nate watched Saeed's face closely and he could see him thinking. A second later, Saeed's eyes met his.

"Yours?"

"Yes."

Both the Yemeni and the Syrian unslung their AK-47s and raised them. Although he didn't look at them directly, Nate could feel the O-shaped muzzles aimed at him like wide-spaced eyes.

Nate said, "I carry it in case I break down in the middle of nowhere. As you know, cell service is spotty deep in the desert. I didn't know what the situation was here, and I didn't want anyone taking my phone." He paused. "Like you did my weapon."

After a moment, Henn's shoulders visibly relaxed and he blew out a long breath. "Well, thank God for that," he said. "I was thinking all kinds of things."

"I still am," Saeed said in a low voice.

"The phone is off," Nate said. "I keep it off. The only time I used it was the other night after someone tried to kill me. I called my woman to tell her I was all right."

Nate didn't further bolster his case. He let it stand.

"I can check that," Saeed said. "I can tell if you're lying."

"Fine by me."

Saeed thumbed the power button on the phone. The display lit up. Nate held his breath while Saeed scrolled through the display menu.

"No incoming calls," he said. "And one thirty-second call out to an unknown number."

"Like I said."

Saeed continued to study the device while he made a decision. As he did, the muzzles of the AKs didn't lower an inch.

"I think we're done here," Henn said. "We're done here, right? I need to get back to the trucks and finalize everything."

Saeed chinned toward the open door, indicating he could go. Then, as Henn backed away, he said, "Get Ibraaheem and come here."

Henn frowned. "Now? You want me to go get Ibby now?"

"Yes."

"I told you, we're doing final tests. I can't spare the time right now."

Saeed said, "Get him and bring him here. It won't take long. Tell him to meet us in the office."

Throughout the conversation, Nate was acutely aware of the live satellite phone Saeed held in his hand. The longer it was live, he knew, the better chance Tyrell or Volk would have to pinpoint his location. But he prayed they wouldn't be stupid enough to call. He could imagine the phone ringing, Saeed punching it up, and receiving a string of *What the fuck have you been doing keeping your phone off* expletives that would not only compromise Nate's position but likely get him killed.

"What is it that can't wait until later?" Henn asked, his face flushed. "We're gonna have two hours sitting in the cab of those trucks on the way to Utah. We can talk about whatever it is then, how about?"

"I said get him," Saeed ordered.

Henn threw up his hands and stormed out.

Nate watched as Saeed turned off the satellite phone. He handed it toward the Syrian and spoke a few words in Arabic. The Syrian nodded, lowered his rifle, and took the phone from him. Saeed dug into the front pocket of his cargo pants and gave the Syrian the keys to Nate's Jeep as well.

From their gestures and body language, Nate guessed Saeed had ordered that his phone and keys be locked away with his gun in the safe. Which meant the Syrian also knew the combination.

The phone had been on for maybe ninety seconds, perhaps two minutes. Nate had no idea if Tyrell or Volk had the technical ability to locate it—and him—in that short of a time frame. Or what they'd do with the knowledge.

"We go to the office," Saeed said to Nate. With his eyes, he ordered the Yemeni to follow them and keep Nate covered.

"Can you tell me why?" Nate asked.

Saeed hesitated for a moment, then said, "I'm in command now. I owe it to Ibraaheem to tell him of the change of plans."

Nate felt that stab again in his chest as he pondered the words *I'm in command now* and *change of plans*.

IBBY LOOKED VISIBLY ANNOYED when he threw open the door to the office with Henn on his heels. Nate was in a hard-backed chair in the corner, where he'd been ordered to sit, and the Yemeni kept his rifle trained on him from fifteen feet away—far enough that Nate couldn't throw himself on the weapon without taking several rounds en route.

The Syrian stood in the other corner a few feet from the panel door that hid the safe. His back was to the wall and his AK-47 was held muzzle-down but with his hand holding the grip and his trigger finger extended. He could swing it up and fire in less than a second. He was carefully watching Ibby and Henn as they entered the room.

"What's going on?" Ibby asked Saeed. "You know we're about ready to . . ." His voice trailed off as he saw Nate in the corner and noticed the positioning of the Yemeni and the Syrian. Saeed stood in the center of the room with his arms folded across his chest. There was no doubt he had taken control.

Saeed said, "Shut the door behind you."

Henn did, and turned back with questions written all over his face. He looked from Ibby to Saeed, then back to Ibby.

Saeed said something in Arabic that sounded both firm and apologetic.

Ibby shook his head as if to deny what he'd heard. He said, "Speak English. We'll talk in English. What do you mean there's a change in our plans?"

"We will knock out the data center," Saeed said. "After all, there are conversations stored there our people don't want analyzed. But after that we're taking the EMP trucks to use for other targets."

Ibby's eyes flashed and he balled his fists. "No. Absolutely not. We're making this statement and that'll be the end of it. We are *not* using those weapons for other targets."

Saeed said, "It's out of your hands now, Ibraaheem. It's out of *my* hands. My commanders say it would be a blasphemy not to use these weapons against the American infidels. It would be *unholy* not to use them, and I agree."

Saeed reverted back to Arabic and spoke for several minutes. His voice was measured, but Nate could see that whatever he said hit Ibby like hammer blows. Nate could pick out a few words—*jihad, dhimmitude, Allah*—but the rest was incomprehensible.

"The money to develop these devices didn't come from the Middle East," Ibby interrupted with anger rising in his voice. "They're not yours. They don't belong to you."

Saeed shrugged as if to say, *So what?*

"You know this is what we do, you know that," Saeed said, switching back to English. "We don't need to build our own weapons and spend our own money and time. Not when we can let them develop the technology and *we can just take it from them*. It's an arms race, but they provide our arms."

"But you're not taking it from them," Ibby pleaded. "You're taking it from *me*."

"I don't see a difference."

"You're missing the entire point," Ibby said. "We aren't making war. We're making a powerful statement. This is the most important thing I've ever done in my life and the only one that's worth anything. You can't take that away from me, or from all the people who believe in this cause, and turn it into something . . . brutal. Something medieval."

"It is right with God," Saeed said. "The rest of our army is on the way. They should be here any minute."

"SO YOU'VE BEEN PLANNING this for a long time," Ibby said. It wasn't a question. "Tell me, was this the plan years ago when we met? When I told you what I wanted to do and you agreed to come here and provide security?"

Saeed didn't need to answer. Instead, he turned to the Syrian and nodded, giving him the go-ahead for something obviously prearranged, Nate thought. The Syrian nodded back and shouldered past Ibby and Henn toward the door. The back pocket of his cargo pants bristled with scores of white plastic zip ties.

"Where is he going?" Ibby asked.

"We need to make sure all of your team and those stupid volunteers are under control," Saeed said. "He's going to herd them outside the third shed for now."

"And then what?" Ibby asked, panic in his face.

Saeed didn't answer. He didn't need to.

"You can't do this," Ibby said, pleading. "This is against everything I stand for, everything I believe. We've got to get past this kind of thing, don't you understand? I thought when we talked about this, you agreed with me. You *acted* like you agreed with me."

Saeed nodded. "You know as well as I do that lying for a righteous cause is not lying at all. You do remember the lesson of *taqiyya* from your studies at the madrassa, don't you? You of all people who received the highest level of education?"

Ibby said, "*Taqiyya* is lying to unbelievers in order to defeat them. I'm *not* an unbeliever."

"In our judgment you are."

"Please don't do this," Ibby said.

Saeed simply shrugged. To Henn, he said, "I'll need you to come with us in case something goes wrong with the devices."

Henn went pale.

"Your wife will stay here. If you want to see her again, you'll help us and you'll do what we ask."

Turning to Ibby, Saeed said, "You can come along until we are done in Utah, and you can stay with us if you'll pledge your loyalty. But not if you keep this up. You've been too long in the West, my friend. Your mind has become filthy with bad ideas."

Nate noticed that *his* future wasn't addressed. The Yemeni obviously caught that as well, because he tightened his grip on his rifle.

He was obviously waiting for a nod from Saeed to pull the trigger, Nate thought.

But what really concerned him was what the Syrian had been sent to do. He could imagine the team of unarmed engineers and volunteers—including Sheridan—being "herded" outside the third shed at gunpoint. Would they be lined up? Ordered to get on their knees?

Ibby squared his stance. "If you try to take over this operation, it will be over my dead body."

Saeed simply nodded his head. Agreed.

Nate noted a nervous tic in Ibby's mouth for the first time. It was as if he was finally comprehending what was happening and he could feel his world spinning out of control.

He said, "What other targets?"

Saeed's face softened. "We have a long list. Hospitals, airports, server farms that would take down the Internet, police headquarters, military bases. But along the way we've identified power substations and power plants. The electrical grid in this country isn't secure. If we aren't stopped, we can take it down."

"My God," Ibby said.

"Did you know that if we hit just nine key transformer substations it could cause a nationwide blackout for eighteen months? *Eighteen months.* A lot can happen in eighteen months."

"Yes," Ibby said. "Millions will die."

"Will you come with us?"

Ibby lowered his head and his breathing got deep. Nate had a hard time believing that Ibby would go along with it.

Beyond the walls of the office, he could hear the startled voices.

The Syrian was obviously moving the engineering team and the volunteers from underground and the third shed to outside.

"This can't be happening," Ibby said. "You're not helping our people, you're hurting them. We have to get beyond this."

Saeed didn't respond.

"For forty-seven months, I planned this and got it funded," Ibby said, his voice breaking. "We've been working nonstop on it—twelve to eighteen hours a day. We've got a permanent group of fifteen patriots who have given up their normal lives for this one thing."

He's lost it, Nate thought. *He's babbling.*

Saeed listened, but he was growing impatient. Ibby was talking quickly, maybe too quickly in English for him to follow. Plus, it made no sense.

"Forty-seven months of work. Twelve to eighteen hours a *day*," Ibby repeated. "Fifteen good men and women who have devoted their entire lives to this *one thing*. This one thing—not to use the EMPs to murder innocent people by depriving them of power, transportation, and the ability to communicate."

"Stop," Saeed said firmly. "What you say shows how weak these infidels truly are. They're not ten feet tall like we used to think, but we've known that for a while now. Once we hit them, they'll collapse. They're soft. If they can't call or text or turn on the lights, they'll give up. They're cowards, after all."

Ibby looked up with tears in his eyes.

"You'll come outside with me now."

Henn covered his face in his hands. He knew he was going, too.

Saeed nodded to the Yemeni covering Nate, as if to tell him, *You know what to do now.*

. . .

NATE HEARD THE RUSH of excited voices as Saeed prompted Ibby and Henn to lead the way outside by prodding them with the barrel of his rifle. Saeed reached back and pulled the door closed behind him.

Nate looked up at the Yemeni. The man seemed torn between keeping his muzzle aimed at Nate's chest and looking outside the window to see what was happening.

When the Yemeni's eyes flicked toward the window, Nate launched from his chair and juked left, batting the rifle muzzle away and grasping the barrel. When the Yemeni bent forward to pull it away, Nate head-butted him, crunching the man's nose and right eye socket.

The Yemeni dropped to his knees, but held tight to the rifle. Nate forced his right index finger into the back of the trigger guard so that when the Yemeni pulled hard on it, he pinched Nate's flesh—but the rifle didn't fire. Nate reached down with his left hand and found the leather-wrapped handle of a serrated knife the Yemeni wore on his belt and, before the man could react, pulled it out and plunged it to the hilt under the Yemeni's sternum and into his heart.

The Yemeni stiffened, his tongue lolled out, and his last breath rattled through his open mouth.

Nate pulled the AK-47 free and shook his right hand. His index finger was already painful and swelling up.

He pointed the muzzle at the dirt floor next to the twitching body of the Yemeni and fired twice. The rifle shots were incredibly loud in the closed room and there was no doubt they were heard outside. They would tell Saeed that the Yemeni had completed his task.

It smelled of bitter gunpowder and he peered outside the cloudy window as he ran across the room. The scene was as he envisioned it: all of Ibby's team and the ragtag group of volunteers stood against the broad and weathered outside wall of the third shed with the Syrian guarding them with his rifle out.

Saeed had marched Ibby and Henn before them as if Ibby were to once again address them with a pep talk. But as Ibby raised his hands and voice to warn them, Saeed stepped behind him and cut his throat from ear to ear. He was sending the message that Ibby was no longer in charge. The collective gasp was chilling. A couple of the women shrieked.

When Nate ducked down from the window, the last thing he viewed was Saeed sawing at Ibby's neck and the cascade of blood. He'd seen a lot, but he knew that the savagery of the act and the writhing and wailing of the observers would remain a singular horror in his mind for as long as he lived.

But there were things to do.

He threw the panel door aside and leaned toward the safe. It had taken a moment, but he'd realized Ibby had sent him a last message before being led out to what he must have known would be his certain death.

Nate spun the combination dial to clear it and then took a deep breath to calm himself. He tried to recall the exact sequence of Ibby's message to him.

Forty-seven, twelve, eighteen, fifteen, one . . .

While he carefully turned the dial, he heard a low rumbling outside that gradually overtook the sound of wailing.

Vehicles arriving on the ranch.

He looked over his shoulder through the window and saw them pass by, one by one. Four white pickups—one more than in his dream—with armed men in the back, just like in his dream. A couple of the fighters in the back of one of the trucks glared into the window as they went by, but Nate was certain they couldn't see him in the dark room.

Suzy Gudenkauf had called it.

Now he learned what was on the hood of the lead vehicle: the severed head of a grizzly bear. Bear paws were wired to the grilles of the second and third trucks.

He thought: *Where did they find a bear?*

27

A HALF HOUR BEFORE, JOE AND JAN STALKUP HAD WATCHED the four white pickups caravan south in the distance while they hid on their bellies in a shallow cactus-rimmed hollow on the desert floor. The depression had been carved out of the sandstone by thousands of years of wind, and it would no doubt fill with rainwater when thunderstorms opened up. He had told her to keep her head down while the trucks passed in the distance.

They had found the hollow after they'd heard another round of very distant gunshots. It was difficult for Joe to figure out the direction the shots had come from since they wafted to them in the breeze. Jan wasn't even sure she'd heard anything, she said.

But Joe certainly recognized the faint *pop-pop-pop* for what it was. He'd spent his career hearing shots and then trying to pinpoint where they'd originated.

When the fourth and last pickup was out of sight and only the spoor of dust kicked up by the trucks' tires remained, Joe scrambled to his feet.

"Let's go," he said. "They're headed straight to the ranch."

"I thought that's where they were going before," she said, standing and brushing fine dust from the thighs of her jeans.

"Me too. Something must have distracted them or maybe they got lost. But I'm glad to see they haven't reached the ranch yet."

"Did they see us?"

"Nope."

He guessed—and it was only a guess—that he and Jan were fifteen miles from the old sheep ranch. Even if they picked up their pace to a near jog, it would still take them more than three hours to get there. Three hours, he thought, of worrying himself sick over what Sheridan might be experiencing. If the men in the trucks were capable of beheading Cooter as well as a grizzly bear, they were capable of anything . . .

"WHAT'S THAT?" Jan asked suddenly once they'd set off again on foot.

Joe wheeled and followed her gesture.

On the same two-track road the white pickups had taken, far enough back that it couldn't be seen but close enough that it traveled within the last wisp of dust contrail, a green pickup slowly limped along.

Joe raised his binoculars and said, "I'll be damned."

"What is it?" Jan asked while lowering instinctively to her haunches.

"I think it's one of ours," he said.

"One of 'ours'?"

Although the heat undulated through his field of vision, he recognized the cowcatcher mounted to the front grille, the abbreviated light bar on top of the cab, and the badge-shaped decal on the door.

"It's got to be Phil Parker," Joe said with a grin.

"Really?"

"Who else could it be out here?"

Jan shook her head and said, "I never thought I'd be happy to see that guy."

"I need to get his attention. I don't think he sees us."

Joe couldn't risk firing his rifle in case the men in the white pickups could hear it, and there was no way to radio Parker in the truck.

He hoped Parker had decided to come check on him after all. If so, Joe could borrow Parker's gear and call radio dispatch as well as Governor Rulon's office. Obviously, the other Game and Fish pickup had not been targeted by either the people on the sheep ranch with their truck-mounted EMP device or the men in the white pickups.

"Hold this," Joe said to Jan as he handed her his rifle. He quickly stripped his uniform shirt off to his T-shirt and waved it, hoping the red color could be seen by Phil Parker.

Jan said, "I bet if I took off *my* shirt, he'd be here in seconds."

Joe laughed at that. His spirits had swelled. Seeing Phil Parker out there was the first good thing that had happened to him in thirty-six hours.

He jumped up and down and waved the red shirt over his head.

Parker continued to slowly roll forward. He was traveling much slower than the pickups had been. Joe thought that it didn't fit that

Parker would creep along so slowly unless he had a reason for it. He guessed that Parker was driving just fast enough to follow the four white pickups by their fresh tire tracks and dust but slow enough so that they wouldn't know they were being pursued. It made sense.

"Phil, you idiot, look over here!" Jan shouted when the green truck continued on.

If he progressed much farther along the distant road, Parker might not look back to see them, so Joe took off running across the hard-packed terrain at a forty-five-degree angle in front of the pickup, waving his red uniform shirt over his head.

He thought, *I'm getting too old to do much running*. But he ran, his T-shirt clinging to his skin from sweat.

Finally, when Joe was too winded to continue and he stopped to catch his breath, Parker's truck slowed to a stop.

"Yes!" Joe shouted back to Jan.

"He's turning," she yelled. "Here he comes."

IT TOOK TEN MINUTES for the pickup to get close enough to them for Joe to realize something was wrong. It was Parker's unit, all right, but the pickup was damaged in some way and barely crawling toward them.

He raised his binoculars and saw dents made by holes in the door and front fender, the windshield spider-webbed with bullet holes, and a man wearing a black face cover behind the wheel.

Phil Parker wasn't driving, but it was Phil's truck.

Joe turned and looked behind him. Jan was about fifty yards away, struggling ungainly under the weight of her pack, the pack that

Joe'd discarded, and the firearms she had clamped under her arms. He didn't know if he could get to her before the pickup arrived.

"Jan, it's not Phil. Somebody's got his truck," he shouted.

She stopped, squinting her confusion. "Who is it?"

"I don't know."

"Well . . . fuck," she said.

Joe wheeled around to face the vehicle. It was nearly to him. There were holes in the front grille as well, and the left headlight had been shot out.

Although the glass was destroyed and nearly white with cracks and damage, he could see that the driver was alone. There was no passenger. All he could make out in regard to the driver was a pair of dark eyes bordered on the top and bottom by a black cloth.

"Oh no," Jan said. "What do we do? Joe?"

When the pickup was ten yards away, it stopped, but the driver kept it running. The driver's-side door opened and the man jumped down. He was in all-black fatigues, like the men Joe had seen around the bear, and he had an AK-47 with an extended magazine.

While he raised his rifle, he spat a stream of Arabic that Joe couldn't understand.

Joe was fully exposed and unarmed. He regretted leaving his .40 Glock handgun in his pack, even though he was a notoriously poor pistol shot.

"Please . . ." Joe said. In an instant, he thought of Sheridan, Marybeth, Lucy, and April.

He'd always wondered what he would think of the second before he was killed.

Joe heard the boom of his shotgun and then the black-clad driver froze in motion, his rifle stock not yet mounted to his shoulder. In the distance behind the driver, Joe saw errant shotgun pellets kick up dirt from the desert floor.

Was the man hit?

Then, as if to answer the question, the driver sidestepped quickly away from the truck, as if he were doing a dance routine, until he was practically running. Then he crashed to the ground on his side. Only then did Joe see small tears in the fabric of the man's black shirt and blood glistening in the sun.

Joe had seen game animals react like that when they were hit through the lungs: a last burst of manic energy before death.

The man let out a long moan that ended with an "*Ung*" sound. Bright red foam seeped through his mask where his mouth was. The rifle he still held out dropped into the sand.

Joe ran to him and kicked the rifle away. Then he bent over and stripped off the black head covering and tossed it over his shoulder. The man was olive-skinned, black-bearded, gaunt, young, and dead, having taken a chest full of double-ought buckshot.

Joe stood and turned to Jan. "Wow."

The two packs and Joe's carbine were at her feet, but she still held the shotgun. She was frantically pulling on the front stock to expel the spent shell and reload it, but she didn't know how.

"It's okay," he said. "Don't worry about that now." Then: "That was a good shot. You saved my life."

"I saved both of our lives," she said, matter-of-fact. "And it wasn't as hard as I thought it would be. Killing a man, I mean."

He wasn't sure how to respond.

She continued to pull and tug on the shotgun to rearm it. Her movements became frantic and he realized that delayed shock had begun to set in. She wasn't as callous as she had appeared, after all.

He walked to her and gently pulled the shotgun from her hands. He saw that there were tears in her eyes.

"You did the right thing," he said.

"I killed a man. I don't know if he had a wife or a mom or a family. I don't know anything about him."

"We know that he was going to kill *us*," Joe said. "That's enough."

She wiped at her eyes for a moment and he pulled her close. She fell into his arms.

Joe felt guilty and strange embracing a woman that wasn't his wife. Jan felt oddly unfamiliar. But he thought that, given the circumstances, Marybeth would understand.

"What happened to Phil?" she asked.

HE FOUND PHIL PARKER'S BODY sprawled facedown in the bed of his pickup. Fist-sized exit wounds pocked his back, neck, and thighs. If he'd been thrown into the back alive, he'd bled out in the past half hour, Joe thought, judging by the amount of still-wet blood in the channels of the floor.

Joe stepped back and breathed deeply so he wouldn't get sick. The death of the fighter right in front of his eyes and the sight of Phil Parker's body had been a one-two punch to his gut.

In his peripheral vision, he saw Jan approaching and he held out his hand to stop her.

"You don't want to see this," he said.

"Phil?" she asked, tearing up again.

"Yup."

"Is he . . ."

"Yup."

After a beat, she said, "Those *bastards*. I'm glad I killed that one over there."

AFTER HIS LEGS FIRMED UP, Joe slid into the front, which was still tacky with Parker's blood. The wires to the radio had been jerked out and they hung to the truck floor like streamers. Parker's cell phone was on the floor in several pieces after a bullet had passed through it. Not that there would be a signal anyway . . .

On the console was Parker's blood-flecked legal pad. On the top page were the scrawled words:

> Gov. Rulon's office
> Find JP. OOR since Thurs. night
> Call 777-7434

Joe knew that OOR was an acronym for "out of range." He thought: *If only they knew how out of range I am.*

But the message was important and reassuring. It meant that someone, probably Marybeth, had alerted Rulon's office that he was off the grid. And it meant Rulon or someone in the executive branch had contacted Parker. So they knew he was in some kind of trouble.

Then it hit him. Phil Parker was dead because he'd been asked to come find him.

"I'm sorry, Phil," he said aloud. "I really am. You were just doing your job."

. . .

JOE WAS ROOTING THROUGH Parker's gearbox when Jan asked, "What are you hoping to find?"

"A satellite phone," he said. "All of us are supposed to have one. But we're also all supposed to have a GPS transceiver so the suits in Cheyenne know our every move, and I know Phil threw his in a ditch right after they installed it. Now I wish he'd kept it on."

Like Joe's gearbox, the back was packed with extra clothing, camping gear, a necropsy kit, several pairs of boots . . . and a large stash of pornographic magazines. Joe didn't have *those* in his truck, but he didn't fault Parker. He imagined how lonely it must get on patrol in the desert.

"What was he doing out here? Why did those men kill him and take his truck?"

"I can only guess what happened," Joe said. "Poor Phil stumbled onto the four trucks and they saw he was law enforcement and took him out before he could radio for help. Then they decided to take his body and the truck to the ranch and get rid of the evidence."

Joe stepped back when he'd located the battered case he recognized as a satellite phone box.

"The truck's shot up and barely running," he said as he opened the case. "It's a good thing that dead guy kept it running. He probably knew that if he shut it off, it might not start again."

He placed the case on the hood of the pickup and opened it.

"Thank God," he said, removing the phone from its foam packing and powering it on.

"Who are you calling?" Jan asked.

"My boss. Then my wife."

Jan said, "I wish you wouldn't."

Surprised, Joe looked up to see her leveling the shotgun at him.

She said, "I can't let you do that, Joe. Ibby has devoted his life to this project. I've devoted *my* life to this. I've raised hundreds of thousands of dollars and coordinated all those volunteers. What we're doing is important. We can't screw it up before we know there's nothing else we can do."

"There's nothing else we can do," Joe said. "Those pickups are on their way to the ranch as we speak. You saw them. I don't think they're friends of Ibby, do you?"

She hesitated, and confusion passed over her face.

He knew that if she said no, it meant the men in the trucks could not only derail their mission to take out the Utah Data Center but hurt Ibby and the volunteers in the process. If she said no, it meant she'd been deceived by Ibby all along.

"Okay," she said finally. She lowered the shotgun. "I don't see where we have a choice."

"We don't," Joe said, lifting the phone to his ear.

He held it there and waited for the device to pick up a satellite signal.

"I'm just so . . . disappointed," Jan said, as much to herself as to Joe.

He'd never felt so excited to hear a dial tone in his life.

At last, he heard "Governor Rulon's office, this is Lisa . . ."

28

AFTER SEPARATING THE MEN FROM THE WOMEN OUTSIDE, THE fighters marched each group into the second shed and ordered everyone to sit down in the dirt with an aisle of about five feet between them.

Although no English was spoken, it was clear enough to Sheridan through their barks and gestures that everyone was to keep their head down and not speak. There were three of them with rifles: one was familiar to her because she'd seen him with Saeed that morning, but the other two had arrived with the four pickups and stayed.

The arrival of the four trucks had frightened her for three reasons. Saeed had shouted a greeting to the fighters as they scrambled to the ground, meaning he knew them. He did it while wiping the blood from his hands on the clothing of Ibby's body. That meant their arrival had been preplanned and timed for the exact day the EMP weapons were ready and operational. Plus, there were so many of them that it looked unlikely that she, or any of the engineering team or the student volunteers, could try to slip away without being seen.

She felt suddenly stupid, scared, and vulnerable—a pawn in a game much larger and more horrific than she could ever have imagined.

ONE OF THE NEW MEN stood behind the seated volunteers and team members with his rifle out. The second man was in front. And the third, Saeed's man, walked between and through the hostages as if daring someone to try to defy him.

Sheridan watched as Seth raised his head across the aisle to say something to Saeed's man, and the gesture was met with a brutal boot kick in his face. Seth cried out and sank over to his side with his hands covering his broken nose. Blood streamed out between his fingers.

Kira Harden sat next to Sheridan with wide, terrified eyes. She'd seen what had happened to Seth as well, and she and Sheridan exchanged frightened glances.

Sheridan was disgusted when one of her fellow volunteers, one of the sixth-year seniors from the University of Colorado, cried out that he, too, was a Muslim and he should be spared.

Saeed's man nodded and approached the student, who started to stand up. The student looked like he was ready to switch sides and grab a rifle if he could get one, but Saeed's man raised his own and shot the student—*BLAM!*—in the head, and he dropped like a sack of sand. The male students around him recoiled in horror and turned away as the dead man's body twitched. The odor of blood combined with the acrid smell of gunpowder within the shed.

Sheridan's ears rang from the sound and proximity of the rifle shot.

Suzy Gudenkauf, whom Sheridan had come to understand as someone who was very close to Ibby, could not stop sobbing. Suzy's head was buried between her knees and her entire body trembled. Sheridan watched with alarm as Saeed's man heard her, walked over, and said something to her in Arabic. Suzy didn't respond.

Sheridan closed her eyes and waited for another gunshot.

She was grateful when the sound of huge diesel motors started up in the shed next to them and apparently distracted the killer. The sound shook the walls and made the ground vibrate as the two eighteen-wheelers backed out one after the other and stopped outside with their motors idling.

Sheridan could hear a half-dozen individual conversations going on through the walls. The men who'd just arrived spoke in guttural and urgent tones. It was obvious they were charged up and ready to leave.

To do what? she wondered.

"We're all fucking going to die," Kira said to her as she leaned in close. The rumbling of the motors outside obscured the sound of her voice from the killer. In fact, Sheridan could barely hear her.

Kira said, "Dude, I've seen some of those videos. The ones where they march a whole bunch of guys in orange jumpsuits out on the beach and cut their throats all at once like it's been choreographed. Have you seen those?"

Sheridan quickly shook her head. She wanted Kira to stop talking.

"Or they have us all get on our knees and get behind us and shoot us all in the head. At least it'll be quick, I guess. We won't know what's coming until it comes.

"I just hope they don't do some of the other things they do to people, like burn us alive or crucify us and leave us out here in the desert."

After a pause, she said, "Maybe they'll just do that to the men. Maybe they'll spare us for a while. You know what I'm talking about, right?"

Then: "This is officially the worst fucking weekend of my entire life."

"Shhhhhhh, please."

"Are you scared they'll kill us?"

"Of course," Sheridan said. "You saw what they did to Ibby and that CU idiot."

"Kicking Seth in the head wasn't so bad, though, was it?"

Sheridan looked over to see if it was even possible Kira was joking at a time like this. She was, although her eyes were oddly vacant. She was either in shock or she was the coldest and toughest person Sheridan had ever met. Probably a mixture of both.

Kira was a piece of work, she decided.

SHE FELT like she was inside someone else's nightmare—not hers. Maybe it was the lack of sleep the night before and the strange new environment she'd encountered that morning. Certainly being herded outside to watch Ibby's head get cut off had created the sense of unreality she now felt.

The new men who had arrived, as well as Saeed and his two thugs, seemed not to be real people but *others*, she thought. She had no idea how to communicate with them or to engage them on a human level. They seemed to be from a different century and a different culture, even though they carried modern weapons and cell phones. They had nothing but contempt for Ibby and for their hostages.

Sheridan realized that, to them, the students sitting around her weren't real people, either. To them, they were all enemies, throwaway units of a world they despised. Or even lower than that.

She should be wailing like Suzy or losing her grip on reality like Kira, she thought. Instead, she seemed to be sleepwalking through it; letting herself be herded here and there, sitting on the dirt as ordered, wondering who was going to die next. Maybe it *was* shock that had taken over Kira as well as herself, she thought. Maybe her brain was not letting her absorb and react to what was happening around her, but somehow keeping her at a distance from it.

It was Saturday, she knew. She thought of Lucy, April, her mom and dad. She liked to think they were all somewhere together, but she knew it was unlikely. The older she got, the less her family was actually all together at once.

She never realized she would miss being with all of them so much.

But she was glad in a way that none of them even knew where she was.

If they knew, she thought, it would be too horrible to bear.

OUTSIDE, ONE OF THE MOTORS raced and there was a grinding sound as an eighteen-wheeler was clumsily put into gear. As it pulled out, Sheridan could smell diesel fumes waft into the shed. The smell made her nauseous.

She noticed that the fighter in front of the room had turned around and was looking out the window. He apparently wanted to watch the trucks as they passed by. Saeed's man shouted at him and the man turned around. He looked both embarrassed and angry at the same time for not having paid attention to the hostages.

It darkened momentarily inside the shed as the first big semi-trailer rumbled out and blocked the light from the window. Then the second truck. Four white pickups followed. She could see the forms of men in the back. They were shouting *"Allahu Akbar"* and pumping their rifles up and down in the air as they passed.

It all looked like a bad cartoon, but it wasn't.

"Where do you think they're going?" Kira asked. "Do you think they're still going to Utah?"

"I don't know."

"You know what?" Kira asked too loudly. "I just realized I don't know, either, and I don't care anymore, because I'm going to die right *here*. I'm going to die while on *a fucking camping trip.*"

"Kira, please."

"No," she said with sarcasm. "I can't die while doing something really cool like swimming with dolphins or helping to achieve world peace. No way. No, I have to die doing something I hate more than anything in the world. It's kind of ironic, don't you think?"

Sheridan looked around. The killer was turning toward them. Toward the sound of talking.

"I don't even have anyone to pray to," Kira said. "I just fucking realized that."

"Shhhh, please."

"Sheridan," Kira said as her voice choked with sudden tears, "I'm so sorry I brought you here."

"Me too, but please stop talking."

Sheridan shut her eyes and tried to recall the feeling she'd had while visualizing her family together a few moments before. It had briefly comforted her.

And there they all were at the breakfast table—Lucy looking angelic, April being annoying, her mom refereeing between the two, her dad looking on with a befuddled expression from the stove, where he was making pancakes.

Only this time, she noticed the presence of Nate leaning against the doorframe, watching them all. She couldn't remember him being there before.

When she opened her eyes and saw him flash by the shed window, she thought she was still in the grip of her dream.

Then she realized she wasn't when the side door to the shed was kicked in and there he was.

29

To Nate's surprise, in the safe he'd found a scoped .454 Casull by Freedom Arms, as well as three boxes of ammunition, next to his .500 and the encrypted satellite phone. There were scores of other arms—semiautomatic pistols, grenades, a half-dozen Heckler & Koch UMP submachine guns—but he left them behind.

Semiautomatics and automatic weapons were for those who couldn't hit what they aimed at.

That the .454 was there, just like in his dream, only reinforced a sense of doom and inevitability that hung over him.

He'd powered on the phone, strapped on his shoulder holster, checked the loads in his .500 Wyoming Express, and waited for the two semitrucks and the convoy of pickups to rumble up and over the rise. Then he scrambled out of the third shed and ran to the second one, peering through a smudged corner of a window.

Seated on the dirt floor next to Suzy Gudenkauf was Sheridan Pickett. Her eyes were shut tight. She looked terrified.

. . .

THERE IS A MOMENT when a peregrine falcon, hundreds of feet in the sky, identifies a target below. The raptor stalls for a moment in the thermal current, draws in its wings, and gracefully does a 180-degree rotation to its back.

Now bullet-shaped and sleekly aerodynamic, the peregrine falls through the sky, gaining more and more velocity until its speed reaches more than two hundred miles an hour. It is the fastest creature on earth, and as it shrieks through layers of changing crosscurrents and atmosphere, it subtly keeps a perfect bead on its prey by slightly shifting a wing or moving its head a degree. As it drops, the falcon's focus narrows until the target—whether an unsuspecting duck rising from a pond or a rabbit foraging for young shoots of grass—becomes the *one true thing* to the exclusion of everything else.

As the peregrine closes in on its target at tremendous speed, its talons descend like the landing gear of an airplane on final approach. The talons are balled into fists.

It is known as the state of *yarak* to falconers, and the end result is a concussion of blood and tissue from the target as the peregrine strikes home.

For Nate, at the moment he kicked in the shed door and dropped low to his haunches, the *one true thing* consisted of three men, including the Syrian, who were standing over the people inside the shed, guarding them with AK-47 rifles.

There were two gunmen inside he'd never seen before and he assumed they'd arrived in one of the pickups. The first stood at the

315

front of the hostages with his back to Nate. The second was in the back, positioned so he could view the hostages. The Syrian paced among the men and women. At the sound of the door being crashed open, the Syrian, like Nate, dropped to make himself a smaller target.

Nate shot the man in back of the gathering first because he was the most immediate threat. Nate went for center mass and the gunman flipped over backward in the air and landed with a thud on the dirt, his rifle clattering to the side.

At the sound of the explosion, the gunman in front wheeled around, turning on his heel, and fired two quick, wild shots that sailed over Nate's head—where his head *should* have been—and through the open doorway.

Nate had cocked his .500 while he brought it down level from its tremendous kick and he fired and hit the gunman on the side of his nose. The force of the .50-caliber slug threw the already-dead body into the seated males.

There were screams and shouts from the hostages, but Nate tuned them out. He leaped to the left inside the shed so his body would no longer be silhouetted within the doorframe and be an easy target.

Sun streamed in behind him and he counted on the Syrian being temporarily blinded inside the dark shed. Nate hoped the Syrian's eyes wouldn't have time to adjust now that he was inside. He scrabbled low along the wall until he found cover behind an ancient rusted tractor body mounted on cinder blocks.

The Syrian had chosen not to try to outgun Nate but to stop him from firing again by other means. He did it by snatching up a young woman from the group and pulling her up in front of him as a shield. The Syrian held the hostage erect by clamping his arm around her throat and lifting her off her feet in front of him. She was thin, dark, and birdlike. Nate recognized her from when he saw her sitting next to Sheridan.

Nate's sense of *yarak* was interrupted when a voice he recognized—Sheridan's—cried out: "Kira!"

The Syrian stuck his rifle out between the girl's body and her right arm. The muzzle wavered and Nate ducked down behind the tractor. He knew the man hadn't yet located him.

Nate ignored the sounds of panic inside the shed: males scuttling away in a crabwalk from the Syrian, but not yet bold enough to rise up to their feet and run; women crying out and extending their arms as if their bare palms would ward off bullets.

He knew he had only a second or two more before the Syrian found him and blasted away, hoping for a direct hit through the gaps of the tractor body or for a ricochet that might do the same damage. Either that, or he could shoot his human shield and turn his weapon on the other hostages.

Nate quickly exchanged the revolvers in his hand so that he had the .454 with the scope in his right. He rose and rested his arm on the cowl of the tractor. The magnified left brown eye of Kira dominated his scope. It blinked with tears.

He couldn't fire without hitting her.

That's when Sheridan launched herself at her friend and hugged her around the waist, pulling her down out of the Syrian's grip. Nate moved the weapon slightly until all he could see in the scope was the Syrian's right eye. He fired.

The Syrian stepped back with only the left half of his head still attached. Sheridan was on top of Kira on the ground, shielding her.

Although it wasn't necessary, Nate also shot the Syrian in the chest, if only to make sure he went down hard and didn't squeeze off any involuntary rounds from his rifle at the hostages.

He heard shouts of relief and shrieks of terror as he stepped out from behind the tractor. He yelled, *"Are there any more of them?"*

The volunteers and engineering team members were in various stages of grief, terror, and pure anger. Women hugged each other and cried; several of the men simply stood and stared at him, not sure who he was or if he'd turn on them next.

"I said . . ."

"No, Nate. There were three of them and you got them all." It was Sheridan, looking up from where she was with Kira on the ground.

"Is she hurt?"

Sheridan untangled herself from her friend. "No, no injuries."

"That was a good move," Nate said to Sheridan.

"I nearly *died*," Kira said, choking on a sob.

"She means, thank you for saving her life," Sheridan said.

"Could have been worse," he said.

Sheridan's eyes widened and she said, "I can't believe you're here. Is my dad with you?"

"No. Why would he be?"

"I don't know," she said. "I know you two work together some-times . . ."

"We can talk about it later," Nate said, stepping forward to ad-dress the former hostages.

"Okay, everybody," he said. "It's time to get out now. Don't gather up your things, don't stand around talking about what just happened. Just get the hell away from here and go home."

He had their attention. "The keys to all the four-wheelers you

---

drove out here are in the safe in the third shed. There are guns there, but don't take them. Just grab a set of keys, find the right ATV, and *go*."

Suzy had recovered enough to ask, "What about our work here?"

"It's done," Nate said. "It's been hijacked."

"But . . ."

"*It's over,*" he said. "Go with them. Everybody."

Nate gestured toward the bodies of the three dead gunmen. "They were keeping you here just long enough to make sure they could get the trucks out and on their way. They were waiting for word to kill you all."

A few of the males hesitated, unsure of what to do. So did Suzy, who obviously didn't want to leave the place where she'd dedicated her last year and a half.

Nate said to them, "Do you want to be here if they come back?"

"Fuck no," Seth said through broken teeth. His left eye was swollen shut from being kicked in the head.

"Then go," Nate told him. To Sheridan, he said, "Not you. You're coming with me."

"What about Kira?"

Kira looked up at Nate with pleading eyes. So did several of the other volunteers. Apparently, they wanted to be with the guy with the guns.

"She seems like a pain in the ass," he said.

"Oh, she *is*," Sheridan said, nodding, "but we're roommates . . ."

"I've got room in my Jeep for you two only," Nate said. "I need space for my birds."

As Sheridan led Kira toward Nate, he saw that Suzy hadn't moved.

"Okay, you too," he said.

Reluctantly, she followed Sheridan and Kira.

"My Jeep is here," he told them. "Hang with me here for a minute, then we'll make our way there. Right now, I need to make a call."

Nate dug the satellite phone out of his back pocket and punched the solitary number on the speed-dial list.

TYRELL ANSWERED on the first ring.

"So you've got my location," Nate said.

"That we do," Tyrell said. "We got a ping on you about a half hour ago, then nothing. Now we've got you on the screen."

"Good."

"Have you now decided to keep your phone on and follow instructions?"

Nate didn't respond.

"Did you find Ibby?"

"Affirmative."

"Is he up to no good?"

"He was," Nate said. "But there's a much bigger problem now."

Tyrell hesitated for a moment, then said, "We're on our way. Don't take any action—I need for you to sit tight and wait for the cavalry to arrive. Then you can brief them. Do you copy?"

"Roger that," Nate said, even though he bristled as always when someone—anyone—told him what to do without saying why, and used the phrase "I need you . . ." to do *anything*. The connection ended abruptly before he could ask how much Tyrell knew about Ibby, the sheds, and the EMPs.

He started to call back but thought better of it. The brief conversation was all wrong. Tyrell hadn't asked what Ibby had been doing or what threat might still be out there.

To Sheridan and Kira, he said, "We're leaving now. *Run, don't walk.*"

"But—" Suzy argued.

"Now," he said as he holstered one of his revolvers and snatched her up around her waist and carried her, running, toward the door.

Before they got to the door, though, he heard the distant deep-bass chug of oncoming helicopters.

30

Ten minutes before, Joe looked through the bullet-punched windshield of Phil Parker's pickup and thought he was seeing things. The shattered glass, he thought, had surely distorted and enlarged the images of oncoming vehicles into what looked like a convoy that included two full-sized eighteen-wheel tractor-trailers.

He leaned his head out the open driver's-side window and squinted.

It had not been an illusion. On the horizon, the sun glinted off the toothy chrome grille of a semitruck, then another right behind it. Two of the white pickups he'd seen earlier led the two big rigs, and pickups number three and four trailed the procession.

"Oh no," Jan said. "Those are the trucks I was telling you about. The ones with the EMP devices in them."

"Your pal Ibby," Joe said.

"They must be headed to Utah."

"Along with some escorts. Which means either the trucks have been hijacked or your pal Ibby was waiting for them to escort him to the promised land."

"Please stop saying 'your pal Ibby' like that. It's demeaning to him."

"Boy, he's got you sold, doesn't he?"

"Wait until you meet him," she said. "He's something you just don't see anymore: a real, honest-to-God leader."

Joe said, "If we've seen them, they've seen us. Now we need to figure out what we're going to do."

"I'll talk to him," Jan said with confidence.

"Who?"

"Ibby, of course."

"So you think he's in this with them? That he's in one of the trucks coming right toward us?"

Joe shook his head as he drove. Parker's pickup was so shot-up it wouldn't go more than twenty miles an hour. The oil pressure gauge had dropped into the dead zone and the needle on the temperature gauge was well into the red. If he turned and retreated, he'd lose a chase in minutes. And if he stopped, the engine might not start up again.

"What if Ibby isn't with them?" Joe said. "What if they've taken his weapons from him and they're on their own now?"

"Then they'll probably kill us," she said. "After all, they killed Phil for no good reason. They don't want us to report them."

"I agree."

"So what do we do?" There was cold fear in her voice and a good reason for it, he thought. A ball of ice was forming inside his chest and his fingers were going numb on the wheel.

Joe said, "That guy you shot back there didn't have a radio on him and Phil's doesn't work. They don't know what happened to him. As far as they know, he's still in this pickup headed back to the ranch with a dead game warden in the back."

She nodded, waiting for more.

"If they think he's still driving it, they might give us a pass," he said.

She said, "We need his black scarf to cover your face."

"We don't have it," Joe said.

"Let me see what I can find," she said, turning around so she could dig through Parker's gear on the back bench seat.

Joe continued to drive right at the oncoming convoy. They were a mile away, but closing on him faster than he'd like. There was no doubt they'd seen him and assumed it was their man because the lead truck had not taken any aggressive action. He peered to the right and left through the open windows as if searching for a road he could take that would somehow speed the truck up or hide it.

That kind of road only existed in his imagination, he knew.

"There's a couple of red shirts," she said, "but no black scarves."

"I'm not surprised," Joe said.

There were more than a dozen armed men coming right toward him, he thought. He was vastly outnumbered and outgunned. Even if he could take out a couple of them before they realized who he was, the rest would overrun him in seconds.

Stopping and begging for mercy seemed out of the question. The men who beheaded Cooter and the grizzly bear wouldn't even consider it.

"Hey," she said, "I found something."

It was a musty black Jack Daniel's Tennessee Whiskey T-shirt that had been balled up on the floor.

"This might be our only chance," she said. "Here, let's get that red shirt off . . ."

He continued to drive while she helped him strip off his red shirt to the T-shirt below. She balled up his uniform and threw it behind the seat. Then she turned the Jack Daniel's T-shirt inside out and pulled it over his head as far as his shoulders. He suddenly couldn't see as she tugged on it until he was peering through an armhole. It smelled of sweat, alcohol, and Parker's musky cologne. Joe could imagine Parker wearing it to the bars in Rawlins after he was off duty.

She yanked down on it until the armhole formed into a kind of balaclava opening.

"It might work," she said, appraising him.

"Maybe," he said, his voice muffled. "Grab Daisy and get down on the floorboards. We can't let them see you."

She understood and nodded quickly. Daisy didn't mind being engulfed on the floor by her.

"If they want to talk to me, I'll pretend I don't hear them," Joe said. "And if they stop us . . ."

"I know," she finished for him. "I know."

JOE CONTINUED TO DRIVE. His hands were getting slick on the wheel and his breath came in shallow gasps. Keeping the front tires firmly in the sandy ruts was getting harder to maintain.

When the lead white pickup was fifty yards away, he eased

Parker's vehicle out into the desert beyond the shoulder of the two-track to give the convoy a wide berth. The driver of the lead truck and his passenger both nodded in his direction as they got close, and Joe nodded back.

The grizzly bear's huge head was wired to the truck like a bizarre hood ornament. Its thick hair was matted with dried blood and dust, and its tongue lolled out between sharp yellow teeth. Joe fought back the twin emotions of revulsion and gut-churning fear.

The fighters in the back of the pickup had a higher angle on Parker's truck, but instead of looking inside the cab and possibly seeing Jan and Daisy, they were more interested in the dead game warden in the back. One of them pointed his finger at the body and re-created the act of shooting at it. Another one laughed.

Joe tried not to stare at the drivers of the semitrucks as they rumbled past him.

The two eighteen-wheelers created so much rolling dust that he was able to get by the two trailing white pickups without anyone in them looking at him too closely. He extended his left hand and waved through the dust and a couple of the fighters waved wearily back.

As the third pickup passed, Joe got a glimpse of the bear paws when there was a break in the rolling dust.

"Stay down," Joe croaked to Jan.

"Okay."

AFTER THE CONVOY HAD PASSED, he eased Parker's pickup back onto the two-track. His heart was still beating so hard he was surprised she couldn't hear it.

He watched the convoy get farther away through his rearview mirror. After two minutes, he said, "I think we did it."

"Can I come up now?" Jan asked.

"Yup."

She crawled back onto the front seat, and Daisy came with her and sat between them.

"That was way too close," he said. He was suddenly very tired. The adrenaline rush he'd felt as the convoy went by was receding into dread.

"I can't believe the T-shirt worked," she said a few minutes later. "You'll probably want to wear that for the rest of your life. It's your lucky T-shirt."

"It didn't work for Phil," he said, peeling it off.

"Did you see Ibby?" she asked.

"Maybe. There were a lot of guys. I don't know what he looks like."

"Fuck."

"Describe him to me," Joe said.

She looked at him suspiciously, then said, "Tall, dark, and handsome. Intelligent and refined."

"Age?"

"Late twenties, early thirties," she said while reaching back into her jeans pocket. "Here, I've got a photo of us together in San Francisco."

He expected her to extract a smartphone but instead she pulled out a thin wallet.

"Remember photographs?" she asked. She riffed through some plastic-coated photos and held one out. In it, Jan embraced a sharply handsome man. In the background was the Golden Gate Bridge.

———

"I can't say for sure, because most of them wore black masks. But I don't recognize him from those I saw."

"They murdered him," she said.

"We don't know that."

"If he wasn't with them, they murdered him," she said. "He'd *never* let anyone take those trucks."

"Sorry."

She covered her face in her hands and screamed. The sound alarmed Daisy, who looked up at Joe for an explanation.

The scream faded into sobs. "They're fucking animals," she said. "They've ruined everything. Are you sure you didn't see him?"

"Ninety-five percent," Joe said.

"We need to kill them all," she hissed.

"First things first."

"LISTEN," JAN SAID. Her eyes were wide with alarm as she reached over and grasped Joe's shoulder. "They're coming back to kill us." Her manner had turned from mourning to anger and now to shock. Her voice was leaden.

He heard it, too. A low rumble.

"That's not them," he said.

"Then what is it?"

Before he could answer, a formation of four helicopter gunships appeared over the southern horizon. They were coming fast and appeared to be headed to the dry valley where the old sheep ranch was located.

"It's the good guys," Joe said. "Rulon must have come through and let the feds know to send the choppers up from a base in Colorado."

"Thank God for that," she said.

"Yup," he said, and they exchanged a delirious glance.

She started to say something, but her words were drowned out by a tremendous series of high-pitched *whoosh* sounds as missiles were launched from the sides of the choppers.

Joe said, "Good-bye, convoy."

But instead of watching the first wave of Hellfire missiles scream through the sky overhead, the earth shook from multiple explosions on the dry valley floor.

He thought: *They're going after the ranch.*

Then he thought: *Sheridan.*

THE DESTRUCTION of the structures on the old ranch was remarkably quick, complete, and devastating.

Joe stopped the pickup on the ridge above the valley and watched swooping helicopters unleash hell on the buildings. He felt dead inside, but he couldn't look away.

The ground shook with explosions as each of the three big sheds was blown up one after the other. The old ranch house had taken a direct hit and was no more than a smoking crater. Black rolls of smoke and dirt punched up from the desert floor like fists and the old, dry barn wood of the sheds, now simply piles of matchsticks, roared with fire.

AS SWIFTLY as they had come, the helicopters rose, turned, and formed into a V, headed south. They were done.

Mission accomplished.

———

Joe slumped against the side of the battered pickup for support. He wasn't sure his legs would hold him up.

His ears rang from the concussions and he almost didn't hear Jan say aloud, "I wonder if anyone got out."

Then: "Why, Joe? Why did they destroy the *ranch*?"

He was too numb to speak.

THE SHARP SMELL of the smoke reached them within a minute. Joe turned from it because it made his eyes water. At least, he blamed the smoke.

Before he turned around, he scanned the valley below to the east and west. He'd seen no vehicles, no sign of anyone who might have gotten away from the buildings before they were pulverized.

Jan continued to ask him questions as if he knew the answers to them. Her questions no longer registered and he kept his back to her. He stared north across the vast desert landscape, seeing nothing, hearing nothing, feeling a hard, cold dread ball up in the back of his throat that would likely grow until it enveloped him.

BECAUSE OF JAN'S QUESTIONS and the ringing in his ears, Joe didn't hear the rumble of a vehicle approaching or the crunching sound of footsteps.

But when he heard Nate say, "I've got Sheridan right here with me," his head snapped up. His friend said, "But who is going to tell her mom? I don't think I want to be in *that* room."

Joe wheeled and flopped his arms across the hood of the

pickup with relief. He needed the support or his legs might have given out.

Oddly, the vision of Sheridan that came to him that instant was from when she was seven years old and all blond hair, missing teeth, gangly arms and legs, and wide green eyes.

But there she was, his twenty-two-year-old college girl. She was climbing out of the back of Nate's Jeep through a tangle of arms that belonged to two others: her roommate from Laramie, whom Joe had met only once and instantly disliked, and a disheveled woman in her thirties who looked distraught. The woman looked up and waved to Jan, who waved back. They knew each other.

"Dad, I'm so sorry," Sheridan said, hanging behind Nate as if ashamed to be seen in full.

"You should be."

"If it weren't for Nate . . ." she said, stopping to look over her shoulder at the rolls of black smoke rising from where the ranch had been minutes before.

"Thank you for getting her out of there," Joe said to Nate. Then: "I've been looking for both of you."

"And you found us," Nate said. "Rather, we found you."

"What the hell just happened here?"

Nate's manner was stoic. Joe knew that when Nate was dead calm he was at his most dangerous.

"What happened was four Boeing AH-64E Apache Guardians armed with Hellfire Two air-to-ground missiles," he said. "They came to wipe everybody out—bad guys, engineers, everyone. We were all supposed to be collateral damage."

Joe shook his head, puzzled.

"What about the team?" Jan asked the woman who had emerged from the Jeep.

"They got out on the ATVs," Suzy Gudenkauf said. "Less one volunteer and . . . Ibby."

Jan and Suzy embraced. One or both were crying. Joe turned back to Nate.

"Why didn't they go after the convoy?"

"Not sure, although I have a theory," Nate said.

"Is it possible they didn't know about it? That they were trying to kill it in the nest but they were fifteen minutes too late?"

"Anything is possible," Nate said.

At that moment, the motor under the hood of Phil Parker's pickup shuddered and died.

"Of course," Joe said sourly.

Nate turned so his back was to Joe. He was staring intently at the fire down below in the valley with his hands on his hips. Thinking.

"DOES MOM KNOW?" Sheridan asked Joe after they'd hugged and stepped back to assess each other. Joe thought Sheridan seemed dirty but safe. There was a faraway look in her eyes that he recognized from when she was young, when she'd seen things that bothered her but she was determined not to fall to pieces. In that way, he thought, she was like her mother. She stayed strong and in the moment.

"No," he said.

"Are you going to tell her?"

"You know the answer to that."

Sheridan closed her eyes briefly, then said, "I hope she doesn't freak out. I had no idea what I was getting into. Nobody did."

"Blame it all on me," Sheridan's roommate Kira said as she crossed her arms and leaned back against the Jeep. "It won't be the first time everything was all my fault."

"Please," Sheridan said to her. "Not now. Let's not make everything about you for right now, okay?"

Kira huffed and looked away.

"How about we worry about that later?" Joe said. "Right now we've got six people, three falcons, and a dog, and we need to try and get out of here in one Jeep. Not to mention, there are trucks out there filled with killers on the way to the interstate highway system."

Nate laughed grimly. Without looking over his shoulder, he said, "Other than that, Mrs. Lincoln, how was the play?"

Kira said, "What's that supposed to mean?"

Nate ignored her when he turned back around. If anything, he was even calmer than before. Joe knew something was about to happen.

To Joe, he said, "I think I know what's going to happen next. Are you okay if I take control of our situation?"

"Will it get us out of here without anyone else getting hurt?"

"I can't guarantee it, if that's what you're asking."

Joe hesitated a moment. "Go ahead," he said. "You know more about what's going on than I do."

Nate said, "Okay. Sheridan, lead the three ladies to the northeast, toward those distant rocks." He pointed across the desert toward the only visible landmark on the desert floor. "That's Adobe Town.

There are plenty of places to hide there. Don't show yourselves, no matter what you hear or see."

Sheridan looked to Joe and raised her eyebrows. He nodded, then waited for Nate to provide an explanation that didn't come.

"Go now," Nate said to her. "We don't have that much time."

"Why can't we take the Jeep?" Kira asked.

"Because I know how this goes," Nate said. "I had a dream about it. In my dream, I have the Jeep."

"A dream?" Kira asked, incredulous. "What are you, some kind of mystic?"

"He's the guy who saved our lives twice already today," Sheridan said to Kira. "Now shut up and follow me so he can try to do it again."

Jan and Suzy didn't comment. They were still too much in shock to argue, Joe thought.

Sheridan kissed Joe on the cheek and said, "I love you, Dad. Thanks for coming for me."

"Of course," he said. "I love you, too, sweetie. Just don't make me ever have to do it again, okay?"

She laughed.

"Take this," he said, handing her the shotgun. "You know how to use it if you need to. And take Daisy with you."

Sheridan rested the shotgun on her shoulder and said, "Follow me, ladies."

As the group gathered, she looked back and said, "Be careful, Dad."

"I will."

"And you, too, Nate."

He grunted.

. . .

JOE WATCHED as the four walked away toward Adobe Town. Daisy stuck close to Sheridan. It had gotten warm enough that their forms began to undulate in waves of heat.

"Are you sure you know what you're doing?" Joe asked.

"No."

"So what is your plan?"

Nate reached into his shirt and withdrew a satellite phone and powered it on.

When someone answered on the other end, Nate said, "I bet you're surprised to hear from *me* right now."

Joe couldn't hear the other side of the conversation.

"Tyrell, I have to admit I didn't realize what an evil bastard you are, and the same with your buddy Keith Volk, or whatever your real names are. But you shot your wad and you have no idea what kind of trouble you've caused. If you don't sit down and listen to me right now, a lot of people are going to die. It'll be the biggest thing since 9/11, and maybe bigger.

"I'll deal with both of you when this is over, but for now you need to listen to *me*."

FOR THE NEXT FIVE MINUTES, Joe stared at the tops of his boots while Nate described the two tractor-trailers—one painted with the logo of a battery company and the other a familiar commercial carrier—as well as what was inside each of them. He estimated their coordinates and argued with the man on the other end of the line about how the helicopters could take them out.

"I know you've fired all the missile ordnance," Nate said with impatience, "but turn them around right now. Those Apaches are fitted with thirty-millimeter cannons. That's more than enough to take out those EMPs. The bad guys have small arms, as far as we know.

"And whatever you do, don't let them fire up the EMP devices or they could take the Apaches out of the sky. Tell your pilots to hit them hard and fast and rake over whatever is left. Tell them if they see the back doors of the trailers opening, that means they're priming the EMPs.

"Tell your guys to *kill them all—*"

"Look," Nate said, cutting through whatever was being said to him. "You don't have time to send other aircraft or drones. If you don't turn those Apaches around right now, you'll lose them on the highway or you'll target the wrong trucks and kill even more civilians than you tried to here. I-80 is a sea of semitrucks and passenger cars. If you don't destroy that convoy before they get there, it'll be your ass in federal prison, and you know it. You'll be famous for all the wrong reasons.

"I'll keep this phone on so you can tell me how it goes," Nate said.

After a long pause, he said, "Oh, don't worry about us. We've got this end handled if they come back."

Then he punched off and grinned at Joe.

Joe said, "We've got this handled?"

Nate shrugged.

Joe took a long breath and looked out across the desert to the north.

"Get in," Nate said, nodding toward his Jeep. "Be careful not to rile up my birds."

As the Jeep rumbled down from the ridge on the two-track, Joe said, "It's been a while, Nate."

"That it has, Joe."

"You know, Marybeth had the same dream. She told me about it the next morning."

Nate said, "Hmmm."

"You know how much stock I put in dreams and your other woo-woo crap, right?"

"I do. That's one reason I've always liked you, Joe."

"Will this be the end for us?"

Nate pondered the question and said, "Probably. I wish to hell I knew how that dream ended."

PART EIGHT

DESERT SOLITAIRE

The fear of death follows from the fear of life. A man who lives fully is prepared to die at any time.

—Edward Abbey, *A Voice Crying in the Wilderness*

31

"HERE COME THE HORSES," NATE SAID. "RIGHT ON SCHEDULE."

Joe looked up from where he'd positioned himself on the rocky ridge fifty yards behind Nate and his Jeep. To the north, he could see rolls of dust on the horizon.

"Just like my dream," Nate added.

Joe nodded.

It had been an hour and a half since Sheridan led the other three toward Adobe Town—about three miles away. Joe had tracked their progress until their forms melted into the heat waves, catching a glimpse of clothing here and there. He could no longer see them and he assumed they had made it and were crouched behind the columns and boulders of the red rock cathedral. At least he hoped so.

He'd stuffed his daypack between two football-sized rocks on the top of the ridge and placed the M14 carbine in the fold. A spare thirty-round magazine was placed on the top of the right-hand rock for easy retrieval. He had half a box of ammunition remaining, although he wondered, if a firefight happened, if he'd even get a chance to reload an empty magazine.

He could not get over how isolated he felt. There was no way to communicate with Sheridan, with the governor, with dispatch, with Marybeth. The Red Desert was a stark and fascinating place and he wished he knew it better. But he didn't want to die there.

Below him, Nate tended to his falcons and looked up occasionally to sweep the horizon with his eyes. Joe watched him check the loads of his two handguns more than once.

"Hey, Nate," Joe called out. "This is like something out of the 1870s."

"We're just a couple of lone cowboys," Nate agreed.

"Is there a plan B?" Joe asked hopefully.

"Nada," Nate said. "I only had one dream."

Joe let that sink in. "Well, I guess that's good to know."

Nate shrugged.

THEY HAD BOTH PAID close attention, fifteen minutes before, when several series of heavy booms echoed from the north. Joe assumed it was the sound of cannon fire from the Apaches. Interspersed within the booms were snappy single shots from small arms and the long cloth-ripping sounds of automatic-weapon fire in return.

Then silence.

JOE HEARD AN ELECTRONIC BURR and looked down to see Nate pull the satellite phone from his pocket and hold it to his ear. He listened for nearly a minute before lowering it and cursing out loud.

Nate said to Joe, "Tyrell said the Apaches knocked out one of the two tractor-trailers a half mile from the interstate, but the second one got on the highway going west in the middle of heavy truck traffic, so they couldn't keep firing on it. The choppers have eyes on the semi, but they're nearly out of ordnance and fuel. One of the pickups got blown to hell, but the other three got away."

"Headed our direction?" Joe asked.

"Of course," Nate said. "If the idiots in charge of this operation had geared up for taking out the convoy instead of blowing up the ranch, this show would be over by now."

Joe said, "So the semi is headed to Utah after all?"

"Yes."

"How are they going to stop it?"

"Don't know, don't care," Nate said.

"I do," Joe groused to himself.

THE HERD OF WILD HORSES turned into nearly liquid form before they overran Nate and the Jeep. Joe was fascinated by them as they thundered past. They were rough and feral beasts, their hides scarred and manes tangled with brush, but the sheer weight and power of the herd shook the ground as it passed. He glimpsed white panicked eyes, yellow teeth, and clumps of dirt thrown into the air from flying hooves.

When their dust finally dissipated, Joe saw that Nate had taken his large gyrfalcon out of his Jeep and was holding it on his gloved fist. The satellite phone was strapped to the back of the bird by several lengths of red baling twine.

Then he let it go.

The falcon flapped its wings clumsily at first as it gained altitude, apparently figuring out how to accommodate the unnatural weight on its back. It flew toward Joe and he ducked as it whooshed over his head so close that he felt the air pound down on his hat from its long wings. He turned to watch it climb toward a distant cirrus cloud that strung across the blue sky.

"I never really bonded with that bird in the first place," Nate said after the falcon was gone. "I always thought of it as a spy. I want nothing to do with it whatsoever."

Joe had no idea how to respond to that.

"Tyrell and his gang will never find us by the phone's GPS now," Nate said. "They'll track the flight of the gyrfalcon. That bird will be in Colorado or Utah airspace by this afternoon."

After a beat, Joe said, "Are you working for the good guys or the bad guys?"

"Right now I'm not sure there's a difference."

Joe pondered that while Nate stripped the hoods and jesses off both of his other falcons and released them to the sky.

"They'll do fine one way or the other," Nate said.

Joe knew the significance of the act, and it deepened his sense of dread.

Then Nate said, "Listen. Here they come. Get ready."

Joe scrambled back behind the rocks and lay prone. The hum of engines came in wafts of breeze. He lifted his binoculars and focused on the northern horizon.

There they were: the three white pickups.

NATE STOOD IN FRONT OF his Jeep and limbered up. He grasped his hands in front of him and pushed his fists downward, then reached behind his back and did the same thing to loosen up his shoulders. He flexed his fingers and balled them again and again. While he did it, he never took his eyes off the approaching vehicles.

There were extra cartridges in each of his front pockets, .50-caliber rounds in the right, .454 in the left. They were each the size of a woman's lipstick, although much heavier.

Even though he'd known Ibby for a very short time, he couldn't yet think of him in the past tense, as extinguished. What Saeed and his men had done was so awful, so savage, that there was only one way to respond.

Kill the snake.

JOE FELT HIS BREATH getting shorter as the pickups neared. He tried to calm himself and ward off a fear so strong it could blind him, so he forced himself to think about Sheridan, Marybeth, Lucy, and April. He mentally placed each one of them: Sheridan safe at Adobe Town, Marybeth working at the library, Lucy in class, April . . . he couldn't place April. Never could.

He wondered if he'd ever see any of them again. A cold chill ran down his back from his scalp to his tailbone.

There were so many of them coming, he thought. And they were coming fast. He was a decent shot with the carbine and he'd used the weapon primarily to dispatch wounded game, but could he shoot accurately when it came to trying to hit swiftly moving objects? He wasn't sure he could provide Nate the cover fire his friend needed. He wasn't sure anyone could.

As the trucks got closer, he couldn't help but think of the men driving them and in the back. He wondered who they really were and what they must be thinking about. They must have loved ones at home somewhere, he thought. They, like Joe, must have families waiting for them. They were human beings with dreams and ambitions and they loved their god and their mission.

Then he shook his head. Whether they were from ISIS or al-Qaeda or some other offshoot, whether they were husbands, fathers, and sons, didn't matter right now. They were the enemy, and if given the opportunity, they'd kill him and Nate and the women at Adobe Town without a second thought. They'd treat him the way they treated the grizzly bear, and Ibby, and Cooter.

His mouth was dry and his heart pounded. He looked over the weapon and realized the safety was on. Joe angrily thumbed it off and seated a cartridge in the chamber.

He was ready.

NATE HAD THE .454 in his left hand and the .500 in his right, then thought better of it and switched weapons. Although he had a big revolver in each hand, he wouldn't fire both at the same time because that would result in two poor shots. This wasn't the movies. Instead, he would aim and fire with his right hand and rotate the weapons when he needed to.

He wanted the scoped revolver first.

There was a reason, he thought, why the U.S. Secret Service purchased .454 Casull handguns from Freedom Arms. The reason was that one could *kill a car*. The round had so much power and velocity that, if properly placed, it could literally penetrate the engine block of a vehicle and knock it out.

The pickups were side by side and coming fast. Nate squinted and recognized Saeed driving the truck on the far left. *Good,* he thought. *Good.*

Several errant AK-47 shots snapped out from the gunmen in the back of the trucks firing wildly over the top of the cabs. Nate didn't move. Aiming true from a moving truck was as ridiculous as shooting from the back of a galloping horse. The 7.62x39mm rounds sizzled over his head and thumped into the hill behind him.

He and Joe had the advantage until the vehicles stopped and the gunmen got out so that they could aim. Still, though, he heard a round *thwack* off the hood of his Jeep right behind him and carom into the hill beneath Joe.

Nate raised the .454 and put the crosshairs squarely on the upper third of the grille of the center truck—the closest one—and fired. The kick of the blast jerked the .454 straight over his head. Without hesitating, he thumbed back the hammer while lowering it and fired again.

The center pickup slowed dramatically and was now rolling forward with momentum but without the aid of its engine. Steaming green radiator fluid billowed out from under the hood and spattered the desert floor. The truck was soon enveloped in almost impenetrable steam.

He then turned to Saeed's pickup on the left, but the man had anticipated that he would be next and he'd hit his brakes and slammed his truck into reverse. He made the maneuver so abruptly that two of the gunmen in the back were thrown out of the bed of the truck.

But Nate was on him, and he fired twice through the roll of steam into the engine of Saeed's vehicle, disabling it.

The pickup on the right had veered away from the dead trucks, and Nate swung the weapon across his body and tried a passing shot above the front right tire into the motor that did little or no damage.

Then he holstered the red-hot .454 under his left arm and switched to the .500.

Joe watched breathlessly as Nate took out the first and second pickups. *Boom-boom. Boom-boom. Boom.*

The gunmen in back of both trucks scrambled out over the bed wells, some hiding behind the vehicles for cover, others just standing there inexplicably, shouting to one another. There were too many to count, it seemed.

He placed his attention on the third truck, the one that had turned away from the others and was now speeding away from the disabled vehicles from left to right, parallel to Nate. If the driver turned sharply and looped back, he could get behind Nate, where Joe's friend would be caught in a cross fire. If that happened, Joe's shooting lane would be destroyed, because he'd have to expose himself on the rim to fire down at the third truck.

So if it managed to flank Nate, he thought, it would be the end.

As the pickup moved, Joe leaned in on the peep sight. Although the carbine was steady, the vehicle bounced up and down over rocks and brush and he couldn't get a good bead on it. He fired anyway— *pop-pop-pop-pop-pop*—in the general direction of the windshield and front passenger window. He continued to fire as fast as he could pull the trigger.

Spent brass casings ejected and bounced off the rock to his right. One casing ricocheted back and into his open collar. As it burned the bare skin in the crook of his neck, his aim got screwy and wild, but he kept pulling the trigger. Finally, the hot brass stung so bad he had to pause and slap it out of his clothing.

When he looked back up, he saw that two bodies writhed in the tracks behind the pickup. His errant shots had apparently hit them.

And by the way the pickup slowed down for no apparent reason and didn't try to outflank Nate, Joe thought he might have hit the driver. Gunmen leaped out of the pickup as it lost speed, some tumbling on impact, others landing on their feet.

The truck stopped suddenly as if the brake pedal had been stomped, throwing the remaining gunmen in the back over the top of the cab and over the sides. Then the passenger door flew open and a black-clad man jumped out, screaming and pointing toward Joe's location.

He felt panic, and for the first time in his life understood the phrase "fog of war." Below him, the black-clad enemy ran and juked through swirling smoke and steam. It was hard to concentrate on legitimate targets, or get a good feel for what was going on.

Joe aimed carefully at the center mass of the man who had been in the cab and pulled the trigger. Nothing. He was out of rounds.

He rolled to his back and ejected the empty magazine and jammed the fresh one in.

Before he could right himself, the top of the ridgeline began to explode around him. Bullets were kicking up dirt and splattering into the rocks he hid behind. His pack jumped as if alive. A round hit the forestock of his carbine and left a notch that looked like someone had taken a bite out of it.

The remaining fighters in the third truck had been organized and were concentrating on *him*.

Below him came furious snaps from the AKs and heavy, measured *boom*s from the .500 as Nate engaged the occupants of the first two vehicles.

CROUCHING NOW BEHIND THE JEEP as rounds shredded its ragtop and thudded into the body, Nate loaded both weapons and glanced up the hill toward Joe's position. It was getting shredded by rifle fire.

And he couldn't see Joe.

Nate had been hit twice, once through the muscle of his left thigh and the other in his right buttock cheek. His thigh wound was a through-and-through and it bled freely down his leg into his boot. If he hadn't seen it, he wouldn't have known it happened, because the butt wound was much worse: it just sat back there, burning like a hot coal that would not cool down.

Rather than appear over the top of the hood of the Jeep like the gunmen had expected, Nate crouched and wheeled around the back. As he did, he glimpsed inside his vehicle and saw that the dowel rods he'd fashioned for his falcons had been blown to bits.

At least, he thought, his birds would live through the day.

He'd expected the gunmen who had not been hit, which was the majority of them, to be huddled behind their own smoking vehicles, taking aim. That's what rational soldiers, well-trained soldiers, would have done, he thought.

But these guys were *crazy*.

Instead, five of them were advancing on foot toward his position. They were screaming, *"Allahu Akbar!"*

Saeed wasn't with them, which didn't surprise Nate one bit.

He waited until three of the five were lined up front to back and he fired one shot center-mass on the first gunman. All three went down.

It was his first triple.

The act seemed to stun the other two, who stopped and stared. He took them out with two head shots.

They were crazy, all right, he thought. But there were still too many of them.

He wasn't sure he could hold out against them all before he bled out.

The gunmen from the third truck continued to keep up heavy fire on the hilltop where Joe had been. Nate had heard no return fire.

His ears began to roar. He couldn't trace the source. Had he been hit in the head? The neck?

Was this rising cacophony the last thing he would ever hear?

JOE WAS FLAT on his back and bleeding. AK-47 rounds snapped through the air inches from his eyes.

Although he didn't think he'd been hit by a bullet, he wasn't sure. So many rounds had struck the rocks around him and fragmented that he'd taken splinters of rock and hot lead in his arms, chest, legs, and face. His entire body was numb.

When there was a momentary pause, he used it to roll to his belly again so he could shoot back. As he did, his left shoulder must have been just high enough on the horizon that they saw him and fired. A round hit the top of his shoulder and it felt like the blow of a baseball bat.

The animal sound that he heard was his own.

When the orange spangles of pain finally faded from his eyes, he turned his head and looked at the wound. He had trouble focusing.

The round had torn back a flap of his red uniform fabric and dark blood was pulsing out of a scorched hole in his flesh. His entire arm was numb, and he doubted he could shoulder the carbine and aim again.

Joe closed his eyes, said a prayer, and painfully pulled the butt of the stock to his injured shoulder and found the peep sight. He wasn't sure he could endure the pain the kick of the weapon would have on his wound when he pulled the trigger again.

As he inched back into the notch in the rocks and stuck the barrel out over his daypack, he seemed to swoon.

There was a roar above him in the sky. Dirt began to lift up from the rocks around him and float through the air.

Suddenly, there was a maelstrom of dust swirling around him and he closed his eyes tight so they wouldn't fill with grit.

Then, .30mm cannon fire.

THE OBLITERATION of the gunmen in and around the three pick-ups by the lone returning Apache helicopter gunship was awesome to behold, Nate thought.

Bad guys were cut into pieces and the three white vehicles were reduced to smoking wrecks of torn sheet metal and twisted frames.

He briefly saw Saeed run out from behind his pickup and raise his hands in the air toward the low helicopter to surrender.

Nate thought about how Saeed had urged his own men to sacrifice themselves but he'd hung back himself, both at Nate's camp several nights before and now when the Apache arrived. Saeed was at his best when others were doing the hard work, or when his victim—like Ibby—was bound and unarmed.

Nate hated him at that second like he'd never hated anyone before, and he quickly raised his weapon and put the front sight on Saeed's jaw and squeezed the trigger.

Saeed's now headless body stood for a moment, slightly swaying, before a cannon round turned him into a smoking grease spot on the desert floor.

Damn, Nate thought. *We killed him twice. Too bad we can't make it three times.*

NATE PLACED both of his empty weapons on the hood of his Jeep so that they were in plain sight and raised his hands, palms out, toward the Apache as it descended. He was weak with loss of blood and he had to lean against the front of his vehicle to stay upright.

His long blond hair whipped behind him from the backwash as the Apache landed. He kept his eyes closed until he could feel it begin to dissipate as the blades slowed and whined.

When he opened them, he saw two airmen in pilot helmets and green jumpsuits approach from the helicopter. They were carrying automatic rifles. They walked cautiously through the battleground, heads on swivels, making sure none of the bodies scattered around them came back to life.

One of the airmen approached Nate and slid his face mask up. He was young and pale and he had freckles across his nose. His gray eyes were cool and steady.

"Good thing we decided to take a shortcut home or we would have never stumbled on your situation here," he said.

Nate expressed his thanks, then chinned toward the top of the ridge. "I've got a friend up there," he said. "I don't know if he made it."

The second pilot nodded and broke off from the first, headed toward the ridge.

"I'm out of fuel and out of ammo," the first pilot said, looking Nate over and unable to keep the concern off his face. "I'll help you to the aircraft so we can get our kit out and get that bleeding stopped."

Nate looked down. His left leg was black with blood and it beaded on the dry desert floor.

"My buddy . . ." Nate said, barely able to stay conscious.

"Put your arm around my shoulder," the pilot said. "We've got to get you over there."

Nate resisted. He'd put Joe into this situation and he didn't want to leave him up there. Suddenly, he felt an overwhelming sense of loss.

"I found a man up here," the other pilot shouted from the top of the hill. "Not sure if he's alive or dead . . ."

32

A week later, Joe Pickett and Nate Romanowski sat in a large windowless room in the basement of the Wyoming Homeland Security building on Bishop Boulevard in Cheyenne. They had been asked to wait for the governor to arrive. The governor and a "special guest," as Rulon had put it to Joe in a voicemail.

The table was long and coffin-shaped with twenty empty rolling chairs spaced neatly around it. Brass-framed placards were placed in front of each chair and Joe recognized the names of local, state, and federal officials. There were monitors mounted end to end on the walls and ports in the table itself where communications equipment could be plugged in.

This was the room, he guessed, where all of the big shots would meet in the event of a civil or natural catastrophe. At the head of the table was the placard for Governor Spencer Rulon. A sign above the threshold to the room read SITUATION ROOM.

Rulon's administrative assistant, Lisa Casper, was the only other person there, and she sat to the right of the empty governor's chair.

She was reading over a sheaf of papers with a nervous intensity that was designed, Joe thought, to discourage questions.

The situation room hummed very softly with recirculated air and the banks of harsh white fluorescent light tubes that lined the ceiling. The walls were constructed of cinder block painted pale green. The floor was covered with dark gray carpet with as much give as asphalt.

Everything about the room and the building itself was bloodless, institutional, and bureaucratic.

This, Joe thought, was why he could never work nine to five in an office.

"So who is the special guest?" Joe asked Casper.

She didn't look up from her very important papers, but her cheeks flushed slightly.

"Can't say, or won't?"

"Please, Joe."

"Got it."

He looked at Nate across the table. Nate had the ability to go as still as one of his hooded falcons when he wanted to. Joe couldn't even tell if he was breathing.

"You know, this building used to be the headquarters for the Wyoming Game and Fish," Joe said. "I used to come here every now and then in the old days."

Nate didn't even acknowledge that Joe had spoken to him.

"Every state has one of these buildings now," Joe said. "Since 9/11."

Nate's crutches were leaned into a corner of the room and his left leg was extended straight out under the table so that he sat with a list to the side. When he came out of his self-induced coma every minute or so, he'd adjust himself in the chair to relieve the pressure on his buttocks. While he did it, he grimaced.

Joe himself still suffered from various wounds and abrasions all over his body. At the hospital in Cheyenne, where they'd been airlifted, the surgeon had removed more than a dozen small shards of rock and bullet fragments, including one from his throat that had missed his carotid artery by half an inch. At the time, he didn't even know he'd been hit there.

He was covered with stitches and bandage strips and he walked like he was seventy years old. After seeing him when he was released from the hospital, Sheridan suggested they cover him in bubble wrap for a week or two. Marybeth endorsed the idea. Joe took it in stride.

His hat was crown-down on the table in front of him. It had been vented by shrapnel. He had awakened the first night in the hospital to find two nurses sticking their fingers through the holes and giggling.

"So what happens now?" Joe asked Casper.

"Please, Joe . . ."

"When does the governor get here?"

"Soon, I would guess. I can't call him because I had to surrender my cell phone before I came down here to the secure room."

"Why are we meeting here?" Joe asked. "Who would be spying on us?"

JOE AND NATE HAD GOTTEN together in a dark corner of the family lounge area on the third floor of the hospital the second night they were both there. Joe had painfully walked down the quiet hall and Nate had wheeled there in his chair. They took two hours to catch each other up on what had led them both to the Red Desert.

Nate's story about the dream, the Wolverines, Ibby and Saeed, and shooting his way into the third shed was so outlandish that Joe of course believed it.

"I'm going back to prison," Nate had told him. "The entire deal was based on their lies. They had an agenda, all right, but it had nothing to do with what they told me."

When Joe tried to argue, Nate hushed him and said, "Sheridan can have my birds if she can catch them. It's time she stepped up. Better that than hanging around with trust-fund anarchists."

Joe had agreed.

THERE WERE FOOTFALLS on the stairwell outside the room and Lisa Casper looked up. Joe followed her eyes to the door.

He heard Rulon say to someone, "You stay out here until we're ready for you. I'll call you in in a minute."

The governor entered the room in full bluster, carrying a medium-sized box wrapped with ribbon. He kicked the door shut behind him with his cowboy boot heel and it locked with an audible *clunk*.

"Greetings, heroes," he said with a grin. "You've looked better, but it could have been worse! Thank God the cavalry showed up in the nick of time."

He blew through the room toward the head of the table. Joe thought it remarkable how one man could fill a room that moments before had seemed empty.

He stopped behind Joe. "I was never in a firefight in the military," he said. "What's it like, Joe?"

"Horrible."

Rulon nodded. "That's what I thought. What about you, Mr. Romanowski?"

Nate's silence said he'd been in more battles than he cared to talk about.

"That's what I thought, too."

He continued around the room, pulled out his chair, sat down in it heavily, and slid the box the length of the table, where it stopped next to Joe.

"Open it," Rulon said.

Joe untied the ribbon and removed a brand-new black Resistol Cattle Baron.

"That's a nine-hundred-dollar hat," Rulon beamed. "One hundred percent beaver, size seven and a quarter. It repels the rain and it sits on your bean like a pillow. If it ever gets beat up, you just send it back and they'll recondition it to look like new. Look inside."

Joe turned the hat over. The sweat brim was inscribed:

To My Range Rider Joe Pickett
From Wyoming Governor Spencer Rulon

"If it doesn't fit, let me know and I'll get it resized," Rulon said. "Your lovely wife gave me your size. Not that she was eager to do so, because she's still mad at me. Maybe she'll forgive me one day, I hope and pray."

"I can't wear it," Joe said. "It's too . . ."

"Wear the damned thing," Rulon said. "Just try not to get it shot up like the last one. I don't think they can fix bullet holes."

Then he threw back his head and laughed.

Joe smiled in return. He carefully placed the new hat near his old one. The battered one he would still wear every time he went out in the field.

"You need to wear it," Rulon said emphatically, "because I'm afraid that's the only thing you're going to get out of what happened in the Red Desert. No medals, no bonuses, no press conference where I can go on and on about your loyalty, patriotism, or devotion to duty."

Before Joe could say that was fine by him and that it had all really been about finding Nate and saving Sheridan, Rulon said, "None of it ever happened. Do you understand me?"

Joe shook his head.

"Pretend the last week and a half was a fever dream, Joe. Nothing happened in the Red Desert. You went down there to find your buddy and you finally located him flying his birds around. You lost another truck when it broke down—no surprise there, given your track record—and the two of you had to hike out, a little worse for wear. But there were no terrorists, no goofball team of anarchists, no EMP devices built into semitrailers. And no rescue by the cavalry."

Joe was dumbfounded. But when he looked over to Nate, he found his friend nodding wryly.

"You get it, don't you?" Rulon said to Nate.

"I'm afraid I do," Nate said. "So that's Tyrell and Volk outside, then?"

"Just Tyrell," Rulon said, sitting back in his chair. "Mr. Volk is apparently in federal custody. They had to draw straws on which one got thrown under the bus, and Mr. Volk—not his real name, as I'm sure I don't need to tell you—drew the short straw."

Joe looked from Rulon to Nate. He was confused. When he turned to Lisa Casper, she avoided his eyes.

"Crazy thing about that bear," Rulon said to Joe. "That grizzly made a beeline straight south for hundreds of miles. What was it thinking?"

Joe shrugged, puzzled that the governor suddenly brought up GB-53.

"That's a difference between us and them, when you think about it," Rulon said. "We do everything in our power to save a bear—we throw money and manpower at keeping that creature alive. And they show up and kill it the first chance they get for no good reason at all except to cut off its damned head."

He paused. "Maybe when I can somehow figure that out, those people will make some kind of sense to me. But I don't know if I really want to know."

He let the last sentence hang there.

Then Rulon stood up and said, "Enough of that. Let's bring in our special guest."

BRIAN TYRELL, wearing a gray suit and a green tie, sat down in one of the chairs directly across from Nate and on the same side of the table as Joe. He leaned forward and clasped his hands and said to Nate, "You're a hell of an operator. Better than I even expected."

Nate glared at him.

Tyrell said, "I won't go on and on. What is, is. What happened,

happened. I'm glad you got out alive and that casualties were minimal—considering. I'm sure you haven't heard that the Utah Data Center was knocked out by the EMP that got away. There is a complete press blackout on that one. There was some collateral damage, but less than we thought there would be."

He gave a *What you gonna do* shrug. "Nothing ever works as perfectly as planned."

"Which is lucky for us," Nate said, "since your plan included obliterating all of the people at that sheep ranch in one fell swoop."

"Nothing personal," Tyrell said. "Loose ends."

Nate narrowed his eyes.

Tyrell continued. "We took out the truck as soon as they finished their work. Two dead, two in federal custody—including Bill Henn, who has agreed to cooperate. In fact, I wouldn't be surprised to find out he's back working for us in the near future. He figured out some technical issues on a mobile EMP device our own people have been struggling with for years."

"Hold it," Joe interrupted. "They destroyed the Utah Data Center?"

Tyrell nodded, followed by a slow smile.

"That was the plan all along," Nate said to Joe. "They let that truck get away on purpose."

"I don't understand," Joe said.

"They knew what Ibby was up to," Nate said to Joe. "They sent me down there to get in the middle of it so they could have a man on the inside. They knew about Saeed's connections, but they didn't know when he'd try to take over, or that he'd bring a small army with him. That part was a surprise, right, Tyrell?"

Tyrell nodded. He said, "It was. We knew Saeed was dirty, but we didn't know how many bad guys he could bring across the border. This was the first time we know of that five loosely affiliated terrorist groups got together for a joint overseas operation. They entered Mexico in twos and threes and joined up at a camp in the desert twenty miles from the Texas border.

"And if it weren't for you two here pinning them down in one place," he said, gesturing to Nate and Joe, "we'd have lone-wolf jihadis running all over the place. Believe me, we've got enough of them as it is."

Joe pressed Tyrell. "Why would you want to take down your own data center?"

"Ever heard of the Fourth Amendment?" Tyrell replied. "Oh, the UDC was conceived with worthwhile intentions, like all programs. But too many politicos and campaign consultants in both parties were getting access to that data and it's getting too close to the elections to let them have it. To those types, politics comes first and national security is an afterthought. This will keep their hands off private information for a while, so the electoral process can work as it should."

Joe sat back, stunned.

Tyrell said, "In the meanwhile, we've stopped another plot. The credit goes to you guys, not that anyone will ever know."

"Why not?" Joe asked. "I'm not looking for credit, but why is it a secret?"

Tyrell exchanged a knowing glance with Nate, then with the governor, who didn't seem to like Tyrell much.

"There have been five incidents of similar magnitude just this year in the homeland," Tyrell said. "And we've disrupted terrorist activities across the country before they happened. Granted, this was the first one using sophisticated mobile EMP devices. We've always thought they'd try to take down our electrical grid with a bomb exploded in the atmosphere, not by trucks that can blast specific targets. But without getting into specifics, we've shut down the manufacture of a dirty bomb, an anthrax factory, and three other plots that you've never heard about and never will. The word from on high is that no one will *ever* hear about them. Otherwise, our leaders figure the sheeple will panic or get angry at them for their fecklessness or start discriminating against specific ethnic or religious groups and we can't have that, can we?"

The last sentence dripped with sarcasm.

"One of these days, we'll foul up," Tyrell said. "They only have to be lucky once. But our batting average is pretty damned good so far. We just hope we can keep it up until smart people are in charge. In the meantime, we do our best on the inside and take our shots when we can—like letting the data center melt down. The politicos are mad as hell about that, so we had to give them poor Keith Volk."

Tyrell raised his fingers in the air. "Keith is a 'rogue' operator," he said, making air quotes around the word *rogue*. "We knew he'd take it like the soldier he is, and he'll be back with us as soon as we can work it within the system."

Joe said, "We aren't the only people who know what happened out there. What about the engineers and the volunteers who got away? They won't stay quiet."

"We've just about gotten to all of them already. We work fast," Tyrell said. "The few credible ones among them—Jan Stalkup and Suzy Gudenkauf, for example—know we can destroy their credit, identity, and reputation if they squeal to the media or unfriendly politicians. The lunatics and hippie types, we don't even worry about. They just come off as the raving cuckoo birds that they are."

Tyrell chuckled, and said, "Besides, seeing Muhammad Ibraaheem get his head cut off right before their eyes put the fear of God into them, so to speak."

"He was a good man," Nate said to Tyrell. "Unlike you."

Tyrell shrugged and did the *What you gonna do* gesture again.

Before Joe could ask, Tyrell said to him, "We're trusting you to speak to your daughter. That way, we won't have to."

Joe felt a blast of anger behind his eyes, but tried to stanch it.

"Easy now," Tyrell said. "It's all good. It's all cool. Right, Governor?"

Rulon had been unnaturally quiet the entire time, Joe thought.

Rulon said, "We arrived at an agreement I can live with, Mr. Tyrell and me."

"That we did," Tyrell said. He said it with a kind of disingenuous bravado, Joe thought. But Joe wasn't thinking clearly—he was still smoldering from the fact that Tyrell had threatened Sheridan.

"First," Rulon said, looking from Tyrell to Nate, "Mr. Tyrell will keep his word to you. As of this morning, your case files have been wiped clean. As far as the federal charges go, you no longer exist as a target. You can go out of this room today an innocent man."

Nate didn't react. Joe thought, *He's been burned before.*

"Of course, our deal that you not commit any more crimes in the state while I'm in office is still in effect," Rulon said. "The election is in less than two weeks, so you'll have to deal with the next governor on that."

Nate nodded, but still seemed wary.

———

Rulon turned to Joe. "And we were able to take care of your in-surance bill problem quicker than I thought possible, thanks to Mr. Tyrell and his compatriots. The medical bills for your daughter have been lost within the system. Correct, Mr. Tyrell?"

Tyrell nodded his head.

"Lisa, can you confirm that both of these actions have taken place?" Rulon asked.

"Yes. We checked again this morning," she said. "DCI confirmed that Mr. Romanowski no longer exists in any federal criminal data-base, and Joe's situation has been resolved."

Joe closed his eyes and let relief wash over him, even though it was dirty relief. Marybeth would be thrilled.

"I thought you guys would be happier," Tyrell said to Nate and Joe.

Nate leaned forward and winced from his injuries as he did so.

He said to Rulon, "And you trust him to keep his word?"

"Of course not!" Rulon laughed.

Joe looked up to see Tyrell flush red.

"Of course I don't trust him, or any of the other federal jackals I have to deal with. But Tyrell here, like all of them, only cares about self-preservation and the accumulation of power. I threaten both if I, as a sitting governor, call a press conference and describe in detail what went on in the middle of the Red Desert in my state. He knows I'd provide evidence and name names, his included.

"Right, Mr. Tyrell?"

Tyrell looked away angrily.

"And don't think we don't know your real name and title and the agency you work for, because we do," Rulon said.

Then the governor raised one finger in the air. "Additionally, everything that has been said in this room today has been videotaped and recorded."

Tyrell's head snapped back around and he glared at Rulon. His palms were pressed flat on the table as if he was prepared to push himself up and attack at any moment.

"Oh, yes," Rulon said, nodding toward the monitors and electronic devices lining the walls. "This is a security zone, as far as anyone on the outside trying to listen in, but it's also wired to record anything that happens here. That way, my people and future officials will be held accountable for the actions they take in an emergency. It would be nice if that happened in Washington, but I'll work on that as a lawyer instead of as the governor. It'll give me something to do."

He beamed and grinned wolfishly. "Installing this system was the best use of federal Homeland Security funds I've made to date. I'd pat myself on the back if I could do it. Lisa, do you want to pat me on the back?"

"No, sir," she said, trying not to smile.

"So you can leave now," he said to Tyrell. "Don't show your face in my state for the rest of your life."

Tyrell shook his head, but didn't get up. He said to Rulon, "You're good. You're devious. We might have a place for you in the Wolverines."

"No thank you," Rulon said. "We ex-politicians in Wyoming don't go to Washington to lobby or work for hedge funds. We go back to work here like real people. So, on your way, Mr. Tyrell."

Tyrell looked sheepishly at Joe, then at Nate, then at Lisa Casper. Without a word, he stood up and walked to the door.

After it wheezed shut and locked, Rulon said to Casper, "When will Colter Allen get here? I told him I'd walk him through the situation room and show him how it worked."

She looked at her watch. "He should be here any minute, Governor."

"Good," Rulon said. Then to Joe and Nate: "We need to clear the room."

Joe was still slightly stunned by what he'd heard that morning, both from Tyrell and Rulon.

He stood shakily.

"Don't forget your hat," Rulon said. "And don't be a stranger. I won't be your governor anymore, but I can be your lawyer."

"Thank you, sir," Joe mumbled.

Nate thanked him as well.

"I'm the one that should be thanking you two," Rulon said. "That was a hell of a thing you did out there."

Joe clamped on his old hat and put his new one back in the box to carry outside. Nate hopped on his good leg to retrieve his crutches.

"You two try to stay out of trouble," Rulon said. Then he laughed again, and said, "I don't know what I'm saying, do I . . . You two don't know how to stay out of trouble."

Joe smiled and held the door open for Nate. As his friend swung through the door, he heard Rulon say to Lisa:

"That idea about using Homeland Security money to put in a recording system is a damned good one, isn't it? We should recommend that to Colter Allen so he can do it."

Joe stopped and looked back over his shoulder.

Rulon grinned, put his finger to his lips, and said, *"Shhhhhhhh."*

Joe knew he was going to miss him.

———

. . .

A LIGHT RAIN was falling outside in the parking lot of the Homeland Security building and the sky had dropped gray and close. Water beaded on the paint and glass of Joe's newest Game and Fish Department pickup. It was a brand-new Ford F-150 SuperCrew with less than a hundred miles on it. Another parting gift from the governor.

"Need a ride?" Joe asked Nate. Joe planned to get in and drive straight to his home five and a half hours north. Marybeth and his daughters had returned home the day before, and a very contrite Sheridan was back at school in Laramie in the process of looking for her own apartment.

"To the airport," Nate said. "I'm going to meet Liv in Louisiana."

Joe nodded. "How long since you've flown commercial as a real person?"

"It's been a while."

"Then what?" Joe asked.

Nate hopped around the truck to the passenger side on his crutches. When he climbed in, he said, "I guess we'll come back."

ON THE SHORT RIDE to the Cheyenne airport, Joe said, "Think our deals will hold?"

Nate shrugged. He said, "We'll see."

"Rulon is on our side."

"That he is. I trust him. He's one of the greatest men I've met." He paused. "I might put Ibby right up there with him."

Joe raised his eyebrows and kept driving.

"It'll be you and me again," Nate said. "I never thought that would happen."

JOE'S PHONE BURRED once in his breast pocket while he dropped Nate off at the small airport. He recognized the alert as an incoming email, but he ignored it.

"I've got a favor to ask," Nate said.

"Shoot."

"Can you come in with me and buy me a ticket? I'll pay you back."

"That's right," Joe said, "you don't have a credit card."

After buying the ticket at the counter, Nate said, "Give Marybeth my best."

"And give my best to Liv," Joe said.

"This will be . . . strange."

"What will?"

Nate said, "Showing my ID to everyone who asks, going through security. Making phone calls, maybe even getting a credit card with my name on it. I'm not sure I'm looking forward to getting back on the grid at all."

"It's not so bad."

Nate paused a moment and said, "I didn't think we were going to make it, Joe. I thought we'd die in the desert."

"Well," Joe said, shaken. "We didn't."

JOE WAS NEARING CHUGWATER, north of Cheyenne on I-25, when he pulled out his cell phone to call Marybeth. He couldn't wait to

---

get home. It was still hunting season and he wanted to get out on patrol, smell the fall, descend back into some kind of routine.

It felt like he'd been gone for months.

As he raised the phone to his face, he noted the little red *1* on his mail icon and he clicked it.

It was from the Wyoming Department of Corrections and the subject line was *Dallas Cates*.

Joe didn't want to read any further.

Not now.

ACKNOWLEDGMENTS

The author would like to thank the experts who provided information for this novel, including Gary New and Marijke Unger of the National Center for Atmospheric Research–Wyoming Supercomputing Center and Jim Frank and Lynn Budd of the State of Wyoming Office of Homeland Security, and Paul Bellotti. Source material used in this novel includes (on tracking grizzly bears) *Montana Outdoors* and the *Billings Gazette*; (on the Red Desert) *Backpacker* magazine, the BLM Rawlins Field Office, and the Biodiversity Conservation Alliance; (on the Utah Data Center) *Wired* magazine and *Esquire* magazine. The devastating effects of an EMP came from a variety of sources, including "Heading Toward an EMP Catastrophe," by Ambassador R. James Woolsey and Dr. Peter Vincent Pry.

Special thanks to my first readers Laurie Box, Molly Donnell, Becky Reif, and Roxanne Woods.

Thanks to Molly Donnell and Prairie Sage Creative for cjbox.net and Jennifer Fonnesbeck for social media expertise and merchandise sales.

It's a sincere pleasure to work with professionals at Putnam, including the legendary Neil Nyren, Ivan Held, Alexis Welby, Christine Ball, and Katie Grinch.

And thanks, of course, to my wonderful agent and friend, Ann Rittenberg.